Carsten Stemm

Confessions of a psychosaurus

Nuts of thoughts to nibble on

Bibliografische Information der Deutschen Nationalbibliothek:
Die Deutsche Nationalbibliothek verzeichnet diese Publikation in der
Deutschen Nationalbibliografie; detaillierte bibliografische Daten sind
im Internet über http://dnb.dnb.de abrufbar.

© 2020 Carsten Stemm

Herstellung und Verlag: BoD – Books on Demand, Norderstedt

ISBN: 978-3-7519-1431-4

Table of Contents

The Psychosaurus introduces itself:

I think poetically and did not become the victim of a biofant. These alien phantas illegally enter from space in the dark and use their long proboscis to suck the sleepy people's imaginations out of their brains. I only reluctantly use words that others have already said. I find that unsanitary. That's why I often invent new words, which creates the problem that nobody understands me anymore. Consequently, I have to use used words again, which the German vernacular has formed only imprecisely. Language can speak because it contains the general images of existence. The main thing in language is to give the pictures of the world a home. It is tragic when a person follows the words of the language and then thinks this is thinking. Real thinking actively shapes language. Language is the I of a psychosaurus, it is its center. The world really comes alive in language, because speaking means: create the world. In the beginning was the word!

Scaredy

A scaredy rabbit is on the way to becoming an Easter bunny. On the way he wanted to visit his uncle, but he's in the pepper again. The scared rabbit is not a frog, it faces the monkey, even if the monkey laughs at it. The louse runs over the flea's liver. The hare hears this flea coughing, which now shoots cannons at sparrows. The scared rabbit overcomes its inner bastard and then turns the flea into a snail. On the left he sees a donkey that is too comfortable. The donkey goes on ice in the middle of summer. That doesn't work on cowhide, and the chickens laugh at the donkey. On the right hand, a gray mouse gets the moths because the moose smacked them. The mosquitoes in the air are harmless in themselves if they do not become elephants and behave like them in the china shop. Mr.

Specht runs like a rabbit and takes out his watered poodle so that it doesn't go crazy in the pan. Mister and dog probably have a bird, but no rooster crows after them, because this is in the basket with his hens. On its way the scared rabbit finds a monkey tooth that no longer harms a fly. Now the scaredy has done it, he has arrived at the Easter bunny.

a conversation

Mole: Say Psychosaurus, what is this book about?

Psychosaurus: In this book, language speaks itself. And there is language talks about everything, so this book has every topic.

Duck: A personal question: what's the difference between that Psychosaurus and Carsten?

Psychosaurus: I don't want to talk about it the topic is totally stressing me.

Duck: It's bent, dude!

Mole: This book is obviously a automatic translation.

Psychosaurus: So it is. This increases the bizarre beyond measure. The language says more than a thousand words.

Giggle: If I want to write to Carsten, he has one too Online or something?

Psychosaurus: At the moment he has the email address

carsten-stemm@web.de and he also has his own online.

Werewolf: Sunt reprimat de această carte!

Giggle: I don't understand a word, not even the train station.

Rabe: You don't have to understand everything. Sometimes it is enough to let the words carry you through the irrational.

Detlef double dooid

Detlef Doppeldoid cannot think properly with both halves of the brain. Detlef thinks faster than light, which leads to space-time swellings in his logosphere. Then he swaps right with left, in with out, and gross with net. He doesn't know if you go in or out of a room. It is bad about Detlef Doppeldoid: the other day he thought people were people. Detlef also cannot remember the difference between Albert Einstein and Konrad Adenauer. Detlef wonders: Aren't " the same " and " the same " the same? Sometimes Mr. Doppeldoid also makes spelling mistakes. If he is completely confused, Detlef even remembers the future.

Detlef says:

" Whenever I no longer know who I am, I look at my identity card: I also have my own number there; a number, all for me alone, just for me. Unique and unmistakable. The state loves me. But does that help me? Who is behind the name Detlef Doppeldoid? And what does a small plastic card prove? It is easy to forge plastic cards. You can fake everything today. You can even fake an identity. I am becoming quite flowery. "

Speaking bunny

The rabbit that can speak is called the speaking rabbit. The speaking rabbit eats while speaking and speaks while nibbling. Word roots are not unknown to him. He is currently consuming love. Love is just a word to him, mugg, mampf. You can eat love without eating, that's wisdom of the hare.

There are ducks!

The biologist is interested in the feathers of the ducks, the ontologist is interested in the being of the ducks. Who gives the ducks? Answer: The 'it'. 'It' and giving result in being. Alternatively, the question could be answered as follows: evolution gives ducks, duck eggs give ducks, duck sex gives ducks, God gives ducks. It's raining. One should actually say: The cloud is raining. This 'it' is not even up to God, because it means: There is a God. This in turn means: The 'It' is greater than God. Another conclusion would be: The 'It' is the real God who gives God first. There are ducks. One does not say: it takes ducks. Giving is happier than taking. Giving is probably more ontological than taking. The 'it' is so unclear that you can no longer see its fog. As a result, you no longer think about where the ducks actually come from. The 'it' is deceptive. It pretends to be knowledge. If we no longer know that the cloud is raining,

then it rains. The negation also gives the 'it': " There is no Elwittitsche! " Who can only be this 'it' who is able to give these non-ducks?

Goldmarie and Pechmarie

Once there was a motivational trainer who had two daughters, both of whom were named Marie. One was hardworking, the other lazy. One day the hardworking woman came to a well that said:

"No drinking water!"

" It's only there for legal reasons, " thought the thirsty woman. The girl drank from the water and accidentally fell into the fountain, causing her to lose consciousness. At some point she woke up in a completely unknown area.

An old woman stood at the window of a house in need of renovation and shook her pillow out. Ms. Holle, as the tenant's name was, said to the girl: "Competent nurses for the elderly like you are rare these days, I have a lot of work to do."

After a while, however, the girl became homesick and expressed the desire to be allowed to return home. Frau Holle granted her this wish. The old woman led the girl to a gate through which she should go. As the hard-working woman walked through the gate, it was raining down on her from the top, dioxin-contaminated pitch that no longer came off her skin. The girl said: " Fucking bullshit! I will take my revenge bitterly on fate. I study mathematics and do my PhD on paradox theories. "

When the mother saw her daughter smeared with pitch, she called her child Pechmarie. For reasons of social compensation, the mother now also sent her lazy daughter to the well. It happened almost the same. Only her second daughter came to another house in which a certain Frau Hölle lived instead of Frau Holles Haus.

After ten minutes of work, the lazy girl's work discipline waned considerably. Ms. Hell said: 'At your age I was pretty lazy too. I don't even have a secondary school leaving certificate. We are now running towards a Château Mouton-Rothschild 1945, which my son-in-law stole himself.

Fortunately, the whole cellar is full of it. " After a week-long binge drinking, the lazy also got homesick and wanted to be left home. Frau Hölle led her to the same gate through which Pechmarie had passed. When the lazy girl went through the gate, it was raining gold on her. Now the girl was a lot more valuable, because the gold could not be removed either. When she got home, she was called Goldmarie by her mother. Out of anger at the injustice of life, the mother left the church and went to a secular judgment. Pechmarie later became the first professor of logic with dioxin scars on her face. Her life was completely botched. Goldmarie, however, lived happily ever after. > Happy ending

Cheese of the sheep

Shepherd: Tell me, what kind of book are you carrying under your arm?

Wolfgang: One of your sheep gave me the book for my birthday. Its title is: Make sheep cheese yourself!

Shepherd: Is that supposed to be a joke?

Wolfgang: Jokes are not to be trifled with. I am never joking. Whoever jokes is just too cowardly to be serious. I was never kidding. And if anyone does laugh, I'll slap my ass on the mouth.

A sheep: Excuse me if I interfere, but I'm genetically modified, so I can talk. Is there a new tax on sheep cheese soon?

another sheep: I too am a genetically improved product of the creator, and I tell you: men are like women, only the other way around.

Wolfgang: I always thought it would be different!

Shepherd: I get dizzy from such complicated conversations. .. Ah, look who's coming! He's limping!

Wolfgang: Then it can only be a comparison!

Shepherd: Why is that?

Wolfgang: Because you always say: every comparison lags!

a shorn sheep: meaning is always ambiguous. So the speaker quickly promises himself in his speech. The double German is a Lapsus Freudianikus, the leak in the overly smooth self-portrayal.

Wolfgang: What kind of talker is that?

Shepherd: The sheep studied. Psycholinguistics or something.

(The limping has now arrived at the discussion group.)

Limping: You are after me. My stolen trade

Plutonium from Russian nuclear power plants has been blown up!

Shepherd: Don't do things, Otto!

Sheep: can you eat plutonium?

Shepherd: Not all sheep have studied!

all sheep together: Mähhhh!

Otto: I have only one way out: suicide!

Wolfgang: I would have an alternative way out. I know a good magician at the circus. He suffers from an allergy, but he's technically fine.

Otto: Who is this magician?

Wolfgang: He is everything you think he is, because he has a lot

Planets in the seventh house, including Pluto.

Otto: I don't believe in astrology!

Wolfgang: But the stars believe in you!

Otto: Fine, I want to try it, because I have nothing left to lose. I am enchanted in a rabbit and write my name backwards so that nobody recognizes me.

Shepherd: great thing! Now that's a really happy ending!

In an emergency, the apple eats pears.

Homicide

Monkey: Good afternoon, weird eye, you have slanted eyes.

Weird eye: And you're a monkey, you monkey.

Monkey: I have a stick of dynamite here.

Who do we put them in the ass?

Weird eye: Of course! At TNT I don't say no!

You brilliant monkey, you deserve the Nobel Prize!

(The monkey pushes the slant in the dynamite's ass and lights the fuse. After nerve-wracking seconds of waiting, there is a violent detonation: dust, debris and remains of meat cover the location of the explosion.)

Monkey: cool! It crashed!

There are no counts or paragraphs for us animals.

Now we're going to eat a banana. Haha!

Steel chick

Once there was a small squeaky car that drives through plump and mild nature. The wagon moves, it is pulled by a horse. A vehicle that no longer drives today. When the companion started to be driven by the motor, the trolley became steel, when the trolley was still being pulled, flowers bloomed and the water rushed to it. The secret of life lived in the mill wheel, here the wheel ran in the water. The automobile was the birth of the steel girl. The sky stretches, the sky stretches, he is excited. Steel chick shoots into the sky with a defense cannon. It is World War II, a senseless attempt by steel to become a horse again. Steel chick is now a horse herself, so she wears a ponytail. Horses are really elegant, as elegance is no longer known in the age of steel. Plastic is also steel. Everything that is not pulled by the horse is steel. You get awe of a beauty who is not a fashion doll.

More space

A multi-room is a room that is larger inside than outside. The multi-cupboard, for example, looks like an ordinary bedroom cupboard. But if you have to hide in the cupboard if necessary, you will be amazed to find that there are entire galaxies in the cupboard. And these are not hallucinations as a result of a lack of oxygen. The world is full of holes in reality. And there are more and more.

danger

Danger threatens you. The accident has not yet struck. But it could strike in the future; that's a risk. Life is insecure. You don't know if life will be broken the next moment. Danger is at the door, danger is unpredictable, it can become a nightmare. Predators are dangerous; Capitalists too. It is dangerous to lay power cables in a tub full of water. Getting married is risky too. Life insurance, on the other hand, promises protection: if you've lost a life, you'll get a new one. But beware of insurance fraud: insurance companies cheat a lot!

Think

Thinking wanders in the land of meaning. The ways of thinking run into the forest of knowledge. Through his hike, thinking becomes more difficult and finally merges with his thought trees and his dream snow.

Olympus

Fred sees a god on cell phone on Olympus:

Fred: Hello God!

How long have the gods been using a cell phone?

God: yes mei, you just adjust. I could also communicate telepathically with my colleagues, but we gods want to make people understandable.

Fred: So, I don't understand it!

Egg heads

Brain wankers are the rabbits of pneumatic agglation. They are also called egg heads. Your neurolants are not very supple, but they are very long. Throw bare walnuts at their bald heads because they contain a lot of brainwax. Neurolants are the rods of the mind. Neurolants can also be the trunks of trees through which you can no longer see the forest for the sheer number of them. But actually Neurolanten are the chopsticks for eating intellectual sushi.

Some brainwaves are called philosophers. Philosophy thinks without drinking, it is light without love. The thinker can joke badly in the desert of knowledge. Cacti never laugh. Philosophy is as hard as old cheese. Philosophers on the path to healing are beginning to write poetry.

Demigod

Fred: You know what Detlef, I was promoted to demigod.

Detlef: Really?

Fred: It's like that! I can now find an answer to every question, if only imprecisely, but I can find out the answer.

Detlef: Who promoted you?

Fred: The big boss!

Detlef: Aha!

Fred: I'm just demigod. I'm not immortal yet, but I'm working on it.

Detlef: Mm, do that.

Fred: I finally know, for example, why the banana is crooked.

Detlef: Yes, why then?

Fred: She longs for unity, the banana wants to go back to paradise, she would like to be a circle, but the Fall forbids her, only her strength extends to the curve.

Detlef: What a demigod knows!

ghost

The term " spirit " is a very lonely word. The word has to explain so many things. Intelligence chops stones; the mind connects. Spirit illuminates the parts of the world like a sun and gives them a shape. The mind is the image for things. Mind dresses the smallest particles with more. The mind can think, intelligence can only think or combine.

cause and effect

A billiard player hits a ball with his stick, which in turn hits another ball. This cause and effect thinking is the original logic of science. Logic justifies it, it doesn't explain anything. The free will of the billiard player is completely hidden in this world view. The causes are dull animals, almost bulls. Causes convince through energy, not through meaning.

logic

Fred: I believe in logic. The entire cosmos is logically structured. However, women are not part of the cosmos. Logical thinking gives you access to every puzzle. You just have to put a lot of effort into thinking.

Arnold Heitermann: Logic does not advance us in knowledge. An example: Three crows sit on a fence. A bird killer comes by and shoots one of the birds.

Arnold: How many birds are still on the fence now?

Fred: There are two crows on the fence.

Arnold: Wrong! There is still a crow on the fence!

Fred: It's completely illogical!

Arnold: That is logical. The shot bird fell dead to the ground. The second crow was startled by the loud bang and flew away immediately. The third crow was terrified by the bang and remains the only bird to sit.

Fred: This case seems very constructed to me, but it is logical.

Arnold: Well, you can explain everything and nothing with logic.

Fred: First of all, afterwards.

Arnold: Yes, always afterwards.

However, the reality was there before.

Fred: What if five crows had suddenly sat on the fence after the shot?

Arnold: Then a few life-tired crows would have sat in the hope of being shot too.

Fred: Really great, what is logical.

Arnold: You can explain everything with logic, even the illogical.

Fred: Man, man, I really have to think about it.

Arnold: But please stay strictly logical!

Fred: Uh ... yes ... well ...

dialog

Socrates: What do you look like shit again this morning, Plato!

Plato: Shut up, ass!

Socrates

Bullet

A bullet is terribly constricted in itself. It would have the desire to give birth if it were ignited. But nobody ignites them. The ball remains dull like mud and does not know each other. Why do balls roll? They roll the way, but they do not change their shape. Ultimately, they are rolled over by the movement. Bullet remains bullet. Now I remember: bullets are female!

(in) perfect

The dog itself is the idea of a dog. Does the idea of a dog now look like a dachshund, a golden retriever, a sheepdog, or even a poodle? We know what a circle looks like in itself. There is only one circle and it is completely round. Triangles already make it more difficult: What angle does the idea of a triangle have? The circle is the only idea that can be drawn exactly. The dog itself cannot be drawn, only a specific dog. The circle itself can be drawn. Shall we worship the circle? Is there any "in itself"? Things only show up "for me"? - The perfect in reality would be too imperfect for life. Life needs a corner in a circle or a hole in a square. The perfect exists only as an idea, because in reality the perfect cannot exist. The circle has corners in the perfection of life. A chestnut is an angular ball. It bears in imperfect perfection as perfect life. Nevertheless, a chestnut tree is somehow sick. Why this? Only the hedgehog knows that!

circle

A circle cannot breathe. Nowhere does he have a hole through which he could breathe. The circle itself can be seen as a hole. Is the circle the gateway to another world? I can't check that because the circle doesn't let me in. It's just too closed. One should not deal with such types. The circle doesn't talk to me, it will always remain mysterious. The circle probably doesn't even have anything to hide: it is naive, boring and empty. - The round is the color of the circle. This color is very rare and has no name. The easiest way to name the color is " colorful ". The round can go on an adventure without a circle and an arc. Life itself is an adventure. Today the group thinks something new. But the round is so old that his thinking of the new can never produce madness. However, philistines never hang around. It's too bumpy for that. The group wanted to become a circle and asked the employment agency for a retraining. The clerk was a square. It ended badly.

The apple thinks and pear guides.

Hitting is awesome

Striking is the most universal verb there is. Hitting is really awesome. This activity was already fully developed in the Stone Age. You can open your eyes, a book alike. Look up in the duden, smash the window, or punch someone in the face. Musicians make noise with the drums. The blow hits you. The 1.FC meniscus beats the Rosenheim flat feet 2-1. Whoever beats wins. The best way to hit is with stones. A noble stone is called a hammer. Hitting is raw and rough. A blow is mindless and atomic. Hitting smashes, breaks, hitting separates. A child of hitting is cutting. A bad child. Another child of hitting is thrusting. This child is more likeable because it has more sun in the forward. Beating makes a fist, so his actions get a belly.

Tool

A work of art is the deposition of all ultimate human experience. There is experience that has been confirmed so that it solidifies as a work of art. The work treasure orientates all beings like a magnetic field from the spiritual. The Werkschatz is the natural

Wikipedia of life. Unfortunately there are also black sheep in the treasure of knowledge: they are called factory dirt.

For King Orthos, to rule means to arrange things according to their own inner self. Orthos does not impart its own will to people. The king does not want to force things, but explores their idiosyncrasies and lets them arrange them themselves. People, goats and other beings live in Orthos Reich, all standing and walking in their right place. After his death, King Orthos will flow into the water of his favorite river, which will eventually pour into the sea. From the sea, his work will continue to orient people.

hunger and thirst

Hunger wants to eat something all the time. Hunger is completely dependent on the object of his desire. But that is exactly what makes hunger so pleasant. He is full of life, some even say that he is life itself. Hunger also has a sister: her name is "" thirst "". But that's only for very crazy types.

Need is the abstraction of hunger and thirst. Need is poor and in need. Need is very secular and always looks the same gray. You can store your needs at any temperature. Need never bears fruit, it always remains lean. If you need something, you go shopping.

Who needs fiber? Above all, if they only consist of ballast. Burden fillers. They fill the void, but remain hollow themselves. It is the essence that shines.

The Psychosaurus is completely at the end:

An ice power as a figure has raised her arm. A stair of water rolls down from the cold face. The shadow woman's eyes shine like two suns at night. Not for long. Your lights have now gone out. The shadow woman flies into the sky as a black angel. The unknown place is orphaned. Where there has never been anyone, there is no one now. My knowledge of not being is next to the empty space. I am warm, but only as heat, because I have no other body. A scream without a tongue goes around desperately in the empty room. There is only emptiness everywhere, where something should actually be. Where there is nothing, you cannot see anything, especially if you have no eyes. But I see the horror and I don't know why.

hole

A hole means a rather round absence. Holes are empty. A hole is often a passage that goes in and out. Sometimes the view goes out through the hole and the view comes in through the hole. Holes are hungry, they would like to be stuffed. The urge of all being is well to be satisfied. Reality has holes. These are so transparent that nobody can see them, not even a physicist with his great apparatus. The lack of clothing can be seen in naked people. The lack of a gap, on the other hand, remains hungry and invisible. Surface tends to be empty. If this emptiness is filled, the surface disappears quickly, it becomes thin. The esthete prescribes color on the surface so that it becomes more confident.

animal

The classic animal has four legs, it "meows" or barks. The term animal is a type case for many beings who have little in common. Animals do not carry leaves and they cannot build atomic bombs. Animals are backward people. However, one day animals will also understand Godel's incompleteness theorem. - But when?

Nature can be raw and rough. There is also the nature of the dreamers: this nature is people's paradise even before the Fall. The nature of the Germanic Charles Darwin looks like this: A fight of the strong against an even stronger. Our second nature is culture. Our third realm is called artificiality. Nobody likes to live there.

Ice flower

A foreign power from Sweden is made of the coldest ice. This power goes on earth in the form of an old girl named Eisblume. A flower made of ice, a beautiful flower. Flowers are reminiscent of spring, because during this time fresh flowers usually bloom in young warmth. However, our ice flower blooms in the murderous cold of winter. All other people who are also made of ice are enraptured by ice flower. Agnis is also out of the cold, out of burning ice. Agnis sees ice flower and is thrilled. The frigids are always the hottest. Mr. Sumpfstein is a stunner as a seller of ice cream. His ice cream balls contain explosives, which ignite when he's long over all mountains. Eisblume sees Mr. Sumpfstein: She gets a shock, the roulette ball rolls in her head. Nobody knows that the ball will stop in the compartment of the seventeen. At Agnis it will be the three. Ice balls or roulette balls, balls are all the same. Bullets are the bad bank of fate. And now we break into this bank and free the madness. Everyone is going crazy: Eisblume, Agnis and Herr Sumpfstein are in one box. You breathe insanity: Ah, that's good. Finally they are free!

blood

Blood flows inside as a thick and powerful heat. Human blood is very personal as long as it still circles in its veins. The blood circles, so it's round. Blood powers in his circle. External blood in the cold and heartless doctor's syringe is already dead. How terrible! Only reptiles bleed cold. Unless the sun is shining on the reptile's green fur. Every vampire knows: When the moon shines, blood is black. You don't see anything during the day.

Fire

Fire dances with violent flames. Wild burning smashes the durability of the fuel. Heat spikes peck into the room, fever teeth bite themselves. The power of the red storm gives its surroundings an aura of warmth. The fire's embers die to ashes. Fire is impressive, but it borrows its substance from the fuel. His food was eaten faster than cooked, much faster. The fire's warmth sleeps fluffy in the space of immortality. When heat goes crazy, it becomes heat.

general

The general shows just as much face as necessary. The special features show much clearer edges. The general is the same everywhere, it is often expressed through the same. In the landscape of everything, the general can be found in every place. The gray uncle of the general is called average. The general has to adjust to the special again and again, which creates stress. The general gives security when you go on an unusual vacation.

Standing shadow

A standing shadow must always stop, although it can go wherever it wants. If the standing shadow wants to move, the environment moves past him instead of past him, he himself stops. The standing shadow can move around and still have to stay in the same place forever. A standing shadow has no company. Of course there are other standing shadows, but they are somewhere else.

Short circuit

The path leads to the goal as long as no esoteric is walking on it. A short circuit shortens the path of life. He quickly follows a path that does not exist. As a result, he lacks experience. Its success is hot and empty and without meat, but the short circuit has a charismatic effect. The shortest route is always a short-circuit, its goal is to be nonexistent. The short circuit acts without growth, it goes without a path. Joachim Ernst Berendt wrote a book: " There is no way, just go: BE in nature ". On the way to the presentation of his book, he was run over by a car.

Go

You get afraid that walking might fall over. But walking has it great: it always stays in balance. Standing moves in the corridor. However, lying never runs.

sky

Peak mountains have no problems and are happy that they are so big and big. Heaven is also happy when it receives visitors from the mountains. The big sky also needs conviviality.

reason

The reason is below. It is the basis, floor, base and justification. If you look into the bottom, it becomes an abyss. You can't discover gravity there. Bottom and abyss calm the nerves immensely. The best job for humans is to get to the bottom of things. Only scaredy rabbits prefer to do something useful because the world perishes in a useful way.

Underworld

The underworld is below the world. It is almost no longer part of the world, you do not know it, which is why it is uncomfortable. The dead lie beneath the ground, there is also the source of fertility. How else should all the plants grow?

cloud

The cloud is a sheep in heaven. Clouds are always sad. They often have to cry. But they also protect cattle from the aggressive sun. A cloud absorbs people's good and evil. You can see from their shapes what the hour has struck. Movement and water dance together in the cloud.

dirt

You shouldn't put dirt in the salad. Otherwise illness threatens! Dirt is the physical equivalent of sin. A wound can be regarded as contamination, because the wound often forms a nasty crust on the edge that looks like dirt. Contamination or stains in turn indicate guilt. Someone is stained. Did we get hurt because we were too imperfect? Or are we imperfect because we were hurt? Or are we guilty of violating something, a law or a person? But we don't hurt! We are perfect and innocent! Whoever claims something like that is hurtful, therefore guilty.

Sex in jail

The walls of the prison form a heart. Its outer walls are black on the outside and red on the inside. The prisoner Rasputin is no longer the youngest, but also not the oldest, because after all he still has acne. Germania is also imprisoned: Rasputin and Germania go to bed together. Rasputin fears that Germania will contract syphilis. Germania leaves Rasputin. She probably only has to do Pippi for a short time, but she won't get very far because we are in the prison of the heart. A prison is a building that you cannot escape. Rasputin stands in front of the mirror and expresses his pimples. The pus splashes on the silver innocence: icky, ey.

Rat and atomic bomb

Rats are mice that have become megalomaniac. They best tolerate radioactivity from all living things. Surely one day they will become kings of the earth. Rats kill each other, they are very similar to humans. Rat yourself who can! However, rats are smarter than humans, because they learn very quickly not to eat toxic food if they notice that their peers are killing it. That is why rat poison is not a permanent solution to exterminate these hell creatures. In the Middle Ages, rats were used to torture people; today, rats are tortured in scientific laboratories. It is a victory for mankind! From victim to perpetrator! Cute rats are cared for and cared for in the Indian Karni Mata Temple. In the West, however, there are only bad sewer rats. In China, the rat even exists as a zodiac sign. But the germ-free Psychosaurus says: "We are no longer living in the Middle Ages! Away with the nasty infection carriers! Why don't the politicians do anything? They never do anything! "

Kink

You can't touch a kink because it is so far from the row from which it dances. If nothing breaks, there are things. A line goes from here to there. It is so normal that it makes you depressed. Scientists and architects like lines. A line doesn't eat life. The line jams life and gains energy from it to be able to heat the room up to a moderate 20 degrees.

Tilt

The slope is a slope that slopes according to the popularity of the slope, turns to an angle that corresponds to the slope of the slope. Such a tilt is not arbitrary, but corresponds to the love of the inclined.

Well

The good is a tree that bears fruit all year round. Its wood is made of solid blood; its leaves can laugh. The colorful is good, the gray is bad. The devil eats the good. The good can consist of itself. However, evil depends on the destruction of good. Therefore, evil can never prevail.

consist

Salt consists of sodium and chlorine. Standing is on your own two feet, but existence needs a substance as a floor. An existence needs parts of which it consists, it cannot be by itself. The coarsest exists. The term "stock" comes very close to that of substance.

Mouse and bat

Mice have four legs and run around in the way that God's order. However, some mice have disregarded their destination and have blown up. They hang out lazily all day (head down) and partying at night (drinking blood and stuff). The mouse as a bat is blind. That is God's punishment for their sins. As a makeshift solution, the flying mice must now see with their ears. It is completely blatant.

thin

Thin women quickly sit on the anorexia dock. Accused of flabby and fat fellows. If the thin wants to gain weight, then it has to call itself "slim". The thin one sometimes has a more intense effect than the thick one because it can hold a lot of essence in its sweet tummy. Therefore, the thin is often more intelligent than the thick. This does not apply to thin board drills, because they have a thick board in front of their heads.

Pyrrhic victory

My name is Schmidt and I am dead. I lived a sinful life. At my workplace at the Satan & Sons company, my greedy boss turned into a 100-euro note. I sensed my chance for a blissful life after death: I quickly put my banknote in my wallet and painted a crucifix on its outer leather. My boss was caught. Only after his assurance that I would not go to hell after my death did I remove the cross again. Shortly afterwards I slipped unhappily on a banana peel in front of the AOK and fell on the hard pavement with the back of my head. I was dead straight away. As promised, I didn't go to hell, but they didn't want to let me into heaven either, since I had defeated evil but still hadn't done good. Now I am constantly going back and forth between heaven and hell and do not know anymore.

To suffer

Fred: Suffering is totally superfluous. Which idiot created the world?

Detlef: Suffering protects against idiotic acts. It prevents you from drinking too much beer. Evil leads to good.

Fred: Isn't that another way? Kind of loving?

Pope: God is infallible (like me), he will know why he created the world.

Mephisto: I am part of that power that always wants evil and always creates good.

Bert Hellinger: On a higher level, evil is also good.

Fred: I live on earth; the earth is a lower level, the higher level is of no use to me. All of this is not very convincing.

Detlef: The sun god also suffered. He died on the cross as a human being and rose again on the third day.

Fred: That is in solidarity with him. I feel much better already.

Allahu Akbar

God is greater than ... God is always greater than a human being can imagine. For safety's sake I don't want to write anything bad about God, you never know. Unless God is the devil. Are evil gods real gods? Or does their existence feed on eating good? If there is only one God, one can actually only call him Allah. The two neutral and all-encompassing A sounds flank the infinite L sound. If there are several gods, then it becomes more colorful and loving and also more understandable for humans. Each god among other gods has his own area of responsibility. Allah doesn't need to have 99 names anymore because there are 99 gods. And the hundredth god will probably unite all gods again, so one suspects. The fanatical polarization in good and evil dissolves in the multitude of gods. Sometimes the gods are also called angels, archangels or higher entities.

garlic

Garlic is stale freshness. His toes are split. A real personality split has its roots. On the outside, however, the onion demonstrates uniformity. Garlic helps against vampires and witches. The tuber strengthens the blood and makes it so inedible for parasites that even the vampires lose their appetite. The schizophrenic leek also kills physical parasites such as tapeworms or putrefactive bacteria. Garlic splits humanity like cigarette smoke. Some like it: these are the good people. However, the bad guys (e.g. vampires, witches, Nazis, childfuckers, capitalists and Greens voters) feel repelled by his smell.

Contract with the devil

You can quickly become one of the rich and beautiful by making a small contract in the service office of Satan & Söhne: the contractor (Teufel) fulfills every worldly wish. In return, the contractor bequeathed his post-mortem soul to the anatomists of hell for research purposes. The contract is legally valid through a drop of blood from the contractor.

Plague

Arnold imagines a plague that comes over the earth and kills all bad people. The good guys don't get sick at all or easily survive the infection. Arnold is of course one of the good guys. How can he be so sure about that? How about if the plague actually only kills the good guys? That would be mean, but typical of the injustice of this world. Arnold gets scared and wants to get vaccinated against fate, even though he knows that it can't be done.

to cut

Consciousness cuts being into things. Cutting is more elegant than stinging, which is why a mosquito does not have a noble title. Strong souls have the courage to face it, cowards have no blade at all. You shouldn't cut your finger! So folks: just be careful! The color of the cutting is called sharpness. Hot peppers and sex bombs can sometimes be a little spicy, too.

poor

Arms stretch out. The arms begin to bloom in the hands. Arms refine in the hands, the hands are strengthened in the tool. Branches are the arms of the trees.

border

A border separates one from the other. It starts at the border or it ends. The border forms a vessel for life. The blood needs veins to live. A house limits living by its walls. When living moves out of his house, he drowns in the sea of homelessness.

The plate has a round edge. In contrast to the frame, the edge completes the growth of its owner. A frame is jewelry, it is a compulsion to stop usury.

The term "world" is used to describe the landscape of everything. The world can be understood as a murderous greatness. This world has no end. The eyes of man cannot find a stop in the endless streets. A secure world is closed in its edges. There the secure world embraces the boundlessness with the arms of finitude.

bright and dark

Gustav is blind on both corns. His feet can't see anything. That's a good thing, because if you don't see anything, you won't get depressed. Therefore Gustav is happy. There are people who have a blind date. You are too blind to meet. Bats also see black, but they hear brightly. Is the light blind to the dark? Does the dark see the light?

the moon

The moon laughs in the dark. It can be seen in full. As a full moon, he is male. Otherwise, she is female. Or was it the other way around? The moon scurries across the sky fearfully. He doesn't like to be seen; only werewolves, bats and ravens are allowed to do this. The moon rules secretly in the realm of evil, it is the trickster with round cheeks, it is an old love, a shining darkness called moon. The moon shines most brightly when decent people sleep.

moment

There is only one moment and it is always the same. Only the moment is a moment. The majority of "moments" makes no sense. So there is no time. And yet the clock is ticking. That is why watches are liars.

memory

People cannot remember at all. We see the past from our present moment. Every day you remember a different past. The way it really was is irretrievably lost.

Original cow

In the beginning there was milk. The universe was created from milk, which is why we speak of the Milky Way. The milk came from the udder of the Urkuh, the large MUU.

fresh

The freshness sings as light in the moisture of life. Fresh meat is healthier than rotten meat. Fruit juice is fresher than blood, because the animal is rotting in its greed.

Turtles

Turtles are ancient embryos. They are from a time when there was no time at all. Their matter is also different. It does not consist of the smallest particles, but milder pulp as hardness runs in a line from here to there. Real earth never dies.

ruin

The wind blows secretly through the ruins of the crumbling castle. Dark walls are empty of events. Firestorms were yesterday, the scars are today. A mouse can write and tells the paper the story of the dead ruin. Birds fly over the red evening sun and disappear into nowhere.

Great

The primal always comes first. The cause, the origin, the primordial soup, the Uranus, the primeval cattle, the ancestor, the primeval forest, the Big Bang, and of course documents and quaint great-grandparents. The latter did not yet know the term dangerous. In Vienna, dangerous means something that is particularly dangerous.

fake news

The earth is flat! If the earth were a sphere, people in New Zealand would fall off the earth. Should NASA stick its fake photos up its ass? They have sniffed too much moon air!

Beginning

A start can suddenly start like a sprint or creep up like the fog in autumn. Plants germinate and babies are born germ-free in the hospital. A beginning requires an end: the birth of a baby ends the pregnancy. The beginning does not yet know itself: only at the end does the beginning know who it was.

children

Children eat children's chocolate. Adults eat adult chocolate. Both products taste like chocolate. You can see: children are nothing special. They are chocolate eaters like you and me. Children don't need to be watered either, even though they go to kindergarten.

Agaric

A toadstool loves its freedom. It needs rain from above. But the red mushroom refuses to receive God's impulses. The fly agaric would like to keep everything under control. It is even an owner of a whip. Dominance is important to it. Rain falls on the fly agaric. The fungus notices, that there are other things than dominance, but the agaric does not dare to open itself. Then he does it, because he is brave. Fear comes from the top down into the mushroom. Hey this. He is now no longer a toadstool, but a little mouse, who wants to live a middle class life in its cave. But this does not work. The mouse studies philosophy and renews the world and becomes famous.

lightning

Martin Luther and Paul were struck by lightning. As quickly as lightning, they became enlightened people. Does a lightning strike improve us? Or is the flash just a short circuit that creates hypocrisy? You would have to try that during the next thunderstorm.

JF Kennedy in Bielefeld

An alleged conspiracy theory says that the city of Bielefeld doesn't even exist. From a certain point of time it was no longer possible for the shadows to cover up the non-existence of Bielefeld. That is why they were keen to present the conspiracy as a mere theory or a joke so that no one would get the idea that the fake of Bielefeld was the bare truth. Fortunately, there is Bill. On July 24, 1963, Bill Clinton visited American President John F. Kennedy in the White House and shook his hand. Clinton exclaimed, "I'm going to be President!" Through this magical act, Clinton stole his fate and identity from

President Kennedy at the time. The result: Kennedy had to die. Or rather his lookalike. The real Kennedy was frozen. When the fake existence of Bielefeld threatened to come to light, Kennedy was thawed again. After a cosmetic surgery and intensive training in German, Kennedy is today under the false name Pit Clausen the mayor of the shadow city of Bielefeld.

The beards

Sindbart: Hey you, I can see you!

Windbart: Madness! I also you. Amazing when you consider that we both don't exist.

Sindbart: When two people meet that don't even exist, they become real in relation to each other and for each other, because they both meet on the same level, namely the level of nonexistence.

Windbart: You rarely meet anyone like you. You rarely become real. We should take the opportunity to have a detailed discussion about deception and truth.

Sindbart: Great, I'm there.

sea

The sea can allow itself greatness because it keeps secrets. The sea is made up of the trenches of the gods (tears contain salt). The sea is food for the earth. The thirst of the desert has long since dried up, the desert no longer needs to live.

Information society

Arnold Heitermann does not see television and does not read a newspaper. Just the headlines. For Otto Normal, what's current is important, everything else is unimportant. Arnold is interested in the bigger picture, not in the mayflies. In addition, you never know if information is correct. If the heading should say: 'Tomorrow the world will end!', Mr. Heitermann would certainly read the entire information. Such a doomsday can really affect you, for personal reasons alone.

water

Water likes to move. If nature allows it, then it flows. Water is fresh and sings in itself. Light sparkles with the movements of its waves. Water is everywhere where there is life. Water is unsteady as long as it is not still in the bottom. The water is wet, the water's nudity remains untouchable.

frogs

You shouldn't be a frog, not a fear frog. Anyone who is built as close to the water as the frog lives in the soul. Soul and lake are the same water, fish and frog know that. You can't really get scared in the water, only dry animals can. Ask the scaredy rabbit! Not the fear frog! Frogs never get out of puberty. The frog is a fish that has not made it to the land animal: a failure of evolution. It is no longer fish, but it was not enough for monkeys either. Frogs are still green behind the ears, and not only there. Frogs often get pimples, but then they are called toads.

Wild boar

Wild boars jump from the roof of a house in the foggy city of Rome. The wild pigs hit their backs on the pavement below. The wild boar has not broken anything, it grunts loosely and lives on. Such a wild boar is really robust. Your blood does not wither. In strong strokes, their fire juice pulsates timelessly through the race track of their veins.

Feelings

Feelings have no color. They are unfaithful bums, their only hold is impermanence. Would you rent your heart to feelings? Feelings are great for quantity and mass, they get stronger and weaker, they come back uninspired like the horses on the carousel.

Doom

The width of the world sinks into the depth. Everything goes to sleep and the moon is in the sky. Its silver light flows into the doom. One hand wants to grab the moon and does it too: It crushed the moon. Silver blood, which is equally black, runs down from a sphere that was once the moon. The world trembles.

kill

Death denies life and enables it equally. What should the eagle live on? What should he shit in the back? He can only live by killing other animals. Like man! Vegans are good people. But they too must follow the call of nature. After all, plants are also living beings. Vegans have a vitamin deficiency. Their innocence makes them pale in the face, they are biovampires. Vegans drink the blood of morality. The biggest predator is humans.

The dead television viewer

The television is on and there is a skeleton in front of it. His empty skull bones are no longer aware of the program. Someone turns off the television: The bone man now realizes that he is missing something and gets angry. Only in withdrawal does death realize that he is dead.

meaning of life

The purpose of life is to feed the great agricultural economist. In any case, that is the view of Dr. Lightbrain. He believes the following: from a distant sky, the great agricultural economist sows the seeds of our soul into the soil of realization. Through life experience, the soul germ grows into a productive ear of soul. The great agricultural economist harvested and consumed this ear after our death. Dr. Brainlight is Dr.'s twin brother Lightbrain. Every morning Dr. Brainlight throws up after the whole grain muesli when he thinks of his brother's crude theory.

Sun

The sun is the heart of the world, there is more space in it than in outer space. She has a big, shiny stomach. The sun gives birth to the world. The sun eats the world. Both equally. The sun is everything. It's white with old people, it's yellow with young people. The sun has no wrinkles on the face.

rabies

A vampire looks in the mirror: a man with black hair and glasses looks out of the silver, he has a pale face. The vampire thinks she looks like a normal person in the mirror. The undead only recognizes itself in the mirror, however, if it looks directly at its hands and body, it sees no one. This is not normal, not even for vampires. Surely he has rabies.

plants

Plants are green animals that cannot walk. Its leaves are stones of water. The sunlight turns them completely green. Stone, water and sun suddenly give life. A plant consists mainly of growth, it enjoys its growth. Growing has no genes, it gets to know them every moment. A plan doesn't grow, even if you carry it out. Plants, on the other hand, grow haphazardly with life.

tough

Some thick skulls have already hit their heads with the hardness. Hardness offers resistance and durability. A skeleton is hard. Usually the hard remains hard. However, a penis is only hard at times. - Just why? - The edge of hardness is an imposing line in the room. Edges should not be overlooked, you could hit your head on them. When two walls collide, the collision is called an edge. An edge is therefore the result of a carom. It is therefore not for the fainthearted. Stones are hard too. A stone is a thing, it has no face, because a stone looks like other stones. In their being, all things are the same. Closet, table or toothbrush are all just things. The stones that lie everywhere are called reality. A stone can be used to hammer in other people's skulls. It was important in the Stone Age. Today some stones can speak, these stones are called "cell phones". If I think about it correctly: There are also beautiful stones, namely gemstones. Dragons collect them.

collect

The collected is dense, sometimes narrow. The collected provides security as a permanent existence. Or it's a burden. It is harder to collect than to collect. If collecting is more difficult than what is collected, one speaks of "hunting".

rubbish

The superfluous is not integrated in the grown. The superfluous did not get to know the superfluous during its growth. While the overflowing can be rich, it sometimes donates, so the superfluous is not only useless, it also hinders the living substance in its progress. The superfluous is just garbage.

Macke

Hugo has a problem. His quirk is that the quirk bothers him on his screen. That drives Hugo crazy. Hugo had a flaw in his face for decades. Standing in front of the mirror, he looked at his quirk until his dermatologist lasered the knob away. Hugo has a quirk with quirks. But only for individual quirks. If everything has a quirk, such as a totally scratched window, Hugo doesn't mind. Hugo really has a problem.

crackhead

The empty thought feeds his withered snow woman. The gray snow woman is called neurosis. She is completely harmless, she is Woody Allen. You can laugh about a neurosis, because weirdos are funny people. But the old snow isn't really that harmless. No blood flows in the snow woman, but yesterday's snow is bored in it. The old snow goes into psychotherapy. Such therapy is also a neurosis, it is white like new snow.

Couple therapy

Dog and cat go into couple therapy. The therapist is a hyena. Dog and cat want to save their relationship. The therapy fails. Just why? What can that be? Certainly on the therapist, they all have a problem themselves.

No humor

Cheplin goes to the basement to laugh to keep his bodies company. He had to kill a lot of people to get money. The suffering of this world and women is not to be trifled with. Cheplin advocates a general ban on humor for all of Germany, with the exception of so-called laughing centers, where people can laugh out loud after paying a humor fee.

Laugh

Laughter is happy with his lips. Serious laughter gets a laughing fit. Humoresque laughter cannot rise from the sofa of the bourgeoisie. Real laughter isn't funny, it's just happy. Only compulsive jokes tear jokes from the tree of suffering.

totally funny

Isolde: Detlef, you never know if you're just kidding or if you're serious.

Detlef: It's very simple: If I'm fun, I'm serious, and if I'm serious, it's just fun.

Isolde: How can I differentiate one from the other?

Detlef: The first is the case on even days and the latter on odd days. Or was it the other way around? I am totally confused.

Isolde: I'm going crazy with the guy!

Climate change

Otto farts.

Miss Dr. Kackebart-Struller: Otto! Do you actually know what you're doing to the ozone layer? With every fart left not only your asshole gets bigger, but also the ozone hole. With each fart, methane flows into the atmosphere, which heats up the earth. Don't fart! We have to save our environment!

Otto Struller: You are right, Mausi, quite right. I'm going to the attic now, feeding the pigeons.

in the wild forest

In the wild forest, the roots of the trees leave their soil and run across the country. Calm does not return, but goes on an adventure. It goes over mountains, it goes in the valleys. Sometimes she jumps too.

roll

Rolling or circling is the movement of a round around its center. The wheel is caught. The roll itself does not roll, it remains immobile in relation to its center. If the rolling would move from a circle to a square, it would move freely. The bike only notices that the landscape is moving past it, the bike itself stops.

Rest and exercise

Quiet enjoys its identity. One can define rest as the absence of compulsive external movement. There is therefore no rest in the disco. Not on the highway either. Movement from the inside with calm is quite possible. Existence has peace. There is also the compulsive calm of Zen Buddhism. Such calm is cultivated death on earth, it is based on the suppression and killing of fidgeting. Real calm, however, lives in freedom.

rogue

The hummingbird flies to a fun palace where people spin. 52 crownless people live in the palace. None and everyone is king and fool at the same time. The people in the palace are all hermaphrodite. You could do it yourself if you wanted to. But they are more interested in creating game worlds: they are fun. Spooling is serious gaming. They are joking here with Jojos, the kings. The kings cast their crowns as fools in the great hall under the fountain. The crowns serve as a nest for the hummingbirds. King Purple writes serious nonsense. You can't talk to a man like that.

job

Work sweats in their no man's land, which is exhausting, because instead of a backbone, work has a chest of appreciation, decorated with pride. Your fulfillment finds work in the heart attack. Those who work can quickly forget their bodies in the basement. Work longs for redemption, but she would never admit that. Work is blind, it does not notice that it is working, it only knows. Christ as Redeemer has long been out. People redeem themselves through work: in psychotherapy, you work on yourself.

True movement is inside. A horse moves itself, but a car is driven by the horsepower of its engine. Movement tends to move in a serpentine manner, namely in waves. Walking, swimming, flying or driving are all movements. Nowadays you mainly get around. You could also move there. But no one can stand it on site. You stay on site.

wind

The wind sweeps Frigg's face. The time is running out. The water disappears into the hole. Everything is running, it is running away. The urine runs, the tears run. No one is with Frigg, just the wind. Her feet are covered by thick shoes. How about if she went bare feet? Then the wind would carry them up, and Frigg would be free. Her heavy shoes are the burden of her past. A wind called Wahuna runs through her hair. Sleipnir, an eight-legged horse, glides past Frigga. Frigga is fascinated, she can be put on the horse to the wind god and can be carried freely, barefoot, with no.

Better a pear in your hand

than an apple tree on the roof.

The machine does the purest. A machine feels nothing, so it works out of sheer despair. It does all the manipulations that the blunt workers did in the old days. Handles without feeling and life, mechanics, movement without meaning, only purpose. How nice it is when a machine does the stupid work for us. But the creators of the machines once planted the stupidity themselves. The machines will continue to bully us from the outside with their stupidity. Artificial intelligence is differentiated, but it remains stupid. We ourselves are only a cog of the big world machine.

The owner calls his hands his own. The atoms of his hands do not belong to the owner. The atoms in his hand are only suitable for the shape of his ego on loan. After the owner's death, the former atoms in his hand are suitable for another appearance. The owner feels at home in his hand, he is rooted in his hand. This root is his identity. It is not the hand itself.

The crazy apple

In the apple, the skin and pulp live together. Are they both married? Much more lives together in the apple: the spherical, the green, the fruity, its hanging on the tree. The apple thinks: `` I have properties, but I am not my properties. If I look at myself, I only find properties, but no being. " The apple becomes angry with this self-knowledge: " All kidding! I don't exist! " Each property of the apple now goes its own way. The spherical goes north, the green goes south. The fruity to the west, and the hanging of the apple to the east. It is no longer an apple, it never existed. The apple has divorced its fake identity. He was just thrown out of his That-Belongs-To-Me. Where's the freshness of the apple? She is sitting in the pub and can be run!

poetry

Poetry means to concentrate the meaning on its concentrate. However, the writer's poetry is sometimes so sealed that the reader can no longer open the meaning box. Only the author understands the content of the poem while he is writing. And even the author's can is too tight the next morning.

transparent

Obviously, what is transparent flies around freely without having to hide. Holes are mainly transparent. Although the see-through can be weighty, it is not easy to see through. The transparent becomes transparent when it becomes clumsy.

to catch

Catching successfully reaches for its prey while being mobile. This is why fish are particularly caught. They are slippery and live in moving water, but can still be caught.

jail

Crimes are only worthwhile if you don't get caught. A monkey comes to the zoo even if it hasn't done anything wrong. A zoo is a proper prison for animals. Some wild animals are imprisoned in the circus. Children sit in prison of their parents' pedagogy. Wives sit in prison of financial dependence on their husbands.

top secret

The secret must not see the eyes of others. It sits alone (or with conspirators) in its bunker and may do the following there: it decomposes, it festers, it rejoices, it turns wrong things, it ignites, it ignites others, it laughs at you, it is afraid, it protects itself, it refuses, or it gives birth to a child. The secret: we don't know what it does. That remains a secret.

to fly

Flying glides through the sea of vastness without feet. In flying, top and bottom are played against each other. A bird has power without raping the world. This is genius. Toadstools, however, cannot fly, their wings are enchanted. The wings of the birds stretch into the daring. They are at home there. The wings are the arms of flying, they are by force. A bird can fly freely without colliding with a cat in the air. An employee, however, very quickly collides with his boss or with the seriousness of life.

light

The light flies easily over puzzles, it just goes past heavy bellies. The light thing tends to be found in the top. Wood floats on water because it is lighter than water. The hot air balloon floats in the blue sky. The light quickly becomes frivolous. Something stupid happens easily.

Snowflake

A snowflake falls carefully. It is quiet. The flake comes from another world. It gives structure to this world, otherwise all magnetic fields would collapse. At the north and south poles, the magnetic field falls into the snow. From the Earth's poles, snow organizes secret changes in the world. Its magnetism permeates the earth's inhabitants and makes them heavy citizens.

protection

Protection is a fine thing. Protection is the first thing you need: constitutional protection, hall protection, crop protection products, data protection and thought protection. You haven't had a visit from Mind Protection yet? It will come, just wait.

Intestine

Digest chews and chews and chews. Digest chews ever finer until the food is so fine that it can be integrated into your own meat. However, the food always remains a bit toxic. The earth is poisonous. It is not our home. Animals can digest better than humans, they live closer to the earth.

earth

What we stand on is called earth. Sometimes it is called floor. Standing and earth are firm. Earth can also mean humus or stone. The substance of the earth is particularly striking, it is dense and heavy. The floor is peaceful, the floor is stupid. The great great mother has no face. Does she have warmth? Roots reach into the earth, they also understand the earth. Roots are one with the calm of the earth.

Bees

Bees live in the thick of matter, inwardly. A bee goes outside where it is cold. It falls dead to the ground as a snowflake. The bees have expressed their inwardness as cold flakes. As long as the snowflake is frozen, it is Christmas tree time. If the flake thaws, the loneliness is naked. In slurping the nectar, the bees connect all parts of the world and master gravity, they chew gravity. The nectar was a book that had not yet been read. Not even by its author.

Heaviness

Heaviness is usually large in quantity. In the lead, however, heaviness is small. Heaviness powers. It has an effect only by its mass, not by its color, because heaviness is far too dark to be colorful. Heaviness does not understand the funny. Only in sugar can the funny and the heavy sleep together. Does gravity come from above or from below? When heat becomes stronger, it becomes gravity. What about the stone that you can't roll? Is it too heavy or too firm? It is too brutal! Heaviness is softer than the brutal. Is it easy then? That's how it is!

wind

The wind runs disembodied over trees and houses. The force of the wind is not visible, only its effects can be seen. The wind blows away the stock. A dandelion blows in the wind, the ashes alike. The wind is very fleeting. But it always blows.

Cracks in the brain

Property is unique. It is peculiar to his thing. Quantity is relative, it is always measured from the comparison. Quantity has no owner. Isolde has a big belly, but she doesn't own the fat. Everything superfluous has a lot. It doesn't matter how many cracks Einstein's brain had. It is the brain's characteristic that makes it unique, not the number of its cracks. You can't compare apples and pears, just their weight.

sand

The fragments of the stones are called sand. Sand fragments are so small that they form a unity again as a community of the isolated. The sand is then felt as a whole. The whole thing is crying, but the sand cannot cry because it is too dry. Stones have neither blood nor water, not even as sand. The tears of sad giants donate salt water as the sea. That is why sand is often found as a beach where there is sea.

People

People only exist in the plural. A person cannot be alone. Man as a herd animal becomes " people ". A crowd consists of people. The blood of the people is the blood of their clan. A person, on the other hand, has his own bloodstream. With the old Jews, the blood of Abraham runs down to his late grandsons. People and archaic peoples have their identity in the group, not in themselves.

Babylon

Babylon was not a baby: it was too big for the tallest. There are also skyscrapers in New York. But these have to be destroyed by terrorists because they want to scratch God. You dance around the golden calf, about economic growth and the cosmetic surgeon. When will God's anger finally come and sweep the sinful people into the trash can?

smallest particles

Fred has gained unauthorized access to the large particle accelerator near Geneva at night and is now crawling into the round ring: he sees bright green particles flying by.

Fred: Hello particles, can you speak too?

Green particle: I have a headache, which is bad because I am only a head. Since the physicists discovered me, I can no longer really weave the world. Even politics is getting out of control.

A red particle flies past: it sticks out its tongue, which is even redder than the particle itself.

red particle: I light the money under my ass. Usually money is just information. My fire gives value to information. A triangle flies by, it has an eye on its forehead.

Triangle: I am the largest particle there is. Really small particles only exist in the hell of physics. The little has no reality. The more comprehensive things become, the more real they become. - Fred is just amazed.

Chaos is a confusion that creative extraterrestrials use to get out of mind protection into the world unstopped. Chaos is colorful. Chaos removes the rubbish of the past. Chaos dances and don't know what for.

write

In writing, the language speaks silently in the sound, but bright in consciousness. Writers are the sculptors of certainty. Writing is always written, even while writing. The writing is final and lasts longer than good wine. The word writes through all times.

to dance

Dancing is daring. Anyone who dances is insane. Dancing can also be cool if you are a reckless person. Thinkers shouldn't dance. The dance shatters her clarity of mind. Desperate for lack of love food, the insanity as a tiger eats the corrupt order of evil: Sweet Miezi make Fressi-Fressi!

Erwin

Drops of tears fall from the sky. They gather on earth to form a brook that swells into a river. Erwin sits in a canoe and paddles through the teardrop. The river flows uphill. Fires burn in honor of Wotan on the right bank of the river. On the left bank is a tree with a stone bird sitting on it. Erwin continues paddling uphill in a canoe. Now it is snowing. The canoeist sees a snowman on the bank between the pine needles. The snowman's eyes are alive, they are the eyes of a potent teddy bear. Erwin continues to paddle up the river. Someone on the left is playing the harp. God is close.

volcano

A woman in black with colorful splinters fights with the cool. They fly together over stars, under stars, between stars. The life of the Titanic appears in its sinking. A paper folding boat floats casually in the water, it drifts cautiously towards a marsh water spring: Peng! Ash falls from above. The Eyjafjallajökull has finally burst.

fit

On the contrary, fit can be found as love. As a related thing, Fit complements one and the other with similar service. Everything fits together in one structure. Beer, cigarettes and ashtrays are on Mr. Alki's kitchen table. That makes sense, it fits. Mr. Alki's kitchen table is a structure. Hinz and Kunz are in the big world catalog together on the Internet. Hinz and Kunz are only connected by their mere existence. The internet is not a structure, but nonsense.

thing

A thing is gray in its being; it is nothing more. Things are impersonal. The faceless world machine of things rules the earth: the internet of things. Things pile up to the world thing. Satan has long had the world in its claws. Living things are not spoken of because they move themselves. However, a young thing can move itself. It's a thing.

Measure

A measure can be the right one, lovingly baked by friendly gods. As a teacher, a sick measure sets limits to the pupil's power. The pupil is then full, his life is backlogged, and industry can generate electricity from the dam.

everything

All of this is an addition of many things to the limit of restlessness. Is this all the whole thing now? The whole thing is at least a round thing. As expected, the whole thing should shine on its edge, but it remains gray there. Then the industrial priest says: "The whole is more than the sum of its parts!" Even after this sentence, everything does not shine, more cannot be seen. The whole remains the naked addition of everything. There is only one more in this book.

Nothing

Nothingness is the world of all non-things. A cup is not a chair. A dress is not a cloud. Not to mention the dog: A dog is just a non-cat like a sparrow. All non-things come together in the world of nothing. Some say that nothing comes after death. Do you want to live there among all the non-things? It will be pretty tight in the closet of non-things.

enjoyment

Enjoyment needs more than what is necessary. So enjoyment is related to happiness. But while happiness is a gift of life, enjoyment is arbitrary. Enjoyment lingers and stays. Enjoyment is greasy. Pleasure is lust that has overeat. Enjoyment doesn't think, enjoyment is too sluggish for that. When the intestines digest more than it needs, it's happy. Satisfaction is a sweetener, but sugar is happiness.

साइकोसॉरस ने अपना परिचय दिया:

मुझे लगता है कि काव्यात्मक रूप से और एक जैव ईंधन का शिकार नहीं हुआ। ये विदेशी फैंटस अवैध रूप से अंधेरे में अंतरिक्ष से प्रवेश करते हैं और अपने लंबे समय के सूबों का उपयोग कर अपने दिमाग के लोगों की नींद को सोख लेते हैं। मैं केवल अनिच्छा से उन शब्दों का उपयोग करता हूं जो दूसरों ने पहले ही कह दिए हैं। मुझे वह अस्वाभाविक लगता है। इसलिए मैं अक्सर नए शब्दों का आविष्कार करता हूं, जिससे यह समस्या पैदा होती है कि कोई भी मुझे अब और नहीं समझता है। नतीजतन, मुझे फिर से उपयोग किए गए शब्दों का उपयोग करना होगा, जो कि जर्मन वर्नाक्यूलर ने केवल अभेद्य रूप से बनाया है। भाषा बोल सकती है क्योंकि इसमें अस्तित्व की सामान्य छवियां हैं। भाषा में मुख्य बात दुनिया की तस्वीरों को घर देना है। यह दुखद है जब कोई व्यक्ति भाषा के शब्दों का अनुसरण करता है और फिर सोचता है कि यह सोच है। वास्तविक सोच सक्रिय रूप से भाषा को आकार देती है। भाषा एक साइकोसॉरस की । है, यह इसका केंद्र है। दुनिया वास्तव में भाषा में जीवित है, क्योंकि बोलने का अर्थ है: दुनिया का निर्माण करना। शुरुआत में शब्द था!

scaredy बिल्ली

एक डरावना खरगोश एक ईस्टर बनी बनने के रास्ते पर है। रास्ते में वह अपने चाचा से मिलना चाहता था, लेकिन वह फिर से मिर्ची में है। डरा हुआ खरगोश मेंढक नहीं है, वह बंदर का सामना करता है, भले ही बंदर उस पर हंसता हो। पिस्सू पिस्सू के जिगर पर चलता है। हरे इस पिस्सू खाँसी सुनता है, जो अब गौरैया पर तोपों की शूटिंग करता है। डरा हुआ खरगोश अपने अंदरूनी कमीने पर काबू पाता है और फिर पिस्सू को घोंघे में बदल देता है। बाईं ओर वह एक गधा देखता है जो बहुत आरामदायक है। गधा गर्मियों के बीच में बर्फ पर चला जाता है। यह काउहेड पर काम नहीं करता है, और मुर्गियां गधे पर हंसती हैं। दाहिने हाथ पर, एक ग्रे माउस को पतंगे मिलते हैं क्योंकि मूस ने उन्हें स्मैक दी थी। हवा में मच्छर अपने आप में हानिरहित हैं यदि वे हाथी नहीं बनते हैं और चीन की दुकान में उनके जैसा व्यवहार

करते हैं। मिस्टर स्पैच खरगोश की तरह चलता है और अपने पानी से भरे पुडल को बाहर निकालता है ताकि वह कड़ाही में पागल न हो। मिस्टर और कुत्ते के पास शायद एक पक्षी है, लेकिन उनके बाद कोई मुर्गा नहीं उड़ता है, क्योंकि यह टोकरी में उसके मुर्गों के साथ है। इसके रास्ते में डरा हुआ खरगोश एक बंदर के दांत को ढूंढता है जो अब एक मक्खी को परेशान नहीं करता है। अब डरा हुआ है, वह ईस्टर बनी पर आ गया है।

एक वार्तालाप

मोल: साइकोसॉरस कहो, इस किताब के बारे में क्या है?

साइकोसॉरस: इस पुस्तक में भाषा स्वयं बोलती है। और भाषा है

हर चीज के बारे में बात करता है, इसलिए इस किताब में हर विषय है।

बत्तख: एक व्यक्तिगत प्रश्न: इसमें क्या अंतर है

साइकोसॉरस और कार्स्टन?

साइकोसॉरस: मैं इसके बारे में बात नहीं करना चाहता

विषय पूरी तरह से मुझे तनाव दे रहा है।

बतख: यह तुला है, यार!

तिल: यह पुस्तक स्पष्ट रूप से एक है

स्वचालित अनुवाद?

साइकोसॉरस: तो यह है। इससे माप से परे विचित्रता बढ़ जाती है।

भाषा एक हजार से अधिक शब्द कहती है।

खीस: अगर मैं कार्स्टन को लिखना चाहता हूं, तो उसके पास भी एक है

ऑनलाइन या कुछ और?

साइकोसॉरस: फिलहाल उसका ईमेल पता है

carsten-stemm@web.de और उसका अपना ऑनलाइन भी है।

वेयरवोल्फ: सन्ट रेप्रिमेट डे एक्सटीए कार्टे!

टमटम: मैं एक शब्द भी नहीं समझती, ट्रेन स्टेशन भी नहीं।

Rabe: आपको सब कुछ समझने की ज़रूरत नहीं है। कभी-कभी यह शब्द आपको तर्कहीन के माध्यम से ले जाने के लिए पर्याप्त है।

डिटेल डबल ड्ड

Detlef Doppeldoid मस्तिष्क के दोनों हिस्सों के साथ ठीक से नहीं सोच सकता है। डेटलेफ प्रकाश की तुलना में तेजी से सोचता है, जिसके कारण उसके लॉगोस्फीयर में अंतरिक्ष-समय की सूजन होती है। फिर वह दाएं से बाएं, बाहर से और सकल के साथ शुद्ध स्वैप करता है। वह नहीं जानता कि आप एक कमरे में या बाहर जाते हैं। यह Detlef Doppeldoid के बारे में बुरा है: दूसरे दिन उसने सोचा कि लोग लोग थे। डेटलेफ को अल्बर्ट आइंस्टीन और कोनराड एडेनॉयर के बीच का अंतर भी याद नहीं है। Detlef चमत्कार: " वही " और " वही " समान नहीं हैं? कभी-कभी मिस्टर डोपेलॉइड भी वर्तनी की गलतियाँ करते हैं। यदि वह पूरी तरह से भ्रमित है, तो डेटलेफ को भी भविष्य याद है।

डेटलेफ कहते हैं:

" जब भी मुझे नहीं पता कि मैं कौन हूं, तो मैं अपना पहचान पत्र देखता हूं: मेरा भी अपना नंबर है; एक संख्या, मेरे लिए सब अकेले, सिर्फ मेरे लिए। अद्वितीय और अचूक। राज्य मुझे प्यार करता है। लेकिन क्या इससे मुझे मदद मिलती है? Detlef Doppeldoid नाम के पीछे कौन है? और एक छोटा प्लास्टिक कार्ड क्या साबित करता है? प्लास्टिक कार्ड बनाना आसान है। आप आज सब कुछ नकली कर सकते हैं। तुम भी एक पहचान नकली कर सकते हैं। मैं काफी फूल बन रहा हूं। "

बोनी बोला

जो खरगोश बोल सकता है, उसे बोलने वाला खरगोश कहा जाता है। बोलने वाला खरगोश बोलते समय भोजन करता है और निबोलते समय बोलता है। शब्द की जड़ें उसके लिए अज्ञात नहीं हैं। वह वर्तमान में प्रेम का उपभोग कर रहा है। प्रेम उसके लिए एक शब्द मात्र है, मग, ममफ। आप बिना खाए प्यार कर सकते हैं, यही हरेक की समझदारी है।

बत्तख हैं!

जीवविज्ञानी बतख के पंखों में रुचि रखते हैं, ऑन्कोलॉजिस्ट बतख के अस्तित्व में रुचि रखते हैं। बत्तखें कौन देता है? उत्तर: 'यह'। 'यह' और होने में परिणाम दे रहा है। वैकल्पिक रूप से, इस प्रश्न का उत्तर निम्नानुसार दिया जा सकता है: विकास बतख देता है, बतख अंडे बतख देता है, बतख सेक्स बतख देता है, भगवान बतख देता है। बारिश हो रही है। वास्तव में कहना चाहिए: बादल बरस रहा है। यह 'यह' ईश्वर तक नहीं है, क्योंकि इसका अर्थ है: एक ईश्वर है। इसका अर्थ यह है कि: यह 'ईश्वर' से बड़ा है। एक और निष्कर्ष होगा: 'इट' वास्तविक भगवान है जो पहले भगवान को देता है। बत्तख हैं। एक नहीं कहता: यह बतख लेता है। देने से ज्यादा खुशी मिलती है। देना शायद लेने से ज्यादा ontological है। 'यह' इतना अस्पष्ट है कि अब आप इसका कोहरा नहीं देख सकते हैं। नतीजतन, आप अब यह नहीं सोचते कि बतख वास्तव में कहां से आते हैं। The यह 'भ्रामक है। यह ज्ञान होने का दिखावा करता है। अगर हम अब नहीं जानते कि बादल बरस रहा है,

फिर बारिश होती है। नकार भी neg इस े देता है ation its कोई एल्विच्चेस नहीं है!' 'Can यह क ` वल ऐसा कौन हो सकता है जो इन-बत्तखों को देने में सक्षम हो?

गोल्डी और पचेमरी

एक बार एक प्रेरक प्रशिक्षक था जिसकी दो बेटियाँ थीं, दोनों का नाम मैरी था। एक मेहनती था, दूसरा आलसी। एक दिन एक मेहनती महिला के पास एक कुआं आया, जिसने कहा:

" पीने का पानी नहीं! "

" यह केवल कानूनी कारणों से है, " प्यासी औरत ने सोचा। लड़की ने पानी पी लिया और गलती से फव्वारे में गिर गई, जिससे वह होश खो बैठी। कुछ बिंदु पर वह पूरी तरह से अज्ञात क्षेत्र में जाग गई।

एक वृद्ध महिला को एक घर की खिड़की पर रेनोवेशन की जरूरत थी और उसने अपना तकिया बाहर निकाल दिया। सुश्री होले, जैसा कि किरायेदार कहा जाता था, ने लड़की से कहा: "आप जैसे बुजुर्गों के लिए सक्षम नर्सें इन दिनों दुर्लभ हैं, मेरे पास बहुत काम है।"

हालांकि, थोड़ी देर बाद, लड़की होमिक हो गई और घर लौटने की अनुमति देने की इच्छा व्यक्त की। फ्राउ होल ने उसे यह इच्छा दी। बूढ़ी औरत ने लड़की को एक गेट तक ले जाया जिसके माध्यम से उसे जाना चाहिए। जैसा कि कड़ी मेहनत करने वाली महिला गेट के माध्यम से चली, ऊपर से उस पर बारिश हो रही थी, डाइऑक्सिन-दूषित पिच जो अब उसकी त्वचा से दूर नहीं हुई थी। लड़की ने कहा: " बकवास बकवास! मैं भाग्य पर अपना बदला फूटा लूँगा। मैं गणित का अध्ययन करता हूं और विरोधाभास सिद्धांतों पर पीएचडी करता हूं। "

जब माँ ने देखा कि उसकी बेटी पिच से लिपट गई है, तो उसने अपने बच्चे को पचेमरी कहा। सामाजिक मुआवजे के कारणों के लिए, माँ ने अब अपनी आलसी बेटी को भी कुँए में भेज दिया। यह लगभग वैसा ही हुआ। केवल उसकी दूसरी बेटी दूसरे घर में आई, जिसमें फ्राउ हॉल्स हौस के बजाय एक निश्चित फ्राउ हॉले रहते थे।

दस मिनट के काम के बाद, आलसी लड़की के काम का अनुशासन काफी कम हो गया। सुश्री हेल ने कहा: 'आपकी उम्र में मैं बहुत आलसी भी थी। मेरे पास एक

माध्यमिक विद्यालय प्रमाणपत्र भी नहीं है। अब हम एक चेट्टू माउटन-रोथस्चाइल्ड 1945 की ओर भाग रहे हैं, जिसे मेरे दामाद ने खुद चुराया था।

सौभाग्य से, पूरा तहखाना इससे भरा हुआ है। " एक हफ्ते तक लगातार पीने के बाद, आलसी भी होमसिक हो गया और घर छोड़ना चाहता था। फ्राउ होले ने उसे उसी गेट तक ले जाया, जिसके माध्यम से पचेमरी गुज़री थी। जब आलसी लड़की गेट से गुज़री तो उस पर सोने की बारिश हो रही थी। अब लड़की बहुत अधिक मूल्यवान थी, क्योंकि सोना भी नहीं निकाला जा सकता था। जब वह घर गया, तो उसे उसकी माँ ने गोल्डमरी कहा। जीवन के अन्याय पर क्रोध से, माँ ने चर्च छोड़ दिया और एक धर्मनिरपेक्ष निर्णय पर चली गई। Pechmarie बाद में उसके चेहरे पर डाइऑक्सिन के निशान के साथ तर्क के पहले प्रोफेसर बन गए। उसका जीवन पूरी तरह से अस्त-व्यस्त था। हालाँकि, गोल्डमरी कभी खुशी से रहते थे। > हैप्पी एंडिंग

भेड़ों का पनीर

शेफर्ड: मुझे बताओ, आप अपनी बांह के नीचे किस तरह की किताब ले जा रहे हैं?

वोल्फगैंग: आपकी एक भेड़ ने मुझे मेरे जन्मदिन के लिए किताब दी। इसका शीर्षक है: भेड़ का पनीर खुद बनाओ!

शेफर्ड: यह एक मजाक माना जाता है?

वोल्फगैंग: चुटकुलों के साथ छेड़ा नहीं जाना चाहिए। मैं कभी मजाक नहीं कर रहा हूं। जो कोई भी मजाक करता है वह गंभीर होने के लिए बहुत कायर है। मैं कभी मजाक नहीं कर रहा था। और अगर कोई हंसता है, तो मैं अपनी गांड को मुंह पर मारूंगा।

एक भेड़: क्षमा करें अगर मैं हस्तक्षेप करता हूं, लेकिन मैं आनुवंशिक रूप से संशोधित हूं, तो मैं बात कर सकता हूं। क्या भेड़ के पनीर पर जल्द ही कोई नया कर लगता है?

एक और भेड़: मैं भी निर्माता के आनुवंशिक रूप से बेहतर उत्पा ???, और मैं आपको बताता हूं: पुरुष महिलाओं की तरह हैं, केव सेबरीके से।

वोल्फगैंग: मैंने हमेशा सोचा था कि यह अलग होगा!

शेफर्ड: मुझे इस तरह की जटिल बातचीत से चक्कर आते हैं। .. आह, देखो कौन आ रहा है! वह लंगड़ा कर चल रहा है!

वोल्फगैंग: तब यह केवल एक तुलना हो सकती है!

शेफर्ड: वह क्यों है?

वोल्फगैंग: क्योंकि आप हमेशा कहते हैं: हर तुलना!

एक कंटीली भेड़: जिसका अर्थ हमेशा अस्पष्ट होता है। इसलिए वक्ता अपने भाषण में खुद से वादा करता है। डबल जर्मन ए   पैराडायिडियानिकस है , अत्यधिक चिकनी आत्म-चित्रण में रिसाव।

वोल्फगैंग: वह किस तरह का बातूनी है?

चरवाहा: भेड़ों का अध्ययन किया। मनोचिकित्सा या कुछ और।

(लंगड़ा अब चर्चा समूह में आ गया है।)

झींगा: तुम मेरे बाद हो। मेरा चोरी का व्यापार

रूसी परमाणु ऊर्जा संयंत्रों से प्लूटोनियम को उड़ा दिया गया है!

शेफर्ड: चीजें मत करो, ओटो!

भेड़: क्या आप प्लूटोनियम खा सकते हैं?

चरवाहा: सभी भेड़ों ने अध्ययन नहीं किया है!

सभी भेड़ें एक साथ: Mähhhh!

ओटो: मेरे पास केवल एक ही रास्ता है: आत्महत्या!

वोल्फगैंग: मेरे पास एक वैकल्पिक रास्ता होगा। मैं सर्कस में एक अच्छे जादूगर को जानता हूं। वह एक एलर्जी से पीड़ित है, लेकिन वह तकनीकी रूप से ठीक है।

ओटो: यह जादूगर कौन है?

वोल्फगैंग: वह सब कुछ है जो आपको लगता है कि वह है, क्योंकि उसके पास बहुत कुछ है

प्लूटो सहित सातवें घर में ग्रह।

ओटो: मुझे ज्योतिष पर विश्वास नहीं है!

वोल्फगैंग: लेकिन सितारे आप पर विश्वास करते हैं!

ओटो: ठीक है, मैं इसे आज़माना चाहता हूं, क्योंकि मेरे पास खोने के लिए कुछ नहीं बचा है। मैं एक खरगोश में मुग्ध हूं औ पनऩाम पीछे की ओ खता हूं ताकि कोई मुझे पहचान न सके।

चरवाहा: बड़ी अच्छी बात है! अब यह वास्तव में सुखद अंत है!

एक आपात स्थिति में, सेब नाशपाती खाता है।

मानव हत्या

बंदर: शुभ दोपहर, अजीब आंखें, आपने आँखें धीमी कर ली हैं।

अजीब आँख: और तुम एक बंदर हो, तुम बंदर हो।

बंदर: मेरे यहाँ डायनामाइट की एक छड़ी है।

हम किसको गांड में डालते हैं?

अजीब आँख: बेशक! टीएनटी में मैं नहीं कहता हूँ!

आप शानदार बंदर, आप नोबेल पुरस्कार के लायक हैं!

(बंदर डायनामाइट के गधे में तिरछा धक्का देता है और फ्यूज को जलाता है। प्रतीक्षा के तंत्रिका-विकट सेकंड के बाद, एक हिंसक विस्फोट होता है: धूल, मलबे और मांस के अवशेष विस्फोट के स्थान को कवर करते हैं।)

बंदर: अच्छा! यह दुर्घटनाग्रस्त हो गया!

हमारे लिए जानवरों की कोई गिनती या पैराग्राफ नहीं हैं।

अब हम एक केला खाने जा रहे हैं। Haha!

स्टील का चूजा

एक बार एक छोटी-सी चीख़ी कार थी, जो प्लंप और सौम्य स्वभाव से चलती थी। वैगन चलता है, इसे घोड़े द्वारा खींचा जाता है। एक वाहन जो आज नहीं चला। जब साथी को मोटर से चलाया जाने लगा, तब ट्रॉली स्टील बन गई, जब ट्रॉली को फिर भी खींच लिया गया, तो फूल खिल गए और पानी रूक गया। जीवन का रहस्य चक्की के पहिये में रहता था, यहाँ पहिया पानी में चलता था। ऑटोमोबाइल स्टील गर्ल का जन्म था। आकाश खिंचता है, आकाश खिंचता है, वह उत्तेजित होता है। स्टील चिक एक रक्षा तोप के साथ आकाश में गोली मारता है। यह द्वितीय विश्व युद्ध है, फिर से एक घोड़ा बनने के लिए स्टील द्वारा एक बेहूदा प्रयास। स्टील चिक अब खुद एक घोड़ा है, इसलिए वह एक पोनीटेल पहनती है। घोड़े वास्तव में सुरुचिपूर्ण हैं, क्योंकि लालित्य अब स्टील के युग में नहीं जाना जाता है। प्लास्टिक भी स्टील है। घोड़े द्वारा खींची गई हर चीज स्टील नहीं होती है। आपको एक ऐसी सुंदरता मिलती है जो एक फैशन डॉल नहीं है।

अधिक स्थान

एक बहु-कमरा एक कमरा है जो बाहर से अंदर से बड़ा है। बहु-अलमारी, उदाहरण के लिए, एक साधारण बेडरूम अलमारी जैसा दिखता है। लेकिन यदि आवश्यक हो तो आपको अलमारी में छिपाना होगा, आप यह जानकर आश्चर्यचकित होंगे कि अलमारी में पूरी आकाशगंगाएं हैं। और ये ऑक्सीजन की कमी के परिणामस्वरूप मतिभ्रम नहीं हैं। दुनिया वास्तविकता में छेदों से भरी है। और तो और हैं।

ख़तरा

खतरा आपको धमकाता है। हादसा अभी तक नहीं हुआ है। लेकिन यह भविष्य में हड़ताल कर सकता था; यह एक जोखिम है। जीवन असुरक्षित है। आप नहीं जानते कि अगले पल जीवन टूट जाएगा या नहीं। खतरे दरवाजे पर है, खतरा अप्रत्याशित है, यह एक बुरा सपना बन सकता है। शिकारी खतरनाक होते हैं; पूँजीपति भी। पानी से भरे टब में पावर केबल बिछाना खतरनाक है। शादी करना जोखिम भरा भी है। दूसरी ओर, जीवन बीमा, सुरक्षा का वादा करता है: यदि आपने एक जीवन खो दिया है, तो आपको एक नया मिलेगा। लेकिन बीमा धोखाधड़ी से सावधान रहें: बीमा कंपनियां बहुत धोखा देती हैं!

सोच

सोच अर्थ की भूमि में भटकती है। सोचने के तरीके ज्ञान के जंगल में चलते हैं। उसकी वृद्धि के माध्यम से, सोच और अधिक कठिन हो जाती है और अंत में उसके विचार पेड़ों और उसके सपने बर्फ में विलीन हो जाते हैं।

ओलिंप

फ्रेड ओलिंप में सेल फोन पर एक भगवान देखता है:

फ्रेड: नमस्ते भगवान!

देवता कितने समय से एक सेल फोन का उपयोग कर रहे हैं?

भगवान: हाँ मेई, आप बस एडजस्ट कर लो मैं अपने सहयोगियों के साथ टेलीपैथिक रूप से भी संवाद कर सकता था, लेकिन हम देवता लोगों को समझने लायक बनाना चाहते हैं।

फ्रेड: तो, मैं इसे समझ नहीं!

अंडे का सिर

ब्रेन वैंकर्स न्यूमेटिक एग्लिकेशन के खरगोश हैं। उन्हें अंडे का सिर भी कहा जाता है। आपके न्यूरोलेंट्स बहुत अधिक कोमल नहीं हैं, लेकिन वे बहुत लंबे हैं। अपने गंजे सिर पर नंगे अखरोट फेंक दें क्योंकि उनमें बहुत सारे दिमाग होते हैं। न्यूरोलेंट्स मन की छड़ें हैं। न्यूरोलॉट्स पेड़ों की चड्डी भी हो सकते हैं, जिसके माध्यम से आप उनमें से सरासर संख्या के लिए जंगल नहीं देख सकते हैं। लेकिन वास्तव में बौद्धिक सुशी खाने के लिए न्यूरोलेंटेन चॉपस्टिक हैं।

कुछ दिमागी तरंगों को दार्शनिक कहा जाता है। दार्शनिक बिना पिए सोचता है, यह प्रेम के बिना हल्का है। विचारक ज्ञान के रेगिस्तान में बुरी तरह से मजाक कर सकता है। कैक्टि कभी नहीं हंसा। दर्शन उतना ही कठिन है जितना पुराना पनीर। हीलिंग की राह पर दार्शनिक कविता लिखने लगे हैं।

यक्ष

फ्रेड: तुम्हें पता है क्या Detlef, मैं demigod के लिए पदोन्नत किया गया था।

Detlef: वाक़ई?

फ्रेड: यह ऐसा है! मैं अब हर सवाल का जवाब पा सकता हूं, अगर केवल अभेद्य रूप से, लेकिन मैं इसका जवाब खोज सकता हूं।

Detlef: आपको किसने प्रमोट किया?

फ्रेड: बिग बॉस!

Detlef: अहा!

फ्रेड: मैं बस निंदा कर रहा हूँ। मैं अभी अमर नहीं हूं, लेकिन मैं इस पर काम कर रहा हूं।

Detlef: एमएम, ऐसा करो।

फ्रेड: मैं अंत में जानता हूं, उदाहरण के लिए, केला क्यों टेढ़ा है।

Detlef: हाँ, फिर क्यों?

फ्रेड: वह एकता के लिए तरसता है, केला स्वर्ग वापस जाना चाहता है, वह एक सर्कल बनना चाहेगा, लेकिन फॉल ने उसे मना किया, केवल उसकी ताकत वक्र तक फैली हुई थी।

Detlef: क्या एक डेमो जानता है!

आत्मा

'ि' स्परिट शब्द बहुत अकेला शब्द है को इतनी सारी चीजों को समझाना है। बुद्धिमत्ता ने पत्थर काट दिए; मन जोड़ता है। आत्मा सूर्य की तरह दुनिया के कुछ हिस्सों को रोशन करती है और उन्हें एक आकार देती है। मन चीजों के लिए छवि है। मन सबसे छोटे कणों को अधिक से अधिक कपड़े पहनाता है। मन सोच सकता है, बुद्धि केवल सोच सकती है या गठबंधन कर सकती है।

कारण और प्रभाव

एक बिलियर्ड खिलाड़ी अपनी छड़ी के साथ एक गेंद को हिट करता है, जो बदले में दूसरी गेंद को हिट करता है। यह कारण और प्रभाव सोच विज्ञान का मूल तर्क है। तर्क इसे सही ठहराता है, यह कुछ भी स्पष्ट नहीं करता है। बिलियर्ड खिलाड़ी की स्वतंत्र इच्छा पूरी तरह से इस विश्व दृष्टिकोण में छिपी हुई है। कारण सुस्त जानवर हैं, लगभग बैल। कारण ऊर्जा के माध्यम से मनाते हैं, अर्थ के माध्यम से नहीं।

तर्क

फ्रेड: मैं तर्क में विश्वास करता हूं। संपूर्ण ब्रह्मांड तार्किक रूप से संरचित है। हालांकि, महिलाएं ब्रह्मांड का हिस्सा नहीं हैं। तार्किक सोच आपको हर पहेली तक पहुँच देती है। आपको बस सोच-समझकर बहुत प्रयास करने होंगे।

अर्नोल्ड हेइटरमैन: तर्क हमें ज्ञान में आगे नहीं बढ़ाता है। एक उदाहरण: एक बाड़ पर तीन कौवे बैठते हैं। एक पक्षी हत्यारा आता है और पक्षियों में से एक को गोली मारता है।

अर्नोल्ड: कितने पक्षी अभी भी बाड़ पर हैं?

फ्रेड: बाड़ पर दो कौवे हैं।

अर्नोल्ड: गलत! अभी भी बाड़ पर एक कौवा है!

फ्रेड: यह पूरी तरह से अतार्किक है!

अर्नोल्ड: यह तर्कसंगत है। शॉट बर्ड जमीन पर गिर गया। दूसरा कौआ जोर से धमाके से चौंका और तुरंत उड़ गया। तीसरा कौआ धमाके से घबरा गया और बैठने वाला एकमात्र पक्षी रह गया।

फ्रेड: यह मामला मुझे बहुत लगता है, लेकिन यह तर्कसंगत है।

अर्नोल्ड: ठीक है, आप तर्क के साथ सब कुछ और कुछ भी समझा सकते हैं।

फ्रेड: सबसे पहले, बाद में।

अर्नोल्ड: हाँ, हमेशा बाद में।

हालांकि, वास्तविकता पहले भी थी।

फ्रेड: क्या होगा अगर पांच कौवे शॉट के बाद अचानक बाड़ पर बैठ गए थे?

अर्नोल्ड: फिर कुछ जीवन-थकाने वाले कौवे भी गोली लगने की उम्मीद में बैठ गए होंगे।

फ्रेड: वास्तव में महान, तार्किक क्या है।

अर्नोल्ड: आप तर्क के साथ सब कुछ समझा सकते हैं, यहां तक कि अतार्किक भी।

फ्रेड: यार, यार, मुझे वास्तव में इसके बारे में सोचना है।

अर्नोल्ड: लेकिन कृपया सख्ती से तार्किक रहें!

फ्रेड: उह ... हाँ ... अच्छी तरह से ...

संवाद

सुकरात: तुम आज सुबह फिर से क्या देख रहे हो, प्लेटो!

प्लेटो: चुप रहो, गधा!

सुकरात: तुम बस संवाद करने में सक्षम नहीं हो!

गेंद

एक बुलेट अपने आप में बहुत सीमित है। यदि इसे प्रज्वलित किया जाता है, तो इसे जन्म देने की इच्छा होगी। लेकिन कोई भी उन्हें प्रज्वलित नहीं करता है। गेंद कीचड़ की तरह सुस्त रहती है और एक दूसरे को नहीं जानती। बॉल्स क्यों रोल करते हैं? वे रास्ते को रोल करते हैं, लेकिन वे अपना आकार नहीं बदलते हैं। अंततः, वे आंदोलन से लुढ़क गए। गोली चली। अब मुझे याद आया: बुलेट मादा हैं!

(इन) परफेक्ट है

कुत्ता ही कुत्ते का विचार है। क्या एक कुत्ते का विचार अब एक डछशंड, एक सुनहरा कुत्ता, एक भेड़ का बच्चा या एक पूडल जैसा दिखता है? हम जानते हैं कि एक चक्र अपने आप में कैसा दिखता है। केवल एक चक्र है और यह पूरी तरह गोल है। त्रिकोण पहले से ही इसे और अधिक कठिन बनाते हैं: त्रिकोण का विचार किस कोण का है? सर्कल एकमात्र ऐसा विचार है जिसे बिल्कुल खींचा जा सकता है। कुत्ते को केवल एक विशिष्ट कुत्ता ही नहीं बनाया जा सकता है। सर्कल को ही खींचा जा सकता है। हम चक्र की पूजा करेंगे? क्या कोई "अपने आप में" है? चीजें केवल "मेरे लिए" दिखाती हैं? - वास्तविकता में परिपूर्ण जीवन के लिए बहुत ही अपूर्ण होगा। जीवन को एक चक्र में एक कोने या एक वर्ग में एक छेद की आवश्यकता होती है। परिपूर्ण केवल एक विचार के रूप में मौजूद है, क्योंकि वास्तव में परिपूर्ण मौजूद नहीं हो सकता है। सर्कल में जीवन की पूर्णता में कोने हैं। चेस्टनट एक कोणीय गेंद है। यह पूर्ण जीवन के रूप में अपूर्ण पूर्णता में है। फिर भी, एक शाहबलूत का पेड़ किसी तरह बीमार है। ऐसा क्यों? केवल हेजहोग जानता है कि!

वृत्त

एक वृत्त साँस नहीं ले सकता। कहीं उसके पास एक छेद नहीं है जिसके माध्यम से वह सांस ले सकता था। सर्कल को ही छेद के रूप में देखा जा सकता है। क्या सर्कल दूसरी दुनिया का प्रवेश द्वार है? मैं इसकी जांच नहीं कर सकता क्योंकि सर्कल ने मुझे अंदर नहीं जाने दिया। यह अभी भी बंद है। किसी को इस प्रकार के व्यवहार नहीं करना चाहिए। सर्कल मुझसे बात नहीं करता है, यह हमेशा रहस्यमय रहेगा। सर्कल में शायद छिपाने के लिए कुछ भी नहीं है: यह भोला, उबाउ और खाली है। - गोल घेरे का रंग है। यह रंग बहुत दुर्लभ है और इसका कोई नाम नहीं है। रंग को नाम देने का सबसे आसान तरीका " रंगीन " है। गोल एक सर्कल और एक आर्क के बिना एक साहसिक पर जा सकता है। जीवन अपने आप में एक रोमांच है। आज समूह कुछ नया सोचता है। लेकिन दौर इतना पुराना है कि नए के बारे में उसकी सोच कभी पागलपन पैदा नहीं कर सकती। हालांकि, परोपकारी कभी भी घूमते नहीं हैं। यह उसके लिए बहुत ऊबड़ है। समूह एक सर्कल बनना चाहता था और रोजगार एजेंसी से मुकरने के लिए कहा। क्लर्क एक वर्ग था। यह बुरी तरह से समाप्त हो गया।

सेब सोचता है और नाशपाती गाइड।

हिटिंग कमाल की है

प्रहार सबसे सार्वभौमिक क्रिया है। मारना वास्तव में बहुत बढ़िया है। यह गतिविधि पहले से ही पाषाण युग में पूरी तरह से विकसित थी। आप अपनी आँखें खोल सकते हैं, एक जैसे किताब। ड्रूडेन में देखें, खिड़की को तोड़ें, या चेहरे पर किसी को पंच करें। संगीतकार ड्रूम के साथ शोर करते हैं। झटका तुम्हें मारता है। 1.FC मेनिस्कस, रोसेनहाइम फ्लैट पैर 2-1 से धड़कता है। जो जीतता है वह जीतता है। हिट करने का सबसे अच्छा तरीका पत्थरों से है। एक महान पत्थर को हथौड़ा कहा जाता है। मारना कच्चा और खुरदरा होता है। एक झटका नासमझ और परमाणु है। स्मैश मारना, टूटना, मारना अलग हो जाता है। मार का एक बच्चा काट रहा है। एक बुरा बच्चा। मार का एक और बच्चा जोर है। यह बच्चा अधिक संभावना है क्योंकि इसमें आगे सूरज है। पिटाई करने वाला मुट्ठी बांधता है, इसलिए उसकी हरकत से पेट फूल जाता है।

कारखाने खजाना

कला का एक काम सभी परम मानवीय अनुभव का चित्रण है। ऐसा अनुभव है कि इसकी पुष्टि की गई है ताकि यह कला के काम के रूप में जम जाए। कार्य खजाना सभी प्राणियों को आध्यात्मिक क्षेत्र से चुंबकीय क्षेत्र की तरह उन्मुख करता है। Werkschatz जीवन का प्राकृतिक विकिपीडिया है। दुर्भाग्य से ज्ञान के खजाने में काली भेड़ें भी हैं: उन्हें कारखाने की गंदगी कहा जाता है।

राजा ऑर्थोस के लिए, शासन करने का मतलब अपने स्वयं के आंतरिक के अनुसार चीजों की व्यवस्था करना है। ऑर्थोस लोगों को अपनी मर्जी नहीं देता। राजा चीजों को मजबूर नहीं करना चाहता है, लेकिन अपनी मूर्खताओं को तलाशता है और उन्हें खुद को व्यवस्थित करने देता है। ऑर्थोस रीच में लोग, बकरियां और अन्य लोग रहते हैं, सभी अपने सही स्थान पर खड़े हैं और चल रहे हैं। उनकी मृत्यु के बाद, राजा ऑर्थोस अपनी पसंदीदा नदी के पानी में बह जाएगा, जो अंततः समुद्र में डाल देगा। समुद्र से, उसका काम लोगों को उन्मुख करना जारी रखेगा।

भूख और प्यास

भूख हर समय कुछ खाना चाहती है। भूख पूरी तरह से उसकी इच्छा की वस्तु पर निर्भर है। लेकिन यह वही है जो भूख को इतना सुखद बनाता है। वह जीवन से भरा है, कुछ तो यह भी कहते हैं कि वह स्वयं जीवन है। भूख की एक बहन भी है: उसका नाम "" प्यास "" है। लेकिन यह केवल बहुत पागल प्रकारों के लिए है।

आवश्यकता है भूख और प्यास का अमूर्त होना। जरूरत गरीब की है और जरूरत में। आवश्यकता बहुत धर्मनिरपेक्ष है और हमेशा एक ही ग्रे दिखता है। आप अपनी आवश्यकताओं को किसी भी तापमान पर संग्रहीत कर सकते हैं। कभी फल की आवश्यकता नहीं होती है, यह हमेशा दुबला रहता है। अगर आपको कुछ चाहिए, तो आप खरीदारी करने जाएं।

फाइबर की जरूरत किसे है? इन सबसे ऊपर, यदि वे केवल गिट्टी से बने होते हैं। बोझ भरने वाला। वे शून्य को भरते हैं, लेकिन स्वयं खोखले रहते हैं। वह सार है जो चमकता है।

साइकोसॉरस पूरी तरह से अंत में है:

आकृति के रूप में एक बर्फ की शक्ति ने उसकी बांह बढ़ा दी है। ठंडे चेहरे से पानी की एक सीढ़ी लुढ़क जाती है। छाया वाली महिला की आँखें रात में दो सूरज की तरह चमकती हैं। लंबे समय तक नहीं। तुम्हारी रोशनी अब बाहर जा चुकी है। छाया औरत आसमान में एक काली परी के रूप में उड़ती है। अज्ञात स्थान अनाथ है। जहाँ कभी कोई नहीं रहा, वहाँ अब कोई नहीं है। नहीं होने का मेरा ज्ञान खाली जगह के बगल में है। मैं गर्म हूं, लेकिन केवल गर्मी के रूप में, क्योंकि मेरे पास कोई दूसरा शरीर नहीं है। एक जीभ के बिना एक चीख खाली कमरे में चारों ओर जाती है। हर जगह केवल खालीपन है, जहां कुछ वास्तव में होना चाहिए। जहां कुछ भी नहीं है, आप कुछ भी नहीं देख सकते हैं, खासकर अगर आपकी कोई आंख नहीं है। लेकिन मुझे डर लगता है और मुझे नहीं पता कि क्यों।

छेद

एक छेद का मतलब है एक गोल अनुपस्थिति। छेद खाली हैं। एक छेद अक्सर एक मार्ग है जो अंदर और बाहर जाता है। कभी-कभी दृश्य छेद के माध्यम से बाहर निकलता है और छेद के माध्यम से दृश्य आता है। छेद भूखे हैं, वे भरवां होना चाहेंगे। सभी के आग्रह से संतुष्ट होना अच्छा है। वास्तविकता में छेद होते हैं। ये इतने पारदर्शी होते हैं कि कोई भी इन्हें नहीं देख सकता है, अपने महान तंत्र के साथ एक भौतिक विज्ञानी भी नहीं। नग्न लोगों में कपड़ों की कमी देखी जा सकती है। दूसरी ओर, एक अंतराल की कमी, भूख और अदृश्य बनी हुई है। सतह खाली हो जाती है। यदि यह खालीपन भर जाता है, तो सतह जल्दी से गायब हो जाती है, पतली हो जाती है। एस्थेट सतह पर रंग निर्धारित करता है ताकि उसे अधिक आत्मविश्वास मिले।

पशु

क्लासिक जानवर के चार पैर होते हैं, यह "मेव्स" या छाल होता है। जानवर शब्द कई प्राणियों के लिए एक प्रकार का मामला है जिनके पास बहुत कम है। जानवर पत्तियां नहीं ढोते हैं और वे परमाणु बम नहीं बना सकते हैं। जानवर पिछड़े लोग हैं। हालांकि, एक दिन जानवर भी गोडेल के अधूरे प्रमेय को समझेंगे। - केवल कब?

प्रकृति कच्ची और खुरदरी हो सकती है। सपने देखने वालों की प्रकृति भी है: यह प्रकृति पतन से पहले ही लोगों का स्वर्ग है। जर्मिनक चार्ल्स डार्विन की प्रकृति इस तरह दिखती है: एक मजबूत के खिलाफ मजबूत की लड़ाई। हमारी दूसरी प्रकृति संस्कृति है। हमारे तीसरे दायरे को कृत्रिमता कहा जाता है। किसी को भी वहां रहना पसंद नहीं है।

बर्फ का फूल

स्वीडन की एक विदेशी शक्ति सबसे ठंडी बर्फ से बनी है। यह शक्ति पृथ्वी पर एक बड़ी लड़की के रूप में जाती है जिसका नाम ईस्बल है। बर्फ से बना एक फूल, एक खूबसूरत फूल। फूल वसंत की याद ताजा करते हैं, क्योंकि इस समय के दौरान ताजा फूल आमतौर पर युवा गर्मी में खिलते हैं। हालांकि, सर्दियों की जानलेवा ठंड में हमारा बर्फ का फूल खिलता है। अन्य सभी लोग जो बर्फ से बने होते हैं, वे बर्फ के फूल से घिर जाते हैं। अग्नि ठंड से भी बाहर है, जलती हुई बर्फ से। अग्नि बर्फ के फूल को देखता है और रोमांचित होता है। फ्रिज हमेशा सबसे गर्म होते हैं। श्री Sumpfstein आइसक्रीम के विक्रेता के रूप में एक स्टनर है। उनकी आइसक्रीम गेंदों में विस्फोटक होते हैं, जो तब जलते हैं जब वे सभी पहाड़ों पर लंबे समय तक रहते हैं। इस्ब्लम मिस्टर सम्पफस्टीन को देखता है: उसे एक झटका लगता है, रूले बॉल उसके सिर में लुढ़क जाती है। किसी को नहीं पता कि गेंद सत्रह के डिब्बे में रुकेगी। अग्नि में यह तीनों होंगे। आइस बॉल हो या रूलेट बॉल, बॉल्स सभी एक जैसे ही होते हैं। गोलियां भाग्य का खराब बैंक हैं। और अब हम इस बैंक को तोड़ते हैं और पागलपन को मुक्त करते हैं। हर कोई पागल हो रहा है: ईस्ब्लम, एग्रिस और हेर सम्पफस्टीन एक बॉक्स में हैं। आप पागलपन की सांस लेते हैं: आह, यह अच्छा है। अंत में वे स्वतंत्र हैं!

रक्त

रक्त एक मोटी और शक्तिशाली गर्मी के रूप में अंदर बहता है। मानव रक्त बहुत ही व्यक्तिगत है क्योंकि यह अभी भी अपनी नसों में घेरे हुए है। रक्त चक्र, इसलिए यह गोल है। उसकी मंडली में रक्त शक्तियाँ। ठंड और हृदयहीन डॉक्टर के सिरिंज में बाहरी रक्त पहले ही मर चुका है। कितना भयानक है! केवल सरीसृप खून बह रहा है। जब तक कि सरीसृप के हरे फर पर सूरज चमक रहा है। हर पिशाच जानता है: जब चंद्रमा चमकता है, तो रक्त काला होता है। आप दिन के दौरान कुछ भी नहीं देखते हैं।

आग

हिंसक लपटों के साथ आग नाचती है। जंगली जलने से ईंधन का स्थायित्व नष्ट हो जाता है। हीट स्पाइक्स कमरे में पैक करते हैं, बुखार के दांत खुद को काटते हैं। लाल तूफान की शक्ति इसके आसपास की गर्मी की आभा देती है। आग के अंगारे जलकर राख हो जाते हैं। आग प्रभावशाली है, लेकिन यह ईंधन से अपना पदार्थ उधार लेती है। उनका भोजन पकाया गया था, बहुत तेजी से पकाया गया था। आग की गर्माहट अमरता के स्थान पर भयंकर रूप से सोती है। जब गर्मी पागल हो जाती है, तो यह गर्मी हो जाती है।

आम तौर पर

सामान्य उतना ही दिखाता है जितना आवश्यक हो। विशेष सुविधाएँ बहुत स्पष्ट किनारों दिखाती हैं। सामान्य हर जगह समान है, यह अक्सर उसी के माध्यम से व्यक्त किया जाता है। सब कुछ के परिदृश्य में, सामान्य हर जगह में पाया जा सकता है। सामान्य के ग्रे अंकल को औसत कहा जाता है। सामान्य को बार-बार विशेष के साथ समायोजित करना पड़ता है, जिससे तनाव पैदा होता है। जब आप असामान्य छुट्टी पर जाते हैं तो सामान्य सुरक्षा देता है।

स्थायी छाया

एक खड़े छाया को हमेशा रोकना चाहिए, हालांकि यह जहां चाहे वहां जा सकता है। अगर खड़ी परछाई हिलना चाहती है, तो वातावरण उसे अतीत की बजाय अतीत की ओर ले जाता है, वह खुद रुक जाता है। खड़ी छाया चारों ओर घूम सकती है और अभी भी उसी स्थान पर हमेशा के लिए रहना है। एक खड़े छाया की कोई कंपनी नहीं है। बेशक अन्य स्थायी छायाएं हैं, लेकिन वे कहीं और हैं।

शॉर्ट सर्किट

रास्ता तब तक लक्ष्य की ओर जाता है जब तक कि कोई गूढ़ व्यक्ति उस पर नहीं चल रहा है। एक शॉर्ट सर्किट जीवन का मार्ग छोटा करता है। वह जल्दी से एक ऐसे मार्ग का अनुसरण करता है जो मौजूद नहीं है। नतीजतन, उसके पास अनुभव की कमी है। इसकी सफलता गर्म और खाली है और मांस के बिना है, लेकिन शॉर्ट सर्किट का करिश्माई प्रभाव पड़ता है। सबसे छोटा मार्ग हमेशा एक शॉर्ट-सर्किट होता है, इसका लक्ष्य कोई भी नहीं होना है। शॉर्ट सर्किट विकास के बिना कार्य करता है, यह बिना किसी मार्ग के चलता है। जोआचिम अर्नस्ट बेरेन्ट ने एक पुस्तक लिखी: " कोई रास्ता नहीं है, बस जाओ: प्रकृति में बीई "। अपनी पुस्तक की प्रस्तुति के रास्ते में, वह एक कार से चला गया था।

जाने

आपको डर लगता है कि चलने पर गिर सकता है। लेकिन चलना बहुत अच्छा है: यह हमेशा संतुलन में रहता है। गलियारे में खड़े कदम। हालांकि, झूठ कभी नहीं चलता है।

स्वर्ग

चोटी के पहाड़ों को कोई समस्या नहीं है और खुश हैं कि वे इतने बड़े और बड़े हैं। स्वर्ग भी खुश है जब यह पहाड़ों से आगंतुकों को प्राप्त करता है। बड़े आकाश को भी विश्वास की आवश्यकता है।

कारण

कारण नीचे है। यह आधार, तल, आधार और औचित्य है। यदि आप नीचे की ओर देखते हैं, तो यह एक रसातल बन जाता है। आप वहां गुरुत्वाकर्षण की खोज नहीं कर सकते। नीचे और रसातल नसों को बेहद शांत करते हैं। इंसानों के लिए सबसे अच्छा काम चीजों की तह तक जाना है। केवल डराने वाले खरगोश कुछ उपयोगी करना पसंद करते हैं क्योंकि दुनिया एक उपयोगी तरीके से नष्ट हो जाती है।

अधोलोक

दुनिया के नीचे अंडरवर्ल्ड है। यह दुनिया का लगभग हिस्सा नहीं है, आप इसे नहीं जानते हैं, यही वजह है कि यह असुविधाजनक है। जमीन के नीचे मृत झूठ, प्रजनन क्षमता का स्रोत भी है। सभी पौधों को कैसे उगाना चाहिए?

बादल

बादल स्वर्ग में भेड़ है। बादल हमेशा उदास रहते हैं। उन्हें अक्सर रोना पड़ता है। लेकिन वे आक्रामक धूप से भी मवेशियों की रक्षा करते हैं। एक बादल लोगों की अच्छाई और बुराई को अवशोषित करता है। आप उनके आकृतियों से देख सकते हैं कि घंटा क्या मारा है। आंदोलन और पानी के बादल में एक साथ नृत्य।

गंदगी

आपको सलाद में गंदगी नहीं डालनी चाहिए। वरना बीमारी का खतरा! गंदगी पाप के भौतिक समतुल्य है। एक घाव को संदूषण के रूप में माना जा सकता है, क्योंकि घाव

अक्सर किनारे पर एक गंदा पपड़ी बनाता है जो गंदगी की तरह दिखता है। बदले में संदूषण या दाग अपराध का संकेत देते हैं। कोई दागदार है। क्या हम इसलिए आहत हुए क्योंकि हम भी असिद्ध थे? या क्या हम असिद्ध हैं क्योंकि हम आहत थे? या हम किसी चीज, किसी कानून या किसी व्यक्ति का उल्लंघन करने के दोषी हैं? लेकिन हम चोट नहीं करते! हम पूर्ण और निर्दोष हैं! जो भी ऐसा दावा करता है, वह आहत होता है, इसलिए दोषी है।

जेल में सेक्स

जेल की दीवारें दिल बनाती हैं। इसकी बाहरी दीवारें बाहर की तरफ काली और अंदर की तरफ लाल हैं। कैदी रासपुतिन अब सबसे छोटा नहीं है, बल्कि सबसे पुराना भी नहीं है, क्योंकि आखिरकार उसे अभी भी मुँहासे हैं। जर्मनिया भी कैद है: रासपुतिन और जर्मनिया एक साथ बिस्तर पर जाते हैं। रासपुतिन को डर है कि जर्मन सिफलिस को अनुबंधित करेगा। जर्मनिया रासपुतिन को छोड़ देता है। उसे शायद केवल थोड़े समय के लिए पिप्पली करना है, लेकिन वह बहुत दूर नहीं जाएगी क्योंकि हम दिल की जेल में हैं। जेल एक ऐसी इमारत है, जिससे आप बच नहीं सकते। Rasputin दर्पण के सामने खड़ा है और अपने pimples व्यक्त करता है। मवाद चांदी निर्दोष पर फूट पड़ता है: icky, आंख।

चूहा और परमाणु बम

चूहे ऐसे चूहे हैं जो मेगालोमनिक हो गए हैं। वे सभी जीवित चीजों से रेडियोधर्मिता को सबसे अच्छी तरह से सहन करते हैं। निश्चय ही एक दिन वे पृथ्वी के राजा बनेंगे। चूहे एक-दूसरे को मारते हैं, वे मनुष्यों के समान हैं। अपने आप को चूहा जो कर सकते हैं! हालांकि, चूहों मनुष्यों की तुलना में अधिक चालाक होते हैं, क्योंकि वे बहुत जल्दी सीखते हैं कि वे विषाक्त भोजन नहीं खाते हैं यदि वे नोटिस करते हैं कि उनके साथी इसे मार रहे हैं। इसीलिए चूहे का जहर इन नरक जीवों को भगाने का स्थायी उपाय नहीं है। मध्य युग में, चूहों का उपयोग लोगों को यातना देने के लिए किया जाता था, आज वैज्ञानिक प्रयोगशालाओं में चूहों को यातना दी जाती है। यह मानव जाति के लिए एक जीत है! पीड़ित से अपराधी तक! प्यारा चूहों की देखभाल और देखभाल भारतीय

करणी माता मंदिर में की जाती है। पश्चिम में, हालांकि, केवल खराब सीवर चूहों हैं। चीन में, चूहे भी राशि चक्र के रूप में मौजूद हैं। लेकिन रोगाणु-मुक्त साइकोसोरस कहता है: "हम अब मध्य युग में नहीं रह रहे हैं! बुरा संक्रमण वाहकों के साथ दूर! राजनेता कुछ क्यों नहीं करते? वे कभी कुछ नहीं करते! "

गुत्थी

आप एक किंक को नहीं छू सकते क्योंकि यह उस पंक्ति से बहुत दूर है जहां से यह नृत्य करता है। कुछ नहीं टूटता तो बातें होती हैं। एक लाइन यहां से वहां तक जाती है। यह इतना सामान्य है कि यह आपको उदास कर देता है। वैज्ञानिक और आर्किटेक्ट लाइन्स पसंद करते हैं। एक लाइन जीवन नहीं खाती है। लाइन जीवन को गति देती है और इससे ऊर्जा प्राप्त करती है जिससे कमरा 20 डिग्री तक गर्म हो सकता है।

Neige

ढलान एक ढलान है जो ढलान की लोकप्रियता के अनुसार ढलान करता है, एक कोण पर मुड़ता है जो ढलान के ढलान से मेल खाती है। ऐसा झुकाव मनमाना नहीं है, लेकिन झुकाव के प्यार से मेल खाता है।

अच्छा

गुड एक ऐसा पेड़ है जो पूरे साल फल देता है। इसकी लकड़ी ठोस रक्त से बनी है; इसकी पत्तियां हंस सकती हैं। रंगीन अच्छा है, ग्रे खराब है। शैतान अच्छा खाता है। अच्छा खुद को शामिल कर सकता है। हालाँकि, बुराई अच्छाई के विनाश पर निर्भर करती है। इसलिए, बुराई कभी भी प्रबल नहीं हो सकती।

मिलकर बनता है

नमक में सोडियम और क्लोरीन होते हैं। अपने दो पैरों पर खड़ा है, लेकिन अस्तित्व को एक मंजिल के रूप में एक पदार्थ की आवश्यकता है। एक अस्तित्व के कुछ हिस्सों की आवश्यकता होती है, जिनमें यह शामिल होता है, यह अपने आप नहीं हो सकता। मोटे मौजूद हैं। "स्टॉक" शब्द पदार्थ के बहुत करीब आता है।

माउस और बल्ले

चूहे के चार पैर हैं और भगवान के आदेश के अनुसार चलते हैं। हालांकि, कुछ चूहों ने अपने गंतव्य की उपेक्षा की है और उड़ा दिया है। वे पूरे दिन (सिर नीचे) और रात को पार्टी करना (खून और सामान पीना) करते हैं। चूहे के रूप में चूहा अंधा है। यह उनके पापों के लिए भगवान की सजा है। एक अस्थायी समाधान के रूप में, उड़ने वाले चूहों को अब अपने कानों से देखना होगा। यह पूरी तरह से धुंधला है।

पतला

पतली महिलाएं जल्दी ही एनोरेक्सिया डॉक पर बैठ जाती हैं। झड़प और वसा के आरोपित। यदि पतला वजन हासिल करना चाहता है, तो उसे खुद को "स्लिम" कहना होगा। पतले वाले को कभी-कभी मोटे की तुलना में अधिक तीव्र प्रभाव पड़ता है क्योंकि यह अपने मीठे पेट में बहुत सार पकड़ सकता है। इसलिए, पतली अक्सर मोटी की तुलना में अधिक बुद्धिमान होती है। यह पतली बोर्ड अभ्यास पर लागू नहीं होता है, क्योंकि उनके सिर के सामने एक मोटी बोर्ड होता है।

पाइरहिक जीत

मेरा नाम शिमट है और मैं मृत हूं। मैंने एक पापी जीवन जिया। शैतान एंड संस कंपनी में मेरे कार्यस्थल पर, मेरा लालची मालिक 100-यूरो के नोट में बदल गया। मैंने मृत्यु के बाद एक आनंदमय जीवन के लिए अपने मौके को महसूस किया: मैंने अपने बैंकनोट को जल्दी से अपने बटुए में डाल दिया और उसके बाहरी चमड़े पर एक क्रूस को चित्रित किया। मेरा बॉस पकड़ा गया। उनके इस आश्वासन के बाद कि मैं अपनी मृत्यु के बाद नरक नहीं जाऊंगा, मैंने फिर से क्रूस को हटा दिया। कुछ ही समय बाद

मैं एओके के सामने एक केले के छिलके पर नाखुश से फिसल गया और अपने सिर के पीछे के हिस्से के साथ कठोर फुटपाथ पर गिर गया। मैं सीधे मर गया था। जैसा कि वादा किया गया था, मैं नरक में नहीं गया था, लेकिन वे मुझे स्वर्ग में नहीं जाने देना चाहते थे, क्योंकि मैंने बुराई को हराया था, लेकिन अभी भी अच्छा नहीं किया था। अब मैं स्वर्ग और नरक के बीच लगातार आगे-पीछे हो रहा हूं और अब नहीं जानता।

भुगतना

फ्रेड: पीड़ित पूरी तरह से अति सुंदर है। किस बेवकूफ ने दुनिया को बनाया?

Detlef: दुखद मूर्खतापूर्ण कृत्यों से बचाता है। यह आपको बहुत अधिक बीयर पीने से रोकता है। बुराई अच्छाई की ओर ले जाती है।

फ्रेड: यह एक और तरीका नहीं है? प्यार की तरह?

पोप: भगवान अचूक है (मेरी तरह), उसे पता चल जाएगा कि उसने दुनिया क्यों बनाई।

मेफिस्टो: मैं उस शक्ति का हिस्सा हूं जो हमेशा बुराई चाहता है और हमेशा अच्छा बनाता है।

बर्ट हेलिंगर: उच्च स्तर पर, बुराई भी अच्छी है।

फ्रेड: मैं पृथ्वी पर रहता हूं; पृथ्वी एक निम्न स्तर है, उच्च स्तर मेरे लिए किसी काम का नहीं है। यह सब बहुत समझाने वाला नहीं है।

Detlef: सूर्य देवता भी पीड़ित थे। वह एक इंसान के रूप में क्रूस पर मर गया और तीसरे दिन फिर से उठा।

फ्रेड: कि उसके साथ एकजुटता में है। मैं बहुत बेहतर महसूस कर रहा हूं।

अल्लाहु अकबर

ईश्वर से बड़ा है ... ईश्वर हमेशा से बड़ा है जिसकी कल्पना मनुष्य कर सकता है। सुरक्षा के लिए मैं भगवान के बारे में कुछ भी बुरा नहीं लिखना चाहता, आप कभी नहीं जानते। जब तक ईश्वर शैतान नहीं है। क्या दुष्ट देवता वास्तविक देवता हैं? या उनका अस्तित्व अच्छा खाने पर फ़ीड करता है? यदि केवल एक ईश्वर है, तो वास्तव में कोई केवल उसे अल्लाह कह सकता है। दो तटस्थ और सभी में शामिल ध्वनियों में अनंत एल ध्वनि बहती है। यदि कई देवता हैं, तो यह अधिक रंगीन और प्रेमपूर्ण हो जाता है और मनुष्यों के लिए भी अधिक समझ में आता है। अन्य देवताओं के बीच प्रत्येक देवता की अपनी जिम्मेदारी का क्षेत्र है। अल्लाह को अब 99 नामों की आवश्यकता नहीं है क्योंकि 99 देवता हैं। और सौवां देवता शायद सभी देवताओं को फिर से एकजुट करेगा, इसलिए एक संदिग्ध। अच्छे और बुरे में कट्टर ध्रुवीकरण देवताओं की भीड़ में घुल जाता है। कभी-कभी देवताओं को स्वर्गदूत, मेहराब या उच्चतर संस्थाएँ भी कहा जाता है।

लहसुन

लहसुन बासी ताजगी है। उसके पैर की उंगलियां फूट गई हैं। एक वास्तविक व्यक्तित्व विभाजन की जड़ें हैं। हालांकि, बाहर की ओर, प्याज एकरूपता प्रदर्शित करता है। लहसुन पिशाच और चुड़ैलों के खिलाफ मदद करता है। कंद रक्त को मजबूत करता है और इसे परजीवियों के लिए इतना अखाद्य बनाता है कि पिशाच भी अपनी भूख खो देते हैं। स्किज़ोफ्रेनिक लीक भी भौतिक परजीवियों जैसे कि टेपवार्म या पुटीय सक्रिय बैक्टीरिया को मारता है। लहसुन सिगरेट के धुएं की तरह मानवता को विभाजित करता है। कुछ इसे पसंद करते हैं: ये अच्छे लोग हैं। हालाँकि, बुरे लोग (जैसे पिशाच, चुड़ैलों, नाज़ियों, बाल-बच्चों, पूँजीपतियों और ग्रीन्स मतदाताओं) को उसकी गंध महसूस होती है।

शैतान के साथ अनुबंध

शैतान और सोहेने के सेवा कार्यालय में एक छोटा अनुबंध करके आप जल्दी से अमीर और सुंदर बन सकते हैं: ठेकेदार (टफेल) हर सांसारिक इच्छा को पूरा करता है। बदले में, ठेकेदार ने अपने पोस्टमार्टम आत्मा को नरक के एनाटोमिस्ट्स के लिए

अनुसंधान उद्देश्यों के लिए रखा। ठेकेदार से रक्त की एक बूंद के माध्यम से अनुबंध कानूनी रूप से वैध है।

महामारी

अर्नोल्ड एक प्लेग की कल्पना करता है जो पृथ्वी पर आता है और सभी बुरे लोगों को मारता है। अच्छे लोग बिल्कुल भी बीमार नहीं होते या आसानी से संक्रमण से बचे रहते हैं। अर्नोल्ड बेशक अच्छे लोगों में से एक है। वह उसके बारे में इतना निश्चित कैसे हो सकता है? कैसे के बारे में अगर प्लेग वास्तव में केवल अच्छे लोगों को मारता है? इसका मतलब यह होगा, लेकिन इस दुनिया के अन्याय के विशिष्ट। अर्नोल्ड डरा हुआ है और भाग्य के खिलाफ टीका लगाना चाहता है, भले ही वह जानता है कि यह नहीं किया जा सकता है।

कमी

चेतना चीजों में कटौती कर रही है। काटना स्टिंगिंग की तुलना में अधिक सुरुचिपूर्ण है, यही वजह है कि एक मच्छर के पास एक महान शीर्षक नहीं है। मजबूत आत्माओं में इसका सामना करने की हिम्मत है, कायरों के पास कोई ब्लेड नहीं है। आपको अपनी उंगली नहीं काटनी चाहिए! तो दोस्तों: बस सावधान! काटने के रंग को तीखापन कहा जाता है। गर्म मिर्च और सेक्स बम कभी-कभी थोड़ा मसालेदार भी हो सकते हैं।

दरिद्र

हथियार बाहर की ओर खिंचते हैं। हाथों में बाहें फूलने लगती हैं। हाथों में हथियार परिष्कृत होते हैं, हाथ उपकरण में मजबूत होते हैं। शाखाएँ वृक्षों की भुजाएँ हैं।

सीमा

एक सीमा एक को दूसरे से अलग करती है। यह सीमा पर शुरू होता है या यह समाप्त होता है। सीमा जीवन के लिए एक पोत बनाती है। जीने के लिए रक्त को शिराओं की आवश्यकता होती है। एक घर अपनी दीवारों से रहने की सीमा। जब जीवित अपने घर से बाहर निकलता है, तो वह बेघर होने के समुद्र में डूब जाता है।

प्लेट में एक गोल किनारे होता है। फ्रेम के विपरीत, किनारे अपने मालिक के विकास को पूरा करता है। एक फ्रेम गहने है, यह सूद को रोकने के लिए एक मजबूरी है।

शब्द "दुनिया" का उपयोग हर चीज के परिदृश्य का वर्णन करने के लिए किया जाता है। दुनिया को एक जानलेवा महानता के रूप में समझा जा सकता है। इस दुनिया का कोई अंत नहीं है। मनुष्य की आंखें अंतहीन सड़कों पर नहीं रुक सकतीं। एक सुरक्षित दुनिया इसके किनारों में बंद है। वहाँ सुरक्षित संसार परिमितता के हथियारों के साथ असीमता को धारण करता है।

प्रकाश और अंधेरा

गुस्ताव दोनों कॉर्न्स पर अंधा है। उसके पैर कुछ भी नहीं देख सकते हैं। यह अच्छी बात है, क्योंकि यदि आप कुछ नहीं देखते हैं, तो आप उदास नहीं होंगे। इसलिए गुस्ताव खुश है। ऐसे लोग हैं जो एक अंधे तारीख है। आप मिलने के लिए बहुत अंधे हैं। चमगादड़ भी काले दिखाई देते हैं, लेकिन वे चमकीले सुनते हैं। क्या प्रकाश अंधेरे से अंधा है? क्या अंधेरा प्रकाश को देखता है?

चाँद

चांद अंधेरे में हंसता है। इसे पूरा देखा जा सकता है। पूर्णिमा के रूप में, वह पुरुष है। अन्यथा, वह महिला है। या यह दूसरी तरह के आसपास था? चाँद डर के मारे पूरे आसमान में उड़ गया। वह देखा जाना पसंद नहीं करता; केवल वेयरव्यू, चमगादड़ और रेवनों को ऐसा करने की अनुमति है। चंद्रमा गुप्त रूप से बुराई के दायरे में शासन करता है, यह गोल गाल के साथ चालबाज है, यह एक पुराना प्यार है, एक चमकदार अंधेरा जिसे चंद्रमा कहा जाता है। जब सभ्य लोग सोते हैं तो चंद्रमा सबसे अधिक चमकता है।

एक मिनट रुकिए

केवल एक पल है और यह हमेशा एक ही है। केवल क्षण ही क्षण है। "क्षणों" के बहुमत का कोई मतलब नहीं है। इसलिए समय नहीं है। और फिर भी घड़ी टिक रही है। इसीलिए घड़ियाँ झूठे होती हैं।

स्मृति

लोग बिल्कुल याद नहीं रख सकते। हम अपने वर्तमान क्षण से अतीत को देखते हैं। हर दिन आपको एक अलग अतीत याद आता है। जिस तरह से यह वास्तव में गैर-कानूनी रूप से खो गया था।

मूल गाय

शुरुआत में दूध था। ब्रह्मांड दूध से बनाया गया था, यही कारण है कि हम मिल्की वे की बात करते हैं। दूध उरुख, बड़े MUU के udder से आया था।

ताज़ा

ताजगी जीवन की नमी में प्रकाश के रूप में गाती है। ताजा मांस सड़े हुए मांस की तुलना में स्वस्थ होता है। फलों का रस खून की तुलना में ताजा होता है, क्योंकि जानवर अपने लालच में सड़ रहा है।

कछुए

कछुए प्राचीन भ्रूण हैं। वे उस समय से हैं जब कोई समय नहीं था। उनकी बात भी अलग है। इसमें सबसे छोटे कण नहीं होते हैं, लेकिन कठोरता लुगदी के रूप में

कठोरता यहाँ से वहाँ तक एक पंक्ति में चलती है। वास्तविक पृथ्वी कभी नहीं मरती है।

विनाश

ढहते महल के खंडहरों के बीच से हवा चुपके से निकलती है। अंधेरी दीवारें घटनाओं से खाली हैं। फायरस्टार कल थे, निशान आज हैं। एक चूहा कागज को मृत खंडहर की कहानी लिख और बता सकता है। पक्षी लाल शाम के सूरज पर उड़ते हैं और कहीं गायब नहीं होते हैं।

उर

प्राण हमेशा सबसे पहले आता है। कारण, मूल, मूल सूप, युरेनस, प्रवाल मवेशी, पूर्वज, प्रज्वलन वन, बिग बैंग, और निश्चित रूप से दस्तावेजों और विचित्र महान दादा-दादी। उत्तरार्द्ध अभी तक खतरनाक शब्द नहीं जानता था। वियना में, खतरनाक का मतलब कुछ है जो विशेष रूप से खतरनाक है।

फर्जी खबर

पृथ्वी एक डिस्क है! अगर पृथ्वी एक गोला होती तो न्यूजीलैंड के लोग धरती से गिर जाते। क्या नासा को अपने नकली फोटो अपनी गांड पर चिपकाने चाहिए? उन्होंने बहुत ज्यादा चाँद की हवा सूँघ ली है!

शुरुआत

एक शुरुआत अचानक स्प्रिंट की तरह शुरू हो सकती है या शरद ऋतु में कोहरे की तरह रेंग सकती है। पौधे अंकुरित होते हैं और बच्चे अस्पताल में रोगाणु मुक्त पैदा होते हैं। एक शुरुआत के लिए एक अंत की आवश्यकता होती है: बच्चे का जन्म

गर्भावस्था को समाप्त करता है। शुरुआत अभी तक खुद को नहीं पता है: केवल शुरुआत में ही पता चल जाता है कि यह कौन था।

बच्चे

बच्चे चॉकलेट खाते हैं। वयस्क वयस्क चॉकलेट खाते हैं। दोनों उत्पादों का स्वाद चॉकलेट की तरह होता है। आप देख सकते हैं: बच्चे कुछ खास नहीं हैं। वे आपके और मेरे जैसे चॉकलेट खाने वाले हैं। बालवाड़ी में जाने पर भी बच्चों को पानी पिलाने की जरूरत नहीं है।

खुंभी

एक टॉडस्टूल अपनी स्वतंत्रता से प्यार करता है। ऊपर से बारिश की जरूरत है। लेकिन लाल मशरूम भगवान के आवेगों को प्राप्त करने से इंकार कर देता है। फ्लाई एगारिक सब कुछ नियंत्रण में रखना चाहेगा। यह एक कोड़ा का मालिक भी है। प्रभुत्व इसके लिए महत्वपूर्ण है। बारिश फ्लाई एगारिक पर गिरती है। कवक नोटिस करता है, कि प्रभुत्व के अलावा अन्य चीजें भी हैं, लेकिन कृषि खुद को खोलने की हिम्मत नहीं करता है। फिर वह ऐसा करता है, क्योंकि वह बहादुर है। डर ऊपर से नीचे मशरूम में आता है। अरे ये तो। वह अब टॉडस्टूल नहीं है, बल्कि एक छोटा चूहा है, जो अपनी गुफा में एक मध्यम वर्ग का जीवन जीना चाहता है। लेकिन यह काम नहीं करता है। माउस दर्शन का अध्ययन करता है और दुनिया को नवीनीकृत करता है और प्रसिद्ध होता है।

बिजली

मार्टिन लूथर और पॉल बिजली की चपेट में आ गए थे। बिजली के रूप में जल्दी से, वे प्रबुद्ध लोग बन गए। क्या बिजली गिरने से हमें सुधार होता है? या फ्लैश सिर्फ एक शॉर्ट सर्किट है जो पाखंड पैदा करता है? आपको यह प्रयास करना होगा कि अगली आंधी के दौरान।

बीएफ कैनेडी बीफेलफील्ड में

एक कथित षडयंत्र सिद्धांत का कहना है कि बीलेफेल्ड शहर भी मौजूद नहीं है। एक निश्चित समय से यह छाया के लिए पर्याप्त नहीं था कि वह बेलेफेल्ड के गैर-अस्तित्व को कवर कर सके। यही कारण है कि वे साजिश को एक सिद्धांत या मजाक के रूप में प्रस्तुत करने के लिए उत्सुक थे ताकि किसी को यह विचार न हो कि बेवफेल्ड का नकली नंगे सच था। सौभाग्य से, वहाँ बिल है। 24 जुलाई 1963 को बिल क्लिंटन ने व्हाइट हाउस में अमेरिकी राष्ट्रपति जॉन एफ कैनेडी का दौरा किया और उनका हाथ हिलाया। क्लिंटन ने कहा, "मैं राष्ट्रपति बनने जा रहा हूं!" इस जादुई कृत्य के माध्यम से, क्लिंटन ने उस समय राष्ट्रपति कैनेडी से अपनी किस्मत और पहचान चुरा ली। परिणाम: कैनेडी को मरना पड़ा। या बल्कि उसकी शक्ल-सूरत। असली कैनेडी जमे हुए थे। जब बीलेफेल्ड के नकली अस्तित्व के प्रकाश में आने की धमकी दी गई, तो कैनेडी को फिर से पिघला दिया गया। जर्मन में एक कॉस्मेटिक सर्जरी और गहन प्रशिक्षण के बाद, कैनेडी आज झूठे नाम बीज़ क्लॉज़ेन के छाया शहर के महापौर के रूप में है।

दाढ़ी

Sindbart: अरे तुम, मैं तुम्हें देख सकता हूँ!

विंडबार्ट: पागलपन! मुझे भी कमाल है जब आप समझते हैं कि हम दोनों मौजूद नहीं हैं।

सिन्डबार्ट: जब दो लोग मिलते हैं जो मौजूद नहीं होते हैं, तो वे एक-दूसरे के लिए और एक-दूसरे के संबंध में वास्तविक हो जाते हैं, क्योंकि वे दोनों एक ही स्तर पर मिलते हैं, अर्थात् कोई भी स्तर नहीं।

विंडबार्ट: आप शायद ही आप जैसे किसी से मिलें। आप शायद ही कभी वास्तविक बनते हैं। हमें धोखे और सच्चाई के बारे में विस्तृत चर्चा करने का अवसर लेना चाहिए।

सिंदबरट: बहुत अच्छा, मैं वहाँ हूँ।

समुद्र

समुद्र खुद को महानता की अनुमति दे सकता है क्योंकि यह रहस्य रखता है। समुद्र देवताओं की खाइयों से बना है (आँसुओं में नमक होता है)। समुद्र पृथ्वी के लिए भोजन है। रेगिस्तान की प्यास लंबे समय से सूख रही है, रेगिस्तान को अब जीने की जरूरत नहीं है।

सूचना समाज

अर्नोल्ड हेइटरमैन टेलीविजन नहीं देखता है और न ही अखबार पढ़ता है। बस सुर्खियां हैं। ओटो नॉर्मल के लिए, वर्तमान क्या महत्वपूर्ण है, बाकी सब कुछ महत्वहीन है। अर्नोल्ड बड़े चित्र में रुचि रखते हैं, मेफ्लाइज़ में नहीं। इसके अलावा, आप कभी नहीं जानते कि क्या जानकारी सही है। यदि शीर्ष को यह कहना चाहिए: 'कल दुनिया खत्म हो जाएगी!', श्री हेइटरमैन निश्चित रूप से पूरी जानकारी पढ़ेंगे। इस तरह के प्रलय का दिन वास्तव में आपको प्रभावित कर सकता है, अकेले व्यक्तिगत कारणों के लिए।

पानी

पानी चलना पसंद करता है। अगर प्रकृति इसकी अनुमति देती है, तो यह बहती है। पानी ताजा है और अपने आप में गाता है। इसकी तरंगों की चाल से प्रकाश चमकता है। हर जगह पानी है जहाँ जीवन है। पानी तब तक अस्थिर रहता है, जब तक वह तल में न हो। पानी गीला है, पानी की नग्रता अछूत है।

मेंढक

आपको मेंढक नहीं होना चाहिए, न कि एक मेंढक। जो कोई भी मेंढक के रूप में पानी के करीब बनाया जाता है वह आत्मा में रहता है। आत्मा और झील एक ही पानी, मछली और मेंढक हैं जो जानते हैं। आप वास्तव में पानी में डर नहीं सकते हैं, केवल

सूखे जानवर ही कर सकते हैं। डराने वाले खरगोश से पूछें! डर नहीं मेंढक! मेंढक कभी भी युवावस्था से बाहर नहीं निकलते। मेंढक एक मछली है जिसने इसे भूमि जानवर के लिए नहीं बनाया है: विकास की विफलता। यह अब मछली नहीं है, लेकिन यह बंदरों के लिए भी पर्याप्त नहीं था। मेंढक अभी भी कानों के पीछे हरे हैं, और न केवल वहां। मेंढकों को अक्सर पिंपल्स होते हैं, लेकिन फिर उन्हें टोड्स कहा जाता है।

जंगली सूअर

रोम के धूमिल शहर में एक घर की छत से जंगली सूअर कूदते हैं। जंगली सुअरों ने नीचे फुटपाथ पर अपनी पीठ ठोकी। जंगली सूअर कुछ भी नहीं टूट गया है, यह शिथिलता से शिकार करता है और जीवित रहता है। इस तरह के एक जंगली सूअर वास्तव में मजबूत है। आपका खून नहीं सूखता है। मजबूत स्ट्रोक में, उनकी आग का रस उनकी नसों के रेस ट्रैक के माध्यम से कालातीत रूप से स्पंदित होता है।

भावनाओं

भावनाओं का कोई रंग नहीं है। वे बेईमान हैं, उनकी एकमात्र पकड़ असमानता है। क्या आप अपने दिल को भावनाओं से भर देंगे? मात्रा और द्रव्यमान के लिए भावनाएं महान हैं, वे मजबूत और कमजोर हो जाते हैं, वे हिंडोला पर घोड़ों की तरह बिना रुके वापस आते हैं।

पतन

दुनिया की चौड़ाई गहराई में डूब जाती है। सब कुछ सो जाता है और चंद्रमा आकाश में है। इसकी चांदी की रोशनी कयामत में बहती है। एक हाथ चाँद को पकड़ना चाहता है और यह भी करता है: उसने चाँद को कुचल दिया। चांदी का रक्त, जो समान रूप से काला है, एक क्षेत्र से नीचे चलता है जो कभी चंद्रमा था। दुनिया कांपती है।

मार

मृत्यु जीवन को नकारती है और समान रूप से सक्षम बनाती है। बाज को क्या जीना चाहिए? उसे पीठ में क्या चीरना चाहिए? वह केवल अन्य जानवरों को मारकर जीवित रह सकता है। आदमी की तरह! शाकाहारी अच्छे लोग हैं। लेकिन उन्हें भी प्रकृति के आह्वान का पालन करना चाहिए। आखिरकार, पौधे भी जीवित प्राणी हैं। शाकाहारी में विटामिन की कमी होती है। उनकी मासूमियत उन्हें चेहरे से पीला कर देती है, वे जीवविज्ञानी हैं। शाकाहारी लोग नैतिकता का खून पीते हैं। सबसे बड़ा शिकारी इंसान है।

मृत टेलीविजन दर्शक

टेलीविजन चालू है और उसके सामने एक कंकाल है। उनकी खाली खोपड़ी की हड्डियों को अब कार्यक्रम के बारे में पता नहीं है। कोई व्यक्ति टेलीविजन बंद कर देता है: हड्डी वाले व्यक्ति को अब पता चलता है कि वह कुछ याद कर रहा है और क्रोधित है। केवल वापसी में मृत्यु का एहसास होता है कि वह मर चुका है।

जीवन का अर्थ

जीवन का उद्देश्य महान कृषि अर्थशास्त्री को खिलाना है। किसी भी मामले में, यह डॉ। लाइट मस्तिष्क। उनका मानना है कि निम्नलिखित: एक दूर के आकाश से, महान कृषि अर्थशास्त्री हमारी आत्मा के बीज को बोध की मिट्टी में बोते हैं। जीवन के अनुभव के माध्यम से, आत्मा रोगाणु आत्मा के उत्पादक कान में बढ़ता है। महान कृषि अर्थशास्त्री ने हमारी मृत्यु के बाद इस कान को काटा और खाया। डॉ ब्रेनलाइट डॉ। का जुड़वां भाई है लाइट मस्तिष्क। हर सुबह डॉ। ब्रेनलाइट पूरे अनाज मूसली के बाद फेंकता है जब वह अपने भाई के कच्चे सिद्धांत के बारे में सोचता है।

सूरज

सूरज दुनिया का दिल है, बाहरी जगह की तुलना में इसमें अधिक जगह है। उसके पास एक बड़ा, चमकदार पेट है। सूरज दुनिया को जन्म देता है। सूरज दुनिया को खा जाता है। दोनों समान रूप से। सूरज ही सब कुछ है। यह पुराने लोगों के साथ सफेद है, यह युवा लोगों के साथ पीला है। चेहरे पर सूरज की झुर्रियां नहीं हैं।

रेबीज

दर्पण में एक पिशाच दिखता है: काले बाल और चश्मे के साथ एक आदमी चांदी से बाहर दिखता है, उसके पास एक पीला चेहरा है। पिशाच सोचता है कि वह दर्पण में एक सामान्य व्यक्ति की तरह दिखता है। मरे केवल खुद को दर्पण में पहचानता है, हालांकि, अगर यह सीधे अपने हाथों और शरीर को देखता है, तो यह कोई नहीं देखता है। यह सामान्य नहीं है, पिशाच के लिए भी नहीं। निश्चित रूप से उसके पास रेबीज है।

पौधा

पौधे हरे रंग के जानवर हैं जो चल नहीं सकते। इसके पत्ते पानी के पत्थर होते हैं। सूरज की रोशनी उन्हें पूरी तरह से हरा कर देती है। पत्थर, पानी और सूरज अचानक जान दे देते हैं। एक पौधे में मुख्य रूप से वृद्धि होती है, इसके विकास में आनंद आता है। बढ़ते हुए कोई जीन नहीं है, यह उन्हें हर पल पता चलता है। एक योजना विकसित नहीं होती है, भले ही आप इसे बाहर ले जाएं। दूसरी ओर, पौधे जीवन के साथ घृणित रूप से विकसित होते हैं।

कड़ा

कुछ मोटी खोपड़ी पहले ही कठोरता के साथ अपने सिर को मार चुकी है। कठोरता प्रतिरोध और स्थायित्व प्रदान करती है। एक कंकाल कठिन है। आमतौर पर कठिन कठिन रहता है। हालांकि, एक लिंग केवल कई बार कठिन होता है। - सिर्फ क्यों? - कठोरता का किनारा कमरे में एक थोपने वाली रेखा है। किनारों को नजरअंदाज नहीं किया जाना चाहिए, आप उन पर अपना सिर मार सकते हैं। जब दो दीवारें टकराती

हैं, तो टक्कर को किनारे कहा जाता है। एक किनारा इसलिए कैरम का परिणाम है। इसलिए यह बेहोश दिल के लिए नहीं है। पत्थर भी कठोर हैं। एक पत्थर एक चीज है, इसका कोई चेहरा नहीं है, क्योंकि एक पत्थर अन्य पत्थरों की तरह दिखता है। उनके होने में, सभी चीजें समान हैं। कोठरी, मेज या टूथब्रश ये सब सिर्फ बातें हैं। हर जगह झूठ बोलने वाले पत्थर को वास्तविकता कहा जाता है। एक पत्थर का उपयोग अन्य लोगों की खोपड़ी में हथौड़ा करने के लिए किया जा सकता है। पाषाण युग में यह महत्वपूर्ण था। आज कुछ पत्थर बोल सकते हैं, इन पत्थरों को "सेल फोन" कहा जाता है। अगर मैं इसके बारे में सही ढंग से सोचता हूं: सुंदर पत्थर भी हैं, अर्थात् रत्न। ड्रेगन उन्हें इकट्ठा करते हैं।

इकट्ठा

एकत्र घना है, कभी-कभी संकीर्ण होता है। एकत्रित सुरक्षा स्थायी अस्तित्व के रूप में सुरक्षा प्रदान करती है। या यह बोझ है। इकट्ठा करने की अपेक्षा इकट्ठा करना कठिन है। यदि एकत्र करने से अधिक कठिन है, तो एक "शिकार" की बात करता है।

बर्बाद

विकसित में एकीकृत नहीं है। सतही को अपने विकास के दौरान अतिशयोक्ति का पता नहीं चला। जबकि अतिप्रवाह समृद्ध हो सकता है, यह कभी-कभी दान करता है, इसलिए अतिप्रकार न केवल बेकार है, यह जीवित पदार्थ को इसकी प्रगति में बाधा डालता है। सतही सिर्फ कचरा है।

मोड़

ह्यूगो में एक समस्या है। उनका क्विक यह है कि क्विक उन्हें अपनी स्क्रीन पर परेशान करता है। जो ह्यूगो को पागल कर देता है। दशकों तक ह्यूगो के चेहरे पर दोष था। आईने के सामने खड़े होकर उसने अपने जिस्म को तब तक देखा जब तक कि उसकी त्वचा विशेषज्ञ ने घुंडी को नहीं हटाया। ह्यूगो में कर्की के साथ एक क्विक है। लेकिन केवल व्यक्तिगत quirks के लिए। अगर सब कुछ एक विचित्र है, जैसे कि

पूरी तरह से खरोंच वाली खिड़की, ह्यूगो को कोई आपत्ति नहीं है। ह्यूगो वास्तव में एक समस्या है।

स्पिनर

खाली विचार उसकी मुरझाई हुई बर्फ औरत को खिला देता है। ग्रे स्नो महिला को न्यूरोसिस कहा जाता है। वह पूरी तरह से हानिरहित है, वह वुडी एलन है। आप एक न्यूरोसिस के बारे में हंस सकते हैं, क्योंकि अजीब अजीब लोग हैं। लेकिन पुरानी बर्फ वास्तव में हानिरहित नहीं है। बर्फ की महिला में कोई रक्त नहीं बहता है, लेकिन कल की बर्फ इसमें ऊब गई है। पुरानी बर्फ मनोचिकित्सा में चली जाती है। ऐसी चिकित्सा भी एक न्यूरोसिस है, यह नई बर्फ की तरह सफेद है।

युगल चिकित्सा

कुत्ते और बिल्ली युगल चिकित्सा में जाते हैं। चिकित्सक एक हाइना है। कुत्ता और बिल्ली अपने रिश्ते को बचाना चाहते हैं। चिकित्सा विफल हो जाती है। केवल क्यों? वह क्या हो सकता है? निश्चित रूप से चिकित्सक पर, वे सभी को एक समस्या है।

कोई हास्य नहीं

चेपलिन अपनी बॉडी कंपनी रखने के लिए हंसने के लिए बेसमेंट में जाती है। पैसा पाने के लिए उसे बहुत से लोगों को मारना पड़ा। इस दुनिया और महिलाओं की पीड़ा से त्रस्त नहीं होना है। चेल्लिन पूरे जर्मनी के लिए हास्य पर एक सामान्य प्रतिबंध की वकालत करता है, अपवाद तथाकथित हंसी केंद्र हैं, जहां लोग हास्य शुल्क का भुगतान करने के बाद जोर से हंस सकते हैं।

हंसी

हँसी उसके होंठों से खुश है। गंभीर हँसी हँसने लायक हो जाती है। हमसफ़र हँसी पूंजीपति वर्ग के सोफे से नहीं उठ सकती। असली हँसी मजाक नहीं है, यह सिर्फ खुश है। केवल अनिवार्य चुटकुले दुख के पेड़ से चुटकुले फाड़ते हैं।

पूरी तरह से मजाकिया

Isolde: Detlef, आपको कभी नहीं पता कि आप सिर्फ मजाक कर रहे हैं या यदि आप गंभीर हैं।

Detlef: यह बहुत सरल है: अगर मैं मज़ेदार हूँ, तो मैं गंभीर हूँ, और अगर मैं गंभीर हूँ, तो यह मज़ेदार है।

Isolde: मैं एक को दूसरे से कैसे अलग कर सकता हूं?

Detlef: पहले दिन पर भी मामला है और बाद के दिनों में अजीब है। या यह दूसरी तरह के आसपास था? मैं सब गड़बड़ कर रहा हूँ।

Isolde: मैं आदमी के साथ पागल हो रहा हूँ!

जलवायु परिवर्तन

ओटो फार्ट्स।

डॉ Kackebart-Struller: ओटो! क्या आप वास्तव में जानते हैं कि आप ओजोन परत के लिए क्या कर रहे हैं? प्रत्येक गोज़ के साथ न केवल आपका गधे बड़ा हो जाता है, बल्कि ओजोन छेद भी होता है। प्रत्येक गोज़ के साथ, मीथेन वायुमंडल में बहता है, जो पृथ्वी को गर्म करता है। गोज़ मत! हमें अपने पर्यावरण को बचाना है!

ओटो स्ट्रॉलर: आप सही हैं, मौसी, बिल्कुल सही। मैं अब अटारी जा रहा हूं, कबूतरों को खाना खिला रहा हूं।

जंगली जंगल में

जंगली जंगल में, पेड़ों की जड़ें अपनी मिट्टी को छोड़कर पूरे देश में चलती हैं। शांत नहीं लौटता है, लेकिन एक साहसिक कार्य पर जाता है। यह पहाड़ों पर जाता है, यह घाटियों में जाता है। कभी-कभी वह कूदती भी है।

रोल

रोलिंग या चक्कर लगाना इसके केंद्र के चारों ओर एक चक्कर है। पहिया पकड़ा जाता है। रोल अपने आप में रोल नहीं करता है, यह अपने केंद्र के संबंध में स्थिर रहता है। यदि रोलिंग एक सर्कल से एक वर्ग में जाती है, तो यह स्वतंत्र रूप से आगे बढ़ेगा। बाइक केवल नोटिस करती है कि लैंडस्केप अतीत से आगे बढ़ रहा है, बाइक अपने आप रुक जाती है।

आराम करें और व्यायाम करें

शांत अपनी पहचान का आनंद लेता है। एक को बाहरी बाहरी आंदोलन की अनुपस्थिति के रूप में आराम को परिभाषित किया जा सकता है। इसलिए डिस्को में कोई आराम नहीं है। हाईवे पर भी नहीं। शांत के साथ अंदर से आंदोलन काफी संभव है। अस्तित्व में शांति है। ज़ेन बौद्ध धर्म का अनिवार्य शांत भी है। ऐसी शांत पृथ्वी पर मौत की खेती की जाती है, यह फिडिंग के दमन और हत्या पर आधारित है। असली शांत, हालांकि, स्वतंत्रता में रहता है।

spaulen

चिड़ियों के झुंड एक मज़ेदार महल में जाते हैं जहाँ लोग घूमते हैं। महल में 52 क्राउनलेस लोग रहते हैं। कोई भी नहीं है और हर कोई एक ही समय में राजा और मूर्ख है। राजमहल के लोग सभी हेर्मैफ्रोडाइट हैं। यदि आप चाहते थे तो आप इसे स्वयं कर सकते थे। लेकिन वे खेल की दुनिया बनाने में अधिक रुचि रखते हैं: वे मज़ेदार हैं। स्पूलिंग गंभीर गेमिंग है। वे यहां जोजोस, राजाओं के साथ मजाक कर रहे हैं। राजाओं ने फव्वारे के नीचे महान हॉल में मूर्खों के रूप में अपने मुकुट

डाले। मुकुट हमिंग बर्ड के लिए एक घोंसले के रूप में सेवा करते हैं। किंग पर्पल गंभीर बकवास लिखते हैं। तुम उस तरह के आदमी से बात नहीं कर सकते।

काम कर रहे

काम उनके आदमी की भूमि में पसीना आता है, जो थकावट भरा होता है, क्योंकि एक रीढ़ की हड्डी के बजाय, काम की सराहना की छाती होती है, जो गर्व के साथ सजाया जाता है। आपकी पूर्ति दिल के दौरे में काम करती है। जो लोग काम करते हैं वे जल्दी से तहखाने में अपने शरीर को भूल सकते हैं। छुटकारे के लिए लंबे समय तक काम करें, लेकिन वह कभी भी यह स्वीकार नहीं करेगी। काम अंधा है, यह ध्यान नहीं देता कि यह काम कर रहा है, यह केवल जानता है। रिडीमर के रूप में क्राइस्ट लंबे समय से बाहर हैं। लोग काम के माध्यम से खुद को भुनाते हैं: मनोचिकित्सा में, आप अपने आप पर काम करते हैं।

सच्चा आंदोलन अंदर है। एक घोड़ा अपने आप चलता है, लेकिन एक कार उसके इंजन की अश्वशक्ति से चलती है। आंदोलन लहरों में अर्थात् सर्पीन तरीके से आगे बढ़ता है। चलना, तैरना, उड़ना या वाहन चलाना सभी आंदोलन हैं। आजकल आप मुख्य रूप से चारों ओर हो जाते हैं। आप वहां भी जा सकते थे। लेकिन कोई भी इसे साइट पर नहीं खड़ा कर सकता है। आप साइट पर बने रहें।

हवा

हवा ने फ्रिग के चेहरे को झपट लिया। समय समाप्त हो रहा है। पानी छेद में गायब हो जाता है। सब भाग रहा है, भाग रहा है। पेशाब चलता है, आँसू दौड़ते हैं। कोई भी फ्रिग के साथ नहीं है, बस हवा है। उसके पैर मोटे जूतों से ढंके हुए हैं। कैसे के बारे में अगर वह नंगे पैर चला गया? फिर हवा उन्हें ऊपर ले जाएगी, और फ्रीग मुक्त होगा। उसके भारी जूते उसके अतीत का बोझ हैं। वाहुना नामक एक हवा उसके बालों से गुजरती है। स्लीपनिर, एक आठ-पैर वाला घोड़ा, फ्रिगा के अतीत को देखता है। फ्रिगा मोहित हो गया है, उसे घोड़े पर हवा देवता के लिए रखा जा सकता है और बिना किसी के साथ, नंगे पैर, स्वतंत्र रूप से ले जाया जा सकता है।

अपने हाथ में एक नाशपाती बेहतर

छत पर एक सेब के पेड़ की तुलना में।

मशीन शुद्धतम करती है। एक मशीन कुछ भी नहीं महसूस करती है, इसलिए यह सरासर निराशा से बाहर निकलती है। यह सभी जोड़तोड़ करता है जो पुराने दिनों में कुंद श्रमिकों ने किया था। भावना और जीवन के बिना संभालती है, यांत्रिकी, बिना अर्थ के आंदोलन, केवल उद्देश्य। कितना अच्छा होता है जब कोई मशीन हमारे लिए बेवकूफी का काम करती है। लेकिन मशीनों के रचनाकारों ने एक बार खुद मूर्खता का बीजारोपण किया। मशीनें अपनी मूर्खता से हमें बाहर से धमकाती रहेंगी। कृत्रिम बुद्धिमत्ता को विभेदित किया जाता है, लेकिन यह मूर्खतापूर्ण है। हम स्वयं केवल बड़ी दुनिया की मशीन के एक दल हैं।

मालिक अपने हाथों को अपना कहता है। उसके हाथों के परमाणु मालिक के नहीं हैं। उसके हाथ में परमाणु केवल ऋण पर उसके अहंकार के आकार के लिए उपयुक्त हैं। मालिक की मृत्यु के बाद, उसके हाथ में पूर्व परमाणु एक अन्य उपस्थिति के लिए उपयुक्त हैं। मालिक अपने हाथ में घर पर महसूस करता है, वह उसके हाथ में निहित है। यह जड़ उसकी पहचान है। यह हाथ ही नहीं है।

पागल सेब

सेब में, त्वचा और लुगदी एक साथ रहते हैं। क्या वे दोनों शादीशुदा हैं? सेब में बहुत अधिक एक साथ रहता है: गोलाकार, हरा, फल, पेड़ पर लटका हुआ। सेब सोचता है: `` मेरे पास गुण हैं, लेकिन मैं अपना गुण नहीं हूं। यदि मैं स्वयं को देखता हूं, तो मुझे केवल गुण ही मिलते हैं, लेकिन कोई भी नहीं। '' सेब इस आत्म-ज्ञान से क्रोधित हो जाता है: '' सभी मजाक! मेरा अस्तित्व नहीं है! '' सेब की प्रत्येक संपत्ति अब अपने तरीके से जाती है। गोलाकार उत्तर की ओर जाता है, हरा दक्षिण की ओर जाता

है। पश्चिम के लिए फल, और पूर्व में सेब की फांसी। यह अब एक सेब नहीं है, यह कभी अस्तित्व में नहीं था। सेब ने अपनी नकली पहचान को तलाक दे दिया है। उसे सिर्फ अपने थाट-बेलोंग्स-टू-मी से बाहर निकाल दिया गया था। सेब की ताजगी कहाँ है? वह पब में बैठी है और उसे चलाया जा सकता है!

कविता

कविता का अर्थ अर्थ को अपने केंद्रित पर केंद्रित करना है। हालांकि, लेखक की कविता कभी-कभी इतनी सील होती है कि पाठक अब अर्थ बॉक्स नहीं खोल सकता है। लिखते समय केवल लेखक ही कविता की सामग्री को समझता है। और यहां तक कि लेखक की अगली सुबह भी तंग हो सकती है।

पारदर्शक

जाहिर है, जो पारदर्शी मक्खियों को छिपाने के बिना स्वतंत्र रूप से चारों ओर है। छेद मुख्य रूप से पारदर्शी होते हैं। हालाँकि, थ्रू थ्रू वज़नदार हो सकता है, लेकिन इसे देखना आसान नहीं है। पारदर्शी हो जाता है जब यह अनाड़ी हो जाता है।

पकड़

मोबाइल होते हुए भी कैचिंग अपने शिकार के लिए सफलतापूर्वक पहुंचता है। यही कारण है कि मछली विशेष रूप से पकड़ी जाती है। वे फिसलन भरे हैं और चलते पानी में रहते हैं, लेकिन फिर भी पकड़े जा सकते हैं।

जेल

यदि आप पकड़े नहीं जाते हैं तो अपराध केवल सार्थक हैं। एक बंदर चिड़ियाघर में आता है, भले ही उसने कुछ भी गलत न किया हो। एक चिड़ियाघर जानवरों के लिए एक उचित जेल है। कुछ जंगली जानवर सर्कस में कैद हैं। बच्चे अपने माता-पिता की

शिक्षा-पद्धति में जेल में बैठते हैं। पत्नियाँ अपने पतियों पर आर्थिक निर्भरता की जेल में बैठ जाती हैं।

शीर्ष रहस्य

रहस्य को दूसरों की आंखों में नहीं देखना चाहिए। यह अकेले (या साजिशकर्ताओं के साथ) अपने बंकर में बैठता है और वहां निम्नलिखित कार्य कर सकता है: यह विघटित होता है, यह उत्सव मनाता है, यह आनन्दित करता है, यह गलत काम करता है, यह प्रज्वलित करता है, यह दूसरों को प्रज्वलित करता है, यह आपको हंसाता है, यह डरता है, यह खुद को बचाता है, यह मना कर देता है, या यह बच्चे को जन्म देता है। रहस्य: हम नहीं जानते कि यह क्या करता है। वह एक रहस्य बना हुआ है।

मक्खी

बिना पैरों के विशालता के समुद्र के माध्यम से उड़ते हुए ग्लाइड। उड़ान में, ऊपर और नीचे एक दूसरे के खिलाफ खेला जाता है। एक पक्षी में दुनिया का बलात्कार किए बिना शक्ति होती है। यह कमाल है। टॉडस्टूल, हालांकि, उड़ नहीं सकते, उनके पंख मुग्ध हैं। पक्षियों के पंख साहसी में फैलते हैं। वे वहां घर पर हैं। पंख उड़ने के हथियार हैं, वे बल से हैं। एक पक्षी हवा में बिल्ली से टकराए बिना स्वतंत्र रूप से उड़ सकता है। एक कर्मचारी, हालांकि, बहुत जल्दी अपने मालिक या जीवन की गंभीरता के साथ टकराता है।

आसान

प्रकाश पहेली के ऊपर आसानी से उड़ जाता है, यह सिर्फ भारी बेलों से गुजरता है। प्रकाश की चीज को शीर्ष में पाया जाता है। लकड़ी पानी पर तैरती है क्योंकि यह पानी की तुलना में हल्का है। गर्म हवा का गुब्बारा नीले आकाश में तैरता है। प्रकाश जल्दी से तुच्छ हो जाता है। कुछ बेवकूफ आसानी से होता है।

Schneeflöckchen

एक बर्फ का टुकड़ा सावधानी से गिरता है। यह शांत है। परत दूसरी दुनिया से आती है। यह इस दुनिया को संरचना देता है, अन्यथा सभी चुंबकीय क्षेत्र ढह जाते। उत्तरी और दक्षिणी ध्रुवों पर, चुंबकीय क्षेत्र बर्फ में गिर जाता है। पृथ्वी के ध्रुवों से, बर्फ दुनिया में गुप्त परिवर्तन आयोजित करता है। इसका चुंबकत्व पृथ्वी के निवासियों की अनुमति देता है और उन्हें भारी नागरिक बनाता है।

सुरक्षा

संरक्षण एक अच्छी बात है। संरक्षण पहली चीज है जो आपको चाहिए: संवैधानिक संरक्षण, हॉल संरक्षण, फसल सुरक्षा उत्पाद, डेटा संरक्षण और विचार संरक्षण। माइंड प्रोटेक्शन से आपकी अभी तक मुलाक़ात नहीं हुई है? यह आएगा, बस इंतजार करो।

आंत

डाइजेस्ट चबाना और चबाना और चबाना। जब तक भोजन इतना महीन न हो जाए तब तक डाइजेस्ट कभी भी बारीक हो जाता है। हालांकि, भोजन हमेशा थोड़ा विषाक्त रहता है। पृथ्वी जहरीली है। यह हमारा घर नहीं है। जानवर मनुष्यों से बेहतर पचा सकते हैं, वे पृथ्वी के करीब रहते हैं।

पृथ्वी

जिस चीज पर हम खड़े होते हैं उसे पृथ्वी कहा जाता है। कभी-कभी इसे मंजिल कहा जाता है। स्थायी और पृथ्वी दृढ़ हैं। पृथ्वी का अर्थ हमस या पत्थर भी हो सकता है। पृथ्वी का पदार्थ विशेष रूप से हड़ताली है, यह घना और भारी है। मंजिल शांतिपूर्ण है, मंजिल बेवकूफ है। महान महान माँ का कोई चेहरा नहीं है। क्या उसके पास गर्मी है? जड़ें पृथ्वी में पहुंचती हैं, वे भी पृथ्वी को समझती हैं। जड़ें पृथ्वी के शांत होने के साथ एक हैं।

मधुमक्खियों

मधुमक्खियां मोटे तौर पर, भीतर की ओर रहती हैं। एक मधुमक्खी ठंडी होने पर बाहर जाती है। यह हिमपात के रूप में जमीन पर गिर जाता है। मधुमक्खियों ने ठंड के गुच्छे के रूप में अपनी आवक व्यक्त की है। जब तक बर्फ़ जमी रहती है, वह क्रिसमस ट्री का समय होता है। अगर फेकते हैं, तो अकेलापन नग्न है। अमृत को घोलने में, मधुमक्खियाँ दुनिया के सभी हिस्सों और गुरुत्व को जोड़ती हैं, वे गुरुत्वाकर्षण को चबाती हैं। अमृत एक किताब थी जिसे अभी तक पढ़ा नहीं गया था। इसके लेखक द्वारा भी नहीं।

तीव्रता

भारीपन आमतौर पर मात्रा में बड़ा होता है। नेतृत्व में, हालांकि, भारीपन छोटा है। भारी शक्ति। इसका प्रभाव केवल इसके द्रव्यमान से होता है, इसके रंग से नहीं, क्योंकि रंगीन होने के लिए भारीपन बहुत गहरा है। भारीपन मजाक नहीं समझता। केवल चीनी में अजीब और भारी नींद एक साथ हो सकती है। क्या गुरुत्वाकर्षण ऊपर से आता है या नीचे से? जब गर्मी मजबूत हो जाती है, तो यह गुरुत्वाकर्षण बन जाता है। उस पत्थर के बारे में जो आप रोल नहीं कर सकते हैं? क्या यह बहुत भारी है या बहुत दृढ़ है? यह बहुत क्रूर है! क्रूरता क्रूर से अधिक नरम होती है। क्या यह आसान है? यह कैसा है!

हवा

हवा पेड़ों और घरों से अलग चलती है। हवा का बल दिखाई नहीं देता है, केवल इसके प्रभाव देखे जा सकते हैं। हवा स्टॉक को उड़ा देती है। एक सिंहपर्णी हवा में उड़ती है, राख समान। हवा बहुत क्षणभंगुर है। लेकिन यह हमेशा उड़ता है।

मस्तिष्क में दरारें

संपत्ति अद्वितीय है। यह उसकी बात के लिए अजीब है। मात्रा सापेक्ष है, इसे हमेशा तुलना से मापा जाता है। मात्रा का कोई स्वामी नहीं है। Isolde का पेट बड़ा है, लेकिन वह मोटा नहीं है। हर चीज में बहुत कुछ होता है। इससे कोई फर्क नहीं पड़ता कि आइंस्टीन के मस्तिष्क में कितनी दरारें थीं। यह मस्तिष्क की विशेषता है जो इसे अद्वितीय बनाता है, न कि इसकी दरारों की संख्या। आप सेब और नाशपाती की तुलना नहीं कर सकते, बस उनका वजन।

रेत

पत्थरों के टुकड़ों को रेत कहा जाता है। रेत के टुकड़े इतने छोटे होते हैं कि वे अलग-थलग पड़े समुदाय के रूप में फिर से एक एकता बनाते हैं। बालू तो एक पूरे के रूप में महसूस किया जाता है। पूरी बात रो रही है, लेकिन रेत रो नहीं सकती क्योंकि यह बहुत सूखा है। पत्थरों में न तो खून होता है और न ही पानी, रेत के रूप में भी नहीं। दुखी दिग्गजों के आँसू समुद्र के रूप में खारे पानी का दान करते हैं। यही कारण है कि रेत को अक्सर समुद्र तट के रूप में पाया जाता है जहां समुद्र है।

लोग

लोग केवल बहुवचन में मौजूद हैं। एक व्यक्ति अकेला नहीं हो सकता। एक झुंड जानवर के रूप में मनुष्य " लोग " बन जाता है। एक भीड़ में लोग शामिल होते हैं। लोगों का खून उनके कबीले का खून है। दूसरी ओर, एक व्यक्ति का अपना खून है। पुराने यहूदियों के साथ, अब्राहम का खून उसके दिवंगत पोते के लिए नीचे चला जाता है। लोग और पुरातन लोग समूह में अपनी पहचान रखते हैं, स्वयं में नहीं।

बेबीलोन

बाबुल कोई बच्चा नहीं था: यह सबसे बड़ा था। न्यूयॉर्क में गगनचुंबी इमारतें भी हैं। लेकिन इन्हें आतंकवादियों द्वारा नष्ट किया जाना है क्योंकि वे भगवान को खरोंचना चाहते हैं। आप आर्थिक विकास और कॉस्मेटिक सर्जन के बारे में सुनहरी बछड़े के

चारों ओर नृत्य करते हैं। परमेश्वर का गुस्सा आखिर कब आएगा और पापी लोगों को कूड़ेदान में फेंक सकता है?

सबसे छोटे कण

फ्रेड ने रात में जेनेवा के पास बड़े कण त्वरक के लिए अनधिकृत पहुंच प्राप्त की है और अब गोल रिंग में रेंग रहा है: वह चमकीले हरे कणों को उड़ते हुए देखता है।

फ्रेड: नमस्ते कण, क्या आप भी बोल सकते हैं?

हरा कण: मेरे सिर में दर्द है, जो बुरा है क्योंकि मैं केवल एक सिर हूं। जब से भौतिकविदों ने मुझे खोजा है, मैं अब वास्तव में दुनिया का वेट नहीं कर सकता। यहां तक कि राजनीति भी नियंत्रण से बाहर हो रही है।

एक लाल कण अतीत में उड़ जाता है: यह अपनी जीभ को बाहर निकालता है, जो कि कण से भी अधिक लाल होता है।

लाल कण: मैं अपनी गांड के नीचे धन रौशनी करता हूँ। आमतौर पर पैसा सिर्फ जानकारी है। मेरी आग सूचना का मूल्य देती है। एक त्रिभुज उड़ता है, इसके माथे पर एक आंख होती है।

त्रिकोण: मैं सबसे बड़ा कण हूं। वास्तव में छोटे कण केवल भौतिकी के नरक में मौजूद हैं। छोटे की कोई वास्तविकता नहीं है। जितनी व्यापक चीजें बनती हैं, उतने ही वास्तविक बन जाते हैं। - फ्रेड बस चकित है।

अराजकता एक भ्रम है जो रचनात्मक बहिर्मुखता का उपयोग दुनिया में मन की सुरक्षा से बाहर निकलने के लिए करता है। अराजकता रंगीन है। अराजकता अतीत की बकवास को दूर करती है। अराजकता नृत्य करती है और न जाने क्या क्या करती है।

लिखने

लेखन में, भाषा ध्वनि में चुपचाप बोलती है, लेकिन चेतना में उज्ज्वल है। लेखक निश्चितता के मूर्तिकार हैं। लिखना हमेशा लिखा जाता है, लिखते समय भी। लेखन अंतिम है और अच्छी शराब से अधिक समय तक रहता है। शब्द हर समय लिखता है।

नृत्य

नाच रहा है। जो भी नाचता है वह पागल है। यदि आप लापरवाह व्यक्ति हैं तो नृत्य भी शांत हो सकता है। विचारकों को नृत्य नहीं करना चाहिए। नृत्य उसकी मन की स्पष्टता को चकनाचूर कर देता है। प्रेम भोजन की कमी के कारण हताश, एक बाघ के रूप में पागलपन बुराई के भ्रष्ट क्रम को खा जाता है: मीठे मीज़ी फ़्रेसि-फ़्रेसी बनाते हैं!

इरविन

अश्रु की बूंदें आकाश से गिरती हैं। वे एक नदी के रूप में घूमने वाले ब्रुक के रूप में पृथ्वी पर इकट्ठा होते हैं। इरविन अश्रु के माध्यम से एक डोंगी और पैडल में बैठता है। नदी ऊपर की ओर बहती है। नदी के दाहिने किनारे पर वॉटन के सम्मान में आग जलती है। बाएं किनारे पर एक पेड़ है जिस पर एक पत्थर का पक्षी बैठा है। इरविन एक डोंगी में चढ़ाई जारी रखता है। अब बर्फबारी हो रही है। डोंगी पाइन सुइयों के बीच बैंक में एक स्नोमैन देखता है। हिममानव की आँखें जीवित हैं, वे एक शक्तिशाली टेडी बियर की आँखें हैं। इरविन नदी को जारी रखता है। बाईं ओर कोई वीणा बजा रहा है। भगवान करीब है।

ज्वालामुखी

रंगीन छींटों के साथ काले रंग की एक महिला शांत से लड़ती है। वे सितारों के बीच, सितारों के बीच, तारों के ऊपर एक साथ उड़ते हैं। टाइटैनिक का जीवन इसके डूबने में दिखाई देता है। एक पेपर फोल्डिंग बोट पानी में लापरवाही से तैरती है, यह

सावधानी से पानी के झरने की ओर बहती है: पेंग! ऊपर से राख गिरती है। आईजफजलजाजोकुल आखिरकार फट गया।

फिट

इसके विपरीत, फिट को प्यार के रूप में पाया जा सकता है। संबंधित चीज़ के रूप में, फ़िट एक और इसी तरह की सेवा के साथ दूसरे को पूरक करता है। सब कुछ एक संरचना में एक साथ फिट बैठता है। श्री अलकी की रसोई की मेज पर बीयर, सिगरेट और ऐशट्रे हैं। यह समझ में आता है, यह फिट बैठता है। श्री अलकी की रसोई की एक संरचना है। Hinz और Kunz इंटरनेट पर एक साथ बड़ी विश्व सूची में हैं। हिंज और कुंज केवल अपने अस्तित्व से जुड़े हुए हैं। इंटरनेट एक संरचना नहीं है, बल्कि बकवास है।

बात

एक चीज अपने ग्रे होने में है; यह और कुछ नहीं है। चीजें अवैयक्तिक हैं। चीजों की फेसलेस वर्ल्ड मशीन पृथ्वी पर राज करती है: चीजों का इंटरनेट। दुनिया की चीजों का ढेर। शैतान के पास लंबे समय से दुनिया है। जीवित चीजों की बात नहीं की जाती है क्योंकि वे खुद को स्थानांतरित करते हैं। हालांकि, एक युवा चीज खुद को स्थानांतरित कर सकती है। बात है।

उपाय

एक उपाय सही हो सकता है, मैत्रीपूर्ण देवताओं द्वारा प्यार से पके हुए। एक शिक्षक के रूप में, एक बीमार उपाय छात्र की शक्ति को सीमित करता है। पुतली तब भरी हुई है, उसका जीवन बैकलॉग है, और उद्योग बांध से बिजली पैदा कर सकता है।

सब कुछ

यह सब बेचैनी की सीमा तक कई चीजों का एक जोड़ है। क्या यह सब अब पूरी बात है? पूरी चीज कम से कम एक गोल चीज है। जैसा कि अपेक्षित था, पूरी चीज को इसके किनारे पर चमकना चाहिए, लेकिन यह वहां ग्रे रहता है। तब औद्योगिक पुजारी कहते हैं: "पूरे इसके हिस्सों की राशि से अधिक है!" इस वाक्य के बाद भी, सब कुछ नहीं चमकता है, देखा जाना नहीं है। पूरा सब कुछ का नग्न जोड़ बना हुआ है। इस पुस्तक में केवल एक और है।

कुछ नहीं

शून्य सभी गैर-चीजों की दुनिया है। एक कप एक कुर्सी नहीं है। एक पोशाक एक बादल नहीं है। कुत्ते का उल्लेख नहीं करना: एक कुत्ता गौरैया की तरह एक गैर-बिल्ली है। सभी गैर-चीजें कुछ भी नहीं की दुनिया में एक साथ आती हैं। कुछ कहते हैं कि मृत्यु के बाद कुछ भी नहीं आता है। क्या आप सभी गैर-चीजों के बीच वहां रहना चाहते हैं? यह गैर-चीजों की अलमारी में बहुत तंग होगा।

आनंद

भोग की जरूरत से ज्यादा जरूरत है। तो आनंद का संबंध आनंद से है। लेकिन जबकि खुशी जीवन का एक उपहार है, आनंद मनमाना है। भोग लिंगा और ठहरता है। आनंद चिकना है। प्रसन्नता वह वासना है जो अति हो गई है। भोग नहीं लगता है, भोग उसके लिए बहुत सुस्त है। जब आंतें जरूरत से ज्यादा पचती हैं, तो वह खुश होती है। संतुष्टि एक स्वीटनर है, लेकिन चीनी खुशी है।

El Psicosaurio se presenta a sí mismo:

Pienso poéticamente y no me convertí en víctima de un biofant. Estas fantasmas alienígenas ingresan ilegalmente desde el espacio en la oscuridad y usan su larga trompa para absorber la imaginación de la gente somnolienta de sus cerebros. Solo uso a regañadientes palabras que otros ya han dicho. Eso me parece insalubre. Es por eso que a menudo invento nuevas palabras, lo que crea el problema que ya nadie me entiende. En consecuencia, tengo que usar palabras usadas nuevamente, que la lengua vernácula alemana se ha formado de manera imprecisa. El lenguaje puede hablar porque contiene las imágenes generales de la existencia. Lo principal en el lenguaje es darles un hogar a las imágenes del mundo. Es trágico cuando una persona sigue las palabras del lenguaje y luego piensa que esto es pensar. El pensamiento real da forma activa al lenguaje. El lenguaje es el yo de un psicosaurio, es su centro. El mundo realmente cobra vida en el lenguaje, porque hablar significa: crear el mundo. En el principio fue la palabra!

Miedo

Un aterrador conejo está en camino de convertirse en un conejito de Pascua. En el camino quería visitar a su tío, pero está nuevamente en el pimiento. El conejo asustado no es una rana, se enfrenta al mono, incluso si el mono se ríe de él. El piojo corre sobre el hígado de la pulga. La liebre oye esta tos de pulgas, que ahora dispara cañones a los gorriones. El conejo asustado vence a su bastardo interno y luego convierte la pulga en un caracol. A la izquierda ve un burro que es demasiado cómodo. El burro se congela en pleno verano. Eso no funciona en piel de vaca, y las gallinas se ríen del burro. En la mano derecha, un ratón gris atrapa las polillas porque el alce las golpeó. Los mosquitos en el aire son inofensivos en sí mismos si no se convierten en elefantes y se comportan como ellos en la tienda de porcelana. Specht corre como un conejo y saca su caniche regado para que no se vuelva loco en la sartén. El señor y el perro probablemente tengan un pájaro, pero ningún gallo los sigue, porque está en la canasta con sus gallinas. En su camino, el conejo asustado encuentra un diente de mono que ya no daña a una mosca. Ahora que el miedo lo ha hecho, ha llegado al conejito de Pascua.

una conversacion

Mole: Di Psychosaurus, ¿de qué trata este libro?

Psicosaurio: en este libro, el lenguaje habla por sí mismo y hay lenguaje

habla de todo, por lo que este libro tiene todos los temas.

Pato: Una pregunta personal: ¿cuál es la diferencia entre eso?

Psicosaurio y Carsten?

Psicosaurio: no quiero hablar de eso

El tema me estresa totalmente.

Pato: ¡Está doblado, amigo!

Mole: este libro es obviamente uno

traducción automática?

Psicosaurio: Así es. Esto aumenta lo extraño más allá de toda medida.

El lenguaje dice más de mil palabras.

Risita: si quiero escribirle a Carsten, él también tiene uno

En línea o algo?

Psicosaurio: por el momento tiene la dirección de correo electrónico

carsten-stemm@web.de y también tiene el suyo en línea.

Hombre lobo: Sunt reprimat de această carte!

Risita: No entiendo una palabra, ni siquiera la estación de tren.

Rabe: No tienes que entenderlo todo. A veces es suficiente dejar que las palabras te lleven a través de lo irracional.

Detlef doble dooid

Detlef Doppeldoid no puede pensar correctamente con ambas mitades del cerebro. Detlef piensa más rápido que la luz, lo que lleva a hinchazones del espacio-tiempo en su logosfera. Luego intercambia derecha con izquierda, adentro con afuera y asqueroso con red. No sabe si entras o sales de una habitación. Es malo sobre Detlef Doppeldoid: el otro día pensó que las personas eran personas. Detlef tampoco puede recordar la diferencia entre Albert Einstein y Konrad Adenauer. Detlef se pregunta: ¿No son "lo mismo" y "lo mismo" lo mismo? A veces, el Sr. Doppeldoid también comete errores ortográficos. Si está completamente confundido, Detlef incluso recuerda el futuro.

Detlef dice:

" Cuando ya no sé quién soy, miro mi tarjeta de identidad: también tengo mi propio número allí; un número, todo solo para mí, solo para mí. Único e inconfundible. El estado me ama. ¿Pero eso me ayuda? ¿Quién está detrás del nombre Detlef Doppeldoid? ¿Y qué prueba una pequeña tarjeta de plástico? Es fácil falsificar tarjetas de plástico. Puedes fingir todo hoy. Incluso puedes fingir una identidad. Me estoy volviendo bastante florido ".

Hablando conejito

El conejo que puede hablar se llama el conejo que habla. El conejo que habla come mientras habla y habla mientras mordisquea. Las raíces de las palabras no son desconocidas para él. Actualmente está consumiendo amor. El amor es solo una palabra para él, mugg, mampf. Puedes comer amor sin comer, eso es sabiduría de la liebre.

Hay patos!

El biólogo está interesado en las plumas de los patos, el ontólogo está interesado en el ser de los patos. ¿Quién da los patos? Respuesta: El "eso". 'Eso' y dando resultado en ser. Alternativamente, la pregunta podría responderse de la siguiente manera: la evolución da patos, los huevos de pato dan patos, el sexo de pato da patos, Dios da patos. Esta lloviendo Uno debería decir: la nube está lloviendo. Este 'eso' ni siquiera depende de Dios, porque significa: Hay un Dios. Esto a su vez significa: "El" es más grande que Dios. Otra conclusión sería: El 'Es' es el Dios verdadero que da a Dios primero. Hay patos No se dice: se necesitan patos. Dar es más feliz que tomar. Dar es probablemente más ontológico que tomar. El 'eso' no está tan claro que ya no se puede ver su niebla. Como resultado, ya no piensas de dónde vienen realmente los patos. El 'eso' es engañoso. Finge ser conocimiento. Si ya no sabemos que la nube está lloviendo,

entonces llueve. La negación también da el 'it': " ¡No hay Elwittitsche! " ¿Quién solo puede ser este 'it' que puede dar a estos no patos?

Goldmarie y Pechmarie

Una vez hubo un entrenador motivador que tenía dos hijas, las cuales se llamaban Marie. Uno era trabajador, el otro perezoso. Un día, la mujer trabajadora llegó a un pozo que decía:

"¡No hay agua potable!"

" Solo está allí por razones legales ", pensó la mujer sedienta. La niña bebió del agua y cayó accidentalmente en la fuente, lo que la hizo perder el conocimiento. En algún momento se despertó en un área completamente desconocida.

Una anciana estaba parada en la ventana de una casa que necesitaba una renovación y sacudió la almohada. La Sra. Holle, así se llamaba el inquilino, le dijo a la niña: `` Las enfermeras competentes para los ancianos como usted son raras hoy en día, hay mucho trabajo para mí ''. Y como la mujer trabajadora estaba tan interesada en el trabajo, hizo la limpieza de la Sra. Holle.

Después de un tiempo, sin embargo, la niña sintió nostalgia y expresó el deseo de que se le permitiera regresar a casa. Frau Holle le concedió este deseo. La anciana condujo a la niña a una puerta por donde debía pasar. Mientras la mujer trabajadora atravesaba la puerta, llovía sobre ella desde arriba, un alquitrán contaminado con dioxinas que ya no se desprendía de su piel. La chica dijo: "¡Maldita mierda! Me vengaré amargamente del destino. Estudio matemáticas y hago mi doctorado en teorías paradójicas ".

Cuando la madre vio a su hija manchada de brea, llamó a su hija Pechmarie. Por razones de compensación social, la madre ahora también envió a su hija perezosa al pozo. Sucedió casi lo mismo. Solo su segunda hija llegó a otra casa en la que vivía cierta Frau Hölle en lugar de Frau Holles Haus.

Después de diez minutos de trabajo, la disciplina laboral de la chica perezosa disminuyó considerablemente. La Sra. Hell dijo: 'A tu edad yo también era bastante vago. Ni siquiera tengo un certificado de finalización de la escuela secundaria. Ahora estamos corriendo hacia un Château Mouton-Rothschild 1945, que mi yerno se robó.

Afortunadamente, toda la bodega está llena de gente ''. Después de una semana de borracheras, los perezosos también echaron de menos su hogar y querían quedarse en casa. Frau Hölle la condujo a la misma puerta por la que había pasado Pechmarie. Cuando la chica perezosa atravesó la puerta, estaba lloviendo oro sobre ella. Ahora la niña era mucho más valiosa, porque el oro tampoco podía ser eliminado. Cuando llegó a casa, su madre la llamó Goldmarie. Enfadada por la injusticia de la vida, la madre dejó la iglesia y fue a un juicio secular. Más tarde, Pechmarie se convirtió en la primera profesora de lógica con cicatrices de dioxina en su rostro. Su vida estaba completamente arruinada. Goldmarie, sin embargo, vivió feliz para siempre. > Final feliz

Queso de oveja

Pastor: Dime, ¿qué tipo de libro llevas bajo el brazo?

Wolfgang: Una de tus ovejas me dio el libro para mi cumpleaños. Su título es: ¡Haz queso de oveja tú mismo!

Pastor: ¿Se supone que eso es una broma?

Wolfgang: No se puede jugar con bromas. Nunca estoy bromeando Quien bromea es demasiado cobarde para hablar en serio. Nunca bromeaba. Y si alguien se ríe, me daré una palmada en la boca.

Una oveja: Disculpe si interfiero, pero estoy genéticamente modificado, para poder hablar. ¿Hay un nuevo impuesto sobre el queso de oveja pronto?

otra oveja: yo también soy un producto genéticamente mejorado del creador, y te digo: los hombres son como las mujeres, pero al revés.

Wolfgang: ¡Siempre pensé que sería diferente!

Pastor: Me mareo por conversaciones tan complicadas. .. Ah, mira quién viene! ¡Está cojeando!

Wolfgang: ¡Entonces solo puede ser una comparación!

Pastor: ¿Por qué es eso?

Wolfgang: Porque siempre dices: ¡cada comparación se queda atrás!

una oveja esquilada: el significado siempre es ambiguo. Entonces el orador se promete rápidamente en su discurso. El doble alemán es un Lapsus Freudianikus, la filtración en el autorretrato demasiado suave.

Wolfgang: ¿Qué tipo de conversador es ese?

Pastor: La oveja estudió. Psicolingüística o algo así.

(La cojera ahora ha llegado al grupo de discusión).

Cojeando: Estás detrás de mí. Mi comercio robado

¡El plutonio de las centrales nucleares rusas ha explotado!

Pastor: ¡No hagas cosas, Otto!

Ovejas: ¿puedes comer plutonio?

Pastor: ¡No todas las ovejas han estudiado!

todas las ovejas juntas: ¡Mähhhh!

Otto: solo tengo una salida: ¡suicidio!

Wolfgang: Tendría una salida alternativa. Conozco un buen mago en el circo. Sufre de alergia, pero técnicamente está bien.

Otto: ¿Quién es este mago?

Wolfgang: Él es todo lo que crees que es, porque tiene mucho

Planetas en la séptima casa, incluido Plutón.

Otto: ¡No creo en la astrología!

Wolfgang: ¡Pero las estrellas creen en ti!

Otto: Bien, quiero probarlo, porque no me queda nada que perder. Estoy encantado en un conejo y escribo mi nombre al revés para que nadie me reconozca.

Pastor: ¡ gran cosa! Ahora que es un final muy feliz!

En una emergencia, la manzana come peras.

Homicidio

Mono: Buenas tardes, ojo extraño, tienes los ojos sesgados.

Ojo extraño: Y eres un mono, mono.

Mono: Tengo un cartucho de dinamita aquí.

¿A quién los metemos por el culo?

Ojo extraño: ¡por supuesto! ¡En TNT no digo que no!

¡Mono brillante, te mereces el Premio Nobel!

(El mono empuja la inclinación en el culo de la dinamita y enciende la mecha. Después de unos segundos de agitación nerviosa de espera, hay una detonación violenta: polvo, escombros y restos de carne cubren el lugar de la explosión).

Mono: genial! Se estrelló!

No hay recuentos ni párrafos para nosotros los animales.

Ahora vamos a comer una banana. Jaja!

Polluelo de acero

Una vez hubo un pequeño automóvil chirriante que atraviesa la naturaleza regordeta y suave. El carro se mueve, es tirado por un caballo. Un vehículo que ya no conduce hoy. Cuando el motor comenzó a conducir al acompañante, el carro se volvió de acero, cuando todavía se tiraba del carro, las flores florecieron y el agua corrió hacia él. El secreto de la vida vivía en la rueda del molino, aquí la rueda corría en el agua. El automóvil fue el nacimiento de la chica de acero. El cielo se estira, el cielo se estira, él está emocionado. Polluelo de acero dispara al cielo con un cañón de defensa. Es la Segunda Guerra Mundial, un intento sin sentido por parte del acero para volver a ser un caballo. La chica de acero ahora es un caballo, por lo que lleva una cola de caballo. Los caballos son realmente elegantes, ya que la elegancia ya no se conoce en la era del acero. El plástico también es acero. Todo lo que no tira del caballo es acero. Te asombra una belleza que no es una muñeca de moda.

Varias habitaciones

Una habitación múltiple es una habitación que es más grande por dentro que por fuera. El armario múltiple, por ejemplo, se parece a un armario de dormitorio ordinario. Pero si tiene que esconderse en el armario si es necesario, se sorprenderá al descubrir que hay galaxias enteras en el armario. Y estas no son alucinaciones como resultado de la falta de oxígeno. El mundo está lleno de agujeros en la realidad. Y hay más y más.

Peligro

El peligro te amenaza. El accidente aún no ha golpeado. Pero podría atacar en el futuro; Eso es un riesgo. La vida es insegura. No sabes si la vida se romperá el próximo momento. El peligro está en la puerta, el peligro es impredecible, puede convertirse en una pesadilla. Los depredadores son peligrosos; Los capitalistas también. Es peligroso tender los cables de alimentación en una bañera llena de agua. Casarse también es arriesgado. El seguro de vida, por otro lado, promete protección: si ha perdido una vida, obtendrá una nueva. Pero cuidado con el fraude de seguros: ¡las compañías de seguros engañan mucho!

Pensando

Pensar vaga en la tierra del significado. Las formas de pensar se topan con el bosque del conocimiento. A través de su caminata, pensar se vuelve más difícil y finalmente se fusiona con sus árboles de pensamiento y la nieve de sus sueños.

Olymp

Fred ve a un dios en el teléfono celular en Olympus:

Fred: hola dios!

¿Cuánto tiempo llevan los dioses usando un teléfono celular?

Dios: sí mei, solo ajústate. También podría comunicarme telepáticamente con mis colegas, pero los dioses queremos que la gente sea comprensible.

Fred: ¡Entonces no lo entiendo!

Cabezas de huevo

Los cerebritos son los conejos de la aglomeración neumática. También se llaman cabezas de huevo. Sus neurolantes no son muy flexibles, pero son muy largos. Lanza nueces desnudas a sus cabezas calvas porque contienen mucha cera cerebral. Los neurolantes son los bastones de la mente. Los neurolantes también pueden ser los troncos de los árboles a través de los cuales ya no se puede ver el bosque por la gran cantidad de ellos. Pero en realidad los neurolanten son los palillos para comer sushi intelectual.

Algunas ondas cerebrales se llaman filósofos. La filosofía piensa sin beber, es luz sin amor. El pensador puede bromear mal en el desierto del conocimiento. Los cactus nunca se ríen. La filosofía es tan dura como el queso viejo. Los filósofos en el camino hacia la curación comienzan a escribir poesía.

Semidiós

Fred: Sabes, Detlef, fui ascendido a semidiós.

Detlef: ¿En serio?

Fred: ¡Es así! Ahora puedo encontrar una respuesta a cada pregunta, aunque sea de manera imprecisa, pero puedo encontrar la respuesta.

Detlef: ¿Quién te promovió?

Fred: ¡El gran jefe!

Detlef: ¡Ajá!

Fred: solo soy un semidiós. Todavía no soy inmortal, pero estoy trabajando en ello.

Detlef: Mm, haz eso.

Fred: Finalmente sé, por ejemplo, por qué el plátano está torcido.

Detlef: Sí, ¿por qué entonces?

Fred: Ella anhela la unidad, el plátano quiere volver al paraíso, le gustaría ser un círculo, pero la Caída se lo prohíbe, solo su fuerza se extiende hasta la curva.

Detlef: ¡Qué sabe un semidiós!

Fantasma

El término "espíritu" es una palabra muy solitaria. La palabra tiene que explicar muchas cosas. La inteligencia corta piedras; La mente se conecta. El espíritu ilumina las partes del mundo como un sol y les da forma. La mente es la imagen de las cosas. La mente viste las partículas más pequeñas con más. La mente puede pensar, la inteligencia solo puede pensar o combinarse.

Causa y efecto

Un jugador de billar golpea una bola con su palo, que a su vez golpea otra bola. Este pensamiento de causa y efecto es la lógica original de la ciencia. La lógica lo justifica, no explica nada. El libre albedrío del jugador de billar está completamente oculto en esta visión del mundo. Las causas son animales aburridos, casi toros. Las causas convencen a través de la energía, no a través del significado.

La lógica

Fred: creo en la lógica. Todo el cosmos está lógicamente estructurado. Sin embargo, las mujeres no son parte del cosmos. El pensamiento lógico te da acceso a cada rompecabezas. Solo tienes que poner mucho esfuerzo en pensar.

Arnold Heitermann: La lógica no nos hace avanzar en el conocimiento. Un ejemplo: tres cuervos se sientan en una cerca. Un asesino de aves viene y dispara a una de las aves.

Arnold: ¿Cuántos pájaros todavía están en la cerca?

Fred: Hay dos cuervos en la cerca.

Arnold: ¡Mal! ¡Todavía hay un cuervo en la cerca!

Fred: ¡Es completamente ilógico!

Arnold: Eso es lógico. El pájaro caído cayó muerto al suelo. El segundo cuervo se sobresaltó por el fuerte estallido y se fue volando de inmediato. El tercer cuervo estaba aterrorizado por la explosión y sigue siendo el único pájaro en sentarse.

Fred: Este caso me parece muy construido, pero es lógico.

Arnold: Bueno, puedes explicar todo y nada con lógica.

Fred: Primero de todo, luego.

Arnold: Sí, siempre después.

Sin embargo, la realidad estaba allí antes.

Fred: ¿Y si cinco cuervos se hubieran sentado de repente en la cerca después del disparo?

Arnold: Entonces algunos cuervos cansados de la vida se habrían sentado con la esperanza de que les dispararan también.

Fred: Realmente genial, lo que es lógico.

Arnold: Puedes explicar todo con lógica, incluso lo ilógico.

Fred: Hombre, hombre, realmente tengo que pensarlo.

Arnold: ¡Pero por favor sigue siendo estrictamente lógico!

Fred: Uh ... si ... bueno ...

Diálogo

Sócrates: ¿Qué aspecto tienes de mierda esta mañana, Platón?

Platón: ¡Cállate, culo!

Sócrates

Bala

Una bala está terriblemente restringida en sí misma y tendría el deseo de dar a luz si se encendiera. Pero nadie los enciende. La pelota permanece opaca como el barro y no se conoce. ¿Por qué ruedan las bolas? Ruedan el camino, pero no cambian su forma. En última instancia, son movidos por el movimiento. La bala sigue siendo bala. Ahora recuerdo: ¡las balas son femeninas!

(en) perfecto

El perro en sí es la idea de un perro. ¿La idea de un perro ahora parece un perro salchicha, un golden retriever, un perro pastor o incluso un caniche? Sabemos cómo se ve un círculo en sí mismo. Solo hay un círculo y es completamente redondo. Los triángulos ya lo hacen más difícil: ¿qué ángulo tiene la idea de un triángulo? El círculo es la única idea que se puede dibujar exactamente. El perro en sí no puede ser dibujado, solo un perro específico. El círculo mismo se puede dibujar. ¿Vamos a adorar al círculo? ¿Hay algún "en sí mismo"? ¿Las cosas solo aparecen "para mí"? - Lo perfecto en realidad sería demasiado imperfecto para la vida. La vida necesita una esquina en un círculo o un agujero en un cuadrado. Lo perfecto existe solo como una idea, porque en realidad lo perfecto no puede existir. El círculo tiene esquinas en la perfección de la vida. Una castaña es una bola angular. Lleva en la perfección imperfecta como vida perfecta. Sin embargo, un castaño está enfermo de alguna manera. ¿Por qué eso? ¡Solo el erizo lo sabe!

Círculo

Un círculo no puede respirar. En ninguna parte tiene un agujero por el que pueda respirar. El círculo en sí mismo puede verse como un agujero. ¿Es el círculo la puerta de entrada a otro mundo? No puedo comprobar eso porque el círculo no me deja entrar. Está demasiado cerrado. Uno no debería tratar con tales tipos. El círculo no me habla, siempre será misterioso. El círculo probablemente ni siquiera tiene nada que ocultar: es ingenuo, aburrido y vacío. - La ronda es el color del círculo. Este color es muy raro y no tiene nombre. La forma más fácil de nombrar el color es "colorido". La ronda puede emprender una aventura sin un círculo y un arco. La vida misma es una aventura, hoy el grupo piensa algo nuevo. Pero la ronda es tan antigua que su pensamiento sobre lo nuevo nunca puede producir locura. Sin embargo, los filisteos nunca andan por ahí. Es demasiado desigual para eso. El grupo quería convertirse en un círculo y le pidió a la agencia de empleo una nueva capacitación. El empleado era un cuadrado. Terminó mal.

La manzana piensa y la pera guía.

Golpear es asombroso

Llamativo es el verbo más universal que existe. Golpear es realmente asombroso. Esta actividad ya estaba completamente desarrollada en la Edad de Piedra. Puedes abrir los ojos, un libro igual. Mira hacia arriba en el duden, rompe la ventana o golpea a alguien en la cara. Los músicos hacen ruido con la batería. El golpe te golpea. El menisco 1.FC supera a los pies planos de Rosenheim 2-1. El que gana gana. La mejor manera de golpear es con piedras. Una piedra noble se llama martillo. Golpear es crudo y áspero. Un golpe es tonto y atómico. Golpear rompe, rompe, golpea separa. Un niño de golpear es cortar. Un niño malo Otro hijo de los golpes es el empuje. Este niño es más simpático porque tiene más sol en la parte delantera. Golpear hace un puño, por lo que sus acciones se desaniman.

Herramienta

Una obra de arte es la deposición de toda la experiencia humana definitiva. Hay experiencia que se ha confirmado para que se solidifique como una obra de arte. El tesoro del trabajo orienta a todos los seres como un campo magnético desde lo espiritual. El Werkschatz es la Wikipedia natural de la vida. Desafortunadamente, también hay ovejas negras en el tesoro del conocimiento: se llaman tierra de fábrica.

Para el rey Orthos, gobernar significa organizar las cosas de acuerdo con su propio ser interior. Orthos no imparte su propia voluntad a las personas. El rey no quiere forzar las cosas, pero explora sus idiosincrasias y les permite organizarlas ellos mismos. Las personas, las cabras y otros seres viven en Orthos Reich, todos de pie y caminando en el lugar correcto. Después de su muerte, el rey Orthos desembocará en el agua de su río favorito, que eventualmente desembocará en el mar. Desde el mar, su trabajo continuará orientando a las personas.

Hambre y sed

El hambre quiere comer algo todo el tiempo. El hambre depende completamente del objeto de su deseo. Pero eso es exactamente lo que hace que el hambre sea tan placentera. Está lleno de vida, algunos incluso dicen que es la vida misma. El hambre también tiene una hermana: su nombre es "sed". Pero eso es solo para tipos muy locos.

La necesidad es la abstracción del hambre y la sed. La necesidad es pobre y necesitada. La necesidad es muy secular y siempre se ve del mismo color gris. Puede almacenar sus necesidades a cualquier temperatura. La necesidad nunca da fruto, siempre permanece magra. Si necesita algo, vaya de compras.

¿Quién necesita fibra? Sobre todo, si solo consisten en lastre. Rellenos de carga. Llenan el vacío, pero se quedan huecos. Es la esencia que brilla.

El Psicosaurio está completamente al final:

Un poder de hielo como figura ha levantado su brazo. Una escalera de agua baja de la cara fría. Los ojos de la mujer sombra brillan como dos soles en la noche. No por mucho tiempo. Tus luces ahora se han apagado. La mujer sombra vuela hacia el cielo como un ángel negro. El lugar desconocido es huérfano. Donde nunca ha habido nadie, ahora no hay nadie. Mi conocimiento de no ser está al lado del espacio vacío. Tengo calor, pero solo como calor, porque no tengo otro cuerpo. Un grito sin lengua da vueltas desesperadamente en la habitación vacía. Solo hay vacío en todas partes, donde algo debería estar realmente. Donde no hay nada, no puedes ver nada, especialmente si no tienes ojos. Pero veo el horror y no sé por qué.

Agujero

Un agujero significa una ausencia bastante redonda. Los agujeros están vacíos. Un agujero es a menudo un pasaje que entra y sale. A veces, la vista sale por el agujero y la vista entra por el agujero. Los agujeros tienen hambre, les gustaría ser rellenados. El impulso de todo ser está bien para ser satisfecho. La realidad tiene agujeros. Son tan transparentes que nadie puede verlos, ni siquiera un físico con su gran aparato. La falta de ropa se puede ver en personas desnudas. La falta de brecha, por otro lado, permanece hambrienta e invisible. La superficie tiende a estar vacía. Si se llena este vacío, la superficie desaparece rápidamente, se vuelve delgada. El esteta prescribe color en la superficie para que tenga más confianza en sí mismo.

Animal

El animal clásico tiene cuatro patas, "maúlla" o ladra. El término animal es un caso tipo para muchos seres que tienen poco en común. Los animales no llevan hojas y no pueden construir bombas atómicas. Los animales son personas atrasadas. Sin embargo, un día los animales también entenderán el teorema de incompletitud de Godel. - ¿Solo cuando?

La naturaleza puede ser cruda y áspera. También existe la naturaleza de los soñadores: esta naturaleza es el paraíso de las personas incluso antes de la caída. La naturaleza del germánico Charles Darwin se ve así: una lucha de los fuertes contra un aún más fuerte. Nuestra segunda naturaleza es la cultura. Nuestro tercer reino se llama artificialidad. A nadie le gusta vivir allí.

Flor de hielo

Una potencia extranjera de Suecia está hecha del hielo más frío. Este poder va a la tierra en forma de una vieja llamada Eisblume. Una flor hecha de hielo, una flor hermosa. Las flores recuerdan a la primavera, porque durante este tiempo, las flores frescas generalmente florecen con calor joven. Sin embargo, nuestra flor de hielo florece en el frío asesino del invierno. Todas las demás personas que también están hechas de hielo quedan cautivadas por la flor de hielo. Agnis también está fuera del frío, del hielo ardiente. Agnis ve flor de hielo y se emociona. Las frígidas son siempre las más calientes. El Sr. Sumpfstein es un aturdidor como vendedor de helados. Sus bolas de helado contienen explosivos, que se encienden cuando es largo sobre todas las montañas. Eisblume ve al Sr. Sumpfstein: Ella se sorprende, la ruleta rueda en su cabeza. Nadie sabe que la pelota se detendrá en el compartimento de los diecisiete. En Agnis serán los tres. Bolas de hielo o bolas de ruleta, las bolas son todas iguales. Las balas son el banco malo del destino. Y ahora entramos en este banco y liberamos la locura. Todos se están volviendo locos: Eisblume, Agnis y Herr Sumpfstein están en una caja. Respiras locura: Ah, eso es bueno. ¡Finalmente son gratis!

Sangre

La sangre fluye dentro como un calor espeso y poderoso. La sangre humana es muy personal mientras siga circulando por sus venas. La sangre circula, entonces es redonda. Poderes de sangre en su círculo. La sangre externa en la jeringa fría y despiadada del médico ya está muerta. ¡Qué terrible! Solo los reptiles se desangran. A menos que el sol brille sobre el pelaje verde del reptil. Todo vampiro sabe: cuando la luna brilla, la sangre es negra. No ves nada durante el día.

Fuego

El fuego baila con llamas violentas. La quema salvaje destruye la durabilidad del combustible. Los picos de calor penetran en la habitación, los dientes febriles se muerden a sí mismos. El poder de la tormenta roja le da a sus alrededores un aura de calor. Las brasas del fuego mueren en cenizas. El fuego es impresionante, pero toma prestada su sustancia del combustible. Su comida se comió más rápido que cocido, mucho más rápido. El calor del fuego duerme esponjoso en el espacio de la inmortalidad. Cuando el calor se vuelve loco, se convierte en calor.

general

El general muestra tanta cara como sea necesario. Las características especiales muestran bordes mucho más claros. El general es el mismo en todas partes, a menudo se expresa a través del mismo. En el paisaje de todo, lo general se puede encontrar en todos los lugares. El tío gris del general se llama promedio. El general tiene que adaptarse al especial una y otra vez, lo que crea estrés. El general brinda seguridad cuando se va de vacaciones inusuales.

Sombra de pie

Una sombra permanente siempre debe detenerse, aunque puede ir a donde quiera. Si la sombra de pie quiere moverse, el entorno se mueve más allá de él que de él, él mismo se detiene. La sombra de pie puede moverse y aún así debe permanecer en el mismo lugar para siempre. Una sombra de pie no tiene compañía. Por supuesto, hay otras sombras permanentes, pero están en otro lugar.

Cortocircuito

El camino conduce a la meta siempre que no haya ningún esotérico caminando sobre ella. Un corto circuito acorta el camino de la vida. Él rápidamente sigue un camino que no existe. Como resultado, le falta experiencia. Su éxito es caliente y vacío y sin carne, pero el cortocircuito tiene un efecto carismático. La ruta más corta siempre es un cortocircuito, su objetivo es no existir. El cortocircuito actúa sin crecimiento, pasa sin camino. Joachim Ernst Berendt escribió un libro: "No hay manera, solo ve: SEA en la naturaleza". En el camino a la presentación de su libro, fue atropellado por un automóvil.

Ir

Tienes miedo de que caminar se caiga. Pero caminar es genial: siempre se mantiene en equilibrio. Movimientos de pie en el corredor. Sin embargo, mentir nunca corre.

El cielo

Las montañas pico no tienen problemas y están felices de que sean tan grandes y grandes. El cielo también es feliz cuando recibe visitantes de las montañas. El gran cielo también necesita convivencia.

Razón

El motivo está abajo. Es la base, piso, base y justificación. Si miras hacia abajo, se convierte en un abismo. No puedes descubrir la gravedad allí. El fondo y el abismo calman los nervios inmensamente. El mejor trabajo para los humanos es llegar al fondo de las cosas. Solo los conejos asustados prefieren hacer algo útil porque el mundo perece de una manera útil.

Inframundo

El inframundo está debajo del mundo. Ya casi no es parte del mundo, no lo sabes, por eso no es cómodo. Los muertos yacen debajo del suelo, también existe la fuente de fertilidad. ¿De qué otra forma deberían crecer todas las plantas?

Nube

La nube es una oveja en el cielo. Las nubes siempre están tristes. A menudo tienen que llorar. Pero también protegen al ganado del sol agresivo. Una nube absorbe el bien y el mal de las personas. Puedes ver por sus formas lo que ha llegado la hora. El movimiento y el agua bailan juntos en la nube.

Suciedad

No deberías poner tierra en la ensalada. De lo contrario, la enfermedad amenaza! La suciedad es el equivalente físico del pecado. Una herida puede considerarse como contaminación, porque la herida a menudo forma una costra desagradable en el borde que parece suciedad. La contaminación o las manchas a su vez indican culpabilidad. Alguien está manchado. ¿Nos lastimamos porque éramos demasiado imperfectos? ¿O somos imperfectos porque nos lastimaron? ¿O somos culpables de violar algo, una ley o una persona? ¡Pero no duele! Somos perfectos e inocentes! Quien dice algo así es hiriente, por lo tanto culpable.

Sexo en la carcel

Los muros de la prisión forman un corazón. Sus paredes exteriores son negras por fuera y rojas por dentro. El prisionero Rasputín ya no es el más joven, pero tampoco el más viejo, porque después de todo, todavía tiene acné. Germania también está encarcelada: Rasputín y Germania se acuestan juntas. Rasputin teme que Germania contraiga sífilis. Germania deja Rasputín. Probablemente solo tenga que hacer Pippi por un corto tiempo, pero no llegará muy lejos porque estamos en la prisión del corazón. Una prisión es un edificio del que no puedes escapar. Rasputin se para frente al espejo y expresa sus granos. El pus salpica a la inocencia plateada: repulsivo, ey.

Rata y bomba atómica

Las ratas son ratones que se han convertido en megalómanos. Toleran mejor la radiactividad de todos los seres vivos. Seguramente algún día se convertirán en reyes de la tierra. Las ratas se matan entre sí, son muy similares a los humanos. ¡Ratéate quién puede! Sin embargo, las ratas son más inteligentes que los humanos, porque aprenden muy rápidamente a no comer alimentos tóxicos si notan que sus compañeros los están matando. Es por eso que el veneno para ratas no es una solución permanente para exterminar a estas criaturas del infierno. En la Edad Media, las ratas se usaban para torturar a las personas; hoy, las ratas son torturadas en laboratorios científicos. ¡Es una victoria para la humanidad! ¡De víctima a perpetrador! Las ratas lindas son cuidadas y cuidadas en el templo indio de Karni Mata. En Occidente, sin embargo, solo hay ratas de alcantarillado malas. En China, la rata incluso existe como un signo del zodiaco. Pero el Psicosaurio libre de gérmenes dice: "¡Ya no vivimos en la Edad Media! ¡Fuera los portadores de infecciones desagradables! ¿Por qué los políticos no hacen nada? ¡Nunca hacen nada!"

Torcedura

No puedes tocar un pliegue porque está muy lejos de la fila desde la que baila. Si nada se rompe, hay cosas. Una línea va de aquí para allá. Es tan normal que te deprime. A los científicos y arquitectos les gustan las líneas. Una línea no come vida. La línea atasca la vida y obtiene energía de ella para poder calentar la habitación hasta 20 grados moderados.

Inclinación

La pendiente es una pendiente que se inclina según la popularidad de la pendiente, se convierte en un ángulo que corresponde a la pendiente de la pendiente. Tal inclinación no es arbitraria, sino que corresponde al amor de los inclinados.

bien

Lo bueno es un árbol que da fruto todo el año. Su madera está hecha de sangre sólida; Sus hojas pueden reír. El colorido es bueno, el gris es malo. El diablo come lo bueno. Lo bueno puede consistir en sí mismo. Sin embargo, el mal depende de la destrucción del bien. Por lo tanto, el mal nunca puede prevalecer.

existir

La sal consiste en sodio y cloro. Pararse está en tus propios pies, pero la existencia necesita una sustancia como piso. Una existencia necesita partes en las que consiste, no puede ser por sí misma. Lo más grueso existe. El término "stock" se acerca mucho al de sustancia.

Ratón y murciélago

Los ratones tienen cuatro patas y corren de la manera que ordena Dios. Sin embargo, algunos ratones han ignorado su destino y han volado. Pasan el día perezosamente (cabeza abajo) y van de fiesta por la noche (beben sangre y otras cosas). El ratón como murciélago es ciego. Ese es el castigo de Dios por sus pecados. Como solución improvisada, los ratones voladores ahora deben ver con sus oídos. Es completamente descarado.

delgado

Las mujeres delgadas se sientan rápidamente en el muelle de anorexia. Acusado de tipos flácidos y gordos. Si el delgado quiere aumentar de peso, entonces debe llamarse "delgado". El delgado a veces tiene un efecto más intenso que el grueso porque puede contener mucha esencia en su dulce barriga. Por lo tanto, lo delgado es a menudo más inteligente que lo grueso. Esto no se aplica a los taladros de tabla delgada, porque tienen una tabla gruesa frente a sus cabezas.

Victoria pírrica

Mi nombre es Schmidt y estoy muerto. Viví una vida pecaminosa. En mi lugar de trabajo en la compañía Satan & Sons, mi codicioso jefe se convirtió en un billete de 100 euros. Sentí mi oportunidad de una vida feliz después de la muerte: rápidamente puse mi billete en mi billetera y pinté un crucifijo en su cuero exterior. Mi jefe fue atrapado. Solo después de su seguridad de que no iría al infierno después de mi muerte, retiré la cruz nuevamente. Poco después me resbalé infelizmente sobre una cáscara de plátano frente al AOK y me caí sobre el pavimento duro con la parte posterior de mi cabeza. Estaba muerto de inmediato. Como prometí, no fui al infierno, pero tampoco querían dejarme entrar al cielo, ya que había derrotado al mal pero aún no había hecho el bien. Ahora estoy constantemente yendo y viniendo entre el cielo y el infierno y ya no lo sé.

El sufrimiento

Fred: El sufrimiento es totalmente superfluo. ¿Qué idiota creó el mundo?

Detlef: El sufrimiento protege contra actos idiotas. Le impide beber demasiada cerveza. El mal lleva al bien.

Fred: ¿No es esa otra forma? Tipo de amor?

Papa: Dios es infalible (como yo), sabrá por qué creó el mundo.

Mephisto: Soy parte de ese poder que siempre quiere el mal y siempre crea el bien.

Bert Hellinger: En un nivel superior, el mal también es bueno.

Fred: vivo en la tierra; la tierra es un nivel inferior, el nivel superior no me sirve de nada. Todo esto no es muy convincente.

Detlef: El dios del sol también sufrió. Murió en la cruz como ser humano y resucitó al tercer día.

Fred: Eso es solidario con él. Me siento mucho mejor

Allahu Akbar

Dios es mayor que ... Dios siempre es mayor de lo que un ser humano puede imaginar. Por razones de seguridad, no quiero escribir nada malo sobre Dios, nunca se sabe. A menos que Dios sea el diablo. ¿Son los dioses malvados dioses reales? ¿O su existencia se alimenta de comer bien? Si solo hay un Dios, uno solo puede llamarlo Alá. Los dos sonidos A neutros y que lo abarcan todo flanquean el sonido L infinito. Si hay varios dioses, entonces se vuelve más colorido y amoroso y también más comprensible para los humanos. Cada dios entre otros dioses tiene su propia área de responsabilidad. Allah ya no necesita tener 99 nombres porque hay 99 dioses. Y el centésimo dios probablemente unirá a todos los dioses nuevamente, así que uno sospecha. La polarización fanática en el bien y el mal se disuelve en la multitud de dioses. A veces los dioses también se llaman ángeles, arcángeles o entidades superiores.

Ajo

El ajo es frescura rancia. Sus dedos están partidos. Una verdadera división de personalidad tiene sus raíces. En el exterior, sin embargo, la cebolla demuestra uniformidad. El ajo ayuda contra vampiros y brujas. El tubérculo fortalece la sangre y la hace tan poco comestible para los parásitos que incluso los vampiros pierden el apetito. El puerro esquizofrénico también mata parásitos físicos como las tenias o las bacterias putrefactas. El ajo divide a la humanidad como el humo del cigarrillo. A algunos les gusta: estas son las buenas personas. Sin embargo, los malos (por ejemplo, vampiros, brujas, nazis, hijos de puta, capitalistas y votantes verdes) se sienten repelidos por su olor.

Contrato con el diablo

Puede convertirse rápidamente en uno de los ricos y hermosos al hacer un pequeño contrato en la oficina de servicio de Satan & Söhne: el contratista (Teufel) cumple todos los deseos mundanos. A cambio, el contratista legó su alma post mortem a los anatomistas del infierno con fines de investigación. El contrato es legalmente válido a través de una gota de sangre del contratista.

Plaga

Arnold imagina una plaga que viene sobre la tierra y mata a todas las personas malas. Los buenos no se enferman en absoluto ni sobreviven fácilmente a la infección. Arnold es, por supuesto, uno de los buenos. ¿Cómo puede estar tan seguro de eso? ¿Qué tal si la peste en realidad solo mata a los buenos? Eso sería malo, pero típico de la injusticia de este mundo. Arnold se asusta y quiere vacunarse contra el destino, aunque sabe que no se puede hacer.

cortar

La conciencia corta el ser en cosas. El corte es más elegante que la picadura, razón por la cual un mosquito no tiene un título noble. Las almas fuertes tienen el coraje de enfrentarlo, los cobardes no tienen espada en absoluto. ¡No deberías cortarte el dedo! Así que amigos: ¡tengan cuidado! El color del corte se llama nitidez. Los pimientos picantes y las bombas sexuales a veces también pueden ser un poco picantes.

Pobre

Los brazos se extienden. Los brazos comienzan a florecer en las manos. Los brazos se afinan en las manos, las manos se fortalecen en la herramienta. Las ramas son los brazos de los árboles.

Límite

Un borde separa uno del otro. Comienza en la frontera o termina. La frontera forma un recipiente para la vida. La sangre necesita venas para vivir. Una casa limita la vida por sus paredes. Cuando la vida se muda de su casa, se ahoga en el mar de personas sin hogar.

La placa tiene un borde redondo. En contraste con el marco, el borde completa el crecimiento de su propietario. Un marco es joyería, es una compulsión para detener la usura.

El término "mundo" se utiliza para describir el paisaje de todo. El mundo puede ser entendido como una grandeza asesina. Este mundo no tiene fin. Los ojos del hombre no pueden detenerse en las calles interminables. Un mundo seguro está cerrado en sus bordes. Allí el mundo seguro abraza lo ilimitado con los brazos de la finitud.

claro y oscuro

Gustav es ciego en ambos callos. Sus pies no pueden ver nada. Eso es bueno, porque si no ves nada, no te deprimirás. Por eso Gustav es feliz. Hay personas que tienen una cita a ciegas. Estás demasiado ciego para encontrarte. Los murciélagos también ven negro, pero escuchan brillantemente ¿Es la luz ciega a la oscuridad? ¿La oscuridad ve la luz?

la luna

La luna se ríe en la oscuridad. Se puede ver en su totalidad. Como luna llena, él es hombre. De lo contrario, ella es mujer. ¿O fue al revés? La luna corre por el cielo con miedo. No le gusta que lo vean; solo los hombres lobo, los murciélagos y los cuervos pueden hacer esto. La luna gobierna secretamente en el reino del mal, es el embaucador con mejillas redondas, es un viejo amor, una brillante oscuridad llamada luna. La luna brilla más cuando la gente decente duerme.

Espera un minuto

Solo hay un momento y siempre es el mismo. Solo el momento es un momento. La mayoría de los "momentos" no tiene sentido. Entonces no hay tiempo. Y, sin embargo, el tiempo corre. Es por eso que los relojes son mentirosos.

Memoria

La gente no puede recordar en absoluto. Vemos el pasado desde nuestro momento presente. Todos los días recuerdas un pasado diferente. La forma en que realmente fue se perdió irremediablemente.

Vaca original

Al principio había leche. El universo fue creado a partir de la leche, por eso hablamos de la Vía Láctea. La leche provenía de la ubre del Urkuh, el gran MUU.

fresco

La frescura canta como luz en la humedad de la vida. La carne fresca es más saludable que la carne podrida. El jugo de fruta es más fresco que la sangre, porque el animal se está pudriendo en su codicia.

Tortugas

Las tortugas son embriones antiguos. Son de una época en que no había tiempo en absoluto. Su asunto también es diferente. No consiste en las partículas más pequeñas, sino en gachas más suaves a medida que la dureza corre en una línea de aquí para allá. La tierra real nunca muere.

Ruina

El viento sopla secretamente a través de las ruinas del desmoronado castillo. Las paredes oscuras están vacías de eventos. Las tormentas de fuego fueron ayer, las cicatrices son hoy. Un ratón puede escribir y le cuenta al periódico la historia de la ruina muerta. Las aves vuelan sobre el sol rojo de la tarde y desaparecen en la nada.

Genial

Lo primario siempre viene primero. La causa, el origen, la sopa primordial, el Urano, el ganado primitivo, el antepasado, el bosque primitivo, el Big Bang, y por supuesto documentos y pintorescos bisabuelos. Este último aún no conocía el término peligroso. En Viena, peligroso significa algo que es particularmente peligroso.

noticias falsas

¡La tierra es un disco! Si la tierra fuera una esfera, la gente en Nueva Zelanda se caería de la tierra. ¿Debería la NASA meter sus fotos falsas en el culo? ¡Han olido demasiado aire de luna!

Comenzando

Un comienzo puede comenzar repentinamente como un sprint o arrastrarse como la niebla en otoño. Las plantas germinan y los bebés nacen libres de gérmenes en el hospital. Un comienzo requiere un final: el nacimiento de un bebé termina el embarazo. El principio aún no se conoce a sí mismo: solo al final el principio sabe quién fue.

Niños

Los niños comen chocolate para niños. Los adultos comen chocolate para adultos. Ambos productos saben a chocolate. Puedes ver: los niños no son nada especial. Son comedores de chocolate como tú y yo. Los niños tampoco necesitan agua, aunque vayan al jardín de infantes.

Agárico

Un toadstool ama su libertad. Necesita lluvia desde arriba. Pero el hongo rojo se niega a recibir los impulsos de Dios. El agárico de mosca quisiera mantener todo bajo control. Incluso es dueño de un látigo. El dominio es importante para ello. La lluvia cae sobre el agárico de mosca. El hongo se da cuenta de que hay otras cosas además del dominio, pero el agárico no se atreve a abrirse. Luego lo hace, porque es valiente. El miedo viene de arriba hacia abajo en el hongo. Hey esto Ahora ya no es un toadstool, sino un ratoncito que quiere vivir una vida de clase media en su cueva. Pero esto no funciona. El ratón estudia filosofía y renueva el mundo y se hace famoso.

Rayo

Martin Luther y Paul fueron alcanzados por un rayo. Tan rápido como un rayo, se convirtieron en personas iluminadas. ¿Un rayo nos mejora? ¿O el flash es solo un cortocircuito que crea hipocresía? Tendría que intentarlo durante la próxima tormenta.

JF Kennedy en Bielefeld

Una supuesta teoría de la conspiración dice que la ciudad de Bielefeld ni siquiera existe. Desde cierto punto, ya no era posible que las sombras cubrieran la inexistencia de Bielefeld. Es por eso que estaban interesados en presentar la conspiración como una mera teoría o una broma para que nadie tuviera la idea de que lo falso de Bielefeld era la pura verdad. Afortunadamente, está Bill. El 24 de julio de 1963, Bill Clinton visitó al presidente estadounidense John F. Kennedy en la Casa Blanca y le estrechó la mano. Clinton exclamó: "¡Voy a ser presidente!" A través de este acto mágico, Clinton le robó su destino e identidad al presidente Kennedy en ese momento. El resultado: Kennedy tuvo que morir. O más bien su parecido. El verdadero Kennedy estaba congelado. Cuando la falsa existencia de Bielefeld amenazó con salir a la luz, Kennedy se descongeló nuevamente. Después de una cirugía estética y un entrenamiento intensivo en alemán, Kennedy se encuentra hoy bajo el nombre falso de Pit Clausen, el alcalde de la ciudad sombra de Bielefeld.

Las barbas

Sindbart: ¡Hola, puedo verte!

Windbart: ¡Locura! Yo tambien Increíble cuando consideras que ambos no existimos.

Sindbart: Cuando dos personas se encuentran que ni siquiera existen, se vuelven reales entre sí y entre sí, porque ambas se encuentran en el mismo nivel, es decir, el nivel de inexistencia.

Windbart: Raramente conoces a alguien como tú. Raramente te vuelves real. Deberíamos aprovechar la oportunidad para tener una discusión detallada sobre el engaño y la verdad.

Sindbart: Genial, estoy ahí.

Mar

El mar puede permitirse grandeza porque guarda secretos. El mar está formado por las trincheras de los dioses (las lágrimas contienen sal). El mar es alimento para la tierra. La sed del desierto se ha secado hace mucho tiempo, el desierto ya no necesita vivir.

Sociedad de la información

Arnold Heitermann no ve televisión y no lee un periódico. Solo los titulares. Para Otto Normal, lo que es actual es importante, todo lo demás no es importante. Arnold está interesado en el panorama general, no en las moscas de mayo. Además, nunca se sabe si la información es correcta. Si el encabezado dijera: "¡Mañana el mundo terminará!", El Sr. Heitermann ciertamente leería toda la información. Tal día del juicio final realmente puede afectarlo, solo por razones personales.

Agua

Al agua le gusta moverse. Si la naturaleza lo permite, entonces fluye. El agua es fresca y canta en sí misma. La luz brilla con los movimientos de sus olas. El agua está en todas partes donde hay vida. El agua es inestable mientras no esté todavía en el fondo. El agua está húmeda, la desnudez del agua permanece intocable.

Ranas

No deberías ser una rana, no una rana de miedo. Cualquiera que esté construido tan cerca del agua como la rana vive en el alma. Alma y lago son la misma agua, los peces y las ranas lo saben. Realmente no puedes asustarte en el agua, solo los animales secos sí. ¡Pregunta al aterrador conejo! ¡No la rana del miedo! Las ranas nunca salen de la pubertad. La rana es un pez que no ha llegado al animal terrestre: un fracaso de la evolución. Ya no es pescado, pero tampoco fue suficiente para los monos. Las ranas todavía están verdes detrás de las orejas, y no solo allí. Las ranas a menudo tienen granos, pero luego se llaman sapos.

Jabalí

Los jabalíes saltan desde el techo de una casa en la brumosa ciudad de Roma. Los cerdos salvajes se golpean la espalda en el pavimento de abajo. El jabalí no ha roto nada, gruñe libremente y sigue vivo. Tal jabalí es realmente robusto. Tu sangre no se marchita. En golpes fuertes, su jugo de fuego late sin tiempo a través de la pista de carreras de sus venas.

Sentimientos

Los sentimientos no tienen color. Son vagos infieles, su único dominio es la impermanencia. ¿Arriesgarías tu corazón a los sentimientos? Los sentimientos son excelentes para la cantidad y la masa, se vuelven más y más débiles, vuelven sin inspiración como los caballos en el carrusel.

Doom

El ancho del mundo se hunde en la profundidad. Todo se va a dormir y la luna está en el cielo. Su luz plateada fluye hacia el destino. Una mano quiere agarrar la luna y también lo hace: aplastó la luna. La sangre plateada, que es igualmente negra, corre desde una esfera que alguna vez fue la luna. El mundo tiembla.

matar

La muerte niega la vida y la habilita por igual. ¿De qué debería vivir el águila? ¿Qué debería cagar en la espalda? Solo puede vivir matando a otros animales. Como hombre! Los veganos son buenas personas. Pero ellos también deben seguir el llamado de la naturaleza. Después de todo, las plantas también son seres vivos. Los veganos tienen una deficiencia de vitaminas. Su inocencia los pone pálidos en la cara, son biovampiros. Los veganos beben la sangre de la moral. El mayor depredador son los humanos.

El televidente muerto

La televisión está encendida y hay un esqueleto frente a ella. Sus huesos del cráneo vacíos ya no son conscientes del programa. Alguien apaga la televisión: el hombre del hueso ahora se da cuenta de que le falta algo y se enoja. Solo al retirarse la muerte se da cuenta de que está muerto.

Sentido de la vida

El propósito de la vida es alimentar al gran economista agrícola. En cualquier caso, esa es la opinión del Dr. Lightbrain Él cree lo siguiente: desde un cielo lejano, el gran economista agrícola siembra las semillas de nuestra alma en el suelo de la realización. A través de la experiencia de la vida, el germen del alma se convierte en un oído productivo del alma. El gran economista agrícola cosechó y consumió este oído después de nuestra muerte. Dr. Brainlight es el hermano gemelo del Dr. Lightbrain Todas las mañanas Dr. Brainlight vomita después del muesli integral cuando piensa en la cruda teoría de su hermano.

Sol

El sol es el corazón del mundo, hay más espacio en él que en el espacio exterior. Ella tiene un estómago grande y brillante. El sol da a luz al mundo. El sol se come al mundo. Ambos por igual. El sol lo es todo. Es blanco con los viejos, es amarillo con los jóvenes. El sol no tiene arrugas en la cara.

Rabia

Un vampiro se mira en el espejo: un hombre con cabello negro y lentes se ve de plata, tiene una cara pálida. El vampiro cree que se ve como una persona normal en el espejo. El no muerto solo se reconoce en el espejo, sin embargo, si mira directamente a sus manos y cuerpo, no ve a nadie. Esto no es normal, ni siquiera para los vampiros. Seguramente tiene rabia.

Plantas

Las plantas son animales verdes que no pueden caminar. Sus hojas son piedras de agua. La luz del sol los vuelve completamente verdes. Piedra, agua y sol de repente dan vida. Una planta consiste principalmente en crecimiento, disfruta de su crecimiento. El crecimiento no tiene genes, los conoce a cada momento. Un plan no crece, incluso si lo llevas a cabo. Las plantas, por otro lado, crecen al azar con la vida.

duro

Algunas calaveras gruesas ya se han golpeado la cabeza con la dureza. La dureza ofrece resistencia y durabilidad. Un esqueleto es duro. Por lo general, lo difícil sigue siendo difícil. Sin embargo, un pene solo es difícil a veces. - ¿Por qué solo? - El borde de la dureza es una línea imponente en la habitación. Los bordes no deben pasarse por alto, podría golpearse la cabeza con ellos. Cuando dos paredes chocan, la colisión se llama borde. Un borde es, por lo tanto, el resultado de una carambola. Por lo tanto, no es para los débiles de corazón. Las piedras también son duras. Una piedra es una cosa, no tiene cara, porque una piedra se parece a otras piedras. En su ser, todas las cosas son iguales. Armario, mesa o cepillo de dientes son solo cosas. Las piedras que se encuentran en todas partes se llaman realidad. Se puede usar una piedra para martillar los cráneos de otras personas. Fue importante en la Edad de Piedra. Hoy algunas piedras pueden hablar, estas piedras se llaman "teléfonos celulares". Si lo pienso correctamente: también hay hermosas piedras, a saber, piedras preciosas. Los dragones los recogen.

recoger

La recogida es densa, a veces estrecha. Lo recogido proporciona seguridad como una existencia permanente. O es una carga. Es más difícil recolectar que recolectar. Si recolectar es más difícil de lo que se recolecta, se habla de "cazar".

Basura

Lo superfluo no está integrado en lo cultivado. Lo superfluo no llegó a conocer lo superfluo durante su crecimiento. Si bien el desbordamiento puede ser rico, a veces dona, por lo que lo superfluo no solo es inútil, sino que también obstaculiza la sustancia viva en su progreso. Lo superfluo es solo basura.

Macke

Hugo tiene un problema. Su peculiaridad es que la peculiaridad lo molesta en su pantalla. Eso vuelve loco a Hugo. Hugo tuvo un defecto en la cara durante décadas. De pie frente al espejo, miró su peculiaridad hasta que su dermatólogo apartó el pomo. Hugo tiene un capricho con caprichos. Pero solo para caprichos individuales. Si todo tiene un capricho, como una ventana totalmente rayada, a Hugo no le importa. Hugo realmente tiene un problema.

Spinner

El pensamiento vacío alimenta a su mujer de nieve marchita. La mujer gris de la nieve se llama neurosis. Ella es completamente inofensiva, es Woody Allen. Puedes reírte de una neurosis, porque los bichos raros son personas divertidas. Pero la nieve vieja no es realmente tan inofensiva. No fluye sangre en la mujer de la nieve, pero la nieve de ayer está aburrida. La vieja nieve entra en psicoterapia. Tal terapia también es una neurosis, es blanca como la nieve nueva.

Terapia de pareja

Perro y gato entran en terapia de pareja. El terapeuta es una hiena. Perro y gato quieren salvar su relación. La terapia falla. ¿Por qué solo? ¿Qué puede ser eso? Ciertamente, en el terapeuta, todos tienen un problema ellos mismos.

Sin humor

Cheplin va al sótano a reír para acompañar a sus cuerpos. Tuvo que matar a mucha gente para obtener dinero. No se puede jugar con el sufrimiento de este mundo y de las mujeres. Cheplin aboga por una prohibición general del humor para toda Alemania, las excepciones son los llamados centros de risa, donde las personas pueden reír a carcajadas después de pagar una tarifa de humor.

Reir

La risa es feliz con sus labios. La risa seria se pone a reír. La risa humoresca no puede levantarse del sofá de la burguesía. La verdadera risa no es divertida, es simplemente feliz. Solo los chistes compulsivos arrancan chistes del árbol del sufrimiento.

totalmente gracioso

Isolda: Detlef, nunca sabes si solo estás bromeando o si hablas en serio.

Detlef: Es muy simple: si soy divertido, lo digo en serio, y si lo digo en serio, es divertido.

Isolda: ¿Cómo puedo diferenciar uno del otro?

Detlef: El primero es el caso en días pares y el último en días impares. ¿O fue al revés? Estoy todo en mal estado.

Isolda: Me estoy volviendo loco con el chico!

Cambio climático

Otto se tira pedos.

Dr. Kackebart-Struller: ¡Otto! ¿Realmente sabes lo que le estás haciendo a la capa de ozono? Con cada pedo que queda, no solo su gilipollas se hace más grande, sino también el agujero de ozono. Con cada pedo, el metano fluye a la atmósfera, que calienta la tierra. No pedo! ¡Tenemos que salvar nuestro medio ambiente!

Otto Struller: Tienes razón, Mausi, tiene toda la razón. Voy al ático ahora, alimentando a las palomas.

en el bosque salvaje

En el bosque salvaje, las raíces de los árboles dejan su suelo y corren por todo el país. La calma no regresa, sino que se va de aventura. Va sobre montañas, va en los valles. A veces ella también salta.

rodar

Rodar o circular es el movimiento de una ronda alrededor de su centro. La rueda está atrapada. El rollo en sí no rueda, permanece inmóvil en relación con su centro. Si el balanceo se moviera de un círculo a un cuadrado, se movería libremente. La bicicleta solo se da cuenta de que el paisaje está pasando, la bicicleta se detiene.

Descansa y haz ejercicio

La tranquilidad disfruta de su identidad. Se puede definir el descanso como la ausencia de movimiento externo compulsivo. Por lo tanto, no hay descanso en la discoteca. Tampoco en la autopista. El movimiento desde el interior con calma es bastante posible. La existencia tiene paz. También existe la calma compulsiva del budismo zen. Tal calma es la muerte cultivada en la tierra, se basa en la represión y la matanza de inquietud. La verdadera calma, sin embargo, vive en libertad.

pícaro

El colibrí vuela a un palacio divertido donde la gente gira. 52 personas sin corona viven en el palacio. Ninguno y todos son reyes y tontos al mismo tiempo. Las personas en el palacio son todas hermafroditas. Podrías hacerlo tú mismo si quisieras. Pero están más interesados en crear mundos de juego: son divertidos. La cola es un juego serio. Están bromeando aquí con Jojos, los reyes. Los reyes echaron sus coronas como tontos en el gran salón debajo de la fuente. Las coronas sirven como nido para los colibríes. El Rey Púrpura escribe serias tonterías. No puedes hablar con un hombre así.

Trabajo

El trabajo suda en la tierra de nadie, lo cual es agotador, porque en lugar de una columna vertebral, el trabajo tiene un cofre de apreciación, decorado con orgullo. Su realización encuentra trabajo en el ataque al corazón. Quienes trabajan pueden olvidar rápidamente sus cuerpos en el sótano. El trabajo anhela la redención, pero ella nunca lo admitiría. El trabajo es ciego, no se da cuenta de que está funcionando, solo lo sabe. Cristo como Redentor ha estado fuera por mucho tiempo. La gente se redime a través del trabajo: en psicoterapia, trabajas en ti mismo.

El verdadero movimiento está adentro. Un caballo se mueve solo, pero un automóvil es impulsado por la potencia de su motor. El movimiento tiende a moverse de manera serpentina, es decir, en olas. Caminar, nadar, volar o conducir son todos movimientos. Hoy en día te desplazas principalmente. También podrías mudarte allí. Pero nadie puede soportarlo en el sitio. Te quedas en el sitio.

Viento

El viento barre la cara de Frigg. El tiempo se acaba. El agua desaparece en el hoyo. Todo se está ejecutando, se está escapando. La orina corre, las lágrimas corren. Nadie está con Frigg, solo el viento. Sus pies están cubiertos por zapatos gruesos. ¿Qué tal si ella se fue descalza? Entonces el viento los llevaría, y Frigg sería libre. Sus zapatos pesados son la carga de su pasado. Un viento llamado Wahuna corre por su cabello. Sleipnir, un caballo de ocho patas, pasa junto a Frigga. Frigga está fascinada, puede llevarla a caballo al dios del viento y puede transportarla libremente, descalza, sin él.

Mejor una pera en tu mano

que un manzano en el techo.

La máquina hace lo más puro. Una máquina no siente nada, por lo que funciona por pura desesperación. Hace todas las manipulaciones que los trabajadores romos hicieron en los viejos tiempos. Manijas sin sentimiento y vida, mecánica, movimiento sin sentido, único propósito. Qué lindo es cuando una máquina hace el estúpido trabajo por nosotros. Pero los creadores de las máquinas una vez plantaron la estupidez ellos mismos. Las máquinas continuarán intimidándonos desde el exterior con su estupidez. La inteligencia artificial se diferencia, pero sigue siendo estúpida. Nosotros mismos somos solo un engranaje de la máquina del gran mundo.

El dueño llama a sus manos las suyas. Los átomos de sus manos no pertenecen al dueño. Los átomos en su mano solo son adecuados para la forma de su ego prestado. Después de la muerte del propietario, los antiguos átomos en su mano son adecuados para otra aparición. El dueño se siente como en casa en su mano, está arraigado en su mano. Esta raíz es su identidad. No es la mano misma.

La manzana loca

En la manzana, la piel y la pulpa viven juntas. ¿Ambos están casados? Mucho más vive en la manzana: lo esférico, lo verde, lo afrutado, lo que cuelga del árbol. La manzana piensa: `` Tengo propiedades, pero no soy mis propiedades. Si me miro a mí mismo, solo encuentro propiedades, pero no ser ". La manzana se enoja con este autoconocimiento:" ¡Broma! ¡No existo! " Cada propiedad de la manzana ahora sigue su propio camino. Lo esférico va hacia el norte, el verde va hacia el sur. El afrutado hacia el oeste y el colgante de la manzana hacia el este. Ya no es una manzana, nunca existió. La manzana se ha divorciado de su identidad falsa. Lo expulsaron de su That-Belongs-To-Me. ¿Dónde está la frescura de la manzana? Ella está sentada en el pub y se puede ejecutar!

Poesía

Poesía significa concentrar el significado en su concentrado. Sin embargo, la poesía del escritor a veces está tan sellada que el lector ya no puede abrir el cuadro de significado. Solo el autor comprende el contenido del poema mientras escribe. E incluso la lata del autor está demasiado apretada a la mañana siguiente.

transparente

Obviamente, lo que es transparente vuela libremente sin tener que esconderse. Los agujeros son principalmente transparentes. Aunque la transparencia puede ser pesada, no es fácil de ver. Lo transparente se vuelve transparente cuando se vuelve torpe.

atrapar

La captura alcanza con éxito a su presa mientras es móvil. Esta es la razón por la cual los peces son particularmente capturados. Son resbaladizas y viven en aguas en movimiento, pero aún pueden ser atrapadas.

Prisión

Los crímenes solo valen la pena si no te atrapan. Un mono llega al zoológico incluso si no ha hecho nada malo. Un zoológico es una prisión adecuada para los animales. Algunos animales salvajes son encarcelados en el circo. Los niños se sientan en prisión por la pedagogía de sus padres. Las esposas se sientan en prisión por dependencia financiera de sus esposos.

alto secreto

El secreto no debe ver los ojos de los demás. Se sienta solo (o con conspiradores) en su búnker y puede hacer lo siguiente allí: se descompone, se pudre, se regocija, da vueltas, enciende, enciende a otros, se ríe de ti, tiene miedo, se protege, se niega o da a luz a un niño. El secreto: no sabemos lo que hace. Eso sigue siendo un secreto.

volar

Volar se desliza por el mar de inmensidad sin pies. En vuelo, arriba y abajo se juegan uno contra el otro. Un pájaro tiene poder sin violar el mundo. Eso es asombroso. Los Toadstools, sin embargo, no pueden volar, sus alas están encantadas. Las alas de los pájaros se extienden hasta la osadía. Están en casa allí. Las alas son los brazos del vuelo, son por la fuerza. Un pájaro puede volar libremente sin chocar con un gato en el aire. Sin embargo, un empleado choca muy rápidamente con su jefe o con la seriedad de la vida.

facil

La luz vuela fácilmente sobre los acertijos, solo pasa barrigas pesadas. Lo ligero tiende a encontrarse en la parte superior. La madera flota sobre el agua porque es más ligera que el agua. El globo de aire caliente flota en el cielo azul. La luz rápidamente se vuelve frívola. Algo estúpido sucede fácilmente.

Copo de nieve

Un copo de nieve cae con cuidado. Es tranquilo El copo proviene de otro mundo. Da estructura a este mundo, de lo contrario todos los campos magnéticos colapsarían. En los polos norte y sur, el campo magnético cae en la nieve. Desde los polos de la Tierra, la nieve organiza cambios secretos en el mundo. Su magnetismo impregna a los habitantes de la tierra y los convierte en ciudadanos pesados.

Protección

La protección es una buena cosa. La protección es lo primero que necesita: protección constitucional, protección de la sala, productos de protección de cultivos, protección de datos y protección del pensamiento. ¿Aún no has recibido una visita de Protección mental? Vendrá, solo espera.

Intestino

Digest mastica y mastica y mastica. La digestión mastica cada vez más fina hasta que la comida esté tan fina que se pueda integrar en su propia carne. Sin embargo, la comida siempre permanece un poco tóxica. La tierra es venenosa. No es nuestro hogar. Los animales pueden digerir mejor que los humanos, viven más cerca de la tierra.

Tierra

Lo que estamos parados se llama tierra. A veces se llama piso. De pie y la tierra son firmes. La tierra también puede significar humus o piedra. La sustancia de la tierra es particularmente llamativa, es densa y pesada. El piso es tranquilo, el piso es estúpido. La tatara madre no tiene cara. ¿Ella tiene calor? Las raíces llegan a la tierra, también entienden la tierra. Las raíces son una con la calma de la tierra.

Abejas

Las abejas viven en el grueso de la materia, interiormente. Una abeja sale afuera donde hace frío. Cae muerto al suelo como un copo de nieve. Las abejas han expresado su interioridad como copos fríos. Mientras el copo de nieve esté congelado, es tiempo de árbol de Navidad. Si el copo se descongela, la soledad está desnuda. Al sorber el néctar, las abejas conectan todas las partes del mundo y dominan la gravedad, mastican la gravedad. El néctar era un libro que aún no había sido leído. Ni siquiera por su autor.

Pesadez

La pesadez suele ser grande en cantidad. En la delantera, sin embargo, la pesadez es pequeña. Pesadez de poderes. Tiene un efecto solo por su masa, no por su color, porque la pesadez es demasiado oscura para ser colorida. La pesadez no entiende lo gracioso. Solo en el azúcar pueden los divertidos y los pesados dormir juntos. ¿La gravedad viene de arriba o de abajo? Cuando el calor se vuelve más fuerte, se convierte en gravedad. ¿Qué pasa con la piedra que no puedes rodar? ¿Es demasiado pesado o demasiado firme? ¡Es demasiado brutal! La pesadez es más suave que la brutal. ¿Es fácil entonces? ¡Así es como es!

Viento

El viento corre desencarnado sobre árboles y casas. La fuerza del viento no es visible, solo se pueden ver sus efectos. El viento sopla el stock. Un diente de león sopla en el viento, las cenizas por igual. El viento es muy fugaz. Pero siempre sopla.

Grietas en el cerebro

La propiedad es única. Es peculiar a su cosa. La cantidad es relativa, siempre se mide a partir de la comparación. La cantidad no tiene dueño. Isolda tiene una gran barriga, pero no posee la grasa. Todo lo superfluo tiene mucho. No importa cuántas grietas haya tenido el cerebro de Einstein. Es la característica del cerebro lo que lo hace único, no la cantidad de grietas. No se pueden comparar manzanas y peras, solo su peso.

Arena

Los fragmentos de las piedras se llaman arena. Los fragmentos de arena son tan pequeños que vuelven a formar una unidad como comunidad de personas aisladas. La arena se siente como un todo. Todo está llorando, pero la arena no puede llorar porque está demasiado seca. Las piedras no tienen sangre ni agua, ni siquiera como arena. Las lágrimas de los tristes gigantes donan agua salada como el mar. Es por eso que la arena se encuentra a menudo como una playa donde hay mar.

Personas

Las personas solo existen en plural. Una persona no puede estar sola. El hombre como animal de rebaño se convierte en "gente". Una multitud se compone de personas. La sangre de la gente es la sangre de su clan. Una persona, por otro lado, tiene su propio torrente sanguíneo. Con los viejos judíos, la sangre de Abraham corre hacia sus difuntos nietos. Las personas y los pueblos arcaicos tienen su identidad en el grupo, no en sí mismos.

Babilonia

Babilonia no era un bebé: era demasiado grande para el más alto. También hay rascacielos en Nueva York. Pero estos tienen que ser destruidos por los terroristas porque quieren arañar a Dios. Bailas alrededor del becerro de oro, sobre el crecimiento económico y el cirujano plástico. ¿Cuándo vendrá finalmente la ira de Dios y arrojará a la gente pecadora a la basura?

partículas más pequeñas

Fred ha obtenido acceso no autorizado al acelerador de partículas grandes cerca de Ginebra por la noche y ahora se arrastra hacia el anillo redondo: ve partículas verdes brillantes volando.

Fred: Hola partículas, ¿puedes hablar también?

Partícula verde: me duele la cabeza, lo cual es malo porque solo soy una cabeza. Desde que los físicos me descubrieron, ya no puedo realmente tejer el mundo. Incluso la política se está saliendo de control.

Una partícula roja pasa volando: saca la lengua, que es aún más roja que la partícula misma.

partícula roja: enciendo el dinero debajo de mi trasero. Por lo general, el dinero es solo información. Mi fuego da valor a la información. Un triángulo vuela, tiene un ojo en la frente.

Triángulo: Soy la partícula más grande que hay. Las partículas realmente pequeñas solo existen en el infierno de la física. Lo pequeño no tiene realidad. Cuanto más se vuelven las cosas, más reales se vuelven. - Fred está asombrado.

El caos es una confusión que los extraterrestres creativos utilizan para salir de la protección mental sin interrupciones. El caos es colorido. El caos elimina la basura del pasado. El caos baila y no sé para qué.

escribir

En la escritura, el lenguaje habla en silencio en el sonido, pero brillante en la conciencia. Los escritores son los escultores de la certeza. La escritura siempre se escribe, incluso mientras se escribe. La escritura es final y dura más que un buen vino. La palabra escribe a través de todos los tiempos.

bailar

Bailar es atrevido. Cualquiera que baila está loco. Bailar también puede ser genial si eres una persona imprudente. Los pensadores no deberían bailar. El baile rompe su claridad mental. Desesperada por falta de comida amorosa, la locura como un tigre se come el orden corrupto del mal: ¡Dulce Miezi hace Fressi-Fressi!

Erwin

Gotas de lágrimas caen del cielo. Se reúnen en la tierra para formar un arroyo que se hincha en un río. Erwin se sienta en una canoa y rema a través de la lágrima. El río fluye cuesta arriba. Los incendios arden en honor a Wotan en la orilla derecha del río. En la margen izquierda hay un árbol con un pájaro de piedra sentado sobre él. Erwin continúa remando cuesta arriba en una canoa. Ahora está nevando. El piragüista ve un muñeco de nieve en la orilla entre las agujas de pino. Los ojos del muñeco de nieve están vivos, son los ojos de un potente oso de peluche. Erwin continúa remando río arriba. Alguien a la izquierda toca el arpa. Dios esta cerca.

Volcan

Una mujer vestida de negro con astillas de colores pelea con la frescura. Vuelan juntos sobre estrellas, bajo estrellas, entre estrellas. La vida del Titanic aparece en su hundimiento. Un bote plegable de papel flota casualmente en el agua, se desplaza con cautela hacia una fuente de agua de pantano: ¡Peng! Ash cae desde arriba. El Eyjafjallajökull finalmente ha estallado.

encajar

Por el contrario, el ajuste se puede encontrar como amor. Como algo relacionado, Fit complementa uno y otro con un servicio similar. Todo encaja en una sola estructura. Cerveza, cigarrillos y ceniceros están en la mesa de la cocina del Sr. Alki. Eso tiene sentido, encaja. La mesa de la cocina del Sr. Alki es una estructura. Hinz y Kunz están juntos en el gran catálogo mundial en Internet. Hinz y Kunz solo están conectados por su mera existencia. Internet no es una estructura, sino una tontería.

Cosa

Una cosa es gris en su ser; No es nada más. Las cosas son impersonales. La máquina mundial sin rostro de las cosas gobierna la tierra: el internet de las cosas. Las cosas se acumulan en la cosa del mundo. Satanás siempre ha tenido al mundo en sus garras. No se habla de los seres vivos porque se mueven. Sin embargo, una cosa joven puede moverse sola. Es una cosa

Medida

Una medida puede ser la correcta, amorosamente horneada por dioses amistosos. Como profesor, una medida enferma establece límites al poder del alumno. El alumno está lleno, su vida está atrasada y la industria puede generar electricidad a partir de la presa.

todo

Todo esto es una adición de muchas cosas al límite de la inquietud. ¿Es todo esto ahora? Todo es al menos una cosa redonda. Como se esperaba, todo debería brillar en su borde, pero allí permanece gris. Entonces el sacerdote industrial dice: "¡El todo es más que la suma de sus partes!" Incluso después de esta oración, todo no brilla, no hay más para ser visto. El todo sigue siendo la simple adición de todo. Solo hay uno más en este libro.

Nada

La nada es el mundo de todas las no cosas. Una taza no es una silla. Un vestido no es una nube. Sin mencionar al perro: un perro no es un gato como un gorrión. Todas las no cosas se unen en el mundo de la nada. Algunos dicen que nada viene después de la muerte. ¿Quieres vivir allí entre todas las no cosas? Estará bastante apretado en el armario de las no cosas.

Disfrute

El disfrute necesita más de lo necesario. Entonces el disfrute está relacionado con la felicidad. Pero si bien la felicidad es un regalo de la vida, el disfrute es arbitrario. El disfrute persiste y se queda. El disfrute es grasiento. El placer es la lujuria que ha comido en exceso. El disfrute no piensa, el disfrute es demasiado lento para eso. Cuando los intestinos digieren más de lo que necesita, es feliz. La satisfacción es un edulcorante, pero el azúcar es la felicidad.

نفسه Psychosaurus يقدم:

أفكر بشاعرية ولم أكن ضحية لعشاق حيوي. تدخل هذه الأطياف الغريبة بشكل غير قانوني من الفضاء في الظلام وتستخدم خرطومهم الطويل لامتصاص خيال الأشخاص النائمين خارج أدمغتهم. أستخدم على مضض الكلمات التي قالها الآخرون بالفعل. أجد أن غير صحي. لهذا السبب غالبًا ما اخترع كلمات جديدة ، مما يخلق مشكلة لم يعد أحد يفهمني. وبالتالي ، يجب علي استخدام الكلمات المستخدمة مرة أخرى ، والتي شكلت العامية الألمانية بشكل غير دقيق فقط. يمكن أن تتحدث اللغة لأنها تحتوي على الصور العامة للوجود. الشيء الرئيسي في اللغة هو إعطاء صور للعالم منزل. إنه لأمر مأساوي عندما يتبع الشخص كلمات اللغة ثم يعتقد أن هذا هو التفكير. التفكير الحقيقي يشكل اللغة بنشاط. اللغة هي أنا من علماء النفس ، هي مركزها. العالم ينبض حقًا باللغة ، لأن التحدث يعني: خلق العالم. في البداية كانت الكلمة!

خائفة

أرنب خائف في طريقه ليصبح أرنب عيد الفصح. في الطريق أراد زيارة عمه ، لكنه في الفلفل مرة أخرى. الأرنب الخائف ليس ضفدعًا ، فهو يواجه القرد ، حتى لو كان القرد يضحك عليه. القمل يمر فوق كبد البراغيث. يسمع الأرنب هذا السعال البراغيث ، الذي يطلق الآن المدافع على العصافير. يتغلب الأرنب الخائف على نذله الداخلي ثم يحول البراغيث إلى حلزون. على اليسار يرى حمارًا مريحًا جدًا. الحمار يجلس على الجليد في منتصف الصيف. هذا لا يعمل على جلد البقر ، ويضحك الدجاج على الحمار. على الجانب الأيمن ، يحصل الفأر الرمادي على العث لأن الضرب صفعهم. البعوض في الهواء غير ضار في حد ذاته إذا لم يصبح فيلة ويتصرف مثلهم في متجر الصين. يدير السيد مثل الأرنب ويخرج كلبه المسقى حتى لا يصاب بالجنون في المقلاة. ربما يكون Specht لدى السيد والكلب طائرًا ، ولكن لا يصبح الديك بعدهما ، لأن هذا في السلة مع دجاجه. في طريقه يجد الأرنب الخائف أسنان قرد لم تعد تؤذي ذبابة. الآن وقد فعل الفزع ذلك ، وصل إلى أرنب عيد الفصح.

محادثة

يقول الخلد Psychosaurus ، ما هو هذا الكتاب؟

Psychosaurus: في هذا الكتاب ، تتحدث اللغة نفسها ، وهناك لغة

يتحدث عن كل شيء ، لذلك يحتوي هذا الكتاب على كل موضوع.

بط: سؤال شخصي: ما الفرق بين ذلك

سيكوسورس وكارستن؟

سيكوسورس: لا أريد الحديث عنه

الموضوع يشدد علي.

بطة: أنها عازمة يا رجل!

الخلد: من الواضح أن هذا الكتاب واحد

الترجمة الآلية؟

Psychosaurus: هكذا هي. هذا يزيد من الغريب لا يمكن قياسه.

تقول اللغة أكثر من ألف كلمة.

الضحكة: إذا كنت أرغب في الكتابة إلى كارستن ، فإن لديه واحدة أيضًا

عبر الإنترنت أو شيء من هذا؟

Psychosaurus: في الوقت الحالي لديه عنوان البريد الإلكتروني

carsten-stemm@web.de ولديه أيضًا موقعه على الإنترنت.

بالذئب: Sunt reprimat de această carte!

الضحكة: لا أفهم كلمة ولا حتى محطة القطار.

ربيع: ليس عليك أن تفهم كل شيء. في بعض الأحيان يكون الأمر كافيًا للسماح للكلمات
بنقلك إلى غير عقلاني.

ديتليف دوويد مزدوج

Detlef التفكير بشكل صحيح مع نصفي الدماغ. يفكر Detlef Doppeldoid لا يستطيع أسرع من الضوء ، مما يؤدي إلى انتفاخات الزمكان في لغته. ثم يستبدل باليمين باليسار ، بالداخل ، بالخسارة بالشبكة. لا يعرف ما إذا كانت تدخل أو تخرج من الغرفة. إنه أمر سيئ في ذلك اليوم اعتقد أن الناس هم أناس. لا يتذكر ديتليف: Detlef Doppeldoid بشأن أليس "نفس" و "نفس" :Detlef أيضًا الفرق بين ألبرت أينشتاين وكونراد أديناور. عجائب أيضًا أخطاء إملائية. إذا كان Doppeldoid نفس الشيء؟ في بعض الأحيان يرتكب السيد مرتبكًا تمامًا ، يتذكر ديتليف المستقبل.

يقول ديتليف:

" كلما لم أعد أعرف من أنا ، أنظر إلى بطاقة هويتي: لدي أيضًا رقم هاتفي الخاص ؛ رقم ، كل شيء لي وحدي ، فقط لي. فريدة من نوعها ولا لبس فيها. الدولة تحبني. لكن هل هذا ؟ وماذا تثبت البطاقة البلاستيكيةDetlef Doppeldoid يساعدني؟ من يقف وراء اسم الصغيرة؟ من السهل تزوير البطاقات البلاستيكية. يمكنك تزييف كل شيء اليوم. يمكنك " .حتى تزييف الهوية. أصبحت منمقة للغاية

يتحدث الأرنب

يسمى الأرنب الذي يمكنه التحدث الأرنب المتكلم. يأكل الأرنب الناطق أثناء التحدث ويتحدث أثناء القضم. جذور الكلمات ليست معروفة له. انه يستهلك الحب حاليا. الحب يمكنك أن تأكل الحب بدون أكل ، هذه هي حكمة .mampf ، mugg ، هو مجرد كلمة له الأرنب.

هناك بط!

يهتـم عـالم الأحيـاء بريـش البـط ، ويهتـم طبيـب الوجـود بوجـود البـط. مـن يعطـي البط؟ الجواب: "هو". "إنه" ويعطي النتيجة في الوجود. بدلا من ذلك ، يمكن الإجابة على

السؤال على النحو التالي: التطور يعطي البط ، بيض البط يعطي البط ، الجنس بطة يعطي البط ، الله يعطي البط. إنها تمطر. يجب على المرء أن يقول في الواقع: إن السحابة تمطر. هذه "الأمر" ليس متروكًا لله ، لأنه يعني: هناك إله. وهذا بدوره يعني: "إنها" أعظم من الله. استنتاج آخر سيكون: "إن" هو الإله الحقيقي الذي أعطى الله أولاً. هناك بط. لا يقول المرء: يتطلب البط. العطاء أكثر سعادة من أخذ. العطاء ربما أكثر وجودي من غير واضح بحيث لم يعد بإمكانك رؤية ضبابه. ونتيجة لذلك ، لم تعد تفكر في 'it'. أخذ ، مصدر البط. إن "هو" خادع. يتظاهر بأنه المعرفة. إذا لم نعد نعلم أن السحابة تمطر

من يستطيع أن يكون "Elwittitsche!" لا يوجد" :"it" ثم تمطر. النفي يعطي أيضًا كلمة هذا "هو" فقط القادر على إعطاء هؤلاء غير البط؟

Pechmarie و Goldmarie

ذات مرة كان هناك مدرب تحفيزي لديه ابنتان ، كلاهما سميت ماري. كان أحدهم يعمل بجد ، والآخر كسول. ذات يوم أتت المرأة الجادة إلى بئر قالت:

"!لا يوجد ماء للشرب"

اعتقدت المرأة المتعطشة "إنها موجودة فقط لأسباب قانونية". شربت الفتاة من الماء وسقطت بالخطأ في النافورة ، مما تسبب في فقدانها للوعي. في وقت ما استيقظت في منطقة مجهولة تمامًا.

وقفت امرأة مسنة عند نافذة منزل بحاجة إلى التجديد وهزت وسادتها. قالت السيدة هولي ، هذا ما تم استدعاء المستأجرة ، للفتاة: "الممرضات الأكفاء لكبار السن مثلك نادرون اليوم ، هناك الكثير من العمل بالنسبة لي." ولأن المرأة المجتهدة كانت حريصة جدًا على العمل ، فقد قامت بالتدبير المنزلي للسيدة هولي.

بعد فترة ، أصبحت الفتاة بالحنين إلى الوطن وعبرت عن رغبتها في السماح لها بالعودة إلى هذه الرغبة. قادت السيدة العجوز الفتاة إلى بوابة Frau Holle المنزل. منحتها السيدة يجب أن تذهب من خلالها. عندما كانت المرأة تعمل بجد عبر البوابة ، كانت تمطر عليها

من أعلى الملعب الملوث بالديوكسين الذي لم يعد يخرج من جلدها. قالت الفتاة: هراء سخيف! سآخذ انتقامي بمرارة على مصير. أدرس الرياضيات وأقوم بدكتوراه في نظريات التناقض. "

عندما رأت الأم ابنتها ملطخة بالنبرة ، اتصلت بابنها بشمري. لأسباب تتعلق بالتعويض الاجتماعي ، أرسلت الأم الآن ابنتها الكسولة إلى البئر. حدث نفس الشيء تقريبا. جاءت Frau Holles معينة بدلاً من Frau Hölle ابنتها الثانية فقط إلى منزل آخر تعيش فيه Haus.

بعد عشر دقائق من العمل ، تضاءل انضباط عمل الفتاة الكسولة إلى حد كبير. قالت السيدة هيل: 'في سنك كنت كسولًا جدًا أيضًا. ليس لدي حتى شهادة تخرج من المدرسة الثانوية. نحن الآن نركض نحو Château Mouton-Rothschild 1945 ، الذي سرقه زوج ابنتي بنفسه.

لحسن الحظ ، القبو بأكمله ممتلئ به. " بعد شرب نهم لمدة أسبوع ، استحوذ الكسل إلى نفس البوابة التي Frau Hölle أيضًا على الحنين إلى الوطن وأراد تركه في المنزل. قادتها عندما مرت الفتاة الكسولة من البوابة ، كانت تمطر الذهب. Pechmarie مر بها عليها. الآن كانت الفتاة أكثر قيمة ، لأنه لا يمكن إزالة الذهب أيضًا. عندما وصلت إلى بدافع الغضب من ظلم الحياة ، تركت الأم الكنيسة. Goldmarie المنزل ، دعتها والدتها لاحقًا أول أستاذة للمنطق مع ندوب Pechmarie وذهبت إلى الحكم العلماني. أصبحت في Goldmarie الديوكسين على وجهها. كانت حياتها فاشلة تمامًا. ومع ذلك ، عاش سعادة دائمة. > نهاية سعيدة

جبن ضأن

الراعي: أخبرني ، ما نوع الكتاب الذي تحمله تحت ذراعك؟

فولفجانج: أعطتني إحدى خرافك كتاب عيد ميلادي. عنوانها: اصنع جبن الأغنام بنفسك!

الراعي: هل يفترض أن تكون مزحة؟

فولفجانج: لا يجب أن تضحك النكات. أنا لا أمزح أبداً. أياً كان النكات فهو جبان جداً لدرجة أنه ليس جاداً. لم أكن أمزح أبداً. وإذا ضحك أي شخص ، سأصفع مؤخرتي على الفم.

خروف: معذرة إذا تدخلت ، لكنني معدلة وراثيا حتى أتمكن من التحدث. هل هناك ضريبة جديدة على الجبن؟

خروف آخر: أنا أيضًا منتج محسّن وراثيًا للخالق ، وأقول لك: الرجال مثل النساء ، فقط بالعكس.

فولفجانج: اعتقدت دائمًا أنه سيكون مختلفًا!

شيبرد: أشعر بالدوار بسبب هذه المحادثات المعقدة. .. آه ، انظر من قادم! انه يعرج!

فولفجانج: إذن يمكن أن تكون مجرد مقارنة!

الراعي: لماذا؟

فولفجانج: لأنك تقول دائمًا: كل مقارنة تتأخر!

خروف مقطوع: المعنى غامض دائمًا. لذا يعد المتحدث نفسه بسرعة في خطابه. الألماني المزدوج Lapsus Freudianikus ، بشكل مفرط السلس الذاتي التصوير في .التسرب هو

فولفجانج: أي نوع من المتكلمين هذا؟

الراعي:. درس الأغنام. اللغويات النفسية أو شيء من هذا.

(وصل العرج الآن إلى مجموعة المناقشة.)

عرج: أنت بعدي. تجارتي المسروقة

تم تفجير البلوتونيوم من محطات الطاقة النووية الروسية!

الراعي:. لا تفعل أشياء ، أوتو!

الأغنام: هل يمكنك أكل البلوتونيوم؟

الراعي:. لم تدرس كل الأغنام!

Mähhhh! :كل الغنم معا

أوتو: لدي مخرج واحد: الانتحار!

فولفجانج: سـيكون لـدي مخـرج بـديل. أنـا أعـرف سـاحر جيـد في السـيرك. يعـاني مـن حساسية ، لكنه بخير من الناحية التقنية.

أوتو: من هو هذا الساحر؟

فولفجانج: إنه كل ما تعتقده هو ، لأنه لديه الكثير

الكواكب في المنزل السابع ، بما في ذلك بلوتو.

أوتو: لا أؤمن بالتنجيم!

فولفجانج: لكن النجوم يؤمنون بك!

أوتو: حسنًا ، أريد تجربتها ، لأنه لم يبق لي ما أخسره. أنا مسحور في أرنب وأكتب اسمي للخلف حتى لا يتعرف علي أحد.

الراعي: شيء عظيم! الآن هذه نهاية سعيدة حقًا!

في حالات الطوارئ ، يأكل التفاح الكمثرى.

القتل

القرد: مساء الخير ، عين غريبة ، لديك عيون مائلة.

عين غريبة: وأنت قرد ، أنت قرد.

القرد: لدي عصا من الديناميت هنا.

من نضعهم في المؤخرة؟

عين غريبة: بالطبع! في TNT لا أقول لا!

أنت قرد رائع ، تستحق جائزة نوبل!

القرد يدفع الميل في مؤخر الديناميت ويضيء الصمامات. بعد ثوان من الانهيار العصبي ،)
(هناك انفجار عنيف: الغبار والحطام وبقايا اللحوم تغطي موقع الانفجار.

القرد: رائع! تحطمت!

لا توجد تهم أو فقرات لنا الحيوانات.

هاها. الآن سنأكل موزة!

كتكوت الصلب

ذات مرة كانت هناك سيارة صرير صغير يقود من خلال طبيعة ممتلئة وخفيفة. تتحرك العربة ، يتم سحبها بواسطة حصان. سيارة لم تعد تقود اليوم. عندما بدأ المرافقة في القيادة بواسطة المحرك ، أصبحت العربة من الفولاذ ، عندما كانت العربة لا تزال تسحب ، ازدهرت الزهور وهرعت المياه إليها. عاش سر الحياة في عجلة الطاحونة ، هنا ركضت العجلة في الماء. كانت السيارة ولادة الفتاة الفولاذية. تمتد السماء ، تمتد السماء ، فهو متحمس. يصطاد كتكوت الصلب في السماء بمدفع دفاع. إنها الحرب العالمية الثانية ، وهي محاولة لا معنى لها من قبل الفولاذ ليصبح حصانًا مرة أخرى. كتكوت الصلب أصبح الآن حصانًا ، لذا فهي ترتدي ذيل حصان. الخيول أنيقة حقًّا ، حيث لم تعد الأناقة معروفة في عصر الفولاذ. البلاستيك هو أيضا الفولاذ. كل ما لا يسحبه الحصان من الفولاذ. تشعر بالرعب من جمال ليس دمية أزياء.

غرف متعددة

الغرفة المتعددة هي غرفة أكبر من الداخل من الخارج. خزانة متعددة ، على سبيل المثال ، تبدو مثل خزانة غرفة نوم عادية. ولكن إذا كان عليك الاختباء في الخزانة إذا لزم الأمر ، فسوف تندهش لتجد أن هناك مجرات كاملة في الخزانة. وهذه ليست هلاوس نتيجة نقص الأكسجين. العالم مليء بالثقوب في الواقع. وهناك المزيد والمزيد.

خطر

175

خطر يهددك. لم يقع الحادث بعد. لكنها يمكن أن تضرب في المستقبل. هذا خطر. الحياة غير آمنة. لا تعرف ما إذا كانت الحياة ستنكسر في اللحظة التالية. الخطر عند الباب ، الخطـر لا يمكــن التنبـؤ بـه ، يمكــن أن يصــبح كابوسّــا. الحيوانـات المفترســة خطيرة ؛ الرأسماليون أيضا. من الخطر وضع كابلات الكهرباء في حوض ملىء بالماء. الزواج محفوف بالمخاطر أيضا. من ناحية أخرى ، يعد التأمين على الحياة بالحماية: إذا فقدت حياة ، فستحصل على حياة جديدة. ولكن حذار من الغش في التأمين: تغش شركات التأمين كثيرا !

اعتقد

التفكير يتجول في أرض المعنى. تصطدم طرق التفكير بغابة المعرفة. من خلال المشي ، يصبح التفكير أكثر صعوبة ويندمج في النهاية مع أشجار فكره وثلوج أحلامه.

أوليمب

يرى فريد إلهًا على الهاتف الخليوي في أوليمبوس:

فريد: مرحبا الله!

منذ متى تستخدم الآلهة الهاتف الخليوي؟

الله: نعم مي ، أنت فقط تعدل. يمكنني أيضًا التواصل عبر زملائي مع زملائي ، لكننا نحن الآلهة نريد أن نجعل الناس مفهومين.

فريد: لذا ، لا أفهم ذلك!

رؤوس البيض

مخابغ الدماغ هي أرانب التراص الهوائية. ويطلق عليهم أيضًا رؤوس البيض. إن الأعصاب ليست مرنة للغاية ، ولكنها طويلة جدًا. قم برمي الجوز العاري على رأسه الأصلع لأنه يحتوي على الكثير من شمع الدماغ. الأعصاب هي قضبان العقل. يمكن للأعصاب أيضًا أن

تكون جذوع الأشجار التي لا يمكنك من خلالها رؤية الغابة لأعدادهم الهائلة. ولكن في الواقع Neurolanten هي عيدان تناول السوشي الفكرية.

تسمى بعض موجات الدماغ الفلاسفة. الفلسفة تفكر بدون شرب ، إنها نور بدون حب. يمكن للمفكر المزاح بشدة في صحراء المعرفة. الصبار لا يضحك. الفلسفة صعبة مثل الجبن القديم. بدأ الفلاسفة على طريق الشفاء بكتابة الشعر.

أنصاف

فريد: أنت تعرف ديتليف ، تمت ترقيتي إلى أنصاف الآلهة.

ديتليف: حقاً؟

فريد: إنه كذلك! يمكنني الآن العثور على إجابة لكل سؤال ، إذا كان ذلك غير دقيق ، ولكن يمكنني معرفة الإجابة.

ديتليف: من روحك؟

فريد: الرئيس الكبير!

Detlef: آها!

فريد: أنا مجرد أنصاف الآلهة. أنا لست خالدة بعد ، لكني أعمل على ذلك.

ديتليف: مم ، افعل ذلك.

فريد: أعلم أخيرًا ، على سبيل المثال ، سبب انثناء الموز.

ديتليف: نعم ، لماذا إذن؟

فريد: إنها تتوق للوحدة ، ويريد الموز العودة إلى الجنة ، وتود أن تكون دائرة ، لكن الخريف يمنعها ، فقط قوتها تمتد إلى المنحنى.

ديتليف: ما يعرفه أنصاف الآلهة!

شبح

مصطلح "الروح" كلمة وحيدة للغاية. يجب أن تشرح الكلمة أشياء كثيرة. المخابرات تقطع الحجارة. يربط العقل. تنير الروح أجزاء العالم مثل الشمس وتعطيها شكلاً. العقل هو صورة الأشياء. العقل يلبس أصغر الجسيمات مع المزيد. يمكن للعقل أن يفكر ، يمكن للذكاء أن يفكر أو يتحد فقط.

السبب والنتيجة

يضرب لاعب البلياردو كرة بعصا ، والتي بدورها تضرب كرة أخرى. هذا التفكير السبب والنتيجة هو المنطق الأصلي للعلم. المنطق يبرر ذلك ، ولا يفسر أي شيء. الإرادة الحرة للاعب البلياردو مخفية تمامًا في هذه النظرة للعالم. الأسباب هي الحيوانات الباهتة ، الثيران تقريبا. الأسباب تقنع من خلال الطاقة ، وليس من خلال المعنى.

المنطق

فريد: أنا أؤمن بالمنطق. الكون كله منظم بشكل منطقي. ومع ذلك ، فإن النساء لسن جزءًا من الكون. يمنحك التفكير المنطقي الوصول إلى كل لغز. عليك فقط بذل الكثير من الجهد في التفكير.

أرنولد هيترمان: المنطق لا يدفعنا إلى المعرفة. مثال: ثلاثة غربان تجلس على السياج. يأتي قاتل الطيور ويطلق النار على أحد الطيور.

أرنولد: كم عدد الطيور التي لا تزال في السياج الآن؟

فريد: هناك غربان على السياج.

أرنولد: خطأ! لا يزال هناك غراب على السياج!

فريد: إنه غير منطقي تمامًا!

أرنولد: هذا منطقي. سقط الطائر بالرصاص ميتا على الأرض. صُدم الغراب الثاني بفعل الانفجار العظيم وطار على الفور. أصيب الغراب الثالث بالرعب من الانفجار ، ولا يزال الطائر الوحيد الذي يجلس.

178

فريد: هذه القضية تبدو لي مبنية للغاية ، لكنها منطقية.

أرنولد: حسنًا ، يمكنك شرح كل شيء ولا شيء بالمنطق.

فريد: بادئ ذي بدء ، بعد ذلك.

أرنولد: نعم ، دائمًا بعد ذلك.

ومع ذلك ، كان الواقع هناك من قبل.

فريد: ماذا لو جلست خمسة غربان فجأة على السياج بعد الطلقة؟

أرنولد: ثم جلست بعض الغربان المتعبة على أمل أن يتم إطلاق النار عليها أيضًا.

فريد: رائع حقًا ، ما هو المنطقي.

أرنولد: يمكنك شرح كل شيء بالمنطق ، حتى غير المنطقي.

فريد: يا رجل ، يجب أن أفكر في الأمر حقًا.

أرنولد: ولكن يرجى البقاء منطقيًا تمامًا!

فريد: آه ... نعم ... حسنا ...

حوار

سقراط: كيف يبدو القرف مرة أخرى هذا الصباح ، أفلاطون!

أفلاطون: اسكت الحمار!

سقراط

رصاصة

الرصاصة مقيدة بشدة في حد ذاتها ، ولديها الرغبة في الولادة إذا أشعلت. لكن لا أحد يشعلهم. تبقى الكرة مملة مثل الطين ولا تعرف بعضها البعض. لماذا تدور

الكرات؟ يتدحرجون في الطريق ، لكنهم لا يغيرون شكلهم. في نهاية المطاف ، يتم تمريرهم من قبل الحركة. رصاصة تبقى رصاصة. الآن أتذكر: الرصاص من الإناث!

في) الكمال)

الكلب نفسه هو فكرة الكلب. هل تبدو فكرة الكلب الآن مثل كلب ألماني أو كلب ذهبي أو كلب رعي أو حتى كلب؟ نحن نعرف كيف تبدو الدائرة في حد ذاتها. هناك دائرة واحدة فقط وهي مستديرة بالكامل. المثلثات تجعل الأمر أكثر صعوبة: ما هي الزاوية التي تمتلكها فكرة المثلث؟ الدائرة هي الفكرة الوحيدة التي يمكن رسمها بالضبط. لا يمكن رسم الكلب نفسه ، فقط كلب محدد. يمكن رسم الدائرة نفسها. هل نعبد الدائرة؟ هل يوجد "في حد ذاته"؟ تظهر الأشياء فقط "بالنسبة لي "؟ - الكمال في الواقع سيكون ناقصِّا جدًا في الحياة. تحتاج الحياة إلى زاوية في دائرة أو حفرة في مربع. الكمال موجود فقط كفكرة ، لأنه في الواقع لا يمكن أن يوجد الكمال. الدائرة لها زوايا في كمال الحياة. الكستناء عبارة عن كرة زاوية. إنها تحمل الكمال الناقص كحياة مثالية. ومع ذلك ، فإن شجرة الكستناء مريضة إلى حد ما. لماذا هذا؟ القنفذ فقط يعرف ذلك!

الدائرة

الدائرة لا تستطيع التنفس. في أي مكان ليس لديه حفرة يمكن من خلالها التنفس. يمكن رؤية الدائرة نفسها على أنها حفرة. هل الدائرة بوابة لعالم آخر؟ لا يمكنني التحقق من ذلك لأن الدائرة لا تسمح لي بالدخول. إنه مغلق للغاية. لا ينبغي التعامل مع مثل هذه الأنواع. الدائرة لا تتحدث معي ، وستظل غامضة دائمًا. من المحتمل أن الدائرة ليس لديها ما تخفيه: إنها ساذجة ومملة وفارغة. - الجولة هي لون الدائرة. هذا اللون نادر للغاية وليس له اسم. أسهل طريقة لتسمية اللون هي "ملونة". يمكن للجولة أن تذهب في مغامرة بدون دائرة وقوس. الحياة نفسها مغامرة ، تفكر المجموعة اليوم في شيء جديد. لكن الجولة قديمة للغاية لدرجة أن تفكيره في الجديد لا يمكن أن ينتج عنه جنودًا. ومع ذلك ، فإن الفلسطينيين لا يتسكعون أبداً. إنه وعرة للغاية لذلك. أرادت المجموعة أن تصبح دائرة وطلبت من وكالة التوظيف إعادة التدريب. الكاتب كان مربع. انتهى بشكل سيئ.

تفكر وتوجه الكمثرى.

الضرب رائع

الضرب هو الفعل الأكثر شمولاً. ضرب رائع حقا. تم تطوير هذا النشاط بالكامل في
العصر الحجري. يمكنك فتح عينيك ، كتاب على حد سواء. انظر في الفجر أو قم بتحطيم
النافذة أو لكمة شخص في وجهه. الموسيقيون يصدرون ضوضاء مع الطبول. الضربة
على قدم روزنهايم المسطحة 2-1. من فاز FC.تضربك. يتفوق الغضب وف الهلالي 1
فاز. أفضل طريقة للضر ب بالحجارة. حجر نبيل يسمى مطرقة. الضر ب خشــن
وخشن. ضربة بلا عقل وذرة. ضرب ضربات ، فواصل ، ضرب يفصل. طفل ضرب يتم
قطع. طفل سيء. طفل آخر من الضرب هو الدفع. هذا الطفل محبوب أكثر لأنه لديه
شمس أكثر في الأمام. الضرب يجعل قبضة اليد ، حتى تحصل أفعاله على بطن.

الأداة

العمل الفني هو ترسيب كل الخبرة الإنسانية المطلقة. هناك خبرة تم تأكيدها بحيث تتعزز
كعمل فني . يوجه كنز العمل جميع الكائنات مثل المجال المغناطيسي مـن
هي ويكيبيديا الحياة الطبيعية. لسوء الحظ هناك أيضًا خروف Werkschatz. الروحاني
أسود في كنز المعرفة: يطلق عليهم اسم التراب المصنع.

لا Orthos. بالنسبة للملك أورثوس ، فإن الحكم يعني ترتيب الأشياء وفقًا لذاتهم الداخلية
ينقل إرادته إلى الناس. لا يرغب الملك في إجبار الأشياء ، ولكنه يستكشف خصوصياتهم
Orthos Reich ويسمح لهم بترتيبها بأنفسهم. يعيش الناس والماعز والكائنات الأخرى في
، وكلهم يقفون ويمشون في مكانهم الصحيح. بعد وفاته ، سوف يتدفق الملك أورثوس في
، مياه نهره المفضل ، والذي سيصب في نهاية المطاف في البحر. من البحر ، سيستمر عمله
لتوجيه الناس.

الجوع والعطش

يريد الجوع أن يأكل شيئًا طوال الوقت. يعتمد الجوع بشكل كامل على هدف رغبته. ولكن
هذا هو بالضبط ما يجعل الجوع لطيفًا جدًا. إنه ممتلئ بالحياة ، حتى أن البعض يقول إنه

حياة في حد ذاتها ، كما أن للجوع أخت: اسمها "" عطش ". ولكن هذا فقط لأنواع مجنون للغاية.

الحاجة هي تجريد الجوع والعطش. الحاجة فقيرة وبحاجة. الحاجة علمانية للغاية وتبدو دائمًا بنفس اللون الرمادي. يمكنك تخزين احتياجاتك في أي درجة حرارة. لا تحتاج أبدًا إلى أن تؤتي ثمارها ، فهي تظل دائمًا هزيلة. إذا كنت بحاجة إلى شيء ، تذهب للتسوق.

من يحتاج الألياف؟ قبل كل شيء ، إذا كانت تتكون فقط من الصابورة. الحشو العبء. يملأون الفراغ ، لكنهم لا يزالون أجوفًا. إنه الجوهر الذي يلمع.

سيكوسورس في النهاية تماما:

قوة الجليد كشخصية رفعت ذراعها. درج من الماء يتدحرج من الوجه البارد. تلمع عيون امرأة الظل مثل شمسين في الليل. ليس لفترة طويلة. انطفأت الأنوار الخاصة بك الآن. تطير امرأة الظل إلى السماء كملاك أسود. يتيم المكان المجهول. حيث لم يكن هناك أي شخص ، لا يوجد أحد الآن. معرفتي بعدم التواجد بجوار المساحة الفارغة. أنا دافئ ، لكن فقط كحرارة ، لأنه ليس لدي جسد آخر. يصرخ يصرخ بلا لسان في غرفة فارغة. لا يوجد سوى فراغ في كل مكان ، حيث يجب أن يكون هناك شيء في الواقع. حيث لا يوجد شيء ، لا يمكنك رؤية أي شيء ، خاصة إذا لم يكن لديك عينان. لكني لا أرى الرعب ولا أعرف لماذا.

هول

الثقب يعني غيابًا دائرّيًا إلى حد ما. ثقوب فارغة. غالبًا ما تكون الحفرة ممرًا يدخل ويخرج. في بعض الأحيان يخرج المنظر من خلال الثقب ويأتي المنظر من خلال الثقب. الثقوب جائعة ، يريدون أن يكونوا محشوين. الرغبة في جميع الكائنات جيدة للرضا. الواقع له ثقوب. هذه شفافية لدرجة أنه لا يمكن لأحد رؤيتها ، ولا حتى فيزيائي بأجهزته العظيمة. يمكن رؤية نقص الملابس في الأشخاص العراة. من ناحية أخرى ، لا إلى أن يكون فارغًا. إذا تم ملء Surface يزال عدم وجود فجوة جائعًا وغير مرئي. يميل هذا الفراغ ، يختفي السطح بسرعة ، ويصبح رقيقًا. يصف الإستي اللون على السطح بحيث يصبح أكثر ثقة بالنفس.

حيوان

الحيوان الكلاسيكي له أربعة أرجل ، إنه "مواء" أو نباح. مصطلح الحيوان هو حالة من نوع للكائنات التي لديها القليل من القواسم المشتركة. لا تحمل الحيوانات أوراق الشجر ولا يمكنها صنع قنابل ذرية. الحيوانات متخلفة. ومع ذلك ، ستفهم الحيوانات يومًا ما أيضًا نظرية عدم اكتمال جودل. - فقط متى؟

يمكن أن تكون الطبيعة خامًا وخشنًا. هناك أيضًا طبيعة الحالمين: هذه الطبيعة هي جنة الناس حتى قبل السقوط. تبدو طبيعة الجرماني تشارلز داروين كما يلي: قتال الأقوياء ضد أقوى. طبيعتنا الثانية هي الثقافة. عالمنا الثالث يسمى اصطناعية. لا أحد يحب العيش هناك.

زهرة الجليد

تتكون قوة أجنبية من السويد من أبرد الجليد. تذهب هذه القوة على الأرض في شكل فتاة زهرة مصنوعة من الثلج ، زهرة جميلة. Eisblume. تشبه الزهور الربيع ، عجوز تدعى لأنه خلال هذا الوقت تتفتح الأزهار الطازجة عادة في دفء الشباب. ومع ذلك ، تتفتح زهرة الثلج لدينا في برد الشتاء القاتل. جميع الأشخاص الآخرين الذين يصنعون أيضًا من الجليد تستثيرهم زهرة الجليد. أجنيس هو أيضا خارج البرد ، من الجليد المحترق. يرى هي دائما الأكثر سخونة. السيد frigids. زهرة الجليد ويشعر بسعادة غامرة Agnis هو مذهل كبائع الآيس كريم. تحتوي كرات الآيس كريم الخاصة به على Sumpfstein متفجرات ، والتي تشتعل عندما يكون طويلاً فوق جميع الجبال. ترى إيزبلوم السيد أصيبت بصدمة ، وتدور كرة الروليت في رأسها. لا أحد يعرف أن الكرة Sumpfstein: ستتوقف في حجرة السبعة عشر . في أجنيس سيكون الثلاثة. كرات الثلج أو كرات الروليت ، الكرات هي نفسها. الرصاص هو بنك مصير سيء. والآن نقتحم هذا البنك في Herr Sumpfstein و Agnis و Eisblume: ونحرر الجنون. الجميع بالجنون صندوق واحد. أنت تتنفس الجنون: آه ، هذا جيد. أخيرا هم أحرار!

الدم

183

يتدفق الدم إلى الداخل كحرارة سميكة وقوية. دم الإنسان شخصي للغاية طالما أنه لا يزال يدور في عروقه. دوائر الدم ، لذا فهي مستديرة. قوى الدم في دائرته. الدم الخارجي في حقنة الطبيب البارد والقلب مات بالفعل. كم هو فظيع! فقط تنزف الزواحف برد. ما لم تشرق الشمس على الفراء الأخضر للزواحف. يعرف كل مصاص دماء: عندما يشرق القمر ، يكون الدم أسود. لا ترى أي شيء خلال النهار.

حريق

رقصات النار مع اللهب العنيف. يحرق الحرق البري متانة الوقود. تتسرب المسامير الحرارية إلى الغرفة ، وتلدغ أسنان الحمى نفسها ، وتعطي قوة العاصفة الحمراء محيطها لهالة من الدفء. تموت جمر النار إلى رماد. النار مثيرة للإعجاب ، لكنها تقترض مادتها من الوقود. كان يؤكل طعامه أسرع من المطبوخ وأسرع بكثير. ينام دفء النار رقيقًا في مساحة الخلود. عندما تصبح الحرارة مجنونة ، تصبح حرارة.

عام

يظهر الجنرال الوجه بقدر الضرورة. تُظهر الميزات الخاصة حواف أكثر وضوحًا. الجنرال هو نفسه في كل مكان ، غالبًا ما يتم التعبير عنه من خلال نفسه. في المناظر الطبيعية لكل شيء ، يمكن العثور على العام في كل مكان. عم العم الرمادي يسمى المتوسط. يجب على الجنرال أن يتكيف مع الخاص مرارا وتكرارا ، مما يخلق الإجهاد. يمنح الجنرال الأمان عندما تذهب في إجازة غير عادية.

ظل واقف

يجب أن يتوقف الظل الدائم دائمًا ، على الرغم من أنه يمكن أن يذهب إلى أي مكان يريده. إذا أراد الظل القائم أن يتحرك ، فإن البيئة تتحرك خلفه بدلاً من تجاوزه ، يتوقف هو نفسه. يمكن للظل القائم أن يتحرك ولا يزال عليه البقاء في نفس المكان إلى الأبد. الظل القائم ليس له شركة. بالطبع هناك ظلال واقفة أخرى ، لكنها في مكان آخر.

ماس كهربائي

يـؤدي المسـار إلى الهـدف طالمـا لا يسـير عليـه الباطني. تقصر الـدائرة القصيرة مـن مسـار الحياة. يتبع بسرعة مسار غير موجود. ونتيجة لذلك ، يفتقر إلى الخبرة. نجاحه حار وفارغ وبدون لحم ، لكن الدائرة القصيرة لها تأثير كاريزمي. أقصر طريق دائمًا ما يكون عبارة عن دائرة كهربائية قصيرة ، وهدفه هو ألا يكون هناك شيء. تعمل الدائرة القصيرة بدون نمو ، كتابّا: "لا توجد طريقة ، فقط Joachim Ernst Berendt وتذهب بدون مسار. كتب اذهب: كن في الطبيعة". في الطريق إلى عرض كتابه ، دهسته سيارة.

يذهب

تخشى أن يسقط المشي. لكن المشي رائع: فهو دائمًا في حالة توازن. التحركات الدائمة في الممر. ومع ذلك ، فإن الكذب لا يعمل أبداً.

الجنة

لا توجد مشاكل في جبال الذروة وهي سعيدة لأنها كبيرة وكبيرة. السماء سعيدة أيضًا عندما تستقبل زوارًا من الجبال. السماء الكبيرة تحتاج أيضًا إلى العيش المشترك.

السبب

السبب أدناه. إنها الأساس والأرضية والقاعدة والتبرير. إذا نظرت إلى الجزء السفلي ، فإنها تصبح هاوية. لا يمكنك اكتشاف الجاذبية هناك. القاع والهاوية تهدئ الأعصاب بشكل كبير. أفضـل وظيفـة للبشر هـي الوصـول إلى الجـزء السفلي من الأشـياء. تفضـل الأرانب المخيفة فقط القيام بشيء مفيد ، لأن العالم يهلك بطريقة مفيدة.

العالم السفلي

العالم السفلي هو تحت العالم. لم تعد جزءًا من العالم تقريبًا ، فأنت لا تعرفه ، ولهذا السبب تشعر بعدم الارتياح. الموتى تحت الأرض ، وهناك أيضا مصدر الخصوبة. وإلا كيف يجب أن تنمو جميع النباتات؟

سحابة

الغيمة خروف في السماء. الغيوم دائما حزينة غالبًا ما يضطرون إلى البكاء. لكنهم يحمون أيضًا الماشية من الشمس العدوانية. سحابة تمتص الخير والشر. يمكنك أن ترى من أشكالهم ما ضربت الساعة. الحركة والرقص المائي معًا في السحابة.

التراب

لا يجب أن تضع الأوساخ في السلطة. وإلا يهدد المرض! الأوساخ هي المعادل المادي للخطيئة. يمكن اعتبار الجرح ملوثًا ، لأن الجرح غالبًا ما يشكل قشرة سيئة على الحافة تشبه الأوساخ. يشير التلوث أو البقع بدورها إلى الشعور بالذنب. شخص ما ملطخ. هل تأذينا لأننا كنا ناقصين للغاية؟ أم أننا ناقصون لأننا أصيبنا؟ أم أننا مذنبون بانتهاك شيء ما ، قانون أم شخص؟ لكننا لا نؤذي! نحن مثاليون وأبرياء! كل من يدعي شيء من هذا القبيل يؤذي ، لذلك مذنب.

الجنس في السجن

تشكل جدران السجن قلبًا. جدرانه الخارجية سوداء من الخارج وأحمر من الداخل. لم يعد السجين راسبوتين أصغرهم ، ولكنه لم يكن الأكبر ، لأنه بعد كل شيء لا يزال يعاني من حب الشباب. تم سجن جرمانيا أيضًا: راسبوتين وجرمانيا يذهبان إلى الفراش معًا. يخشى ريما كان عليها فقط Rasputin. راسبوتين من إصابة جرمانيا بمرض الزهري. جرمانيا يترك لفترة قصيرة ، لكنها لن تذهب بعيدًا جدًا لأننا في سجن القلب. السجن Pippi أن تفعل هو مبنى لا يمكنك الهروب منه. راسبوتين يقف أمام المرآة ويعبر عن البثور. يطرح القيح على البراءة الفضية: icky، ey.

الجرذ والقنبلة الذرية

الفئران الفئران التي أصبحت مصابة بجنون العظمة. إنها تتسامح بشكل أفضل مع النشاط الإشعاعي من جميع الكائنات الحية. بالتأكيد سيصبحون في يوم من الأيام ملوك الأرض. تقتل الفئران بعضها البعض ، فهي تشبه إلى حد كبير البشر. فأجر نفسك! ومع ذلك ، فإن الفئران أذكى من البشر ، لأنها تتعلم بسرعة كبيرة عدم تناول الطعام السام إذا لاحظوا أن أقرانهم يقتلونه. هذا هو السبب في أن سم الفئران ليس حلاً دائمًا لإبادة هذه المخلوقات الجحيم. في العصور الوسطى ، تم استخدام الفئران لتعذيب الناس ؛ اليوم ، يتم تعذيب الفئران في المختبرات العلمية. إنه انتصار للبشرية! من الضحية إلى الجاني! يتم رعاية الفئران اللطيفة ورعايتها في معبد كارني ماتا الهندي. في الغرب ، لا يوجد سوى فئران الصرف الصحي السيئة. في الصين ، يوجد الفأر كعلامة للبروج. لكن الطبيب النفسي الخالي من الجراثيم يقول: "لم نعد نعيش في العصور الوسطى! بعيدا مع ناقلات العدوى السيئة! لماذا لا يفعل السياسيون أي شيء؟ إنهم لا يفعلون أي شيء!"

شبك

لا يمكنك لمس شبك لأنه بعيد جدًا عن الصف الذي يرقص منه ، إذا لم ينكسر شيء ، فهناك أشياء. ينتقل خط من هنا إلى هناك. من الطبيعي أن يجعلك مكتئبًا. العلماء والمهندسون المعماريون يحبون الخطوط. الخط لا يأكل الحياة. يشوش الخط الحياة ويكتسب الطاقة منه ليتمكن من تسخين الغرفة حتى 20 درجة معتدلة.

إمالة

المنحدر هو منحدر ينحدر وفقًا لشعبية المنحدر ، ويتحول إلى زاوية تتوافق مع ميل المنحدر. مثل هذا الميل ليس تعسفيًا ، ولكنه يتوافق مع حب المائل.

جيد

الخير هو شجرة تؤتي ثمارها على مدار السنة. خشبها مصنوع من الدم الصلب. أوراقها يمكن أن تضحك. الملونة جيدة والرمادي سيء. الشيطان يأكل الخير. يمكن أن يتكون

الخير من نفسه. ومع ذلك ، يعتمد الشر على تدمير الخير. لذلك ، لا يمكن أن يسود الشر أبدا.

موجود

يتكون الملح من الصوديوم والكلور. يقف على قدميك ، لكن الوجود يحتاج إلى مادة كأرضية. يحتاج الوجود إلى أجزاء يتكون منها ، ولا يمكن أن يكون بمفرده. الخشن موجود. يقترب مصطلح "المخزون" من المصطلح الجوهري.

الفأر والخفافيش

لدى الفئران أربعة أرجل وتجري في الطريق الذي أمر الله. ومع ذلك ، فقد تجاهلت بعض الفئران وجهتها وتفجرت. وهم يتسكعون طوال اليوم (يتجهون لأسفل) ويحتفلون في الليل (يبثر بون الدماء والأشياء). الفأر مثل الخفاش أعمى. هذا هو عقاب الله لذنوبهم. كحل بديل ، يجب أن ترى الفئران الطائرة الآن بأذنها. إنه صارخ تمامًا.

رقيق

تجلس النساء النحيفات بسرعة على رصيف فقدان الشهية. متهم من الزملاء المترهلين والدهون. إذا كان النحيف يريد زيادة الوزن ، فعليه أن يطلق على نفسه "نحيف". في بعض الأحيان يكون للرقيق تأثير أكثر كثافة من التأثير السميك لأنه يمكن أن يحمل الكثير من الجوهر في بطنه الحلو. لذلك ، غالبًا ما يكون الرقيق أكثر ذكاءً من السميك. لا ينطبق هذا على مثاقيب الألواح الرقيقة ، لأنها تحتوي على لوح سميك أمام رؤوسهم.

انتصار باهظ الثمن

اسمي شميدت وأنا ميت ، عشت حياة خاطئة. في مكان عملي في شركة Satan & Sons ، تحول مديري الجشع إلى ملاحظة بقيمة 100 يورو. شعرت بفرصتي من أجل حياة سعيدة بعد الموت: وضعت بسرعة أوراقي النقدية في محفظتي ورسمت صليبًا على جلدها

الخارجي. تم القبض على مديري. فقط بعد تأكيده أني لن أذهب إلى الجحيم بعد وفاتي ، أزلت الصليب مرة أخرى. بعد ذلك بوقت قصير ، انزلقت بشكل غير سعيد على قشر الموز وسقطت على الرصيف الصلب مع الجزء الخلفي من رأسي . كنت ميتًا على AOK أمام الفور ، كما وعدت ، لم أذهب إلى الجحيم ، لكنهم لم يرغبوا في السماح لي بدخول الجنة أيضًا ، لأني هزمت الشر ولكني لم أقم بعمل جيد. أنا الآن أتنقل ذهابًا وإيابًا بين السماء والجحيم ولا أعرف بعد الآن.

المعاناة

فريد: المعاناة غير ضرورية على الإطلاق. أي أحمق خلق العالم؟

Detlef: الشر. المعاناة تحمي من الأفعال الحمقاء. يمنعك من شرب الكثير من الجعة. الشر يؤدي إلى الخير.

فريد: أليست هذه طريقة أخرى؟ نوع من المحبة؟

البابا: الله معصوم (مثلي) ، سيعرف لماذا خلق العالم.

مفيستو: أنا جزء من تلك القوة التي تريد دائما الشر وتخلق الخير دائما.

بيرت هيلينجر: على مستوى أعلى ، الشر جيد أيضًا.

فريد: أعيش على الأرض. الأرض هي مستوى أدنى ، المستوى الأعلى لا فائدة لي. كل هذا ليس مقنعا للغاية.

ديتليف: عانى إله الشمس أيضا. مات على الصليب كإنسان وقام مرة أخرى في اليوم الثالث.

فريد: هذا تضامن معه. أشعر بتحسن كبير.

الله أكبر

الله أكبر من ... الله أكبر دائمًا مما يتخيله الإنسان. من أجل السلامة ، لا أريد أن أكتب شيئًا سيئًا عن الله ، فأنت لا تعرف أبدًا. ما لم يكن الله هو الشيطان. هل آلهة الشر آلهة

حقيقية؟ أم أن وجودها يتغذى على الأكل الجيد؟ إذا كان هناك إله واحد ، يمكن للمرء أن اللامتناهي. إذا كان L المحايدان والشاملان بالصوت A يدعوه فقط بالله. ويحيط الصوتان هناك العديد من الآلهة ، فعندئذٍ يصبح أكثر ألوانًا ومحبة وأكثر فهمًا للبشر. كل إله من بين آلهة أخرى لديه منطقة مسؤوليته الخاصة. لم يعد الله بحاجة إلى 99 اسمًا لأن هناك 99 آلهة. وربما سيوحد الإله المائة جميع الآلهة مرة أخرى ، لذلك يشتبه المرء. الاستقطاب المتعصب في الخير والشر يذوب في العديد من الآلهة. في بعض الأحيان تسمى الآلهة أيضًا الملائكة أو الملائكة أو الكيانات العليا.

ثوم

الثوم هـو نضـارة قديمـة. يتـم تقسـيم أصـابع قدميـه. انقسـام الشخصـية الحقيقيـة لـه جـذوره. لكـن مـن الخـارج ، يُظهـر البصـل التماثـل. يسـاعد الثـوم ضـد مصاصـي الـدماء والسحرة. يقوي الدرنة الدم ويجعله غير صالح للأكل للطفيليات حتى مصاصي الدماء يفقدون شهيتهم. يقتل الكراث الفصامي أيضًا الطفيليات الفيزيائية مثل الديدان الشريطية أو البكتيريا المتعفنة. يقسم الثوم البشرية مثل دخان السجائر. البعض يحبه: هؤلاء هم الصالحين. ومـع ذلـك ، فـإن الأشـرار (مثـل مصاصـي الـدماء ، والسـحرة ، والنـازيين ، والأطفال ، والرأسماليين ، والناخبين الخضر) يشعرون بالصد من رائحته.

العقد مع الشيطان

يمكنك أن تصبح بسرعة واحدة من الأغنياء والجميلة من خلال إبرام عقد صغير في مكتب يحقق كل الرغبات الدنيوية. في المقابل ، (Teufel) المقاول :Satan & Söhne خدمة ترك المقاول روحه بعد الموت لعلماء تشريح الجحيم لأغراض البحث. العقد صالح من الناحية القانونية من خلال قطرة دم من المقاول.

الطاعون

يتخيل أرنولد الطاعون الذي يخيم على الأرض ويقتل جميع الأشرار. لا يمرض الأخيار على الإطلاق أو ينجو بسهولة من العدوى. أرنولد هو بالطبع أحد الأخيار. كيف يمكنه التأكد من ذلك؟ ماذا لو أن الطاعون يقتل الأخيار فقط؟ هذا سيكون يعني ، ولكن نموذجية

للظلم في هذا العالم. يشعر أرنولد بالخوف ويرغب في التطعيم ضد القدر، على الرغم من أنه يعلم أنه لا يمكن القيام بذلك.

قطع

يقطع الوعي الوجود في الأشياء. القطع أكثر أناقة من اللسع، وهذا هو السبب في أن البعوضة ليس لها لقب نبيل. الأرواح القوية لديها الشجاعة لمواجهتها، والجبناء ليس لديهم شفرة على الإطلاق. لا يجب أن تقطع إصبعك! لذا يا رفاق: فقط كن حذرا! يسمى لون القطع الحدة. يمكن أن يكون الفلفل الحار والقنابل الجنسية حارًا في بعض الأحيان أيضًا.

ضعيف

تمتد الأسلحة. تبدأ الذراعين تتفتح في اليدين. تكرير الأسلحة في اليدين، يتم تعزيز اليدين في الأداة. الفروع هي أذرع الأشجار.

الحد

حد يفصل أحدهما عن الآخر. يبدأ عند الحدود أو ينتهي. تشكل الحدود سفينة مدى الحياة. يحتاج الدم إلى عروق ليعيش. منزل يحد من المعيشة بجدرانه. عندما ينتقل العيش خارج منزله، يغرق في بحر التشرد.

اللوحة لها حافة مستديرة. على النقيض من الإطار، تكمل الحافة نمو مالكها. الإطار هو المجوهرات، إنه إجبار لوقف الربا.

يستخدم مصطلح "العالم" لوصف المناظر الطبيعية لكل شيء. يمكن فهم العالم على أنه عظمة قاتلة. هذا العالم ليس له نهاية. لا يمكن لعيون الإنسان أن تتوقف في الشوارع اللامتناهية. عالم آمن مغلق في حوافه. هناك العالم الآمن يحتضن اللا حدود بأذرع النهايات.

النور والظلام

غوستاف أعمى على كل من الذرة. لا يمكن أن ترى قدميه أي شيء. هذا شيء جيد ، لأنه إذا كنت لا ترى أي شيء ، فلن تصاب بالاكتئاب. لذلك غوستاف سعيد. هناك أناس لديهم تاريخ أعمى. أنت أعمى جدا للقاء. الخفافيش ترى الأسود ، لكنها تسمع بشكل ساطع ، هل الضوء أعمى في الظلام؟ هل يرى الظلام النور؟

القمر

القمر يضحك في الظلام. يمكن رؤيته بالكامل. كقمر ، هو ذكر. وإلا فهي أنثى. أم كان العكس؟ القمر يصرخ عبر السماء بخوف. لا يحب أن يُرى ؛ يسمح فقط للذئاب الضارية ، الخفافيش والغراب ، بالقيام بذلك ، القمر يحكم سراً في عالم الشر ، إنه المحتال مع الخدين المستدير ، إنه حب قديم ، ظلمة مشرقة تسمى القمر. القمر يلمع أكثر عندما ينام الناس المحترمون.

انتظر دقيقة

هناك لحظة واحدة وهي نفسها دائمًا. اللحظة فقط هي لحظة. غالبية "اللحظات" لا معنى لها. لذلك ليس هناك وقت. ومع ذلك فإن الساعة تدق. هذا هو السبب في أن الساعات كاذبة.

الذاكرة

لا يستطيع الناس تذكر على الإطلاق. نرى الماضي منذ لحظتنا الحالية. كل يوم تتذكر ماض مختلف. الطريقة التي كانت بها حقاً ضاعت بشكل لا رجعة فيه.

بقرة أصلية

في البداية كان هناك حليب. تم إنشاء الكون من الحليب ، ولهذا السبب نتحدث عن درب التبانة. Urkuh ، MUU الكبيرة. جاء الحليب من ضرع.

طازج

النضـارة تغني كضـوء في رطوبـة الحيـاة. اللحـوم الطازجـة صـحية أكـثر مـن اللحـوم الفاسدة. عصير الفاكهة طازج أكثر من الدم ، لأن الحيوان يتعفن في جشعه.

السلاحف

السلاحف هي أجنة قديمة. هم من وقت لم يكن فيه وقت على الإطلاق. قضيتهم مختلفة أيضا. لا تتكون من أصغر الجسيمات ، ولكن عصيدة أخف حيث تصلب الصلابة في خط من هنا إلى هناك. الأرض الحقيقية لا تموت أبداً.

الخراب

تهـب الريح سرا مـن خلال أنقـاض القلعـة المتداعيـة. الجـدران الداكنـة خاليـة مـن الأحداث. كانت العواصف النارية أمس ، والندوب اليوم. يمكن للفأر أن يكتب ويحكي للصحيفة قصة الخراب الميت. تطير الطيور فوق شمس المساء الحمراء وتختفي في أي مكان.

عظيم

البدائي دائما يأتي أولا. السبب ، الأصل ، الشوربة البدائية ، أورانوس ، الماشية ما قبل التاريخ ، الجد ، غابة البدائية ، الانفجار الكبير ، وبالطبع الوثائق والأجداد الغريبون. هذا الأخير لم يعرف بعد المصطلح خطير. في فيينا ، يعني الخطورة شيء خطير بشكل خاص.

أخبار مزيفة

الأرض قرص! لو كانت الأرض كرة ، لكان الناس في نيوزيلندا يسقطون عن الأرض. هل يجب على وكالة ناسا أن تلتصق بصورها المزيفة حتى الحمار؟ لقد شموا الكثير من هواء القمر!

البداية

يمكن أن تبدأ البداية فجأة مثل العدو السريع أو تتسلل مثل الضباب في الخريف. تنبت النباتات ويولد الأطفال خالي من الجراثيم في المستشفى. تتطلب البداية نهاية: ولادة طفل ينهي الحمل. البداية لا تعرف نفسها بعد: في النهاية فقط تعرف البداية من كان.

أطفال

يأكل الأطفال شوكولاتة الأطفال. يأكل البالغون شوكولاتة البالغين. كلا المنتجين طعم مثل الشوكولاتة. يمكنك أن ترى أن الأطفال لا شيء خاص. هم أكلة الشوكولاتة مثلي ومثلك. لا يحتاج الأطفال إلى الماء أيضًا ، على الرغم من أنهم يذهبون إلى روضة الأطفال.

أغاريك

كرسي متحرك يحب حريته. يحتاج المطر من فوق. لكن الفطر الأحمر يرفض تلقي نبضات الله. يود غاريق الذباب أن يبقي كل شيء تحت السيطرة. بل هو صاحب سوط. الهيمنة مهمة لها. يسقط المطر على غاريقون ذبابة. يلاحظ الفطر ، أن هناك أشياء أخرى غير على فتح نفسه. ثم يفعل ذلك ، لأنه شجاع. يأتي الخوف agaric الهيمنة ، ولكن لا يجرؤ من القمة إلى الفطر. يا هذا. لم يعد الآن كرسيًا للأطفال ، ولكنه فأر صغير يريد أن يعيش حياة الطبقة المتوسطة في كهفه. لكن هذا لا يعمل. الفأر يدرس الفلسفة ويجدد العالم ويشتهر.

البرق

ضرب مارتن لوثر وبولس البرق. وبسرعة البرق ، أصبحوا مستنيرين. هل البرق يحسن لنا؟ أم أن الفلاش مجرد دائرة قصيرة تولد النفاق؟ عليك أن تجرب ذلك خلال العاصفة الرعدية التالية.

كينيدي في بيليفيلد JF

تقول نظرية المؤامرة المزعومة أن مدينة بيليفيلد غير موجودة حتى. من وقت معين ، لم يعد من الممكن للظلال تغطية عدم وجود بيليفيلد. هذا هو السبب في أنهم كانوا حريصين على تقديم المؤامرة على أنها مجرد نظرية أو نكتة حتى لا يفهم أحد أن مزيفة بيليفيلد كانت الحقيقة العارية. لحسن الحظ ، هناك بيل. في 24 يوليو 1963 ، زار بيل كلينتون الرئيس الأمريكي جون كينيدي في البيت الأبيض وصافح يده. صاحت كلينتون ، "سأكون رئيسًا!" من خلال هذا العمل السحري ، سرق كلينتون مصيره وهويته من الرئيس كينيدي في ذلك الوقت. النتيجة: كان على كينيدي أن يموت. أو بالأحرى نظيره. تم تجميد كينيدي الحقيقي. عندما هدد الوجود المزيف لبيليفيلد بالظهور ، تم إذابة كينيدي مرة أخرى. بعد الجراحة التجميلية والتدريب المكثف باللغة الألمانية ، أصبح كينيدي اليوم تحت الاسم المستعار Pit Clausen عمدة مدينة الظل في بيليفيلد.

اللحى

مرحبًا ، يمكنني رؤيتك :Sindbart!

Windbart: Madness! أنا أيضًا مدهش عندما تفكر في أننا على حد سواء غير موجود.

Sindbart: عندما يلتقي شخصان لا وجود لهما ، يصبحان واقعيين فيما يتعلق ببعضهما البعض ، ولأنهما يلتقيان على نفس المستوى ، وهما مستوى عدم الوجود.

Windbart: نادرًا ما تقابل أي شخص مثلك. نادرًا ما تصبح حقيقيًّا. يجب أن ننتهز الفرصة لإجراء مناقشة تفصيلية حول الخداع والحقيقة.

سندبارت: رائع ، أنا هناك.

البحر

يمكن للبحر أن يسمح لنفسه بالعظمة لأنه يحتفظ بالأسرار. يتكون البحر من دموع الآلهة (تحتوي الدموع على الملح). البحر غذاء للأرض. لقد جف عطش الصحراء منذ فترة طويلة ، ولم تعد الصحراء بحاجة للعيش.

مجتمع المعلومات

أرنولد هيترمان Otto لا يرى التلفزيون ولا يقرأ صحيفة. فقط العناوين. بالنسبة لـ ما هو مهم هو كل شيء آخر غير مهم. أرنولد مهتم بالصورة الأكبر ، وليس في Normal ، الفراشات. بالإضافة إلى ذلك ، لا تعرف أبدًا ما إذا كانت المعلومات صحيحة. إذا كان Heitermann العنوان يجب أن يقول: "غدا سينتهي العالم!" ، فمن المؤكد أن السيد سيقرأ المعلومات بأكملها. مثل يوم القيامة هذا يمكن أن يؤثر عليك حقًا ، لأسباب شخصية فقط.

الماء

يحب الماء أن يتحرك. إذا سمحت الطبيعة بذلك ، فإنها تتدفق. المياه عذبة وتغني في حد ذاتها. يتألق الضوء مع حركات موجاته. الماء في كل مكان توجد فيه حياة. الماء غير مستقر طالما أنه لا يزال في القاع. الماء رطب ، ويظل عُري الماء لا يمكن المساس به.

الضفادع

لا يجب أن تكون ضفدعًا ، لا ضفدع الخوف. أي شخص بني بالقرب من الماء مثل الضفدع يعيش في الروح. الروح والبحيرة هما نفس الماء والسمك والضفدع يعرفون ذلك. لا يمكنك أن تشعر بالخوف حقًا في الماء ، فقط الحيوانات الجافة يمكنها أن تسأل الأرنب الخائف! لا ضفدع الخوف! الضفادع لا تخرج أبدًا من سن البلوغ. الضفدع هو سمكة لم تصل إلى حيوان الأرض: فشل في التطور. لم تعد سمكة ، لكنها لم تكن كافية للقردة أيضًا. الضفادع لا تزال خضراء خلف الأذنين ، وليس فقط هناك. غالبًا ما تحصل الضفادع على البثور ، ولكن بعد ذلك يطلق عليها الضفادع.

خنزير بري

الخنازير البرية تقفز من سطح منزل في مدينة روما الضبابية. ضربت الخنازير البرية ظهورهم على الرصيف أدناه. لم يكسر الخنزير البري أي شيء ، فهو ينهمش بشكل فضفاض ويعيش. مثل هذا الخنزير البري قوي حقًا. دمك لا يذبل. في السكتات الدماغية القوية ، ينبض عصير النار الخاص بهم إلى الأبد عبر مسار سباق عروقهم.

المشاعر

المشاعر ليس لها لون. إنهم متشردون غير مخلصين ، وعقدهم الوحيد هو عدم الثبات. هل ستؤجر قلبك للمشاعر؟ المشاعر رائعة للكمية والكتلة ، فهي تصبح أقوى وأضعف ، وتعود غير ملهمة مثل الخيول الموجودة في دائري.

الموت

عرض العالم يغرق في العمق. كل شيء يذهب للنوم والقمر في السماء. يتدفق ضوءها الفضي إلى الموت. تريد يد واحدة الإمساك بالقمر وتقوم بذلك أيضًا: لقد سحقت القمر. الدم الفضي ، الأسود على حد سواء ، ينساب من كرة كانت في السابق قمرًا. يرتجف العالم.

اقتل

الموت ينكر الحياة ويمكّنها على قدم المساواة. ما الذي يجب أن يعيش عليه النسر؟ ماذا يجب أن يتخبط في الظهر؟ يمكنه أن يعيش فقط بقتل الحيوانات الأخرى. مثل الرجل! النباتيون هم أهل الخير. ولكن يجب عليهم أيضًا اتباع نداء الطبيعة. بعد كل شيء ، النباتات هي أيضا كائنات حية. يعاني النباتيين من نقص فيتامين. إن براءتهم تجعلهم شاحبين في الوجه ، وهم مصاصون حيويون. يشرب النباتيون دم الأخلاق. أكبر حيوان مفترس هو البشر.

مشاهد التلفزيون الميت

التلفزيـون يعمـل وهنـاك هيكـل عظمـي أمامـه. لـم تعـد عظـام جمجمتـه الفارغـة على علـم بالبرنامـج. شـخص مـا يغلـق التليفزيـون: يـدرك رجـل العظـام الآن أنـه يفتقـد شـيئًا ويغضب. فقط في الانسحاب يدرك الموت أنه ميت.

معنى الحياة

الغرض من الحياة هو إطعام الاقتصادي الزراعي الكبير. على أية حال ، هـذه وجهة نظر د. الدماغ الخفيف. يؤمن بما يلي: من سماء بعيدة ، يزرع الاقتصادي الزراعي العظيم بذور روحنا في تربة الإدراك. مـن خلال تجربـة الحيـاة ، تنمـو جرثومـة الـروح إلى أذن منتجـة للـروح. قـام الاقتصـادي الزراعـي الكـبير بحصـد هـذه الأذن واسـتهلكها بعـد وفاتنا. Brainlight د. هو الأخ التوأم للدكتور الدماغ الخفيف. كل صباح د Brainlight ينمو بعد موسلي الحبوب الكاملة عندما يفكر في نظرية شقيقه الخام.

الشمس

الشمس هي قلب العالم ، يوجد فيها مساحة أكبر من الفضاء الخارجي. لديها معدة كبيرة ولامعة. تلد الشمس العالم. تأكل الشمس العالم. كلاهما بالتساوي. الشمس هي كل شيء. إنه أبيض مع كبار السن ، إنه أصفر مع الشباب. الشمس ليس لها تجاعيد على الوجه.

داء الكلب

مصاص دماء ينظر في المرآة: رجل ذو شعر أسود ونظارات ينظر من الفضة ، له وجه شاحب. تعتقد مصاص الدماء أنها تبدو كشخص طبيعي في المرآة. يتعرف أونددى على نفسـه فقط في المرآة ، إذا نظر مباشرة إلى يـديه وجسـمه ، فلن يـرى أحـدًا. هـذا ليـس طبيعيا ، ولا حتى بالنسبة لمصاصي الدماء. بالتأكيد لديه داء الكلب.

النباتات

النباتات حيوانات خضراء لا يمكنها المشي. أوراقها حجارة من الماء. ضوء الشمس يحولهم إلى اللون الأخضر بالكامل. الحجر والماء والشمس يعطي الحياة فجأة. يتكون النبات بشكل رئيسي من النمو ، ويتمتع بنموه. النمو ليس لديه جينات ، بل يتعرف عليها في كل لحظة. لا تنمو الخطة ، حتى لو نفذتها. من ناحية أخرى ، تنمو النباتات بشكل عشوائي مع الحياة.

صعب

لقد أصابت بعض الجماجم السميكة رؤوسها بالفعل بصلابة. توفر الصلابة مقاومة ومتانة. الهيكل العظمي صعب. عادة ما يظل الصعب صعبًا. ومع ذلك ، فإن القضيب يكون صعبًا في بعض الأحيان. - لماذا فقط؟ - حافة الصلابة خط فاصل في الغرفة. لا يجب تجاهل الحواف ، يمكنك ضرب رأسك عليها. عندما يصطدم جداران ، يسمى التصادم حافة. وبالتالي الحافة هي نتيجة كاروم. لذلك فهو ليس لأصحاب القلوب الضعيفة. الأحجار صعبة أيضًا. الحجر شيء ء ، ليس له وجه ، لأن الحجر يبدو مثل الأحجار الأخرى. في كل شيء ، كل الأشياء هي نفسها. خزانة أو طاولة أو فرشاة أسنان كلها أشياء. الحجارة التي تكمن في كل مكان تسمى الحقيقة. يمكن استخدام الحجر لطرق جماجم الآخرين. كانت مهمة في العصر الحجري. اليوم يمكن لبعض الأحجار أن تتكلم ، هذه الأحجار تسمى "الهواتف المحمولة". إذا فكرت في الأمر بشكل صحيح: هناك أيضًا أحجار جميلة ، وهي الأحجار الكريمة. جمعها التنين.

اجمع

المجموعة كثيفة وأحيانًا ضيقة. يوفر المجتمع الأمن كوجود دائم. أو أنه عبء. جمعها أصعب من جمعها. إذا كان الجمع أكثر صعوبة مما يتم جمعه ، يتحدث المرء عن الصيد"""".

قمامة

لا لزوم لها في الزراعة لزوم لها. لم يكن لزومًا معرفة الفائض أثناء نموه. في حين أن الفائض يمكن أن يكون غنيًا ، فإنه يتبرع أحيانًا ، لذا فإن الفائض ليس عديم الفائدة فحسب ، بل يعوق أيضًا المادة الحية في تقدمه. الزائد هو مجرد قمامة.

ماكي

هوغـو لـديه مشكلة. غريبـه هـو أن الغريب يزعجـه على شاشـته. هـذا يقـود هوجـو للجنون. كان لدى هوغو عيب في وجهه لعقود. واقفا أمام المرآة ، نظر إلى غرابته حتى قـام طبيب الأمـراض الجلديـة الخـاص بـه بإزالـة المقبض. هوغـو لـديه مراوغـات مـع المراوغـات. ولكن فقط للمراوغـات الفرديـة. إذا كان كل شيء يحتوي على غريب ، مثل مشكلة حقًا Hugo نافذة مخدوشة تمامًا ، فإن هوجو لا يمانع. لدى.

الدوار

الفكر الفارغ يغذي امرأة الثلج الذابلة. تسمى امرأة الثلج الرمادية العصاب. إنها غير ضارة تمامًا ، إنها وودي ألن. يمكنك الضحك حول العصاب ، لأن غريب الأطوار هم أشخاص مرحون. لكن الثلج القديم ليس في الحقيقة غير ضار. لا يتدفق الدم في امرأة الثلج ، لكن ثلج الأمس مللت فيه. يذهب الثلج القديم إلى العلاج النفسي. مثل هذا العلاج هو أيضًا عصاب ، إنه أبيض مثل الثلج الجديد.

العلاج الثنائي

الكلب والقط يدخلان في علاج الزوجين. المعالج ضبع. الكلب والقط يريدان حفظ علاقتهما. فشل العلاج. لماذا فقط؟ ماذا يمكن أن يكون؟ بالتأكيد على المعالج ، كلهم لديهم مشكلة بأنفسهم.

لا روح الدعابة

يذهب شيبلين إلى الطابق السفلي للضحك للحفاظ على رفقة جسده. كان عليه أن يقتل الكثير من الناس للحصول على المال. إن معاناة هذا العالم والمرأة لا يجب أن تخدع. يدعو شابلن إلى فرض حظر عام على الفكاهة في جميع أنحاء ألمانيا ، باستثناء ما يسمى مراكز الضحك ، حيث يمكن للناس أن يضحكوا بصوت عال بعد دفع رسوم الفكاهة.

اضحك

الضحك سـعيد بشـفتيه. الضحك الشـديد يحصـل على نوبة ضـحك. لا يمكن للضحك الهزلي أن يرتفـع مـن كنبـة البرجوازيـة. الضـحك الحقيقي ليس مضحكا ، إنه سـعيد فقط. فقط النكات القهرية تمزق النكات من شجرة المعاناة.

مضحك تماما

Isolde: Detlef ، أنت لا تعرف أبدًا ما إذا كنت تمزح فقط أو إذا كنت جادًا.

Detlef: الأمر بسيط جدًا: إذا كنت مرحة ، فأنا جاد ، وإذا كنت جادًا ، فهذا أمر ممتع.

Isolde: كيف يمكنني تمييز أحدهما عن الآخر؟

ديتليف: الأول هو الحالة في الأيام الزوجية والأخيرة في الأيام الفردية. أم كان العكس؟ لقد أفسدت كل شيء.

إيزولدي: أنا مجنون مع الرجل!

تغير المناخ

فرتو أوتو.

د. Kackebart-Struller: Otto! مع كل هل تعرف بالفعل ما تفعله لطبقة الأوزون؟ ضرط يسار ليس فقط الأحمق الخاص بك يكبر ، ولكن أيضا ثقب الأوزون. مع كل ضرط ، يتدفق الميثان في الغلاف الجوي ، الذي يسخن الأرض. لاضرطة! علينا أن ننقذ بيئتنا!

أوتو سترولر: أنت محق ، ماوسي ، محق تمامًا. انا ذاهب الى العلية الآن ، وإطعام الحمام.

في الغابة البرية

في الغابة البرية ، تترك جذور الأشجار تربتها وتجري في جميع أنحاء البلاد. الهدوء لا يعود ، لكنه يذهب في مغامرة. يمر فوق الجبال ، يذهب في الوديان. في بعض الأحيان تقفز أيضًا.

لفة

التدحرج أو الدوران هو حركة جولة حول مركزها. تم الإمساك بالعجلة. لا تتدحرج اللفة نفسها ، تظل غير متحركة فيما يتعلق بمركزها. إذا تحركت المتداول من دائرة إلى مربع ، فستتحرك بحرية. تلاحظ الدراجة فقط أن المناظر الطبيعية تتحرك بعدها ، وتتوقف الدراجة نفسها.

الراحة وممارسة الرياضة

يتمتع الهدوء بهويته. يمكن للمرء أن يعرف الراحة على أنها غياب الحركة الخارجية القهرية. لذلك ليس هناك راحة في الديسكو. ليس على الطريق السريع. ايضا الحركة من الداخل بهدوء ممكنة جدا. الوجود له سلام. هناك أيضًا الهدوء القهري لبوذية زن. هذا الهدوء يزرع الموت على الأرض ، ويقوم على قمع التململ وقتله. لكن الهدوء الحقيقي يعيش بحرية.

شرير

يطير الطائر الطنان إلى قصر ممتع حيث يدور الناس. يعيش 52 شخصًا بلا تاج في القصر. لا أحد والجميع ملك وأحمق في نفس الوقت. الناس في القصر كلهم خنثيون. يمكنك أن تفعل ذلك بنفسك إذا أردت ذلك. لكنهم أكثر اهتمامًا بإنشاء عوالم Jojos ، اللعبة: إنها ممتعة. التخزين المؤقت هو ألعاب خطيرة. إنهم يمزحون هنا مع الملوك. يلقي الملوك تيجانهم على أنهم حمقى في القاعة الكبرى تحت النافورة. تيجان

بمثابة عش للطيور الطنانة. يكتب الملك الأرجواني هراء خطير. لا يمكنك التحدث إلى رجل مثل هذا

العمل

تعرق العمل في أرضهم ، وهو أمر مرهق ، لأنه بدلاً من العمود الفقري ، فإن العمل لديه صندوق تقدير ، مزين بالفخر. تجد وفاء بك العمل في النوبة القلبية. يمكن لأولئك الذين يعملون بسرعة نسيان أجسادهم في الطابق السفلي. اشتاق للخلاص ، لكنها لن تعترف بذلك أبدًا. العمل أعمى ، ولا يلاحظ أنه يعمل ، فهو يعلم فقط. المسيح كمخلص كان منذ فترة طويلة. يخلص الناس أنفسهم من خلال العمل: في العلاج النفسي ، تعمل على نفسك.

الحركة الحقيقية في الداخل. الحصان يتحرك ، ولكن السيارة مدفوعة بالحصان لمحركها. تميل الحركة إلى التحرك بطريقة أفعوانية ، أي في الأمواج. المشي أو السباحة أو الطيران أو القيادة كلها حركات. في الوقت الحاضر أنت تتجول بشكل رئيسي. يمكنك أيضًا الانتقال إلى هناك. ولكن لا يمكن لأحد أن يقف في الموقع. يمكنك البقاء في الموقع.

الريح

تجتاح الريح وجه فريج. الوقت ينفد. يختفي الماء في الحفرة. كل شيء يسير ، يهرب. يجري البول ، والدموع تجري. لا أحد مع فريج ، الريح فقط. قدميها مغطاة بأحذية سميكة. ماذا لو ذهبت عارية؟ ثم ستحملهم الرياح ، وستكون فريج تمر عبر Wahuna مجانية. حذائها الثقيل هو عبء ماضيها. رياح تسمى شعرها. سليبنير ، حصان ثمانية أرجل ، ينزلق عبر فريجا. فريقا مفتونة ، ويمكن وضعها على حصان إله الريح ويمكن حملها بحرية ، حافية القدمين ، بلا.

أفضل الكمثرى في يدك

203

من شجرة تفاح على السطح.

الجهاز يفعل أنقى. لا تشعر الآلة بأي شيء ، لذا فهي تعمل بدافع اليأس المطلق. إنه يفعل كل التلاعبات التي قام بها العمال الصريحون في الأيام الخوالي. يعالج دون الشعور والحياة ، والميكانيكا ، والحركة بدون معنى ، والغرض الوحيد. كم هو جميل عندما تقوم الآلة بالعمل الغبي لنا. لكن صانعي الآلات زرعوا الغباء بأنفسهم ذات مرة. سوف تستمر الآلات في التنمر علينا من الخارج بغبائها. يتم تمييز الذكاء الاصطناعي ، لكنه لا يزال غبيًا. نحن أنفسنا فقط مجرد ترس من آلة العالم الكبير.

المالك يدعو يديه بنفسه. لا تنتمي ذرات يديه إلى المالك. الذرات في يده مناسبة فقط لشكل نفسه على سبيل الإعارة. بعد وفاة المالك ، تكون الذرات السابقة في يده مناسبة لمظهر آخر. يشعر المالك في المنزل بيده ، وهو متجذر في يده. هذا الجذر هو هويته. إنها ليست اليد نفسها.

التفاحة المجنونة

في التفاح ، يعيش الجلد واللب معًا. هل كلاهما متزوج معًا؟ يعيش الكثير في التفاحة: كروية ، خضراء ، فاكهية ، معلقة على الشجرة. تفكر التفاحة: `` لدي ممتلكات ، لكني لست ممتلكاتي. إذا نظرت إلى نفسي ، فإنني أجد خصائص فقط ، ولكن لا يوجد كائن. "تغضب التفاحة من معرفة الذات هذه:" كل مزاح! أنا غير موجود! "كل خاصية في التفاحة تسير الآن بطريقتها الخاصة. الكروية تتجه شمالاً والخضراء تتجه جنوباً. فاكهيّة الغرب ، وتعليق تفاحة شرقاً. لم تعد تفاحة ، لم تكن موجودة. لقد فصلت التفاحة هويتها المزيفة. تم طرده للتو من ذلك الذي ينتمي إلي. أين نضارة التفاح؟ إنها تجلس في الحانة ويمكن تشغيلها!

شعر

الشعر يعني تركيز المعنى على تركيزه. ومع ذلك ، يكون شعر الكاتب مختومًا في بعض الأحيان بحيث لم يعد بإمكان القارئ فتح مربع المعنى. المؤلف فقط هو الذي يفهم مضمون القصيدة أثناء كتابته. وحتى علبة الكاتب ضيقة للغاية في صباح اليوم التالي.

شفاف

من الواضح أن ما هو شفاف يطير بحرية دون الحاجة إلى الاختباء. الثقوب شفافة بشكل رئيسي . على الرغم من أن الشفافية يمكن أن تكون ثقيلة ، إلا أنه ليس من السهل رؤيتها. تصبح الشفافية شفافة عندما تصبح خرقاء.

قبض

اصطيادها يصل بنجاح إلى فريستها أثناء التنقل. هذا هو السبب في صيد الأسماك بشكل خاص. إنهم زلقون ويعيشون في مياه متحركة ، ولكن لا يزال يمكن الإمساك بهم.

السجن

تعتبر الجرائم ذات قيمة فقط إذا لم يتم الإمساك بك. يأتي قرد إلى حديقة الحيوان حتى لو لم يرتكب أي خطأ. حديقة الحيوانات هي سجن مناسب للحيوانات. يتم سجن بعض الحيوانات البرية في السيرك. أطفال يجلسون في السجن بسبب تربية والديهم. تجلس الزوجات في سجن الاعتماد المالي على أزواجهن.

سري للغاية

يجب ألا يرى السر أعين الآخرين. يجلس وحده (أو مع المتآمرين) في مخبأه وقد يفعل ما يلي هناك: يتحلل ، يتقيأ ، يفرح ، يتحول إلى أشياء خاطئة ، يشعل ، يشعل الآخرين ، يضحك عليك ، يخاف ، تحمي نفسها ، ترفض ، أو تلد طفلاً. السر: لا نعرف ماذا يفعل. يبقى ذلك سرا.

تطير

الطيران ينساب في بحر واسع بدون أقدام. في الطيران ، يتم لعب الجزء العلوي والسفلي ضد بعضهما البعض. طائر لديه القوة دون اغتصاب العالم. هذا رائع. ومع ذلك ، لا يمكن أن تطير المقاعد العلوية ، وأجنحتها مسحورة. تمتد أجنحة الطيور في الجرأة. هم في المنزل هناك. الأجنحة هي أذرع الطيران ، فهي بالقوة. يمكن للطيور أن تطير بحرية دون أن تصطدم بقطة في الهواء. ومع ذلك ، يصطدم الموظف بسرعة كبيرة مع رئيسه أو بخطورة الحياة.

سهل

يتطاير الضوء بسهولة فوق الألغاز ، حيث يتجاوز مجرد البطون الثقيلة. يميل الشيء الخفيف إلى الوجود في الأعلى. يطفو الخشب على الماء لأنه أخف من الماء. يطفو منطاد الهواء الساخن في السماء الزرقاء. يصبح الضوء سريعًا تافهًا. شيء غبي يحدث بسهولة.

ندفة الثلج

تسقط ندفة الثلج بعناية. إنه هادئ. تأتي الرقائق من عالم آخر. إنه يعطي بنية لهذا العالم ، وإلا ستنهار جميع المجالات المغناطيسية. في القطبين الشمالي والجنوبي ، يقع المجال المغناطيسي في الثلج. من أقطاب الأرض ، ينظم الثلج تغييرات سرية في العالم. جاذبيتها تتغلغل في سكان الأرض وتجعلهم مواطنين ثقليين.

الحماية

الحماية شيء جيد. الحماية هي أول ما تحتاجه: الحماية الدستورية ، حماية القاعة ، منتجات حماية المحاصيل ، حماية البيانات وحماية الفكر. لم تحصل على زيارة من Mind Protection فقط ، انتظر ، سيأتي؟ بعد.

الأمعاء

هضم يمضغ ويمضغ ويمضغ. هضم المضغ أفضل من أي وقت مضى حتى يصبح الطعام جيدًا بحيث يمكن دمجه في لحومك الخاصة. ومع ذلك ، يبقى الطعام دائمًا سامًا بعض الشيء. الأرض سامة. إنه ليس وطننا. يمكن أن تهضم الحيوانات أفضل من البشر ، فهي تعيش بالقرب من الأرض.

الأرض

مـا نقـف عليه يسـمى الأرض. في بعـض الأحيـان يطلـق عليـه الكلمـة. الدائمـة والأرض ثابتة. يمكن أن تعني الأرض أيضًا الدبال أو الحجر. مادة الأرض مذهلة بشكل خاص ، فهي كثيفـة وثقيلـة. الكلمـة سلمية ، الكلمـة غبية. الأم العظيمـة ليس لهـا وجه. هـل لـديها دفء؟ تصل الجذور إلى الأرض ، كما أنها تفهم الأرض. الجذور واحدة بهدوء الأرض.

النحل

يعيش النحل في ثخانة المادة داخليًا. تخرج النحلة حيث تكون باردة. تسقط ميتة على الأرض مثل ندفة ثلج. وقد عبر النحل عن نفوذهم كرقائق باردة. طالما يتم تجميد الثلج ، فقد حان وقت شجرة شجرة عيد الميلاد. في حالة ذوبان القشرة ، تكون الوحدة عارية. عند تحريـك الرحيـق ، يربـط النحـل جميـع أجـزاء العـالم والجاذبيـة الرئيسـية ، ويمضـغ الجاذبية. الرحيق هو كتاب لم يقرأ بعد. ولا حتى من قبل مؤلفها.

ثقل

عـادة مـا تكون الثقل كبيرة في الكمية. في المقدمة ، ومع ذلك ، فإن الثقل صغير. قوى ثقل. له تأثير فقط من خلال كتلته ، وليس من خلال لونه ، لأن ثقله داكن جدًا بحيث لا يكون ملونًا. الثقل لا يفهم المضحك. فقط في السكر يمكن أن ينام المرح والثقل معا. هل تأتي الجاذبية من الأعلى أم من الأسفل؟ عندما تصبح الحرارة أقوى ، تصبح جاذبية. ماذا عـن الحجـر الـذي لا يمكنـك رميـه؟ هـل هي ثقيلـة جـدا أم قويـة جـدا؟ إنهـا وحشـية للغاية! الثقل أنعم من الوحشي. هل من السهل إذن؟ هكذا هي

الريح

الريح تجرد من الأشجار والمنازل. قوة الرياح غير مرئية ، يمكن رؤية آثارها فقط. تهب الرياح الأسهم. تهب الهندباء في الريح ، الرماد على حد سواء. الريح عابرة جدا. لكنها دائما تهب ما.

شقوق في الدماغ

الملكية فريدة من نوعها. إنه غريب على شيء ٠. الكمية نسبية ، يتم قياسها دائمًا من بطن كبير ، لكنها لا تمتلك الدهون. كل شيء Isolde المقارنة. الكمية ليس لها مالك. لدى لا لزوم له الكثير. لا يهم عدد الشقوق التي يعاني منها دماغ آينشتاين. إن خاصية الدماغ هي التي تجعله فريدًا.وليس عدد شقوقه. لا يمكنك مقارنة التفاح والكمثرى ، فقط وزنهم.

رمال

تسمى شظايا الحجارة الرمل. شظايا الرمل صغيرة جدًا لدرجة أنها تشكل وحدة مرة أخرى كمجتمع للعزلة. ثم يتم الشعور بالرمل ككل. كل شيء يبكي ، لكن الرمل لا يمكن أن يبكي لأنه جاف للغاية. الأحجار ليس لها دم ولا ماء ، ولا حتى كالرمل. دموع العمالقة الحزينة تتبرع بالمياه المالحة مثل البحر. هذا هو السبب في أن الرمال غالبًا ما توجد كشاطئ حيث يوجد بحر.

الناس

الناس موجودون فقط في صيغة الجمع. لا يمكن أن يكون الشخص وحده. يصبح الإنسان كحيوان قطيع "الناس". يتكون الحشد من الناس. دم الشعب دم عشيرتهم. الشخص ، من ناحية أخرى ، لديه مجرى الدم الخاص به. مع اليهود القدامى ، يتدفق دم إبراهيم إلى أحفاده المتأخرين. الناس والشعوب القديمة لديهم هويتهم في المجموعة ، وليس في أنفسهم.

بابل

لـم تكـن بابل طفلاً: كانت كبيرة جـدًا على الأطـول. هنـاك أيضًـا ناطحـات السـحاب في نيويورك. لكن هذه يجب أن يدمرها الإرهابيون لأنهم يريدون خدش الله. ترقصين حول العجـل الـذهبي ، حـول النمـو الاقتصادي وجـراح التجميل. متى سـيأتي غضب الله أخيـراً ويجرف الخطاة في سلة المهملات؟

أصغر الجسيمات

تمكن فريد من الوصول غير المصرح به إلى مسرع الجسيمات الكبير بالقرب من جنيف ليلاً. وهو يزحف الآن إلى الحلقة المستديرة: يرى جسيمات خضراء زاهية تتطاير.

فريد: مرحبا جزيئات ، هل يمكنك التحدث أيضًا؟

الجسيمات الخضراء: لدي صداع ، وهذا أمر سيئ لأني مجرد رأس. منذ أن اكتشفني علماء الفيزياء ، لم يعد بإمكاني حياكة العالم. حتى السياسة تخرج عن السيطرة.

يمر جسيم أحمر في الماضي: يخرج لسانه ، الذي يكون أكثر احمرارًا من الجسيم نفسه.

الجسـيمات الحمـراء: أشـعل المـال تحـت مـؤخرتي. عـادة مـا يكـون المـال مجـرد معلومات. ناري يعطي قيمة للمعلومات. يطير المثلث ، وله عين على جبهته.

المثلث: أنا أكبر جسيم موجود. لا توجد جسيمات صغيرة إلا في جحيم الفيزياء. القليل ليس له حقيقة. كلما أصبحت الأشياء أكثر شمولاً ، أصبحت أكثر واقعية. - فريد مندهش للتو.

الفوضى هي الارتباك الذي تستخدمه الكائنات الفضائية الإبداعية للتخلص من حماية العقل في العالم دون توقف. الفوضى ملونة. تزيل الفوضى قمامة الماضي. ترقص الفوضى ولا تعرف لماذا.

اكتب

في الكتابة ، تتحدث اللغة بصمت في الصوت ، ولكنها مشرقة في الوعي. الكتاب هم نحاتو اليقين. الكتابة مكتوبة دائمًا ، حتى أثناء الكتابة. الكتابة نهائية وتستمر لفترة أطول من النبيذ الجيد. تكتب الكلمة طوال الوقت.

ارقص

الرقص شجاع. أي شخص يرقص هو مجنون. يمكن أن يكون الرقص رائعًا أيضًا إذا كنت شخصًا متهورًا. لا يجب على المفكرين الرقص. حطم الرقص وضوح ذهنها. يائسة لعدم وجود حب الطعام ، الجنون كنمر يأكل أمر الشر الفاسد Sweet Miezi يصنع Fressi-Fressi!

اروين

قطرات دموع تسقط من السماء. يجتمعون على الأرض لتشكيل كتلة تتضخم في النهر. يجلس إروين في زورق ومجاذيف من خلال الدمعة. يتدفق النهر صعودًا. الحرائق تحترق تكريما لوتان على الضفة اليمنى للنهر. على الضفة اليسرى توجد شجرة عليها طائر حجري يجلس عليها. يواصل إروين التجديف صعودًا في زورق. الآن تثلج. يرى الزورق رجل ثلج على الضفة بين إبر الصنوبر. عيون رجل الثلج حية ، فهي عيون دب قوي. يواصل إروين تجديف النهر. شخص على اليسار يعزف على القيثارة. الله قريب.

بركان

امرأة سوداء مع شظايا ملونة تحارب البرودة. يطيرون معًا فوق النجوم ، تحت النجوم ، بين النجوم. تظهر حياة تايتانيك في غرقها. زورق قابل للطي يطفو بشكل عرضي في الماء ، ينجرف بحذر نحو نبع ماء الأهوار: بنغ! يقع الرماد من فوق. لقد انفجر Eyjafjallajökull أخيرًا.

مناسب

Fit على العكس من ذلك ، يمكن العثور على النوبة كالحب. كشيء ذي صلة ، يكمل أحدهما والآخر بخدمة مماثلة. كل شيء يتناسب معًا في هيكل واحد. البيرة والسجائر ومنفضة السجائر على طاولة مطبخ السيد ألكي . هذا منطقي ، يناسبه. طاولة المطبخ في كتالوج العالم الكبير معًا على الإنترنت. يرتبط Kunz و Hinz السيد ألكي هي بنية. يوجد هينز وكونز فقط من خلال وجودهما. الإنترنت ليس هيكلًا ، بل هراء.

الشيء

شيء رمادي في وجوده. إنه ليس أكثر. الأمور غير شخصية. إن آلة الأشياء العالمية التي لا وجه لها تحكم الأرض: إنترنت الأشياء. تتراكم الأشياء إلى شيء العالم. لقد كان للشيطان العالم في مخالبه منذ فترة طويلة. لا يتم التحدث عن الكائنات الحية لأنها تتحرك بنفسها. ومع ذلك ، يمكن لشيء صغير أن يتحرك بنفسه. إنه شيء.

التدبير

يمكن أن يكون المقياس هو الإجراء الصحيح ، المخبوز بمحبة من قبل الآلهة الصديقة. كمعلم ، يحدد الإجراء المرضي حدودًا لسلطة التلميذ. عندئذ يكون التلميذ ممتلئًا ، وتتأخر حياته ، ويمكن للصناعة توليد الكهرباء من السد.

كل شيء

كل هذا هو إضافة أشياء كثيرة إلى حد الأرق. هل هذا كل شيء الآن؟ كل شيء على الأقل شيء مستدير. كما هو متوقع ، يجب أن يتألق كل شيء على حافة ذلك ، لكنه يبقى رماديًا هناك. ثم يقول الكاهن الصناعي: "الكل أكبر من مجموع أجزائه!" حتى بعد هذه الجملة ، كل شيء لا يلمع ، لا يمكن رؤية المزيد. الكل يبقى إضافة عارية لكل شيء. لا يوجد سوى واحد آخر في هذا الكتاب.

لا شيء

لا شيء هو عالم كل الأشياء. الكأس ليس كرسي. الفستان ليس سحابة. ناهيك عن الكلب: الكلب ليس مجرد قطة مثل العصفور. كل الأشياء غير مجتمعة في عالم لا شيء. يقول البعض أن لا شيء يأتي بعد الموت. هل تريد أن تعيش هناك بين كل الأشياء؟ سيكون ضيقًا جدًا في خزانة الأشياء غير.

تمتع

المتعة تحتاج إلى أكثر مما هو ضروري. لذا فإن المتعة مرتبطة بالسعادة. ولكن في حين أن السعادة هي هدية الحياة ، فإن الاستمتاع تعسفي. تمتع بالبقاء والإقامة. التمتع دهني . المتعة هي الرغبة في تناول الطعام. المتعة لا تعتقد ، المتعة بطيئة للغاية لذلك. عندما تهضم الأمعاء أكثر مما تحتاجه ، تكون سعيدة. الارتياح مادة تحلية ، لكن السكر هو السعادة.

french / français

Le Psychosaurus se présente:

Je pense poétiquement et je n'ai pas été victime d'un biofant. Ces fantômes extraterrestres pénètrent illégalement de l'espace dans l'obscurité et utilisent leur longue trompe pour aspirer l'imagination des gens endormis de leur cerveau. J'utilise à contrecœur des mots que d'autres ont déjà dit. Je trouve cela insalubre. C'est pourquoi j'invente souvent de nouveaux mots, ce qui crée le problème que personne ne me comprend plus. Par conséquent, je dois à nouveau utiliser des mots utilisés, que la langue vernaculaire allemande n'a formés que de façon imprécise. Le langage peut parler parce qu'il contient les images générales de l'existence. L'essentiel dans la langue est de donner aux images du monde une maison. C'est tragique quand une personne suit les mots de la langue et pense que c'est ce qu'elle pense. La vraie pensée façonne activement le langage. La langue est le je d'un psychosaurus, c'est son centre. Le monde prend vraiment vie dans la langue, parce que parler signifie: créer le monde. Au début était le mot!

Scaredy

Un lapin effrayé est en passe de devenir un lapin de Pâques. En chemin, il voulait rendre visite à son oncle, mais il est à nouveau dans le poivre. Le lapin effrayé n'est pas une grenouille, il fait face au singe, même si le singe en rit. Le pou coule sur le foie de la puce. Le lièvre entend cette toux de puce, qui tire maintenant des canons sur des moineaux. Le lapin effrayé surmonte son bâtard intérieur puis transforme la puce en escargot. A gauche, il aperçoit un âne trop confortable. L'âne part sur la glace au milieu de l'été. Cela ne fonctionne pas sur la peau de vache, et les poulets se moquent de l'âne. Sur la main droite, une souris grise attrape les papillons parce que l'orignal les a frappés. Les moustiques dans l'air sont inoffensifs en eux-mêmes s'ils ne deviennent pas des éléphants et se comportent comme eux dans le magasin de porcelaine. M. Specht court comme un lapin et sort son caniche arrosé pour qu'il ne devienne pas fou dans la poêle. Monsieur et chien ont probablement un oiseau, mais aucun coq ne chante après eux, car il est dans le panier avec ses poules. Sur son chemin, le lapin effrayé trouve une dent de singe qui ne nuit plus à une mouche. Maintenant que le cauchemar l'a fait, il est arrivé au lapin de Pâques.

une conversation

Mole: Dis Psychosaurus, de quoi parle ce livre?

Psychosaurus: Dans ce livre, la langue se parle elle-même. Et il y a la langue

parle de tout, donc ce livre a tous les sujets.

Duck: Une question personnelle: quelle est la différence entre ça

Psychosaurus et Carsten?

Psychosaurus: je ne veux pas en parler

le sujet me stresse totalement.

Canard: Il est courbé, mec!

Mole: Ce livre en est évidemment un

traduction automatique?

Psychosaurus: Il en est ainsi. Cela augmente le bizarre au-delà de toute mesure.

La langue dit plus de mille mots.

Giggle: Si je veux écrire à Carsten, il en a un aussi

En ligne ou quelque chose?

Psychosaurus: Pour le moment, il a l'adresse e-mail

carsten-stemm@web.de et il a également le sien en ligne.

Werewolf: Sunt reprimat de această carte!

Giggle: Je ne comprends pas un mot, pas même la gare.

Rabe: Tu n'as pas besoin de tout comprendre. Parfois, il suffit de laisser les mots vous porter à travers l'irrationnel.

Detlef double dooid

Detlef Doppeldoid ne peut pas penser correctement avec les deux moitiés du cerveau. Detlef pense plus vite que la lumière, ce qui entraîne des gonflements spatio-temporels dans sa logosphère. Puis il échange de droite à gauche, dedans avec dehors, et brut avec net. Il ne sait pas si vous entrez ou sortez d'une pièce. C'est mauvais pour Detlef Doppeldoid: l'autre jour, il pensait que les gens étaient des gens. Detlef ne se souvient pas non plus de la différence entre Albert Einstein et Konrad Adenauer. Detlef se demande: n'est-ce pas " le même " et " le même " le même? Parfois, M. Doppeldoid fait également des fautes d'orthographe. S'il est complètement confus, Detlef se souvient même de l'avenir.

Detlef dit:

" Chaque fois que je ne sais plus qui je suis, je regarde ma carte d'identité: j'y ai aussi mon propre numéro; un certain nombre, pour moi seul, juste pour moi. Unique et indubitable. L'État m'aime. Mais est-ce que cela m'aide? Qui est derrière le nom Detlef Doppeldoid? Et que prouve une petite carte plastique? Il est facile de forger des cartes en plastique. Vous pouvez tout simuler aujourd'hui. Vous pouvez même truquer une identité. Je deviens assez fleuri. "

Lapin qui parle

Le lapin qui peut parler est appelé le lapin qui parle. Le lapin qui parle mange en parlant et parle en grignotant. Les racines des mots ne lui sont pas inconnues. Il consomme actuellement de l'amour. L'amour n'est qu'un mot pour lui, mugg, mampf. Vous pouvez manger de l'amour sans manger, c'est la sagesse du lièvre.

Il y a des canards!

Le biologiste s'intéresse aux plumes des canards, l'ontologue s'intéresse à l'être des canards. Qui donne les canards? Réponse: le «ça». «Ça» et donner le résultat à l'être. Alternativement, la question pourrait être répondue comme suit: l'évolution donne des canards, des œufs de canard donnent des canards, le sexe de canard donne des canards, Dieu donne des canards. Il pleut. Il faut dire: le nuage pleut. Ce «ça» n'est même pas du ressort de Dieu, car cela signifie: Il y a un Dieu. Cela signifie à son tour: Le «Il» est plus grand que Dieu. Une autre conclusion serait: Le «Il» est le vrai Dieu qui donne en premier à Dieu. Il y a des canards. On ne dit pas: il faut des canards. Donner est plus heureux que de prendre. Donner est probablement plus ontologique que prendre. Le «il» est si peu clair que vous ne pouvez plus voir son brouillard. En conséquence, vous ne pensez plus à la provenance réelle des canards. Le «il» est trompeur. Cela prétend être de la connaissance. Si nous ne savons plus que le nuage pleut,

puis il pleut. La négation donne aussi le «ça»: «« Il n'y a pas d'Elwittitsche! »« Qui ne peut être que ce «qui» qui est capable de donner à ces non-canards?

Goldmarie et Pechmarie

Une fois, il y avait un entraîneur de motivation qui avait deux filles, toutes deux nommées Marie. L'un était travailleur, l'autre paresseux. Un jour, la travailleuse est arrivée dans un puits qui a dit:

" Pas d'eau potable! "

" Ce n'est là que pour des raisons légales ", a pensé la femme assoiffée. La jeune fille a bu de l'eau et est tombée accidentellement dans la fontaine, lui faisant perdre connaissance. À un moment donné, elle s'est réveillée dans une zone complètement inconnue.

Une vieille femme se tenait à la fenêtre d'une maison à rénover et a secoué son oreiller. Mme Holle, comme l'appelait le locataire, a dit à la jeune fille: "Les infirmières compétentes pour les personnes âgées comme vous sont rares de nos jours, j'ai beaucoup de travail à faire."

Après un certain temps, cependant, la fille a eu le mal du pays et a exprimé le désir d'être autorisée à rentrer chez elle. Frau Holle lui a accordé ce souhait. La vieille femme a conduit la jeune fille à une porte par laquelle elle devrait passer. Alors que la femme travailleuse passait la porte, il pleuvait sur elle par le haut, du terrain contaminé par de la dioxine qui ne sortait plus de sa peau. La fille a dit: " Putain de conneries! Je prendrai ma revanche amèrement sur le destin. J'étudie les mathématiques et fais mon doctorat sur les théories du paradoxe. "

Lorsque la mère a vu sa fille enduite de poix, elle a appelé son enfant Pechmarie. Pour des raisons de compensation sociale, la mère a également envoyé sa fille paresseuse au puits. C'est arrivé presque pareil. Seule sa deuxième fille est venue dans une autre maison dans laquelle vivait une certaine Frau Hölle au lieu de Frau Holles Haus.

Après dix minutes de travail, la discipline de travail de la fille paresseuse a considérablement diminué. Mme Hell a déclaré: «À votre âge, j'étais aussi assez paresseuse. Je n'ai même pas de certificat de fin d'études secondaires. Nous courons maintenant vers un Château Mouton-Rothschild 1945, que mon gendre s'est volé.

Heureusement, toute la cave en est pleine. " Après une semaine de beuveries, les paresseux ont également eu le mal du pays et ont voulu quitter leur domicile. Frau Hölle la conduisit à la même porte par laquelle Pechmarie était passée. Lorsque la fille paresseuse a franchi le portail, il pleuvait de l'or sur elle. Maintenant, la fille était beaucoup plus précieuse, car l'or ne pouvait pas non plus être retiré. À son retour à la maison, sa mère l'a appelée Goldmarie. Par colère face à l'injustice de la vie, la mère a quitté l'église et s'est rendue à un jugement séculier. Pechmarie est devenu plus tard le premier professeur de logique avec des cicatrices de dioxine sur son visage. Sa vie était complètement bâclée. Goldmarie, cependant, a vécu heureux pour toujours. > Fin heureuse

Fromage de brebis

Shepherd: Dites-moi, quel genre de livre portez-vous sous votre bras?

Wolfgang: Un de vos moutons m'a donné le livre pour mon anniversaire. Son titre est: Faites vous-même du fromage de brebis!

Shepherd: C'est censé être une blague?

Wolfgang: Les blagues ne doivent pas être insignifiantes. Je ne plaisante jamais. Celui qui plaisante est tout simplement trop lâche pour être sérieux. Je ne plaisantais jamais. Et si quelqu'un rit, je me tape le cul sur la bouche.

Un mouton: Excusez-moi si j'interviens, mais je suis génétiquement modifié, donc je peux parler. Y aura-t-il bientôt une nouvelle taxe sur le fromage de brebis?

un autre mouton: Moi aussi, je suis un produit génétiquement amélioré du créateur, et je vous le dis: les hommes sont comme les femmes, seulement l' inverse.

Wolfgang: J'ai toujours pensé que ce serait différent!

Shepherd: J'ai des vertiges à cause de conversations aussi compliquées. .. Ah, regardez qui vient! Il boitait!

Wolfgang: Alors ce ne peut être qu'une comparaison!

Shepherd: Pourquoi ça?

Wolfgang: Parce que vous dites toujours: chaque comparaison est à la traîne!

un mouton tondu: le sens est toujours ambigu. L'orateur se promet donc rapidement dans son discours. Le double allemand est un Lapsus Freudianikus, la fuite dans l'auto-représentation trop lisse.

Wolfgang: Quel genre de locuteur est-ce?

Berger: Les moutons ont étudié. Psycholinguistique ou quelque chose.

(La boiterie est maintenant arrivée au groupe de discussion.)

Boiter: Vous êtes après moi. Mon métier volé

Le plutonium des centrales nucléaires russes a explosé!

Shepherd: Ne fais pas les choses, Otto!

Mouton: pouvez-vous manger du plutonium?

Berger: Tous les moutons n'ont pas étudié!

tous les moutons ensemble: Mähhhh!

Otto: Je n'ai qu'une seule issue: le suicide!

Wolfgang: J'aurais une issue alternative. Je connais un bon magicien au cirque. Il souffre d'une allergie, mais il est techniquement bien.

Otto: Qui est ce magicien?

Wolfgang: Il est tout ce que vous pensez qu'il est, car il a beaucoup

Planètes dans la septième maison, y compris Pluton.

Otto: Je ne crois pas à l'astrologie!

Wolfgang: Mais les stars croient en toi!

Otto: Très bien, je veux l'essayer, car je n'ai plus rien à perdre. Je suis enchanté d'un lapin et j'écris mon nom à l'envers pour que personne ne me reconnaisse.

Berger: une bonne chose! Voilà une fin vraiment heureuse!

En cas d'urgence, la pomme mange des poires.

Homicide

Monkey: Bonjour, œil bizarre, tu as les yeux inclinés.

Oeil bizarre: Et tu es un singe, toi singe.

Singe: J'ai un bâton de dynamite ici.

Qui les mettons-nous dans le cul?

Oeil bizarre: bien sûr! Chez TNT, je ne dis pas non!

Vous, singe brillant, vous méritez le prix Nobel!

(Le singe pousse l'inclinaison dans le cul de la dynamite et allume le fusible. Après des secondes éprouvantes pour les nerfs, il y a une violente détonation: de la poussière, des débris et des restes de viande recouvrent le lieu de l'explosion.)

Singe: cool! Il s'est écrasé!

Il n'y a pas de comptes ou de paragraphes pour nous les animaux.

Maintenant, nous allons manger une banane. Haha!

Poussin en acier

Une fois, il y avait une petite voiture grinçante qui traverse une nature grasse et douce. Le chariot se déplace, il est tiré par un cheval. Un véhicule qui ne roule plus aujourd'hui. Lorsque le compagnon a commencé à être entraîné par le moteur, le chariot est devenu en acier, alors que le chariot était encore tiré, les fleurs ont fleuri et l'eau s'est précipitée vers lui. Le secret de la vie vivait dans la roue du moulin, ici la roue tournait dans l'eau. L'automobile était la naissance de la fille d'acier. Le ciel s'étire, le ciel s'étire, il est excité. Un poussin d'acier tire dans le ciel avec un canon de défense. C'est la Seconde Guerre mondiale, une tentative insensée de l'acier pour redevenir un cheval. Le poussin d'acier est maintenant un cheval elle-même, elle porte donc une queue de cheval. Les chevaux sont vraiment élégants, car l'élégance n'est plus connue à l'ère de l'acier. Le plastique est également l'acier. Tout ce qui n'est pas tiré par le cheval est en acier. Vous obtenez la crainte d'une beauté qui n'est pas une poupée de mode.

Multi-pièces

Une multi-pièce est une pièce plus grande à l'intérieur qu'à l'extérieur. Le multi-placard, par exemple, ressemble à un placard de chambre ordinaire. Mais si vous devez vous cacher dans l'armoire si nécessaire, vous serez étonné de constater qu'il y a des galaxies entières dans l'armoire. Et ce ne sont pas des hallucinations dues à un manque d'oxygène. Le monde est plein de trous dans la réalité. Et il y en a de plus en plus.

Danger

Le danger vous menace. L'accident n'a pas encore frappé. Mais cela pourrait frapper à l'avenir; c'est un risque. La vie est précaire. Vous ne savez pas si la vie sera brisée le moment suivant. Le danger est à la porte, le danger est imprévisible, il peut devenir un cauchemar. Les prédateurs sont dangereux; Les capitalistes aussi. Il est dangereux de poser des câbles d'alimentation dans une cuve pleine d'eau. Se marier est risqué aussi. L'assurance-vie, quant à elle, promet une protection: si vous avez perdu une vie, vous en obtiendrez une nouvelle. Mais attention à la fraude à l'assurance: les compagnies d'assurance trichent beaucoup!

Penser

La pensée erre au pays du sens. Les modes de pensée se heurtent à la forêt de la connaissance. Au fil de sa randonnée, la réflexion devient plus difficile et se confond finalement avec ses arbres de pensée et sa neige de rêve.

Olymp

Fred voit un dieu sur téléphone portable sur Olympus:

Fred: Bonjour mon Dieu!

Depuis combien de temps les dieux utilisent-ils un téléphone portable?

Dieu: oui mei, vous vous ajustez juste. Je pouvais également communiquer par télépathie avec mes collègues, mais nous, les dieux, voulons rendre les gens compréhensibles.

Fred: Donc, je ne comprends pas!

Têtes d'oeufs

Les branleurs de cerveau sont les lapins de l'agglutination pneumatique. Ils sont également appelés têtes d'oeufs. Vos neurolants ne sont pas très souples, mais ils sont très longs. Jetez des noix nues à leur tête chauve car elles contiennent beaucoup de cire cérébrale. Les neurolants sont les bâtonnets de l'esprit. Les neurolants peuvent également être les troncs d'arbres à travers lesquels vous ne pouvez plus voir la forêt pour le nombre d'entre eux. Mais en fait, Neurolanten sont les baguettes pour manger des sushis intellectuels.

Certaines ondes cérébrales sont appelées philosophes. La philosophie pense sans boire, elle est lumière sans amour. Le penseur peut mal plaisanter dans le désert du savoir. Les cactus ne rient jamais. La philosophie est aussi dure que le vieux fromage. Les philosophes sur le chemin de la guérison commencent à écrire de la poésie.

Demigod

Fred: Tu sais quoi Detlef, j'ai été promu demi-dieu.

Detlef: Vraiment?

Fred: C'est comme ça! Je peux maintenant trouver une réponse à chaque question, ne serait-ce que de façon imprécise, mais je peux trouver la réponse.

Detlef: Qui vous a promu?

Fred: Le grand patron!

Detlef: Aha!

Fred: Je suis juste un demi-dieu. Je ne suis pas encore immortel, mais j'y travaille.

Detlef: Mm, fais ça.

Fred: Je sais enfin, par exemple, pourquoi la banane est tordue.

Detlef: Oui, pourquoi alors?

Fred: Elle aspire à l'unité, la banane veut retourner au paradis, elle aimerait être un cercle, mais la Chute l'interdit, seule sa force s'étend jusqu'à la courbe.

Detlef: Ce qu'un demi-dieu sait!

Fantôme

Le terme «esprit» est un mot très solitaire. Le mot doit expliquer tant de choses. Intelligence coupe des pierres; l'esprit se connecte. L'esprit illumine les parties du monde comme un soleil et leur donne une forme. L'esprit est l'image des choses. L'esprit habille les plus petites particules avec plus. L'esprit peut penser, l'intelligence ne peut que penser ou se combiner.

Cause et effet

Un joueur de billard frappe une balle avec son bâton, qui à son tour frappe une autre balle. Cette pensée de cause à effet est la logique originelle de la science. La logique le justifie, elle n'explique rien. Le libre arbitre du joueur de billard est complètement caché dans cette vision du monde. Les causes sont des animaux ternes, presque des taureaux. Les causes convainquent par l'énergie, pas par le sens.

La logique

Fred: Je crois en la logique. Le cosmos tout entier est logiquement structuré. Cependant, les femmes ne font pas partie du cosmos. La pensée logique vous donne accès à chaque puzzle. Il suffit de faire beaucoup d'efforts pour réfléchir.

Arnold Heitermann: La logique ne nous fait pas avancer dans la connaissance. Un exemple: trois corbeaux sont assis sur une clôture. Un tueur d'oiseaux passe et tire sur l'un des oiseaux.

Arnold: Combien d'oiseaux sont encore sur la clôture maintenant?

Fred: Il y a deux corbeaux sur la clôture.

Arnold: Faux! Il y a encore un corbeau sur la clôture!

Fred: C'est complètement illogique!

Arnold: C'est logique. L'oiseau abattu est tombé mort au sol. Le deuxième corbeau a été surpris par la forte détonation et s'est envolé immédiatement. Le troisième corbeau a été terrifié par le coup et reste le seul oiseau à s'asseoir.

Fred: Cette affaire me semble très construite, mais c'est logique.

Arnold: Eh bien, vous pouvez tout expliquer et rien avec de la logique.

Fred: Tout d'abord, après.

Arnold: Oui, toujours après.

Cependant, la réalité était là avant.

manche peut partir à l'aventure sans cercle ni arc. La vie elle-même est une aventure. Aujourd'hui, le groupe pense à quelque chose de nouveau. Mais le cycle est si vieux que sa pensée du nouveau ne peut jamais produire de folie. Cependant, les philistins ne traînent jamais. C'est trop cahoteux pour ça. Le groupe a voulu devenir un cercle et a demandé à l'agence pour l'emploi de se recycler. L'employé était un carré. Ça s'est mal terminé.

La pomme pense et guide la poire.

Frapper est génial

Frapper est le verbe le plus universel qui soit. Frapper est vraiment génial. Cette activité était déjà pleinement développée à l'âge de pierre. Vous pouvez ouvrir les yeux, comme un livre. Levez les yeux dans le vide, brisez la fenêtre ou frappez quelqu'un au visage. Les musiciens font du bruit avec les tambours. Le coup vous frappe. Le ménisque 1.FC bat les pieds plats de Rosenheim 2-1. Celui qui bat gagne. La meilleure façon de frapper est avec des pierres. Une pierre noble s'appelle un marteau. Frapper est brut et brut. Un coup est stupide et atomique. Frapper, casser, casser, séparer. Un enfant de frapper coupe. Un mauvais enfant. Un autre enfant de frapper pousse. Cet enfant est plus sympathique car il a plus de soleil vers l'avant. Battre fait un poing, donc ses actions ont un ventre.

Outil

Une œuvre d'art est le dépôt de toute expérience humaine ultime. Il y a une expérience qui a été confirmée pour qu'elle se solidifie comme une œuvre d'art. Le trésor de travail oriente tous les êtres comme un champ magnétique du spirituel. Le Werkschatz est le

Wikipedia naturel de la vie. Malheureusement, il y a aussi des moutons noirs dans le trésor de la connaissance: on les appelle des saletés d'usine.

Pour le roi Orthos, gouverner signifie arranger les choses selon leur propre moi intérieur. Orthos ne transmet pas sa propre volonté aux gens. Le roi ne veut pas forcer les choses, mais explore leurs particularités et les laisse les organiser elles-mêmes. Les gens, les chèvres et autres êtres vivent à Orthos Reich, tous debout et marchant à leur place. Après sa mort, le roi Orthos se déversera dans l'eau de sa rivière préférée, qui finira par se déverser dans la mer. Depuis la mer, son travail continuera d'orienter les gens.

Faim et soif

La faim veut manger quelque chose tout le temps. La faim dépend complètement de l'objet de son désir. Mais c'est exactement ce qui rend la faim si agréable. Il est plein de vie, certains disent même qu'il est la vie même. La faim a aussi une sœur: son nom est "" soif "". Mais ce n'est que pour les types très fous.

Le besoin est l'abstraction de la faim et de la soif. Le besoin est faible et dans le besoin. Le besoin est très laïque et a toujours le même aspect gris. Vous pouvez stocker vos besoins à n'importe quelle température. Le besoin ne porte jamais de fruit, il reste toujours maigre. Si vous avez besoin de quelque chose, vous allez faire du shopping.

Qui a besoin de fibre? Surtout, s'ils ne sont constitués que de ballast. Charges de charge. Ils comblent le vide, mais restent eux-mêmes creux. C'est l'essence qui brille.

Le Psychosaurus est complètement à la fin:

Une puissance de glace comme une figure a levé son bras. Un escalier d'eau descend du visage froid. Les yeux de la femme de l'ombre brillent comme deux soleils la nuit. Pas pour longtemps. Vos lumières sont maintenant éteintes. La femme de l'ombre vole dans le ciel comme un ange noir. L'endroit inconnu est orphelin. Là où il n'y a jamais eu personne, il n'y a plus personne. Ma connaissance de ne pas être est à côté de l'espace vide. J'ai chaud, mais seulement comme chaleur, car je n'ai pas d'autre corps. Un cri sans langue tourne désespérément dans la pièce vide. Il n'y a que du vide partout où quelque chose devrait être. Là où il n'y a rien, vous ne pouvez rien voir, surtout si vous n'avez pas d'yeux. Mais je vois l'horreur et je ne sais pas pourquoi.

Trou

Un trou signifie une absence plutôt ronde. Les trous sont vides. Un trou est souvent un passage qui entre et sort. Parfois, la vue sort par le trou et la vue entre par le trou. Les trous ont faim, ils aimeraient être bourrés. L'envie de tout être doit être satisfaite. La réalité a des trous. Celles-ci sont si transparentes que personne ne peut les voir, pas même un physicien avec son grand appareil. Le manque de vêtements peut être vu chez les personnes nues. L'absence de fossé, en revanche, reste affamée et invisible. La surface a tendance à être vide. Si ce vide est rempli, la surface disparaît rapidement, elle devient mince. L'esthète prescrit la couleur à la surface pour qu'elle gagne en confiance en soi.

Animal

L'animal classique a quatre pattes, il "miaule" ou aboie. Le terme animal est un cas type pour de nombreux êtres qui ont peu en commun. Les animaux ne portent pas de feuilles et ne peuvent pas construire de bombes atomiques. Les animaux sont des gens arriérés. Cependant, un jour, les animaux comprendront également le théorème d'incomplétude de Godel. - Seulement quand?

La nature peut être brute et rude. Il y a aussi la nature des rêveurs: cette nature est le paradis des gens avant même la chute. La nature du germanique Charles Darwin ressemble à ceci: un combat du fort contre un encore plus fort. Notre seconde nature est la culture. Notre troisième domaine est appelé artificiel. Personne n'aime y vivre.

Fleur de glace

Une puissance étrangère suédoise est constituée de la glace la plus froide. Ce pouvoir va sur terre sous la forme d'une vieille fille nommée Eisblume. Une fleur de glace, une belle fleur. Les fleurs rappellent le printemps, car pendant ce temps, les fleurs fraîches fleurissent généralement dans une jeune chaleur. Cependant, notre fleur de glace fleurit dans le froid meurtrier de l'hiver. Toutes les autres personnes qui sont également faites de glace sont ravies par la fleur de glace. Agnis est également hors du froid, hors de la glace brûlante. Agnis voit une fleur de glace et est ravie. Les frigides sont toujours les plus chauds. M. Sumpfstein est un étonnant en tant que vendeur de crème glacée. Ses boules de crème glacée contiennent des explosifs, qui s'enflamment quand il est long sur toutes les montagnes. Eisblume voit M. Sumpfstein: Elle reçoit un choc, la balle de roulette roule dans sa tête. Personne ne sait que le ballon s'arrêtera dans le compartiment des dix-sept. Chez Agnis, ce seront les trois. Boules de glace ou boules de roulette, les boules sont toutes pareilles. Les balles sont la mauvaise banque du destin. Et maintenant nous entrons dans cette banque et libérons la folie. Tout le monde devient fou: Eisblume, Agnis et Herr Sumpfstein sont dans une même boîte. Vous respirez la folie: Ah, c'est bien. Enfin, ils sont gratuits!

Sang

Le sang coule à l'intérieur comme une chaleur épaisse et puissante. Le sang humain est très personnel tant qu'il tourne encore dans ses veines. Les cercles de sang, donc c'est rond. Pouvoirs sanguins dans son cercle. Le sang extérieur dans la seringue froide et sans cœur du médecin est déjà mort. Seuls les reptiles saignent froid. A moins que le soleil ne brille sur la fourrure verte du reptile. Chaque vampire sait: quand la lune brille, le sang est noir. Vous ne voyez rien pendant la journée.

Le feu

Le feu danse avec des flammes violentes. La combustion sauvage détruit la durabilité du carburant. Des pointes de chaleur pénètrent dans la pièce, des dents de fièvre se mordent, la puissance de la tempête rouge donne à son environnement une aura de chaleur. Les braises du feu meurent en cendres. Le feu est impressionnant, mais il emprunte sa substance au carburant. Sa nourriture était consommée plus rapidement que cuite, beaucoup plus rapidement. La chaleur du feu dort moelleux dans l'espace de l'immortalité. Quand la chaleur devient folle, elle devient chaleur.

général

Le général montre autant de visage que nécessaire. Les caractéristiques spéciales montrent des bords beaucoup plus clairs. Le général est partout le même, il s'exprime souvent par le même. Dans le paysage de tout, le général se retrouve partout. L'oncle gris du général est appelé moyen. Le général doit s'adapter à la spéciale encore et encore, ce qui crée du stress. Le général donne la sécurité lorsque vous partez en vacances insolites.

Ombre debout

Une ombre debout doit toujours s'arrêter, même si elle peut aller où elle veut. Si l'ombre debout veut bouger, l'environnement passe devant lui au lieu de le dépasser, il s'arrête lui-même. L'ombre debout peut se déplacer et doit toujours rester au même endroit pour toujours. Une ombre debout n'a pas de compagnie. Bien sûr, il y a d'autres ombres debout, mais elles sont ailleurs.

Court-circuit

Le chemin mène au but tant qu'aucun ésotérique ne marche dessus. Un court-circuit raccourcit le chemin de la vie. Il suit rapidement un chemin qui n'existe pas. En conséquence, il manque d'expérience. Son succès est chaud et vide et sans viande, mais le court-circuit a un effet charismatique. L'itinéraire le plus court est toujours un court-circuit, son objectif est d'être inexistant. Le court-circuit agit sans croissance, il passe sans chemin. Joachim Ernst Berendt a écrit un livre: " Il n'y a pas moyen, allez-y: SOYEZ dans la nature ". Sur le chemin de la présentation de son livre, il a été renversé par une voiture.

Allez

Vous avez peur que la marche ne tombe. Mais la marche a son avantage: elle reste toujours en équilibre. Debout se déplace dans le couloir. Cependant, le mensonge ne court jamais.

Le paradis

Les montagnes de pointe n'ont aucun problème et sont heureuses qu'elles soient si grandes et grandes. Le ciel est également heureux lorsqu'il reçoit des visiteurs des montagnes. Le grand ciel a aussi besoin de convivialité.

Raison

La raison est ci-dessous. C'est la base, le sol, la base et la justification. Si vous regardez en bas, cela devient un abîme. Vous ne pouvez pas y découvrir la gravité. Le fond et l'abîme calment énormément les nerfs. Le meilleur travail pour les humains est d'aller au fond des choses. Seuls les lapins effrayés préfèrent faire quelque chose d'utile, car le monde périt d'une manière utile.

Underworld

Le monde souterrain est en dessous du monde. Il ne fait presque plus partie du monde, vous ne le savez pas, c'est pourquoi il n'est pas confortable. Les morts gisent sous le sol, il y a aussi la source de fertilité. Sinon, comment toutes les plantes devraient-elles pousser?

Nuage

Le nuage est un mouton dans le ciel. Les nuages sont toujours tristes. Ils doivent souvent pleurer. Mais ils protègent également le bétail du soleil agressif. Un nuage absorbe le bien et le mal des gens. Vous pouvez voir de leurs formes ce que l'heure a sonné. Le mouvement et l'eau dansent ensemble dans le nuage.

Saleté

Vous ne devriez pas mettre de saleté dans la salade. Sinon, la maladie menace! La saleté est l'équivalent physique du péché. Une plaie peut être considérée comme une contamination, car la plaie forme souvent une croûte désagréable sur le bord qui ressemble à de la saleté. La contamination ou les taches indiquent à leur tour la culpabilité. Quelqu'un est taché. Avons-nous été blessés parce que nous étions trop imparfaits? Ou sommes-nous imparfaits parce que nous avons été blessés? Ou sommes-nous coupables d'avoir violé quelque chose, une loi ou une personne? Mais on ne fait pas de mal! Nous sommes parfaits et innocents! Quiconque prétend quelque chose comme ça est blessant, donc coupable.

Sexe en prison

Les murs de la prison forment un cœur. Ses murs extérieurs sont noirs à l'extérieur et rouges à l'intérieur. Le prisonnier Raspoutine n'est plus le plus jeune, mais pas non plus le plus âgé, car après tout il a encore de l'acné. Germania est également emprisonnée: Rasputin et Germania vont se coucher ensemble. Rasputin craint que Germania ne contracte la syphilis. Germania quitte Rasputin. Elle n'a probablement qu'à faire Pippi pour peu de temps, mais elle n'ira pas très loin car nous sommes dans la prison du cœur. Une prison est un bâtiment auquel vous ne pouvez pas échapper. Rasputin se tient devant le miroir et exprime ses boutons. Le pus éclabousse l'innocence argentée: icky, ey.

Rat et bombe atomique

Les rats sont des souris devenues mégalomanes. Ils tolèrent mieux la radioactivité de tous les êtres vivants. Ils deviendront sûrement un jour les rois de la terre. Les rats s'entretuent, ils sont très similaires aux humains. Rat vous-même qui peut! Cependant, les rats sont plus intelligents que les humains, car ils apprennent très vite à ne pas manger de nourriture toxique s'ils remarquent que leurs pairs le tuent. C'est pourquoi le poison à rat n'est pas une solution permanente pour exterminer ces créatures infernales. Au Moyen Âge, les rats étaient utilisés pour torturer les gens; aujourd'hui, les rats sont torturés dans les laboratoires scientifiques. C'est une victoire pour l'humanité! De la victime à l'agresseur! Les rats mignons sont soignés et soignés dans le temple indien de Karni Mata. En Occident, cependant, il n'y a que de mauvais rats d'égout. En Chine, le rat existe même en tant que signe du zodiaque. Mais le Psychosaurus sans germe dit: "Nous ne vivons plus au Moyen Âge! Loin des méchants porteurs d'infection! Pourquoi les politiciens ne font-ils rien? Ils ne font jamais rien! "

Kink

Vous ne pouvez pas toucher un coude car il est si loin du rang à partir duquel il danse. Si rien ne se casse, il y a des choses. Une ligne va d'ici à là. C'est tellement normal que ça vous déprime. Les scientifiques et les architectes aiment les lignes. Une ligne ne mange pas la vie. La ligne brouille la vie et en tire de l'énergie pour pouvoir chauffer la pièce à une température modérée de 20 degrés.

Inclinaison

La pente est une pente qui s'incline en fonction de la popularité de la pente, se transforme en un angle qui correspond à la pente de la pente. Une telle inclinaison n'est pas arbitraire, mais correspond à l'amour des inclinés.

bien

Le bien est un arbre qui porte des fruits toute l'année. Son bois est fait de sang solide; ses feuilles peuvent rire. Le coloré est bon, le gris est mauvais. Le diable mange le bien. Le bien peut consister en lui-même. Cependant, le mal dépend de la destruction du bien. Par conséquent, le mal ne peut jamais prévaloir.

exister

Le sel se compose de sodium et de chlore. La position debout est sur vos deux pieds, mais l'existence a besoin d'une substance comme sol. Une existence a besoin de parties qui la composent, elle ne peut pas être seule. Le plus grossier existe. Le terme «stock» est très proche de celui de substance.

Souris et chauve-souris

Les souris ont quatre pattes et courent dans l'ordre de Dieu. Cependant, certaines souris ont ignoré leur destination et ont explosé. Ils traînent paresseusement toute la journée (tête baissée) et font la fête la nuit (boire du sang et d'autres trucs). La souris comme une chauve-souris est aveugle. C'est la punition de Dieu pour leurs péchés. Comme solution de fortune, les souris volantes doivent maintenant voir avec leurs oreilles. C'est complètement flagrant.

mince

Les femmes minces s'assoient rapidement sur le quai de l'anorexie. Accusé de mecs mous et gros. Si le mince veut prendre du poids, alors il doit s'appeler "mince". Le mince a parfois un effet plus intense que l'épais car il peut contenir beaucoup d'essence dans son ventre doux. Par conséquent, le mince est souvent plus intelligent que l'épais. Cela ne s'applique pas aux perceuses à planches minces, car elles ont une planche épaisse devant leur tête.

Victoire à la Pyrrhus

Je m'appelle Schmidt et je suis mort, j'ai vécu une vie pécheresse. Sur mon lieu de travail au sein de la société Satan & Sons, mon patron gourmand s'est transformé en un billet de 100 euros. J'ai senti ma chance d'une vie heureuse après la mort: j'ai rapidement mis mon billet de banque dans mon portefeuille et peint un crucifix sur son cuir extérieur. Mon patron a été pris. Ce n'est qu'après son assurance que je n'irais pas en enfer après ma mort que j'ai à nouveau enlevé la croix. Peu de temps après, j'ai glissé tristement sur une peau de banane devant l'AOK et je suis tombé sur le trottoir dur avec l'arrière de ma tête. J'étais mort tout de suite. Comme promis, je ne suis pas allé en enfer, mais ils ne voulaient pas non plus me laisser entrer au ciel, car j'avais vaincu le mal mais je n'avais toujours pas fait le bien. Maintenant, je fais constamment des allers-retours entre le ciel et l'enfer et je ne sais plus.

La souffrance

Fred: La souffrance est totalement superflue. Quel idiot a créé le monde?

Detlef: La souffrance protège contre les actes idiots. Cela vous empêche de boire trop de bière. Le mal mène au bien.

Fred: N'est-ce pas une autre façon? Un peu d'amour?

Pape: Dieu est infaillible (comme moi), il saura pourquoi il a créé le monde.

Mephisto: Je fais partie de ce pouvoir qui veut toujours le mal et crée toujours le bien.

Bert Hellinger: À un niveau supérieur, le mal est également bon.

Fred: Je vis sur terre; la terre est un niveau inférieur, le niveau supérieur ne me sert à rien. Tout cela n'est pas très convaincant.

Detlef: Le dieu solaire a également souffert. Il est mort sur la croix en tant qu'être humain et est ressuscité le troisième jour.

Fred: C'est en solidarité avec lui. Je me sens beaucoup mieux.

Allahu Akbar

Dieu est plus grand que ... Dieu est toujours plus grand que ce qu'un être humain peut imaginer. Par sécurité, je ne veux rien écrire de mal sur Dieu, on ne sait jamais. A moins que Dieu ne soit le diable. Les mauvais dieux sont-ils de vrais dieux? Ou leur existence se nourrit-elle d'une bonne alimentation? S'il n'y a qu'un seul Dieu, on ne peut en fait l'appeler qu'Allah. Les deux sons A neutres et globaux encadrent le son infini L. S'il y a plusieurs dieux, alors il devient plus coloré et aimant et aussi plus compréhensible pour les humains. Chaque dieu parmi les autres dieux a sa propre zone de responsabilité. Allah n'a plus besoin d'avoir 99 noms parce qu'il y a 99 dieux. Et le centième dieu réunira probablement tous les dieux encore, alors on soupçonne. La polarisation fanatique du bien et du mal se dissout dans la multitude des dieux. Parfois, les dieux sont également appelés anges, archanges ou entités supérieures.

L'ail

L'ail est une fraîcheur rassis. Ses orteils sont fendus. Une véritable scission de personnalité a ses racines. À l'extérieur, cependant, l'oignon fait preuve d'uniformité. L'ail aide contre les vampires et les sorcières. Le tubercule renforce le sang et le rend si immangeable pour les parasites que même les vampires perdent leur appétit. Le poireau schizophrène tue également les parasites physiques tels que les ténias ou les bactéries putréfactives. L'ail fend l'humanité comme la fumée de cigarette. Certains l'aiment: ce sont les bonnes personnes. Cependant, les méchants (par exemple les vampires, les sorcières, les nazis, les enculés, les capitalistes et les électeurs verts) se sentent repoussés par son odeur.

Contrat avec le diable

Vous pouvez rapidement devenir l'un des riches et des beaux en faisant un petit contrat dans le bureau de service de Satan & Söhne: l'entrepreneur (Teufel) répond à tous les souhaits du monde. En retour, l'entrepreneur a légué son âme post-mortem aux anatomistes de l'enfer à des fins de recherche. Le contrat est juridiquement valable grâce à une goutte de sang de l'entrepreneur.

La peste

Arnold imagine une peste qui vient sur la terre et tue toutes les mauvaises personnes. Les gentils ne tombent pas malades du tout ou survivent facilement à l'infection. Arnold est bien sûr l'un des bons gars. Comment peut-il en être si sûr? Et si la peste ne faisait que tuer les bons? Ce serait méchant, mais typique de l'injustice de ce monde. Arnold a peur et veut se faire vacciner contre le destin, même s'il sait que cela ne peut pas être fait.

couper

La conscience coupe l'être dans les choses. Couper est plus élégant que piquer, c'est pourquoi un moustique n'a pas de titre noble. Les âmes fortes ont le courage de l'affronter, les lâches n'ont pas de lame du tout. Vous ne devriez pas vous couper le doigt! Alors les amis: faites juste attention! La couleur de la découpe est appelée netteté. Les piments forts et les bombes sexuelles peuvent parfois aussi être un peu épicés.

Pauvre

Les bras s'étirent. Les bras commencent à fleurir dans les mains. Les bras s'affinent dans les mains, les mains sont renforcées dans l'outil. Les branches sont les bras des arbres.

Limite

Une bordure sépare l'un de l'autre. Ça commence à la frontière ou ça finit. La frontière forme un vaisseau pour la vie. Le sang a besoin de veines pour vivre. Une maison limite la vie par ses murs. Lorsque la vie quitte sa maison, il se noie dans la mer des sans-abri.

La plaque a un bord rond. Contrairement au cadre, le bord complète la croissance de son propriétaire. Une monture est un bijou, c'est une contrainte pour arrêter l'usure.

Le terme «monde» est utilisé pour décrire le paysage de tout. Le monde peut être compris comme une grandeur meurtrière. Ce monde n'a pas de fin. Les yeux de l'homme ne peuvent pas s'arrêter dans les rues sans fin. Un monde sécurisé est fermé sur ses bords. Là, le monde sûr embrasse l'infini avec les bras de la finitude.

clair et foncé

Gustav est aveugle sur les deux cors. Ses pieds ne peuvent rien voir. C'est une bonne chose, car si vous ne voyez rien, vous ne serez pas déprimé. Gustav est donc heureux. Il y a des gens qui ont un rendez-vous à l'aveugle. Tu es trop aveugle pour te rencontrer. Les chauves-souris voient également le noir, mais elles entendent très bien. La lumière est-elle aveugle à l'obscurité? L'obscurité voit-elle la lumière?

la lune

La lune rit dans le noir. On peut le voir en entier. En pleine lune, il est un homme. Sinon, elle est femelle. Ou était-ce l'inverse? La lune parcourt le ciel avec effroi. Il n'aime pas être vu; seuls les loups-garous, les chauves-souris et les corbeaux sont autorisés à le faire. La lune règne secrètement dans le royaume du mal, c'est la tromperie aux joues rondes, c'est un vieil amour, une obscurité brillante appelée lune. La lune brille plus brillamment lorsque des personnes décentes dorment.

Attends une minute

Il n'y a qu'un instant et c'est toujours pareil. Seul le moment est un moment. La majorité des "moments" n'a aucun sens. Il n'y a donc pas de temps. Et pourtant, l'horloge tourne. C'est pourquoi les montres sont des menteurs.

La mémoire

Les gens ne s'en souviennent pas du tout. Nous voyons le passé de notre moment présent. Chaque jour, vous vous souvenez d'un passé différent. La façon dont c'était vraiment est irrémédiablement perdue.

Vache originale

Au début, il y avait du lait. L'univers a été créé à partir de lait, c'est pourquoi nous parlons de la voie lactée. Le lait provenait du pis de l'Urkuh, le grand MUU.

frais

La fraîcheur chante comme la lumière dans l'humidité de la vie. La viande fraîche est plus saine que la viande pourrie. Le jus de fruit est plus frais que le sang, car l'animal pourrit dans sa cupidité.

Les tortues

Les tortues sont d'anciens embryons. Ils datent d'une époque où il n'y avait pas de temps du tout. Leur question est également différente. Il ne se compose pas des plus petites particules, mais de la bouillie plus douce car la dureté court en ligne d'ici à là. La vraie terre ne meurt jamais.

Ruine

Le vent souffle secrètement à travers les ruines du château en ruine. Les murs sombres sont vides d'événements. Les tempêtes de feu étaient hier, les cicatrices sont aujourd'hui. Une souris peut écrire et raconte au journal l'histoire de la ruine morte. Les oiseaux survolent le soleil rouge du soir et disparaissent nulle part.

Super

Le primal vient toujours en premier. La cause, l'origine, la soupe primordiale, l'Uranus, le bétail préhistorique, l'ancêtre, la forêt vierge, le Big Bang, et bien sûr les documents et les arrière-grands-parents pittoresques. Ce dernier ne connaissait pas encore le terme dangereux. À Vienne, dangereux signifie quelque chose qui est particulièrement dangereux.

fausses nouvelles

La terre est un disque! Si la terre était une sphère, les habitants de la Nouvelle-Zélande tomberaient de la terre. La NASA devrait-elle coller ses fausses photos dans le cul? Ils ont reniflé trop d'air lunaire!

Début

Un départ peut soudainement commencer comme un sprint ou remonter comme le brouillard en automne. Les plantes germent et les bébés naissent sans germes à l'hôpital. Un début nécessite une fin: la naissance d'un bébé met fin à la grossesse. Le commencement ne se connaît pas encore: ce n'est qu'à la fin que le commencement sait qui c'était.

Les enfants

Les enfants mangent du chocolat pour enfants. Les adultes mangent du chocolat adulte. Les deux produits ont le goût du chocolat. Vous pouvez voir: les enfants n'ont rien de spécial. Ce sont des mangeurs de chocolat comme vous et moi. Les enfants n'ont pas non plus besoin d'être arrosés, même s'ils vont à la maternelle.

Agaric

Un champignon adore sa liberté. Il a besoin de pluie d'en haut. Mais le champignon rouge refuse de recevoir les impulsions de Dieu. L'agaric de mouche voudrait tout garder sous contrôle. Il est même propriétaire d'un fouet. La domination est importante pour elle. La pluie tombe à la volée agaric. Le champignon remarque qu'il y a autre chose que la dominance, mais l'agaric n'ose pas s'ouvrir. Puis il le fait, car il est courageux. La peur vient de haut en bas dans le champignon. Hé ça. Il n'est plus désormais un crapaud, mais une petite souris, qui veut vivre une vie bourgeoise dans sa grotte. Mais cela ne fonctionne pas. La souris étudie la philosophie et renouvelle le monde et devient célèbre.

Foudre

Martin Luther et Paul ont été frappés par la foudre. Aussi vite que la foudre, ils sont devenus des gens éclairés. Un coup de foudre nous améliore-t-il? Ou le flash n'est-il qu'un court-circuit qui crée de l'hypocrisie? Il faudrait essayer cela lors du prochain orage.

JF Kennedy à Bielefeld

Une prétendue théorie du complot dit que la ville de Bielefeld n'existe même pas. À partir d'un certain moment, les ombres ne pouvaient plus masquer l'inexistence de Bielefeld. C'est pourquoi ils tenaient à présenter le complot comme une simple théorie ou une blague afin que personne n'ait l'idée que le faux de Bielefeld était la pure vérité. Heureusement, il y a Bill. Le 24 juillet 1963, Bill Clinton a rendu visite au président américain John F. Kennedy à la Maison Blanche et lui a serré la main. Clinton s'est exclamé: «Je vais être président!» Grâce à cet acte magique, Clinton a volé son destin et son identité au président Kennedy à l'époque. Résultat: Kennedy a dû mourir. Ou plutôt son sosie. Le vrai Kennedy était figé. Lorsque la fausse existence de Bielefeld a menacé de se révéler, Kennedy a de nouveau été décongelée. Après une chirurgie esthétique et une formation intensive en allemand, Kennedy est aujourd'hui sous le faux nom de Pit Clausen le maire de la ville fantôme de Bielefeld.

Les barbes

Sindbart: Hé vous, je peux vous voir!

Windbart: Madness! Moi aussi Incroyable quand on considère que nous n'existons pas tous les deux.

Sindbart: Quand deux personnes se rencontrent qui n'existent même pas, elles deviennent réelles l'une par rapport à l'autre et l'une pour l'autre, car elles se rencontrent toutes deux au même niveau, à savoir le niveau de non-existence.

Windbart: Vous rencontrez rarement quelqu'un comme vous. Vous devenez rarement réel. Nous devons profiter de l'occasion pour avoir une discussion détaillée sur la tromperie et la vérité.

Sindbart: Super, je suis là.

Mer

La mer peut s'offrir de la grandeur car elle garde des secrets. La mer est constituée des tranchées des dieux (les larmes contiennent du sel). La mer est la nourriture de la terre. La soif du désert s'est tarie depuis longtemps, le désert n'a plus besoin de vivre.

Société de l'information

Arnold Heitermann ne voit pas la télévision et ne lit pas de journal. Juste les gros titres. Pour Otto Normal, ce qui est actuel est important, tout le reste est sans importance. Arnold s'intéresse à la situation dans son ensemble, pas aux éphémères. De plus, vous ne savez jamais si les informations sont correctes. Si le titre devait dire: "Demain le monde se terminera!", M. Heitermann lirait certainement l'intégralité de l'information. Une telle fin du monde peut vraiment vous affecter, pour des raisons personnelles uniquement.

De l'eau

L'eau aime bouger. Si la nature le permet, elle coule. L'eau est fraîche et chante en soi. La lumière scintille avec les mouvements de ses vagues. L'eau est partout où il y a de la vie. L'eau est instable tant qu'elle n'est pas encore au fond. L'eau est humide, la nudité de l'eau reste intouchable.

Grenouilles

Vous ne devriez pas être une grenouille, pas une grenouille de peur. Quiconque est construit aussi près de l'eau que la grenouille vit dans l'âme. L'âme et le lac sont la même eau, le poisson et la grenouille le savent. Vous ne pouvez pas vraiment avoir peur dans l'eau, seuls les animaux secs le peuvent. Demandez au lapin effrayé! Pas la peur de la grenouille! Les grenouilles ne sortent jamais de la puberté. La grenouille est un poisson qui n'a pas atteint l'animal terrestre: un échec de l'évolution. Ce n'est plus du poisson, mais ce n'était pas suffisant non plus pour les singes. Les grenouilles sont encore vertes derrière les oreilles, et pas seulement là. Les grenouilles obtiennent souvent des boutons, mais elles sont alors appelées crapauds.

Sanglier

Les sangliers sautent du toit d'une maison dans la ville brumeuse de Rome. Les cochons sauvages se sont cognés le dos sur le trottoir en dessous. Le sanglier n'a rien cassé, il grogne vaguement et vit. Un tel sanglier est vraiment robuste. Votre sang ne se flétrit pas. À grands coups, leur jus de feu vibre intemporellement à travers la piste de course de leurs veines.

Sentiments

Les sentiments n'ont pas de couleur. Ce sont des clochards infidèles, leur seule prise est l'impermanence. Souhaitez-vous louer votre cœur aux sentiments? Les sensations sont bonnes pour la quantité et la masse, elles deviennent plus fortes et plus faibles, elles reviennent sans inspiration comme les chevaux sur le carrousel.

Doom

La largeur du monde s'enfonce dans la profondeur. Tout s'endort et la lune est dans le ciel. Sa lumière argentée coule dans le destin. Une main veut saisir la lune et le fait aussi: elle a écrasé la lune. Le sang d'argent, qui est également noir, descend d'une sphère qui était autrefois la lune. Le monde tremble.

tuer

La mort nie la vie et la rend également possible. Sur quoi devrait vivre l'aigle? Que devrait-il chier dans le dos? Il ne peut vivre qu'en tuant d'autres animaux. Comme l'homme! Les végétaliens sont de bonnes personnes. Mais eux aussi doivent suivre l'appel de la nature. Après tout, les plantes sont aussi des êtres vivants. Les végétaliens ont une carence en vitamines. Leur innocence les rend pâles au visage, ce sont des biovampires. Les végétaliens boivent le sang de la moralité. Le plus grand prédateur est l'homme.

Le téléspectateur mort

La télévision est allumée et il y a un squelette devant. Ses os de crâne vides ne sont plus au courant du programme. Quelqu'un éteint la télévision: l'homme osseux se rend compte maintenant qu'il manque quelque chose et se met en colère. Ce n'est que dans le retrait que la mort se rend compte qu'il est mort.

Le sens de la vie

Le but de la vie est de nourrir le grand économiste agricole. En tout cas, c'est l'avis du Dr Cerveau léger. Il croit ce qui suit: d'un ciel lointain, le grand économiste agricole sème les graines de notre âme dans le sol de la réalisation. Grâce à l'expérience de la vie, le germe de l'âme devient une oreille productive de l'âme. Le grand économiste agricole a récolté et consommé cette oreille après notre mort. Dr. Brainlight est le frère jumeau du Dr Cerveau léger. Chaque matin Dr. Brainlight jette après le muesli de grains entiers quand il pense à la théorie brute de son frère.

Soleil

Le soleil est le cœur du monde, il y a plus d'espace en lui que dans l'espace. Elle a un gros ventre brillant. Le soleil donne naissance au monde. Le soleil mange le monde. Les deux également. Le soleil est tout. C'est blanc avec les vieux, c'est jaune avec les jeunes. Le soleil n'a pas de rides sur le visage.

La rage

Un vampire se regarde dans le miroir: un homme aux cheveux noirs et aux lunettes regarde hors de l'argent, il a un visage pâle. Le vampire pense qu'elle ressemble à une personne normale dans le miroir. Les morts-vivants ne se reconnaissent que dans le miroir, cependant, s'ils regardent directement leurs mains et leur corps, ils ne voient personne. Ce n'est pas normal, même pas pour les vampires. Il a sûrement la rage.

Les plantes

Les plantes sont des animaux verts qui ne peuvent pas marcher. Ses feuilles sont des pierres d'eau. La lumière du soleil les rend complètement verts. La pierre, l'eau et le soleil donnent soudain vie. Une plante se compose principalement de croissance, elle profite de sa croissance. La croissance n'a pas de gènes, elle les connaît à chaque instant. Un plan ne se développe pas, même si vous le réalisez. Les plantes, en revanche, poussent au hasard de la vie.

dur

Certains crânes épais ont déjà frappé leurs têtes avec la dureté. La dureté offre résistance et durabilité. Un squelette est dur. Habituellement, le dur reste dur. Cependant, un pénis n'est dur qu'à certains moments. - Pourquoi seulement? - Le bord de dureté est une ligne imposante dans la pièce. Les bords ne doivent pas être négligés, vous pourriez vous frapper la tête dessus. Lorsque deux murs entrent en collision, la collision est appelée arête. Un bord est donc le résultat d'une carambole. Ce n'est donc pas pour les timides. Les pierres aussi sont dures. Une pierre est une chose, elle n'a pas de visage, car une pierre ressemble à d'autres pierres. Dans leur être, toutes choses sont pareilles. Placard, table ou brosse à dents ne sont que des choses. Les pierres qui se trouvent partout sont appelées réalité. Une pierre peut être utilisée pour marteler le crâne des autres. C'était important à l'âge de pierre. Aujourd'hui, certaines pierres peuvent parler, ces pierres sont appelées "téléphones portables". Si j'y pense correctement: il y a aussi de belles pierres, à savoir des pierres précieuses. Les dragons les récupèrent.

recueillir

Le collecté est dense, parfois étroit. Le collecté assure la sécurité comme une existence permanente. Ou c'est un fardeau. Il est plus difficile de collecter que de collecter. Si la collecte est plus difficile que ce qui est collecté, on parle de "chasse".

Déchets

Le superflu n'est pas intégré au cultivé. Le superflu n'a pas connu le superflu pendant sa croissance. Alors que le débordement peut être riche, il donne parfois, donc le superflu n'est pas seulement inutile, il entrave également la substance vivante dans sa progression. Le superflu n'est que des ordures.

Macke

Hugo a un problème. Sa bizarrerie est que la bizarrerie le dérange sur son écran. Cela rend Hugo fou. Hugo avait un défaut sur son visage depuis des décennies. Debout devant le miroir, il regarda sa bizarrerie jusqu'à ce que son dermatologue détourne le bouton. Hugo a une bizarrerie avec des bizarreries. Mais seulement pour des caprices individuels. Si tout a une bizarrerie, comme une fenêtre totalement rayée, cela ne dérange pas Hugo. Hugo a vraiment un problème.

Spinner

La pensée vide nourrit sa femme de neige fanée. La femme des neiges grises est appelée névrose. Elle est complètement inoffensive, c'est Woody Allen. Vous pouvez rire d'une névrose, parce que les cinglés sont des gens drôles. Mais la vieille neige n'est pas vraiment inoffensive. Aucun sang ne coule dans la femme des neiges, mais la neige d'hier s'y ennuie. La vieille neige entre en psychothérapie. Une telle thérapie est aussi une névrose, elle est blanche comme de la neige fraîche.

Thérapie de couple

Le chien et le chat suivent une thérapie de couple. Le thérapeute est une hyène. Le chien et le chat veulent sauver leur relation. La thérapie échoue. Pourquoi seulement? Qu'est-ce que ça peut être? Certainement sur le thérapeute, ils ont tous un problème eux-mêmes.

Pas d'humour

Cheplin se rend au sous-sol pour rire pour tenir compagnie à son corps. Il a dû tuer beaucoup de gens pour gagner de l'argent. La souffrance de ce monde et des femmes ne doit pas être négligée. Cheplin préconise une interdiction générale de l'humour pour toute l'Allemagne, à l'exception des soi-disant centres de rire, où les gens peuvent rire à haute voix après avoir payé des frais d'humour.

Rire

Le rire est content de ses lèvres. Le rire sérieux prend une crise de rire. Le rire humoristique ne peut s'élever du canapé de la bourgeoisie. Le vrai rire n'est pas drôle, il est juste heureux. Seules les blagues compulsives déchirent les blagues de l'arbre de la souffrance.

totalement drôle

Isolde: Detlef, vous ne savez jamais si vous plaisantez ou si vous êtes sérieux.

Detlef: C'est très simple: si je suis amusant, je suis sérieux et si je suis sérieux, c'est juste amusant.

Isolde: Comment puis-je différencier l'un de l'autre?

Detlef: Le premier est le cas les jours pairs et le dernier les jours impairs. Ou était-ce l'inverse? Je suis tout foiré.

Isolde: Je deviens fou avec le gars!

Le changement climatique

Otto pète.

Dr. Kackebart-Struller: Otto! Savez-vous réellement ce que vous faites à la couche d'ozone? Avec chaque pet restant non seulement votre trou du cul grossit, mais aussi le trou d'ozone. À chaque pet, le méthane s'écoule dans l'atmosphère, qui réchauffe la terre. Ne pète pas! Nous devons sauver notre environnement!

Otto Struller: Vous avez raison, Mausi, tout à fait raison. Je vais au grenier maintenant, en train de nourrir les pigeons.

dans la forêt sauvage

Dans la forêt sauvage, les racines des arbres quittent leur sol et traversent le pays. Le calme ne revient pas, mais part à l'aventure. Ça va au-dessus des montagnes, ça va dans les vallées. Parfois elle saute aussi.

rouler

Le roulement ou la rotation est le mouvement d'un rond autour de son centre. La roue est coincée. Le rouleau lui-même ne roule pas, il reste immobile par rapport à son centre. Si le roulement se déplaçait d'un cercle à un carré, il se déplacerait librement. Le vélo remarque seulement que le paysage passe devant lui, le vélo lui-même s'arrête.

Repos et exercice

Le calme jouit de son identité. On peut définir le repos comme l'absence de mouvement externe compulsif. Il n'y a donc pas de repos dans la discothèque. Pas sur l'autoroute non plus. Le mouvement de l'intérieur avec calme est tout à fait possible. L'existence a la paix. Il y a aussi le calme compulsif du bouddhisme zen. Un tel calme est cultivé la mort sur terre, il est basé sur la suppression et la mise à mort de l'agitation. Le vrai calme, cependant, vit en liberté.

voyou

Le colibri vole vers un palais amusant où les gens tournent. 52 personnes sans couronne vivent dans le palais. Personne et tout le monde est roi et fou en même temps. Les gens du palais sont tous hermaphrodites. Vous pouvez le faire vous-même si vous le souhaitez. Mais ils sont plus intéressés par la création de mondes de jeu: ils sont amusants. Le spoulage est un jeu sérieux. Ils plaisantent ici avec Jojos, les rois. Les rois jetaient leurs couronnes comme des idiots dans la grande salle sous la fontaine. Les couronnes servent de nid aux colibris. King Purple écrit un non-sens sérieux. Vous ne pouvez pas parler à un homme comme ça.

Travail

Le travail transpire dans leur no man's land, ce qui est épuisant, car au lieu d'une épine dorsale, le travail a une poitrine d'appréciation, décorée avec fierté. Votre épanouissement trouve du travail dans la crise cardiaque. Ceux qui travaillent peuvent vite oublier leur corps au sous-sol. Le travail aspire à la rédemption, mais elle ne l'admettrait jamais. Le travail est aveugle, il ne remarque pas qu'il fonctionne, il sait seulement. Le Christ Rédempteur est depuis longtemps absent. Les gens se rachètent par le travail: en psychothérapie, vous travaillez sur vous-même.

Le vrai mouvement est à l'intérieur. Un cheval se déplace, mais une voiture est entraînée par la puissance de son moteur. Le mouvement a tendance à se déplacer de manière serpentine, à savoir dans les vagues. Marcher, nager, voler ou conduire sont tous des mouvements. De nos jours, vous vous déplacez principalement. Vous pouvez également vous y déplacer. Mais personne ne peut le supporter sur place. Vous restez sur place.

Le vent

Le vent balaie le visage de Frigg. Le temps presse. L'eau disparaît dans le trou. Tout court, ça fuit. L'urine coule, les larmes coulent. Personne n'est avec Frigg, juste le vent. Ses pieds sont couverts de chaussures épaisses. Et si elle allait pieds nus? Alors le vent les porterait et Frigg serait libre. Ses chaussures lourdes sont le fardeau de son passé. Un vent appelé Wahuna traverse ses cheveux. Sleipnir, un cheval à huit pattes, glisse devant Frigga. Frigga est fascinée, elle peut être mise sur le cheval au dieu du vent et peut être portée librement, pieds nus, sans.

Mieux vaut une poire dans ta main

qu'un pommier sur le toit.

La machine fait le plus pur. Une machine ne ressent rien, alors elle fonctionne par pur désespoir. Il fait toutes les manipulations que les travailleurs brutaux faisaient autrefois. Poignées sans sensation ni vie, mécanique, mouvement sans sens, seul but. Comme c'est agréable quand une machine fait le travail stupide pour nous. Mais les créateurs des machines ont une fois planté la stupidité eux-mêmes. Les machines continueront de nous intimider de l'extérieur avec leur stupidité. L'intelligence artificielle est différenciée, mais elle reste stupide. Nous-mêmes ne sommes qu'un rouage de la grande machine mondiale.

Le propriétaire appelle ses mains les siennes. Les atomes de ses mains n'appartiennent pas au propriétaire. Les atomes dans sa main ne conviennent qu'à la forme de son ego prêté. Après la mort du propriétaire, les anciens atomes dans sa main conviennent à une autre apparence. Le propriétaire se sent chez lui dans sa main, il est enraciné dans sa main. Cette racine est son identité. Ce n'est pas la main elle-même.

La pomme folle

Dans la pomme, la peau et la pulpe cohabitent. Sont-ils tous les deux mariés? Beaucoup plus vit ensemble dans la pomme: la sphérique, la verte, la fruitée, sa pendaison à l'arbre. La pomme pense: `` J'ai des propriétés, mais je ne suis pas mes propriétés. Si je me regarde, je ne trouve que des propriétés, mais pas d'être. " La pomme se met en colère contre cette connaissance de soi: " Je plaisante! Je n'existe pas! " Chaque propriété de la pomme suit désormais sa propre voie. Le sphérique va au nord, le vert au sud. Le fruité à l'ouest, et la pendaison de la pomme à l'est. Ce n'est plus une pomme, elle n'a jamais existé. La pomme a divorcé de sa fausse identité. Il vient d'être expulsé de son That-Belongs-To-Me. Où est la fraîcheur de la pomme? Elle est assise dans le pub et peut être exécutée!

Poésie

La poésie signifie concentrer le sens sur son concentré. Cependant, la poésie de l'écrivain est parfois si scellée que le lecteur ne peut plus ouvrir la boîte de sens. Seul l'auteur comprend le contenu du poème pendant qu'il écrit. Et même la boîte de l'auteur est trop serrée le lendemain matin.

transparent

De toute évidence, ce qui est transparent vole librement sans avoir à se cacher. Les trous sont principalement transparents. Bien que la transparence puisse être lourde, elle n'est pas facile à voir à travers. Le transparent devient transparent quand il devient maladroit.

attraper

Attraper avec succès atteint sa proie tout en étant mobile. C'est pourquoi les poissons sont particulièrement pêchés. Ils sont glissants et vivent dans l'eau en mouvement, mais ils peuvent toujours être capturés.

Prison

Les crimes ne valent la peine que si vous ne vous faites pas prendre. Un singe vient au zoo même s'il n'a rien fait de mal. Un zoo est une véritable prison pour les animaux. Certains animaux sauvages sont emprisonnés dans le cirque. Les enfants sont en prison de la pédagogie de leurs parents. Les femmes sont incarcérées en raison de leur dépendance financière à l'égard de leur mari.

top secret

Le secret ne doit pas voir les yeux des autres. Il est assis seul (ou avec des conspirateurs) dans son bunker et peut y faire les choses suivantes: il se décompose, il festoie, il se réjouit, il tourne mal, il s'enflamme, il enflamme les autres, il se moque de vous, il a peur, elle se protège, elle refuse ou elle donne naissance à un enfant. Le secret: on ne sait pas ce que ça fait. Cela reste un secret.

voler

Le vol glisse à travers la mer de l'immensité sans pieds. En vol, le haut et le bas sont joués l'un contre l'autre. Un oiseau a du pouvoir sans violer le monde. C'est génial. Les crapauds, cependant, ne peuvent pas voler, leurs ailes sont enchantées. Les ailes des oiseaux s'étirent dans l'audace. Ils sont chez eux là-bas. Les ailes sont les bras du vol, elles sont de force. Un oiseau peut voler librement sans entrer en collision avec un chat en l'air. Un employé entre cependant très vite en collision avec son patron ou avec le sérieux de la vie.

facile

La lumière vole facilement au-dessus des énigmes, elle passe juste devant de gros ventres. La chose légère a tendance à se trouver en haut. Le bois flotte sur l'eau car il est plus léger que l'eau. La montgolfière flotte dans le ciel bleu. La lumière devient rapidement frivole. Quelque chose de stupide se produit facilement.

Flocon de neige

Un flocon de neige tombe doucement. C'est calme. Le flocon vient d'un autre monde. Il donne une structure à ce monde, sinon tous les champs magnétiques s'effondreraient. Aux pôles nord et sud, le champ magnétique tombe dans la neige. Depuis les pôles de la Terre, la neige organise des changements secrets dans le monde. Son magnétisme imprègne les habitants de la terre et en fait de lourds citoyens.

La protection

La protection est une bonne chose. La protection est la première chose dont vous avez besoin: protection constitutionnelle, protection des halls, produits de protection des cultures, protection des données et protection de la pensée. Vous n'avez pas encore reçu la visite de Mind Protection? Cela viendra, attendez.

Intestin

Digérer mâche et mâche et mâche. Digest mâche toujours plus fin jusqu'à ce que la nourriture soit si fine qu'elle puisse être intégrée dans votre propre viande. Cependant, la nourriture reste toujours un peu toxique. La terre est toxique. Ce n'est pas notre maison. Les animaux peuvent mieux digérer que les humains, ils vivent plus près de la terre.

La terre

Ce sur quoi nous nous tenons s'appelle la terre. Parfois, il est appelé étage. La position debout et la terre sont fermes. La terre peut également signifier de l'humus ou de la pierre. La substance de la terre est particulièrement frappante, elle est dense et lourde. Le sol est paisible, le sol est stupide. La grande grande mère n'a pas de visage. At-elle de la chaleur? Les racines atteignent la terre, elles comprennent aussi la terre. Les racines ne font qu'un avec le calme de la terre.

Les abeilles

Les abeilles vivent dans l'épaisseur de la matière, intérieurement. Une abeille sort dehors où il fait froid. Il tombe mort au sol comme un flocon de neige. Les abeilles ont exprimé leur intériorité sous forme de flocons froids. Tant que le flocon de neige est gelé, c'est l'heure de l'arbre de Noël. Si le flocon dégèle, la solitude est nue. En avalant le nectar, les abeilles relient toutes les parties du monde et maîtrisent la gravité, elles mâchent la gravité. Le nectar était un livre qui n'avait pas encore été lu. Pas même par son auteur.

Lourdeur

La lourdeur est généralement importante. En tête, cependant, la lourdeur est faible. Pouvoirs lourds. Il n'a d'effet que par sa masse, pas par sa couleur, car la lourdeur est beaucoup trop sombre pour être colorée. La lourdeur ne comprend pas le drôle. Ce n'est que dans le sucre que le drôle et le lourd peuvent dormir ensemble. La gravité vient-elle d'en haut ou d'en bas? Lorsque la chaleur devient plus forte, elle devient la gravité. Et la pierre que tu ne peux pas rouler? Est-il trop lourd ou trop ferme? C'est trop brutal! La lourdeur est plus douce que la brutale. Est-ce que c'est facile alors? C'est comme ça!

Le vent

Le vent coule désincarné sur les arbres et les maisons. La force du vent n'est pas visible, seuls ses effets sont visibles. Le vent emporte le stock. Un pissenlit souffle dans le vent, les cendres pareillement. Le vent est très éphémère. Mais ça souffle toujours.

Des fissures dans le cerveau

La propriété est unique. C'est particulier à son truc. La quantité est relative, elle est toujours mesurée à partir de la comparaison. La quantité n'a pas de propriétaire. Isolde a un gros ventre, mais elle ne possède pas la graisse. Tout ce qui est superflu a beaucoup. Peu importe le nombre de fissures dans le cerveau d'Einstein. C'est la caractéristique du cerveau qui le rend unique, pas le nombre de ses fissures. Vous ne pouvez pas comparer des pommes et des poires, juste leur poids.

Sable

Les fragments des pierres sont appelés sable. Les fragments de sable sont si petits qu'ils forment à nouveau une unité en tant que communauté d'isolés. Le sable est ensuite ressenti dans son ensemble. Le tout pleure, mais le sable ne peut pas pleurer car il est trop sec. Les pierres n'ont ni sang ni eau, pas même sous forme de sable. Les larmes de géants tristes font don d'eau salée comme la mer. C'est pourquoi le sable se trouve souvent comme une plage où il y a de la mer.

Les gens

Les gens n'existent qu'au pluriel. Une personne ne peut pas être seule. L'homme en tant qu'animal de troupeau devient un «peuple». Une foule se compose de personnes. Le sang du peuple est le sang de son clan. Une personne, en revanche, a sa propre circulation sanguine. Avec les vieux juifs, le sang d'Abraham coule jusqu'à ses défunts petits-fils. Les gens et les peuples archaïques ont leur identité dans le groupe, pas en eux-mêmes.

Babylone

Babylone n'était pas un bébé: elle était trop grande pour les plus grands. Il y a aussi des gratte-ciel à New York. Mais ceux-ci doivent être détruits par les terroristes parce qu'ils veulent rayer Dieu. Vous dansez autour du veau d'or, de la croissance économique et du chirurgien esthétique. Quand la colère de Dieu viendra-t-elle enfin et balaiera-t-elle les pécheurs dans la poubelle?

les plus petites particules

Fred a obtenu un accès non autorisé au grand accélérateur de particules près de Genève la nuit et rampe maintenant dans l'anneau rond: il voit des particules vertes brillantes passer.

Fred: Bonjour les particules, pouvez-vous aussi parler?

Particule verte: j'ai mal à la tête, ce qui est grave car je ne suis qu'une tête. Depuis que les physiciens m'ont découvert, je ne peux plus vraiment tisser le monde. Même la politique échappe à tout contrôle.

Une particule rouge vole au-delà: elle sort sa langue, qui est encore plus rouge que la particule elle-même.

particule rouge: j'allume l'argent sous mon cul. Généralement, l'argent n'est qu'une information. Mon feu donne de la valeur à l'information. Un triangle vole, il a l'œil sur le front.

Triangle: Je suis la plus grosse particule qui soit. De très petites particules n'existent que dans l'enfer de la physique. Le petit n'a pas de réalité. Plus les choses deviennent complètes, plus elles deviennent réelles. - Fred est juste étonné.

Le chaos est une confusion que les extraterrestres créatifs utilisent pour sortir de la protection de l'esprit dans le monde sans arrêt. Le chaos est coloré. Le chaos enlève les déchets du passé. Le chaos danse et je ne sais pas pourquoi.

écrire

266

Par écrit, la langue parle silencieusement dans le son, mais brillante dans la conscience. Les écrivains sont les sculpteurs de la certitude. L'écriture est toujours écrite, même pendant l'écriture. L'écriture est finale et dure plus longtemps qu'un bon vin. Le mot s'écrit à tout moment.

danse

Danser, c'est audacieux. Quiconque danse est fou. La danse peut aussi être cool si vous êtes une personne téméraire. Les penseurs ne devraient pas danser. La danse brise sa clarté d'esprit. Désespérée par manque de nourriture d'amour, la folie comme un tigre mange l'ordre corrompu du mal: Sweet Miezi fait Fressi-Fressi!

Erwin

Des gouttes de larmes tombent du ciel. Ils se rassemblent sur terre pour former un ruisseau qui se gonfle dans une rivière. Erwin est assis dans un canoë et pagaie à travers la larme. La rivière coule en montée. Des incendies brûlent en l'honneur de Wotan sur la rive droite de la rivière. Sur la rive gauche, un arbre avec un oiseau en pierre est assis dessus. Erwin continue de pagayer en montée dans un canot. Maintenant, il neige. Le canoéiste voit un bonhomme de neige sur la rive entre les aiguilles de pin. Les yeux du bonhomme de neige sont vivants, ce sont les yeux d'un puissant ours en peluche. Erwin continue de remonter la rivière. Quelqu'un à gauche joue de la harpe. Dieu est proche.

Volcan

Une femme en noir avec des éclats colorés se bat avec le cool. Ils volent ensemble au-dessus des étoiles, sous les étoiles, entre les étoiles. La vie du Titanic apparaît dans son naufrage. Un bateau pliant en papier flotte nonchalamment dans l'eau, il dérive prudemment vers une source d'eau de marais: Peng! La cendre tombe d'en haut. L'Eyjafjallajökull a finalement éclaté.

en forme

Au contraire, l'ajustement peut être trouvé comme l'amour. Comme élément connexe, Fit complète l'un et l'autre avec un service similaire. Tout s'intègre dans une seule structure. La bière, les cigarettes et les cendriers sont sur la table de la cuisine de M. Alki. Cela a du sens, ça va. La table de cuisine de M. Alki est une structure. Hinz et Kunz sont ensemble dans le grand catalogue mondial sur Internet. Hinz et Kunz ne sont liés que par leur simple existence. Internet n'est pas une structure, mais un non-sens.

Chose

Une chose est grise dans son être; ce n'est rien de plus. Les choses sont impersonnelles. La machine du monde sans visage régit la terre: l'Internet des objets. Les choses s'accumulent dans le monde. Satan a longtemps eu le monde entre ses griffes. On ne parle pas des êtres vivants parce qu'ils se déplacent. Cependant, un jeune peut se déplacer. C'est une chose.

Mesurer

Une mesure peut être la bonne, préparée avec amour par des dieux amis. En tant qu'enseignant, une mesure malade fixe des limites au pouvoir de l'élève. L'élève est alors plein, sa vie est en retard et l'industrie peut produire de l'électricité à partir du barrage.

tout

Tout cela est un ajout de beaucoup de choses à la limite de l'agitation. Est-ce tout cela maintenant? Le tout est au moins rond. Comme prévu, le tout devrait briller sur son bord, mais il y reste gris. Alors le prêtre industriel dit: "Le tout est plus que la somme de ses parties!" Même après cette phrase, tout ne brille pas, il n'y a plus rien à voir. L'ensemble reste l'addition nue de tout. Il n'y en a qu'un de plus dans ce livre.

Rien

Le néant est le monde de toutes les non-choses. Une tasse n'est pas une chaise. Une robe n'est pas un nuage. Sans parler du chien: un chien n'est pas un chat comme un moineau. Toutes les non-choses se réunissent dans le monde de rien. Certains disent que rien ne vient après la mort. Voulez-vous y vivre parmi toutes les non-choses? Ce sera assez serré dans le placard des non-choses.

Plaisir

Le plaisir a besoin de plus que ce qui est nécessaire. Le plaisir est donc lié au bonheur. Mais si le bonheur est un don de vie, la jouissance est arbitraire. Le plaisir persiste et reste. Le plaisir est gras. Le plaisir est la luxure qui a trop mangé. Le plaisir ne pense pas, le plaisir est trop lent pour cela. Quand les intestins digèrent plus qu'il n'en a besoin, il est content. La satisfaction est un édulcorant, mais le sucre est le bonheur.

Психозавр представляет себя:

Я думаю поэтично и не стал жертвой биофанта. Эти инопланетные фанты нелегально входят из космоса в темноту и используют свой длинный хоботок, чтобы высосать фантазии сонных людей из их мозга. Я только неохотно использую слова, которые уже говорили другие. Я нахожу это антисанитарным. Вот почему я часто придумываю новые слова, что создает проблему, которую никто меня больше не понимает. Следовательно, я должен снова использовать использованные слова, которые немецкий язык произнес только неточно. Язык может говорить, потому что он содержит общие образы существования. Главное в языке - дать картинам мира дом. Трагично, когда человек следует словам языка и думает, что это мышление. Реальное мышление активно формирует язык. Язык - это я психозавра, это его центр. Мир действительно оживает на языке, потому что говорение означает: создать мир. В начале было слово!

Scaredy кошка

Страшный кролик на пути к тому, чтобы стать пасхальным кроликом. По дороге он хотел навестить своего дядю, но он снова в перце. Испуганный кролик не лягушка, он смотрит на обезьяну, даже если обезьяна смеется над ней. Вошь перебирает печень блох. Заяц слышит этот кашель от блох, который теперь стреляет пушками по воробьям. Испуганный кролик преодолевает своего внутреннего ублюдка и затем превращает блох в улитку. Слева он видит осла, который слишком удобен. Осел выходит на лед в середине лета. Это не работает на коровьей шкуре, и цыплята смеются над ослом. С правой стороны, серая мышь получает бабочки, потому что лось чмокает их. Комары в воздухе безвредны сами по себе, если они не становятся слонами и ведут себя как они в магазине фарфора. Мистер Шпехт бежит как кролик и вынимает своего поитого пуделя, чтобы он не сходил с ума на сковороде. Мистер и собака, вероятно, имеют птицу, но после них нет ворон петуха, потому что это в корзине с его курами. На своем пути испуганный кролик находит зуб обезьяны, который больше не вредит мухе. Теперь испуганный сделал это, он прибыл к пасхальному кролику.

разговор

Крот: Скажи Психозавр, о чем эта книга?

Психозавр: В этой книге язык говорит сам по себе. И есть язык

говорит обо всем, поэтому в этой книге есть все темы.

Утка: личный вопрос: в чем разница

Психозавр и Карстен?

Психозавр: я не хочу об этом говорить

тема полностью меня напрягает.

Утка: Это согнуто, чувак!

Моль: Эта книга, очевидно, одна

автоматический перевод?

Психозавр: Так и есть. Это увеличивает причуды сверх всякой меры.

Язык говорит более тысячи слов.

Хихикать: Если я хочу написать Карстену, у него тоже есть

Онлайн или что-то?

Психозавр: На данный момент у него есть адрес электронной почты

carsten-stemm@web.de и у него тоже есть свой онлайн.

Оборотень: повторяйся!

Хихиканье: я не понимаю ни слова, даже вокзал.

Рабе: Вам не нужно все понимать. Иногда этого достаточно, чтобы слова пронесли вас через иррациональное.

Детлеф двойной дуоид

Детлеф Доппелдоид не может правильно мыслить обеими половинками мозга. Детлеф думает быстрее света, что приводит к пространственно-временным набуханиям в его логосфере. Затем он меняет право с левым, с с, и брутто с сеткой. Он не знает, входите вы или выходите из комнаты. Это плохо о Детлефе Доппелдоиде: на днях он думал, что люди были людьми. Детлеф также не может вспомнить разницу между Альбертом Эйнштейном и Конрадом Аденауэром. Детлеф задается вопросом: «Не одно и то же» и «одно и то же»? Иногда мистер Доппелдоид также делает орфографические ошибки. Если он полностью смущен, Детлеф даже вспоминает будущее.

Детлеф говорит:

«Когда я больше не знаю, кто я, я смотрю на свое удостоверение личности: у меня там тоже есть свой номер; номер, только для меня, только для меня. Уникальный и безошибочный. Государство любит меня. Но поможет ли это мне? Кто стоит за именем Детлеф Доппелдоид? А что доказывает маленькая пластиковая карточка? Пластиковые карты легко подделать. Вы можете подделать все сегодня. Вы даже можете подделать личность. Я становлюсь довольно цветочным.

Говорящий кролик

Кролик, который умеет говорить, называется говорящим кроликом. Говорящий кролик ест во время разговора и говорит, покусывая. Корни слова не известны ему. В настоящее время он поглощает любовь. Любовь - это просто слово для него, магг, мамп. Вы можете есть любовь без еды, это мудрость зайца.

Есть утки!

Биолог интересуется перьями уток, онтолог интересуется существом уток. Кто дает уток? Ответ: «это». «Это» и дает результат в бытии. Кроме того, на вопрос можно ответить следующим образом: эволюция дает уток, утиные яйца дают уток, утиный секс дает уток, Бог дает уток. Идет дождь. На самом деле нужно сказать: облако идет дождь. Это «это» даже не зависит от Бога, потому что это означает: Бог есть. Это, в свою очередь, означает: «Это» больше, чем Бог. Другой вывод: «Это» -

это настоящий Бог, который первым дает Бога. Есть утки. Один не говорит: это требует уток. Дарить счастливее, чем брать. Давать, вероятно, более онтологически, чем принимать. «Это» настолько неясно, что вы больше не можете видеть его туман. В результате вы больше не думаете о том, откуда на самом деле происходят утки. «Это» обманчиво. Это притворяется знанием. Если мы больше не знаем, что облако идет дождь,

тогда идет дождь. Отрицание также дает «это»: «Elwittitsche не существует!» «Кто может быть только этим« этим », кто может дать этих не уток?

Гольдмари и Печмари

Когда-то был мотивационный тренер, у которого было две дочери, обе из которых были названы Мари. Один был трудолюбивым, другой ленивым. Однажды трудолюбивая женщина подошла к колодцу, который сказал:

«Нет питьевой воды!»

«Это только по юридическим причинам», - подумала жаждущая женщина. Девушка выпила из воды и случайно упала в фонтан, в результате чего она потеряла сознание. В какой-то момент она проснулась в совершенно неизвестном месте.

Пожилая женщина стояла у окна дома, нуждающегося в ремонте, и стряхнула подушку. Мисс Холл, вот как назывался арендатор, сказала девушке: «Компетентные медсестры для пожилых людей, таких как вы, сегодня редки, для меня много работы». И поскольку трудолюбивая женщина так увлекалась работой, она занималась уборкой дома для мисс Холл.

Однако через некоторое время девушка стала тосковать по дому и выразила желание вернуться домой. Фрау Холле дала ей это желание. Старуха привела девушку к воротам, через которые она должна была пройти. Когда трудолюбивая женщина проходила через ворота, с нее сверху шел дождь, загрязненная диоксином смола, которая больше не стекала с ее кожи. Девушка сказала: «Черт возьми! Я горько отомщу за судьбу. Я изучаю математику и докторантуру по теории парадоксов.

Когда мать увидела, что ее дочь испачкана смолой, она позвала своего ребенка Печмари. По соображениям социальной компенсации мать теперь также отправила свою ленивую дочь в колодец. Это случилось почти так же. Только ее вторая дочь пришла в другой дом, в котором жила некая фрау Холле, а не фрау Холлес Хаус.

После десяти минут работы дисциплина работы ленивой девушки значительно ослабла. Миссис Хелл сказала: «В твоем возрасте я тоже была довольно ленива. У меня даже нет сертификата об окончании средней школы. Сейчас мы бежим к замку Мутон-Ротшильд 1945 года, который украл сам мой зять.

К счастью, весь погреб полон ».« После недельного пьянства ленивый тоже тосковал по дому и хотел остаться дома. Фрау Хёлле привела ее к тем же воротам, через которые проходила Печмари. Когда ленивая девушка прошла через ворота, на нее шел золотой дождь. Теперь девушка была намного более ценной, потому что золото также не могло быть удалено. Когда она вернулась домой, ее звали ее матерью Голдмари. Из-за гнева из-за несправедливости жизни мать ушла из церкви и пошла на светский суд. Позже Печмари стала первым профессором логики с диоксиновыми шрамами на лице. Ее жизнь была полностью неудачной. Голдмари, однако, жил долго и счастливо. > Счастливый конец

Сыр овечий

Шепард: Скажите, какую книгу вы носите под мышкой?

Вольфганг: Одна из ваших овец дала мне книгу на мой день рождения. Его название: «Сделай овечий сыр сам!»

Шепард: Это должно быть шутка?

Вольфганг: С шутками нельзя шутить. Я никогда не шучу. Тот, кто шутит, слишком труслив, чтобы быть серьезным. Я никогда не шутил. И если кто-нибудь рассмеется, я хлопну по заднице.

Овца: Извините, если я вмешиваюсь, но я генетически изменен, поэтому я могу говорить. Скоро будет введен новый налог на овечий сыр?

другая овца: я тоже генетически улучшенный продукт создателя, и я говорю вам: мужчины похожи на женщин, только наоборот.

Вольфганг: Я всегда думал, что это будет по-другому!

Шепард: У меня кружится голова от таких сложных разговоров. .. Ах, смотри, кто идет! Он хромает!

Вольфганг: Тогда это может быть только сравнение!

Шепард: Почему это?

Вольфганг: Потому что вы всегда говорите: каждое сравнение отстает!

стриженая овца: значение всегда неоднозначно. Поэтому говорящий быстро обещает себя в своей речи. Двойной немец - это Lapsus Freudianikus, утечка в чересчур плавном изображении.

Вольфганг: Что это за болтун?

Пастух: овцы учились. Психолингвистика или что-то.

(Сейчас хромает в дискуссионной группе.)

Хромая: ты за мной. Моя украденная профессия

Плутоний с российских АЭС взорван!

Пастух: Не делай ничего, Отто!

Овцы: вы можете есть плутоний?

Пастух: Не все овцы учились!

все овцы вместе: Mähhhh!

Отто: У меня есть только один выход: самоубийство!

Вольфганг: У меня был бы альтернативный выход. Я знаю хорошего мага в цирке. Он страдает от аллергии, но технически он в порядке.

Отто: Кто этот маг?

Вольфганг: Он - все, о чем ты думаешь, потому что у него много

Планеты в седьмом доме, в том числе Плутон.

Отто: я не верю в астрологию!

Вольфганг: Но звезды верят в тебя!

Отто: Хорошо, я хочу попробовать, потому что мне нечего терять. Я очарован кроликом и пишу свое имя задом наперед, чтобы никто не узнал меня.

Шепард: отличная вещь! Теперь это действительно счастливый конец!

В экстренной ситуации яблоко ест груши.

убийство

Обезьяна: Добрый день, странный глаз, у тебя косые глаза.

Странный глаз: А ты обезьяна, ты обезьяна.

Обезьяна: у меня здесь динамитная шашка.

Кому мы их в задницу положим?

Странный глаз: конечно! В TNT я не говорю нет!

Вы блестящая обезьяна, вы заслуживаете Нобелевскую премию!

(Обезьяна толкает наклон в задницу динамита и зажигает взрыватель. После нервных секунд ожидания происходит сильная детонация: пыль, осколки и остатки мяса покрывают место взрыва.)

Обезьяна: круто! Это разбилось!

Для нас, животных, нет никаких подсчетов или абзацев.

Теперь мы собираемся съесть банан. Ха-ха!

Стальной цыпленок

Когда-то здесь была маленькая скрипучая машина, которая проезжает по пухлой и мягкой природе. Фургон движется, его тянет лошадь. Автомобиль, который больше не ездит сегодня. Когда спутник начал приводиться в движение мотором, тележка стала стальной, когда тележку все еще тянули, цветы расцвели, и вода устремилась к нему. Секрет жизни жил в мельничном колесе, здесь колесо врезалось в воду. Автомобиль был рождением стальной девочки. Небо простирается, небо простирается, он взволнован. Стальной цыпленок стреляет в небо с помощью защитной пушки. Это Вторая мировая война, бессмысленная попытка стали снова стать лошадью. Стальная цыпочка теперь сама лошадь, поэтому она носит хвост. Лошади действительно изящны, поскольку элегантность больше не известна в век стали. Пластик тоже сталь. Все, что не тянет лошадь - это сталь. Вы получаете страх от красоты, которая не кукла моды.

больше пространства

Многокомнатный номер - это комната, которая больше внутри, чем снаружи. Например, мульти-шкаф выглядит как обычный шкаф для спальни. Но если вам придется при необходимости прятаться в шкафу, вы будете удивлены, обнаружив, что в шкафу есть целые галактики. И это не галлюцинации из-за недостатка кислорода. Мир полон дыр в реальности. И их становится все больше и больше.

опасность

Опасность угрожает вам. Авария еще не произошла. Но это может ударить в будущем; это риск. Жизнь небезопасна. Вы не знаете, будет ли жизнь сломана в следующий момент. Опасность у двери, опасность непредсказуема, это может стать кошмаром. Хищники опасны; Капиталисты тоже. Опасно прокладывать силовые кабели в ванне с водой. Жениться тоже рискованно. Страхование жизни, с другой стороны, обещает защиту: если вы потеряли жизнь, вы получите новую. Но остерегайтесь страхового мошенничества: страховые компании обманывают много!

думать

Мышление бродит по земле смысла. Пути мышления натыкаются на лес знаний. Благодаря его походу мышление становится более трудным и, наконец, сливается с деревьями его мыслей и снегом его мечты.

Олимп

Фред видит бога на сотовом телефоне на Олимпе:

Фред: Привет, Боже!

Как долго боги используют мобильный телефон?

Бог: да, мэй, ты просто поправляйся. Я также мог бы телепатически общаться со своими коллегами, но мы, боги, хотим, чтобы людям было понятно.

Фред: Значит, я этого не понимаю!

Яичные головы

Мозговые дрочки - это кролики с пневматической аггляцией. Их также называют головами яйца. Ваши нейроланты не очень гибкие, но они очень длинные. Выбрасывайте голые грецкие орехи в их лысые головы, потому что они содержат много воска для мозга. Нейроланты - это стержни ума. Нейролантами также могут быть стволы деревьев, через которые вы больше не можете видеть лес за их огромным количеством. Но на самом деле Neurolanten - это палочки для еды для интеллектуальных суши.

Некоторые мозговые волны называются философами. Философия мыслит без питья, это свет без любви. Мыслитель может плохо шутить в пустыне знаний. Кактусы никогда не смеются. Философия такая же твердая, как старый сыр. Философы на пути к исцелению начинают писать стихи.

полубог

Фред: Вы знаете, что такое Детлеф, меня повысили до полубога.

Детлеф: Действительно?

Фред: Это так! Теперь я могу найти ответ на каждый вопрос, хотя бы неточно, но я могу найти ответ.

Детлеф: Кто тебя продвинул?

Фред: большой босс!

Детлеф: Ага!

Фред: Я просто полубог. Я еще не бессмертен, но я работаю над этим.

Детлеф: Мм, сделай это.

Фред: Я наконец знаю, например, почему банан изогнут.

Детлеф: Да, почему тогда?

Фред: Она жаждет единства, банан хочет вернуться в рай, она хотела бы быть кругом, но Падение запрещает ей, только ее сила распространяется на изгиб.

Детлеф: Что знает полубог!

дух

Термин «дух» - очень одинокое слово. Слово должно объяснить так много вещей. Интеллект рубит камни; разум соединяется. Дух освещает части света как солнце и придает им форму. Ум - это образ вещей. Разум одевает мельчайшие частицы с большим. Ум может думать, разум может только думать или объединяться.

Причина и следствие

Бильярдист бьет по мячу своей палкой, которая, в свою очередь, бьет по другому. Это причинно-следственное мышление является оригинальной логикой науки. Логика это оправдывает, она ничего не объясняет. Свободная воля бильярдиста полностью скрыта в этом мировоззрении. Причины - скучные животные, почти быки. Причины убеждают через энергию, а не через смысл.

логика

Фред: я верю в логику. Весь космос логически структурирован. Однако женщины не являются частью космоса. Логическое мышление дает вам доступ к каждой головоломке. Вы просто должны приложить много усилий к размышлению.

Арнольд Хайтерманн: Логика не продвигает нас в знании. Пример: три вороны сидят на заборе. Подходит убийца птиц и стреляет в одну из птиц.

Арнольд: Сколько птиц до сих пор на заборе?

Фред: На заборе две вороны.

Арнольд: Неверно! На заборе все еще есть ворона!

Фред: Это совершенно нелогично!

Арнольд: Это логично. Выстрел птицы упал замертво на землю. Вторая ворона была поражена громким взрывом и немедленно улетела. Третья ворона была в ужасе от удара и остается единственной сидящей птицей.

Фред: Этот случай мне кажется очень сконструированным, но он логичен.

Арнольд: Ну, вы можете объяснить все и ничего с помощью логики.

Фред: Прежде всего, потом.

Арнольд: Да, всегда потом.

Однако реальность была там раньше.

Фред: Что, если пять ворон внезапно сели на забор после выстрела?

Арнольд: Тогда бы несколько уставших от жизни ворон сидели бы в надежде быть застреленными.

Фред: Действительно здорово, что логично.

Арнольд: Вы можете объяснить все с помощью логики, даже нелогичного.

Фред: Чувак, я действительно должен подумать об этом.

Арнольд: Но, пожалуйста, оставайтесь строго логичными!

Фред: Э-э ... да ... хорошо ...

диалог

Сократ: Как ты выглядишь снова как дерьмо этим утром, Платон!

Платон: Заткнись, задница!

Сократ: Вы просто не в состоянии диалога!

мяч

Пуля ужасно сжата сама по себе, у нее было бы желание родить, если бы она была зажжена. Но никто не зажигает их. Мяч остается тупым, как грязь, и не знает друг друга. Почему шары катятся? Они катятся, но не меняют свою форму. В конечном счете, они перевернуты движением. Пуля остается пулей. Теперь я помню: пули женские!

(в) идеально

Собака сама по себе является идеей собаки. Выглядит ли идея собаки теперь такса, золотистый ретривер, овчарка или даже пудель? Мы знаем, как выглядит сам круг. Есть только один круг, и он полностью круглый. Треугольники уже усложняют: какой угол имеет идея треугольника? Круг - единственная идея, которую можно нарисовать точно. Сама собака не может быть нарисована, только конкретная собака. Сам круг можно нарисовать. Должны ли мы поклоняться кругу? Есть ли "в себе"? Вещи появляются только «для меня»? - Идеальное в реальности было бы слишком несовершенным для жизни. Для жизни нужен угол в круге или дыра в квадрате. Идеальное существует только как идея, потому что в действительности идеальное не может существовать. Круг имеет углы в совершенстве жизни. Каштан - это угловой шар. Несовершенное совершенство несет в себе совершенную жизнь. Тем не менее, каштан почему-то болен. Почему? Это знает только ежик!

круг

Круг не может дышать. Нигде у него нет дыры, через которую он мог дышать. Сам круг можно рассматривать как дыру. Является ли круг воротами в другой мир? Я не могу это проверить, потому что круг не пускает меня. Это просто слишком закрыто. Не следует иметь дело с такими типами. Круг не говорит со мной, он всегда будет оставаться загадочным. Кругу, вероятно, даже нечего скрывать: он наивен, скучен и пуст. - Раунд это цвет круга. Этот цвет очень редкий и не имеет названия. Самый простой способ назвать цвет «красочным». Раунд может отправиться в приключение без круга и дуги. Сама жизнь - это приключение. Сегодня группа думает что-то новое. Но раунд настолько стар, что его размышления о новом никогда не приведут к безумию. Однако филистимляне никогда не бродят вокруг. Это слишком ухабисто для этого. Группа хотела стать кружком и попросила агентство по трудоустройству пройти переподготовку. Клерк был квадратным. Это плохо кончилось.

Яблоко думает и груша направляет.

Удар это здорово

Ударение - самый универсальный глагол, который есть. Удар действительно потрясающий. Эта деятельность была полностью разработана в каменном веке. Вы можете открыть глаза, как книгу. Посмотрите в пижоне, разбейте окно или ударите кого-нибудь по лицу. Музыканты шумят на барабанах. Удар бьет тебя. Мениск 1.FC бьет плоские ноги Розенхайма 2-1. Тот, кто бьет, побеждает. Лучший способ ударить - это камни. Благородный камень называется молотком. Удар сырой и грубый. Удар бессмысленный и атомный. Удары разбиваются, ломаются, удары отделяются. Дитя удара рубит. Плохой ребенок Другой ребенок удара - это толчок. Этот ребенок более симпатичен, потому что у него больше солнца впереди. Избиение делает кулак, поэтому его действия получают живот.

завод сокровище

Произведение искусства - это отложение всего предельного человеческого опыта. Есть опыт, который был подтвержден, так что он превращается в произведение искусства. Трудовое сокровище ориентирует всех существ как магнитное поле из духовного. Werkschatz - это естественная Википедия жизни. К сожалению, в сокровищнице знаний есть и паршивые овцы: их называют фабричной грязью.

Для царя Ортоса править означает упорядочивать вещи в соответствии с их собственной внутренней сущностью. Ортос не передает свою волю людям. Король не хочет форсировать события, но исследует их особенности и позволяет им самим их устраивать. Люди, козы и другие существа живут в Ортос Рейхе, все стоят и ходят в нужном месте. После его смерти король Ортос будет течь в воду своей любимой реки, которая в конечном итоге выльется в море. С моря его работа продолжит ориентировать людей.

Голод и жажда

Голод хочет все время что-нибудь съесть. Голод полностью зависит от объекта его желания. Но именно это делает голод таким приятным. Он полон жизни, некоторые даже говорят, что он есть сама жизнь. У голода также есть сестра: ее зовут "жажда". Но это только для очень сумасшедших типов.

Нужна абстракция голода и жажды. Нужда бедна и нуждается. Потребность очень светская и всегда выглядит одинаково серой. Вы можете хранить свои потребности при любой температуре. Потребность никогда не приносит плодов, она всегда остается скудной. Если вам что-то нужно, вы ходите по магазинам.

Кому нужно волокно? Прежде всего, если они состоят только из балласта. Бремя наполнителей. Они заполняют пустоту, но сами остаются пустыми. Это сущность, которая сияет.

Психозавр полностью в конце:

Ледяная сила как фигура подняла руку. Лестница из воды скатывается с холодного лица. Глаза теневой женщины сияют, как два солнца ночью. Недолго Ваши огни теперь погасли. Теневая женщина летит в небо как черный ангел. Неизвестное место осиротело. Там, где никогда не было никого, сейчас никого нет. Мое знание небытия находится рядом с пустым пространством. Мне тепло, но только как тепло, потому что у меня нет другого тела. Крик без языка отчаянно ходит в пустой комнате. Везде только пустота, где что-то должно быть. Там, где ничего нет, вы ничего не видите, особенно если у вас нет глаз. Но я вижу ужас и не знаю почему.

отверстие

Отверстие означает довольно круглое отсутствие. Отверстия пусты. Яма часто является проходом, который входит и выходит. Иногда вид выходит через отверстие, а вид входит через отверстие. Дырки голодные, их хочется набить. Стремление всего существа хорошо быть удовлетворенным. У реальности есть дыры. Они настолько прозрачны, что их никто не видит, даже физик с его великолепным аппаратом. Отсутствие одежды можно увидеть у голых людей. Отсутствие разрыва, с другой стороны, остается голодным и невидимым. Поверхность имеет тенденцию быть пустой. Если эта пустота заполнена, поверхность быстро исчезает, она становится тонкой. Эстет предписывает цвет поверхности, чтобы он стал более уверенным в себе.

животное

У классического животного четыре ноги, оно «мяукает» или лает. Термин «животное» является типичным случаем для многих существ, которые имеют мало общего. Животные не несут листья и не могут создавать атомные бомбы. Животные отсталые люди. Однако однажды животные также поймут теорему Гёделя о неполноте. - Только когда?

Природа может быть грубой и грубой. Существует также природа мечтателей: эта природа является раем людей еще до падения. Природа германского Чарльза Дарвина выглядит так: борьба сильных против еще более сильных. Наша вторая натура это культура. Наше третье царство называется искусственностью. Никто не любит там жить.

Ледяной цветок

Иностранная держава из Швеции сделана из самого холодного льда. Эта сила приходит на землю в виде старой девочки по имени Эйсблюм. Цветок из льда, красивый цветок. Цветы напоминают весну, потому что в это время свежие цветы обычно распускаются в молодом тепле. Тем не менее, наш ледяной цветок цветет в смертоносном холоде зимы. Все другие люди, которые также сделаны из льда, восхищены цветком льда. Агнис тоже из холода, из горящего льда. Агнис видит ледяной цветок и взволнован. Фригиды всегда самые горячие. Мистер

Шампфштейн - продавец мороженого. Его шарики с мороженым содержат взрывчатку, которая загорается, когда он над всеми горами. Эйсблюм видит мистера Сампфштейна: она получает удар, шарик рулетки катится в ее голове. Никто не знает, что мяч остановится в купе семнадцати. В Агнисе это будет три. Ледяные шарики или шарики рулетки, шарики все одинаковые. Пули - плохой берег судьбы. И теперь мы врываемся в этот банк и освобождаем безумие. Все сходят с ума: Eisblume, Agnis и Herr Sumpfstein находятся в одной коробке. Вы дышите безумием: Ах, это хорошо. Наконец-то они бесплатны!

кровь

Кровь течет внутрь как густая и мощная жара. Человеческая кровь очень личная, пока она все еще кружит в своих жилах. Кровь кружит, значит, круглая. Кровавые силы в его кругу. Наружная кровь в холодном и бессердечном врачебном шприце уже мертва. Как ужасно! Только рептилии кровоточат холодно. Если солнце не светит на зеленый мех рептилии. Каждый вампир знает: когда светит луна, кровь черная. Вы ничего не видите в течение дня.

огонь

Огонь танцует с сильным пламенем. Дикое горение разрушает долговечность топлива. Вспышки тепла врываются в комнату, зубы лихорадки кусают себя. Сила красного шторма придает окружающей среде ауру тепла. Угли огня умирают в пепле. Огонь впечатляет, но он заимствует свое вещество из топлива. Его еда была съедена быстрее приготовленной, намного быстрее. Тепло огня спит пушистым в пространстве бессмертия. Когда тепло сходит с ума, оно становится жаром.

в целом

Генерал показывает столько лица, сколько необходимо. Специальные функции показывают намного более четкие края. Общее везде одинаково, часто выражается одинаково. В ландшафте всего можно найти общее в любом месте. Серого дядю генерала называют средним. Генерал должен снова и снова приспосабливаться к особому, что создает стресс. Генерал обеспечивает безопасность, когда вы отправляетесь в необычный отпуск.

Стоящая тень

Постоянная тень всегда должна останавливаться, хотя она может идти куда угодно. Если стоящая тень хочет двигаться, окружающая среда движется мимо него, а не мимо него, он сам останавливается. Стоящая тень может двигаться и все равно оставаться вечно на одном месте. У стоящей тени нет компании. Конечно, есть и другие стоящие тени, но они есть где-то еще.

Короткое замыкание

Путь ведет к цели, пока по ней не идет эзотерика. Короткое замыкание сокращает путь жизни. Он быстро идет по пути, которого не существует. В результате ему не хватает опыта. Его успех горячий и пустой и без мяса, но короткое замыкание имеет харизматический эффект. Кратчайший путь - это всегда короткое замыкание, его цель - не существовать. Короткое замыкание действует без роста, оно идет без пути. Иоахим Эрнст Берендт написал книгу: «Нет пути, просто иди: БЫТЬ в природе». По дороге на презентацию своей книги его сбила машина.

идти

Вы боитесь, что ходьба может упасть. Но ходьба имеет большое значение: она всегда остается в равновесии. Стоит движение в коридоре. Однако ложь никогда не убегает.

небо

Пики горы не имеют проблем и рады, что они такие большие и большие. Небеса также счастливы, когда принимают гостей с гор. Большое небо также нуждается в веселье.

причина

Причина ниже. Это основа, пол, основание и обоснование. Если вы посмотрите на дно, оно станет пропастью. Вы не можете обнаружить гравитацию там. Дно и бездна очень успокаивают нервы. Лучшая работа для людей - докопаться до сути. Только испуганные кролики предпочитают делать что-то полезное, потому что мир гибнет полезным способом.

подземный мир

Подземный мир находится под миром. Это почти не часть мира, вы не знаете, поэтому это не удобно. Мертвые лежат под землей, есть также источник плодородия. Как еще должны расти все растения?

облако

Облако - овца на небесах. Облака всегда грустные. Им часто приходится плакать. Но они также защищают скот от агрессивного солнца. Облако поглощает добро и зло людей. По их формам видно, что пробил час. Движение и вода танцуют вместе в облаке.

грязь

Вы не должны класть грязь в салат. Иначе болезнь грозит! Грязь - это физический эквивалент греха. Рана может рассматриваться как загрязнение, потому что рана часто образует неприятную корку на краю, которая выглядит как грязь. Загрязнение или пятна в свою очередь указывают на вину. Кто-то запятнан. Мы пострадали, потому что были слишком несовершенны? Или мы несовершенны, потому что нам было больно? Или мы виновны в нарушении чего-либо, закона или личности? Но нам не больно! Мы совершенны и невинны! Тот, кто заявляет что-то подобное, причиняет боль, поэтому виновен.

Секс в тюрьме

Стены тюрьмы образуют сердце. Его внешние стены черные снаружи и красные внутри. Заключенный Распутин уже не самый молодой, но и не самый старый, потому что у него все еще есть прыщи. Германия также заключена в тюрьму: Распутин и Германия ложатся спать вместе. Распутин опасается, что Германия заразится сифилисом. Германия покидает Распутин. Вероятно, ей нужно сделать Пиппи только на короткое время, но она не очень далеко продвинется, потому что мы в тюрьме сердца. Тюрьма - это здание, от которого нельзя сбежать. Распутин стоит перед зеркалом и выражает свои прыщи. Гной брызгает на серебряную невинность: неприглядный, эй.

Крыса и атомная бомба

Крысы - это мыши, которые стали манией величия. Они лучше всего переносят радиоактивность от всего живого. Конечно, однажды они станут царями земли. Крысы убивают друг друга, они очень похожи на людей. Раскрась себя кто может! Однако крысы умнее людей, потому что они очень быстро учатся не есть токсичную пищу, если замечают, что их сверстники убивают ее. Вот почему крысиный яд не является постоянным решением для уничтожения этих адских существ. В средние века крыс использовали для пыток людей, а сегодня крыс подвергают пыткам в научных лабораториях. Это победа человечества! От жертвы к преступнику! За милыми крысами ухаживают и ухаживают в индийском храме Карни Мата. Однако на западе есть только плохие канализационные крысы. В Китае крыса существует даже как знак зодиака. Но Психозавр без микробов говорит: «Мы больше не живем в средние века! Прочь с противными носителями инфекции! Почему политики ничего не делают? Они никогда ничего не делают!

перегиб

Вы не можете коснуться излома, потому что это так далеко от ряда, из которого он танцует. Если ничего не ломается, есть вещи. *Линия идет отсюда туда.* Это так нормально, что это вызывает у вас депрессию. *Ученые и архитекторы любят линии. Линия не ест жизни. Линия затирает жизнь и получает от нее энергию,* чтобы можно было обогревать комнату до умеренных 20 градусов.

Neige

Склон представляет собой уклон, склон которого в соответствии с популярностью уклона превращается в угол, соответствующий уклону склона. Такой наклон не является произвольным, но соответствует любви склонных.

хорошо

Добро это дерево, которое плодоносит круглый год. Его древесина сделана из твердой крови; его листья могут смеяться. Цвет - это хорошо, серый - плохо. Дьявол ест добро. Добро может состоять из себя. Однако зло зависит от уничтожения добра. Поэтому зло никогда не одолеет.

состоять

Соль состоит из натрия и хлора. Стоять на своих двух ногах, но существованию нужна субстанция как пол. Существование нуждается в частях, из которых оно состоит, оно не может быть само по себе. Самое грубое существует. Термин «запас» очень близок к веществу.

Мышь и летучая мышь

Мыши имеют четыре ноги и бегают так, как Божий приказ. Однако некоторые мыши пренебрегали своим предназначением и взорвались. Они лениво тусуются весь день (головой вниз) и вечеринками по ночам (пьют кровь и прочее). Мышь как летучая мышь слепа. Это Божье наказание за их грехи. Как временное решение, летающие мыши теперь должны видеть своими ушами. Это совершенно вопиюще.

тонкий

Худенькие женщины быстро садятся на док анорексии. Обвиняется в дряблых и толстых парнях. Если худой хочет набрать вес, то он должен называть себя «худым». Тонкий иногда имеет более интенсивный эффект, чем толстый, потому что он может содержать много сущности в своем сладком животике. Поэтому худой часто умнее толстого. Это не относится к сверлам с тонкими досками, потому что у них толстая доска перед их головами.

Пиррова победа

Меня зовут Шмидт и я мертв. Я жил греховной жизнью. На моем рабочем месте в компании Satan & Sons мой жадный босс превратился в банкноту в 100 евро. Я почувствовал свой шанс на блаженную жизнь после смерти: я быстро положил свою банкноту в свой кошелек и нарисовал распятие на его внешней коже. Мой босс был пойман. Только после его заверения, что я не попаду в ад после своей смерти, я снова снял крест. Вскоре после этого я, к несчастью, поскользнулся на банановой кожуре перед АОК и упал на твердый тротуар затылком. Я был сразу же мертв. Как и обещал, я не попал в ад, но они не хотели пускать меня на небеса, так как я победил зло, но все еще не сделал добро. Теперь я постоянно иду вперед и назад между раем и адом и больше не знаю.

страдать

Фред: Страдание совершенно лишнее. Какой идиот создал мир?

Детлеф: Страдание защищает от идиотских поступков. Это мешает вам пить слишком много пива. Зло ведет к добру.

Фред: Разве это не другой путь? Вид любви?

Папа: Бог непогрешим (как и я), он будет знать, почему он создал мир.

Мефисто: Я часть той силы, которая всегда хочет зла и всегда творит добро.

Берт Хеллингер: На более высоком уровне зло тоже хорошо.

Фред: я живу на земле; Земля - это более низкий уровень, более высокий уровень мне не нужен. Все это не очень убедительно.

Детлеф: Бог Солнца тоже пострадал. Он умер на кресте как человек и воскрес на третий день.

Фред: Это солидарно с ним. Я чувствую себя намного лучше.

Аллаху Акбар

Бог больше чем ... Бог всегда больше, чем человек может себе представить. Ради безопасности, я не хочу писать ничего плохого о Боге, ты никогда не знаешь. Если Бог не дьявол. Злые боги настоящие боги? Или их существование питается хорошей едой? Если есть только один Бог, на самом деле можно назвать его только Аллахом. Два нейтральных и всеобъемлющих звука А окружают бесконечный звук Л. Если есть несколько богов, то это становится более красочным и любящим, а также более понятным для людей. Каждый бог среди других богов имеет свою зону ответственности. Аллаху больше не нужно иметь 99 имен, потому что есть 99 богов. И сотый бог, вероятно, снова объединит всех богов, так что можно подозревать. Фанатичная поляризация добра и зла растворяется во множестве богов. Иногда богов также называют ангелами, архангелами или высшими сущностями.

чеснок

Чеснок несвежая свежесть. Его пальцы на ногах расколоты. Настоящий личностный раскол имеет свои корни. Снаружи, однако, лук демонстрирует однородность. Чеснок помогает против вампиров и ведьм. Клубень укрепляет кровь и делает ее настолько несъедобной для паразитов, что даже вампиры теряют аппетит. Шизофренический лук-порей также убивает физических паразитов, таких как ленточные черви или гнилостные бактерии. Чеснок раскалывает человечество, как сигаретный дым. Некоторым это нравится: это хорошие люди. Тем не менее, плохие парни (например, вампиры, ведьмы, нацисты, детективы, капиталисты и избиратели зеленых) чувствуют отталкивание от его запаха.

Контракт с дьяволом

Вы можете быстро стать одним из богатых и красивых, заключив небольшой контракт в сервисном офисе Satan & Söhne: подрядчик (Teufel) выполняет все мирские желания. Взамен подрядчик завещал свою посмертную душу анатомам ада в исследовательских целях. Договор имеет юридическую силу через каплю крови от подрядчика.

эпидемия

Арнольд представляет чуму, которая проникает через землю и убивает всех плохих людей. Хорошие парни вообще не болеют и не переживают инфекцию. Арнольд, конечно, один из хороших парней. Как он может быть так уверен в этом? Как насчет того, если чума на самом деле убивает только хороших парней? Это было бы подло, но типично для несправедливости этого мира. Арнольд пугается и хочет сделать прививку от судьбы, хотя знает, что это невозможно.

вырезать

Сознание врезается в вещи. Резка более элегантна, чем покалывание, поэтому у комара нет благородного названия. Сильные души имеют мужество противостоять этому, у трусов нет клинка вообще. Вы не должны порезать палец! Так что ребята: просто будьте осторожны! Цвет черенка называется резкостью. Острый перец и секс-бомбы тоже иногда могут быть немного пряными.

бедных

Руки вытянуты. Руки начинают цвести в руках. Руки очищают в руках, руки укрепляются в инструменте. Ветви являются руками деревьев.

граница

Граница отделяет одно от другого. Это начинается на границе или заканчивается. Граница образует сосуд для жизни. Кровь нуждается в венах, чтобы жить. Дом ограничивает жизнь своими стенами. Когда жизнь покидает его дом, он тонет в море бездомных.

Тарелка имеет круглый край. В отличие от рамки, край завершает рост своего владельца. Рама - это украшение, это обязательство остановить ростовщичество.

Термин «мир» используется для описания ландшафта всего. Мир можно понимать как убийственное величие. Этот мир не имеет конца. Глаза человека не могут найти остановки на бесконечных улицах. Безопасный мир закрыт по краям. Там безопасный мир охватывает безграничность руками конечности.

свет и тьма

Густав слеп на обоих мозолях. Его ноги ничего не видят. Это хорошо, потому что, если вы ничего не видите, вы не впадете в депрессию. Поэтому Густав счастлив. Есть люди, у которых свидание вслепую. Вы слишком слепы, чтобы встретиться. Летучие мыши также видят черное, но они слышат ярко. Свет слеп к темноте? Видит ли тьма свет?

луна

Луна смеется в темноте. Это можно увидеть в полном объеме. Как полная луна, он мужчина. В противном случае она женщина. Или это было наоборот? Луна со страхом несется по небу. Ему не нравится, когда его видят; это могут делать только оборотни, летучие мыши и вороны. Луна тайно правит в царстве зла, это обманщик с круглыми щеками, это старая любовь, сияющая тьма, называемая луной. Ярче всего светит луна, когда спят приличные люди.

Подожди минутку

Есть только один момент, и он всегда один и тот же. Только момент есть момент. Большинство «моментов» не имеет смысла. Так что времени нет. И все же часы тикают. Вот почему часы лжецы.

память

Люди не могут вспомнить вообще. Мы видим прошлое с нашего настоящего момента. Каждый день ты помнишь другое прошлое. То, как это было на самом деле, безвозвратно потеряно.

Оригинальная корова

В начале было молоко. Вселенная была создана из молока, поэтому мы говорим о Млечном Пути. Молоко пришло из вымени Urkuh, большого MUU.

свежий

Свежесть поет как свет во влаге жизни. Свежее мясо полезнее, чем гнилое. Фруктовый сок свежее крови, потому что животное гниет в своей жадности.

черепахи

Черепахи - это древние зародыши. Они из того времени, когда вообще не было времени. Их дело также в другом. Он состоит не из мельчайших частиц, а из более мягкой каши, так как твердость проходит от одной линии к другой. Настоящая земля никогда не умирает.

разорение

Ветер тайно дует через руины разрушающегося замка. Темные стены пусты от событий. Огненные бури были вчера, шрамы сегодня. Мышь может написать и рассказать газете историю мертвых руин. Птицы летят над красным вечерним солнцем и исчезают в никуда.

ур

Первичное всегда на первом месте. Причина, происхождение, изначальный суп, Уран, первобытный скот, предок, первобытный лес, Большой взрыв, и, конечно, документы и странные прадеды. Последний еще не знал термин опасный. В Вене опасный означает нечто особенно опасное.

поддельные новости

Земля это диск! Если бы земля была сферой, люди в Новой Зеландии упали бы с земли. Должно ли НАСА засунуть свои поддельные фотографии в задницу? Они вдыхали слишком много лунного воздуха!

начало

Старт может внезапно начаться как спринт или подкрасться, как туман осенью. Растения прорастают, а дети рождаются в больнице без микробов. Начало требует конца: рождение ребенка заканчивается беременностью. Начало еще не знает себя: только в конце начало знает, кем оно было.

дети

Дети едят детский шоколад. Взрослые едят взрослый шоколад. Оба продукта на вкус как шоколад. Вы видите: дети ничего особенного. Они едят шоколад, как ты и я. Детей тоже не нужно поливать, даже если они ходят в детский сад.

пластинчатый гриб

Поганка любит свою свободу. Нужен дождь сверху. Но красный гриб отказывается принимать Божьи импульсы. Мухомор хотел бы держать все под контролем. Это даже владелец кнута. Доминирование важно для него. Дождь падает на мухомор. Гриб замечает, что есть и другие вещи, кроме доминирования, но мухомор не осмеливается раскрыться. Тогда он делает это, потому что он смелый. Страх приходит сверху вниз в гриб. Привет это. Теперь он уже не поганка, а маленькая мышка, которая хочет жить в своем пещере средним классом. Но это не работает. Мышь изучает философию, обновляет мир и становится знаменитой.

молния

Мартин Лютер и Пол были поражены молнией. Так быстро, как молния, они стали просветленными людьми. Удар молнии улучшает нас? Или вспышка - это просто короткое замыкание, которое порождает лицемерие? Вы должны попробовать это во время следующей грозы.

Дж.Ф. Кеннеди в Билефельде

Предполагаемая теория заговора гласит, что город Билефельд даже не существует. С определенного момента времени тени уже не могли скрыть несуществование Билефельда. Вот почему они стремились представить заговор как простую теорию или шутку, чтобы никто не мог понять, что подделка Билефельда была чистой истиной. К счастью, есть Билл. 24 июля 1963 года Билл Клинтон посетил американского президента Джона Ф. Кеннеди в Белом доме и пожал ему руку. Клинтон воскликнул: «Я собираюсь стать президентом!» Благодаря этому волшебному действию Клинтон украл свою судьбу и личность у президента Кеннеди в то время. Результат: Кеннеди должен был умереть. Вернее его двойник. Настоящий Кеннеди был заморожен. Когда фальшивое существование Билефельда грозило раскрыться, Кеннеди снова оттаял. После космической операции и интенсивных тренировок на немецком языке Кеннеди сегодня под псевдонимом Пит-Клаузен, мэр теневого города Билефельд.

Бороды

Синдбарт: Эй, я тебя вижу!

Виндбарт: Безумие! Я тебя тоже. Удивительно, если учесть, что нас обоих не существует.

Синдбарт: Когда встречаются два человека, которых даже не существует, они становятся реальными по отношению друг к другу и друг к другу, потому что они оба встречаются на одном уровне, а именно на уровне небытия.

Windbart: Вы редко встречаете таких, как вы. Вы редко становитесь настоящими. Мы должны воспользоваться возможностью, чтобы подробно обсудить обман и правду.

Синдбарт: Отлично, я там.

море

Море может позволить себе величие, потому что оно хранит секреты. Море состоит из окопов богов (в слезах содержится соль). Море - это пища для земли. Жажда пустыни давно высохла, пустыне больше не нужно жить.

Информационное общество

Арнольд Хайтерманн не смотрит телевизор и не читает газеты. Просто заголовки. Для Otto Normal важно то, что актуально, а все остальное неважно. Арнольд интересуется общей картиной, а не подругами. Кроме того, вы никогда не узнаете, верна ли информация. Если заголовок скажет: «Завтра мир закончится!», Мистер Хайтерманн наверняка прочтет всю информацию. Такой конец света может действительно повлиять на вас, только по личным причинам.

вода

Вода любит двигаться. Если природа это позволяет, тогда она течет. Вода свежая и поет сама по себе. Свет сверкает движениями своих волн. Вода везде, где есть жизнь. Вода неустойчива до тех пор, пока она еще не на дне. Вода мокрая, нагота остается неприкосновенной.

лягушки

Вы не должны быть лягушкой, не лягушкой страха. Любой, кто построен так близко к воде, как лягушка, живет в душе. Душа и озеро - это одна и та же вода, рыба и лягушка знают это. Вы не можете действительно испугаться в воде, только сухие животные могут. Спросите испуганного кролика! Не лягушка страха! Лягушки никогда не выходят из полового созревания. Лягушка - это рыба, которая не добралась до наземного животного: провал эволюции. Это уже не рыба, но и обезьянам этого было недостаточно. Лягушки все еще зеленые за ушами, и не только там. Лягушки часто получают прыщи, но тогда их называют жабами.

Кабан

Дикие кабаны прыгают с крыши дома в туманном городе Риме. Дикие свиньи бьют себя по тротуару внизу. Кабан ничего не сломал, хрюкает и живет. Такой кабан действительно крепок. Твоя кровь не увядает. В сильные удары их огненный сок пульсирует бесконечно через ипподром их вен.

чувства

Чувства не имеют цвета. Они неверные задницы, их единственная власть - непостоянство. Вы бы отдавали свое сердце чувствам? Чувства велики по количеству и массе, они становятся сильнее и слабее, они возвращаются без вдохновения, как лошади на карусели.

крушение

Ширина мира погружается в глубину. Все идет спать, а луна в небе. Его серебряный свет проникает в гибель. Одна рука хочет схватить луну и делает это тоже: она раздавила луну. Серебряная кровь, которая одинаково черная, стекает с сферы, которая когда-то была Луной. Мир дрожит.

убить

Смерть отрицает жизнь и позволяет ей в равной степени. На что должен жить орел? Что он должен срать в спину? Он может жить только убивая других животных. Как мужчина! Веганы хорошие люди. Но они тоже должны следовать зову природы. Ведь растения - это тоже живые существа. Веганы имеют дефицит витаминов. Их невинность делает их бледными по лицу, они биовампиры. Веганы пьют кровь морали. Самый большой хищник - люди.

Мертвый телезритель

Телевизор включен, и перед ним есть скелет. Его пустые кости черепа больше не знают о программе. Кто-то выключает телевизор: теперь этот человек понимает, что ему чего-то не хватает, и злится. Только в отречении смерть осознает, что он мертв.

Смысл жизни

Цель жизни - накормить великого аграрного экономиста. В любом случае, это мнение доктора Свет мозга. Он верит в следующее: из далекого неба великий сельскохозяйственный экономист сеет семена нашей души в почву реализации. Благодаря жизненному опыту зародыш души превращается в продуктивное ухо души. Великий экономист сельского хозяйства собрал и съел это ухо после нашей смерти. Д-р Брейнлайт - брат-близнец доктора Свет мозга. Каждое утро доктор Брэйнлайт подбрасывает после всего зерна мюсли, когда он думает о грубой теории своего брата.

солнце

Солнце - это сердце мира, в нем больше пространства, чем в космосе. У нее большой блестящий живот. Солнце рождает мир. Солнце ест мир. Оба одинаково. Солнце это все. У стариков белый, у молодых желтый. Солнце не имеет морщин на лице.

бешенство

Вампир смотрит в зеркало: мужчина с черными волосами и очками смотрит из серебра, у него бледное лицо. Вампир думает, что она выглядит как обычный человек в зеркале. Нежить узнает себя только в зеркале, однако, если она смотрит прямо на свои руки и тело, она никого не видит. Это не нормально, даже для вампиров. Конечно, у него бешенство.

завод

Растения - это зеленые животные, которые не могут ходить. Его листья - камни воды. Солнечный свет делает их полностью зелеными. Камень, вода и солнце вдруг дают жизнь. Растение состоит в основном из роста, оно наслаждается своим ростом. У роста нет генов, они узнают их каждый момент. План не растет, даже если вы его выполняете. Растения, с другой стороны, растут случайно с жизнью.

жесткий

Некоторые толстые черепа уже били по голове твердостью. Твердость предлагает сопротивление и долговечность. Скелет тяжело. Обычно тяжело остается тяжелым. Тем не менее, пенис бывает только твердым время от времени. - Почему только? - Край твердости является внушительной чертой в комнате. Края не следует упускать из виду, вы можете ударить их головой. Когда две стены сталкиваются, столкновение называется ребром. Таким образом, ребро является результатом карома. Поэтому не для слабонервных. Камни тоже жесткие. Камень это вещь, у него нет лица, потому что камень похож на другие камни. В их существе все вещи одинаковы. Шкаф, стол или зубная щетка - это всего лишь вещи. Камни, которые лежат повсюду, называются реальностью. Камень можно использовать, чтобы забивать черепа других людей. Это было важно в каменном веке. Сегодня некоторые камни могут говорить, эти камни называются «сотовые телефоны». Если я правильно об этом думаю: есть и красивые камни, а именно драгоценные камни. Драконы собирают их.

собирать

Собранная плотная, иногда узкая. Собрание обеспечивает безопасность как постоянное существование. Или это бремя. Труднее собирать, чем собирать. Если собирать сложнее, чем собирать, говорят об «охоте».

отходы

Избыточное не интегрируется в выращенное. Избыточное не узнало лишнего во время его роста. Хотя переполнение может быть богатым, оно иногда жертвует, поэтому лишнее не только бесполезно, но и мешает живому веществу развиваться. Лишнее это просто мусор.

выверт

У Хьюго проблема. Его причудой является то, что причуды беспокоит его на экране. Это сводит Гюго с ума. У Хьюго были недостатки на лице в течение десятилетий. Стоя перед зеркалом, он смотрел на его причуду, пока его дерматолог не отпустил ручку. У Хьюго есть причуды со странностями. Но только для отдельных причуд. Если у всего есть причуды, такие как полностью поцарапанное окно, Хьюго не возражает. У Хьюго действительно есть проблема.

волчок

Пустая мысль питает его иссохшую снежную женщину. Серая снежная женщина называется невроз. Она совершенно безвредна, она Вуди Аллен. Вы можете смеяться над неврозом, потому что странные люди смешные. Но старый снег не так уж безопасен. В снегу не течет кровь, но вчера в нем скучает вчерашний снег. Старый снег уходит в психотерапию. Такая терапия тоже невроз, она белая, как новый снег.

Парная терапия

Собака и кошка идут на пару терапии. Терапевт - это гиена. Собака и кошка хотят сохранить свои отношения. Терапия терпит неудачу. Почему только? Что это может быть? Конечно, у психотерапевта все они сами имеют проблемы.

Нет юмора

Чеплин идет в подвал, чтобы посмеяться, чтобы собраться с телом. Он должен был убить много людей, чтобы получить деньги. Страдания этого мира и женщин нельзя шутить. Чеплин выступает за общий запрет на юмор для всей Германии, за исключением так называемых центров смеха, где люди могут громко смеяться после уплаты пошлины за юмор.

смех

Смех счастлив с его губ. Серьезный смех приходит в смех. Юмористический смех не может подняться с дивана буржуазии. Настоящий смех не смешной, он просто счастливый. Только навязчивые шутки рвут шутки с дерева страданий.

совершенно смешно

Изольда: Детлеф, ты никогда не знаешь, шутишь ли ты или серьезно.

Детлеф: Это очень просто: если я веселый, я серьезный, и если я серьезный, это просто весело.

Изольда: Как я могу отличить одно от другого?

Детлеф: Первый случай - в четные дни, а второй - в нечетные. Или это было наоборот? Я все испортил.

Изольда: Я схожу с ума от парня!

Изменение климата

Отто пукает.

Д-р Kackebart-Struller: Отто! Вы действительно знаете, что делаете с озоновым слоем? С каждым пуком не только ваш мудак становится больше, но и озоновая дыра. С каждым пуком метан попадает в атмосферу, которая нагревает землю. Не пукни! Мы должны сохранить нашу окружающую среду!

Отто Струллер: Вы правы, Маузи, совершенно верно. Я сейчас иду на чердак, кормлю голубей.

в диком лесу

В диком лесу корни деревьев покидают почву и бегут по всей стране. Спокойствие не возвращается, но отправляется в приключение. Это идет по горам, это идет по долинам. Иногда она тоже прыгает.

рулет

Вращение или кружение - это движение раунда вокруг его центра. Колесо поймано. Сам рулон не катится, он остается неподвижным относительно своего центра. Если раскат будет двигаться от круга к квадрату, он будет двигаться свободно. Велосипед только замечает, что пейзаж движется мимо него, сам велосипед останавливается.

Отдых и упражнения

Тихо наслаждается своей индивидуальностью. Отдых можно определить как отсутствие навязчивого внешнего движения. Поэтому на дискотеке нет отдыха. Не на шоссе тоже. Движение изнутри со спокойствием вполне возможно. Существование имеет мир. Существует также навязчивое спокойствие дзен-буддизма. Такое спокойствие культивируется смертью на земле, оно основано на подавлении и убийстве ерзанья. Настоящее спокойствие, однако, живет на свободе.

spaulen

Колибри летит в забавный дворец, где вращаются люди. 52 дворца без короны живут во дворце. Никто и каждый не король и не дурак одновременно. Все люди во дворце - гермафродиты. Вы можете сделать это сами, если хотите. Но они больше заинтересованы в создании игровых миров: они веселые. Спулинг - серьезная игра. Они шутят здесь с королями Jojos. Короли бросили свои короны как дураки в большом зале под фонтаном. Короны служат гнездом для колибри. Король Фиолетовый пишет серьезную чушь. Вы не можете разговаривать с таким человеком.

рабочий

Работа потеет на своей ничейной земле, что утомительно, потому что вместо позвоночника у работы есть сундук благодарности, украшенный гордостью. Ваше выполнение находит работу в сердечном приступе. Те, кто работает, могут быстро забыть свои тела в подвале. Работа жаждет искупления, но она никогда этого не признает. Работа слепа, она не замечает, что она работает, она только знает. Христос как Искупитель давно вышел. Люди выкупают себя через работу: в психотерапии вы работаете над собой.

Истинное движение внутри. Лошадь движется сама, но автомобиль управляется лошадиными силами своего двигателя. Движение имеет тенденцию двигаться змеиным образом, а именно волнами. Ходьба, плавание, полет или вождение - все это движения. В настоящее время вы в основном передвигаетесь. Вы также можете переехать туда. Но никто не может выдержать это на месте. Вы остаетесь на сайте.

ветер

Ветер подметает лицо Фригга. Время уходит. Вода исчезает в яме. Все бежит, убегает. Моча течет, слезы текут. С Фриггом никого нет, только ветер. Ее ноги покрыты толстыми ботинками. Как насчет того, чтобы она пошла босиком? Тогда ветер унесет их, и Фригг будет свободен. Ее тяжелые ботинки - это бремя ее прошлого. Ветер, называемый вахуна, пронизывает ее волосы. Слейпнир, восьминогая лошадь, скользит мимо Фригги. Фригга очарована, ее можно посадить на коня богу ветра, и ее можно носить свободно, босиком, без.

Лучше груша в руке

чем яблоня на крыше.

Машина делает самое чистое. Машина ничего не чувствует, поэтому работает от чистого отчаяния. Он делает все манипуляции, которые тупые рабочие делали в старые времена. Ручки без чувств и жизни, механика, движение без смысла, только цель. Как хорошо, когда машина делает глупую работу за нас. Но создатели машин однажды посеяли глупости сами. Машины будут продолжать издеваться над нами со своей глупостью. Искусственный интеллект дифференцирован, но остается глупым. Мы сами являемся винтиком большой мировой машины.

Хозяин называет свои руки своими. Атомы его рук не принадлежат владельцу. Атомы в его руке подходят только для формы его эго. После смерти владельца бывшие атомы в его руке пригодны для другого появления. Хозяин чувствует себя как дома в руке, он укоренен в руке. Этот корень его личность. Это не сама рука.

Сумасшедшее яблоко

В яблоке кожа и мякоть живут вместе. Они оба женаты? В яблоке живет гораздо больше: сферическое, зеленое, фруктовое, оно висит на дереве. Яблоко думает: `` У меня есть свойства, но я не моя собственность. Если я смотрю на себя, я нахожу только свойства, но не существо ».« Яблоко злится от этого самопознания: «Все шутят! Я не существую! »Каждое свойство яблока теперь идет своим путем. Сферический идет на север, зеленый идет на юг. Фруктовый на западе и повешение яблока на востоке. Это больше не яблоко, оно никогда не существовало. Яблоко развелось с поддельной личностью. Он был просто выброшен из своего «То, что принадлежит мне». Где свежесть яблока? Она сидит в пабе и может быть запущена!

поэзия

Поэзия означает сосредоточить смысл на своем концентрате. Тем не менее, поэзия писателя иногда настолько запечатана, что читатель больше не может открыть окно смысла. Только автор понимает содержание стихотворения, когда пишет. И даже банку автора на следующий день слишком туго.

прозрачный

Очевидно, что то, что прозрачно, летает свободно, не прячась. Отверстия в основном прозрачные. Несмотря на то, что прозрачность может быть весомой, ее нелегко увидеть. Прозрачный становится прозрачным, когда становится неуклюжим.

поймать

Поймать успешно достигает своей добычи, будучи мобильным. Вот почему рыба особенно ловится. Они скользкие и живут в движущейся воде, но все же их можно поймать.

тюрьма

Преступления имеют смысл только в том случае, если вас не поймают. Обезьяна приходит в зоопарк, даже если она не сделала ничего плохого. Зоопарк - это настоящая тюрьма для животных. Некоторые дикие животные заключены в цирк. Дети сидят в тюрьме педагогики своих родителей. Жены сидят в тюрьме из-за финансовой зависимости от своих мужей.

совершенно секретно

Секрет не должен видеть глаза других. Он сидит один (или с заговорщиками) в своем бункере и может делать там следующее: он разлагается, он гниет, он радуется, превращает неправильные вещи, он зажигает, он зажигает других, он смеется над вами, он боится, он защищает себя, отказывается или рождает ребенка. Секрет: мы не знаем, что он делает. Это остается секретом.

летать

Полет скользит по морю простора без ног. В полете верх и низ играются друг против друга. Птица обладает силой, не насилуя мир. Это потрясающе. Однако поганки не могут летать, их крылья зачарованы. Крылья птиц тянутся к дерзким. Они там дома. Крылья - это летающие руки, они силой. Птица может свободно летать, не сталкиваясь с кошкой в воздухе. Сотрудник, однако, очень быстро сталкивается со своим начальником или с серьезностью жизни.

легко

Свет легко пролетает над головоломками, он просто проходит мимо тяжелых животов. Легкая вещь, как правило, находится в верхней части. Дерево плавает на воде, потому что оно легче воды. Воздушный шар плавает в голубом небе. Свет быстро становится легкомысленным. Что-то глупое случается легко.

Schneeflöckchen

Снежинка осторожно падает. Тихо Хлопья приходят из другого мира. Он дает структуру этому миру, иначе все магнитные поля разрушатся. На северном и южном полюсах магнитное поле падает в снег. С полюсов Земли снег организует тайные изменения в мире. Его магнетизм пронизывает жителей Земли и делает их тяжелыми гражданами.

защита

Защита это хорошая вещь. Защита - это первое, что вам нужно: защита конституции, защита зала, средства защиты растений, защита данных и защита мыслей. Вы еще не посещали Mind Protection? Это придет, просто подожди.

кишка

Дайджест жует и жует и жует. Переваривайте жевательные продукты до тех пор, пока пища не станет настолько вкусной, чтобы ее можно было добавлять в собственное мясо. Однако еда всегда остается немного токсичной. Земля ядовита. Это не наш дом. Животные могут переваривать лучше, чем люди, они живут ближе к земле.

земля

То, на чем мы стоим, называется землей. Иногда это называется пол. Стоя и земля тверды. Земля также может означать гумус или камень. Особенно поразительно вещество земли, оно плотное и тяжелое. Пол мирный, пол тупой. У великой великой матери нет лица. У нее есть тепло? Корни уходят в землю, они также понимают землю. Корни едины со спокойствием земли.

пчелы

Пчелы живут в глубине материи, внутри. Пчела выходит на улицу, где холодно. Он падает замертво на землю как снежинка. Пчелы выразили свою внутренность как холодные хлопья. Пока снежинка замерзла, настало время рождественской елки. Если хлопья оттаивают, одиночество голое. Разлагая нектар, пчелы соединяют все части света и осваивают гравитацию, жуют гравитацию. Нектар был книгой, которую еще не читали. Даже его автором.

строгость

Тяжесть обычно велика по количеству. В лидерах, однако, тяжесть невелика. Сила тяжести. Он имеет эффект только своей массой, а не цветом, потому что тяжесть слишком темная, чтобы быть красочной. Тяжесть не понимает смешного. Только в сахаре смешные и тяжелые могут спать вместе. Гравитация приходит сверху или снизу? Когда тепло становится сильнее, оно становится гравитацией. А как насчет камня, который ты не можешь свернуть? Это слишком тяжелый или слишком твердый? Это слишком жестоко! Тяжесть мягче, чем жестокая. Это легко? Вот как это!

ветер

Ветер развевается над деревьями и домами. Сила ветра не видна, видны только ее последствия. Ветер уносит запас. Одуванчик дует на ветру, как пепел. Ветер очень мимолетный. Но это всегда дует.

Трещины в мозге

Недвижимость уникальна. Это свойственно его вещи. Количество является относительным, оно всегда измеряется из сравнения. Количество не имеет владельца. У Изольды большой живот, но у нее нет жира. У всего лишнего много. Неважно, сколько трещин было у мозга Эйнштейна. Это особенность мозга, которая делает его уникальным, а не количество трещин. Вы не можете сравнить яблоки и груши, только их вес.

песок

Фрагменты камней называются песком. Фрагменты песка настолько малы, что снова образуют единство как сообщество изолированных. Песок тогда ощущается как единое целое. Все плачет, но песок не может плакать, потому что он слишком сухой. В камнях нет ни крови, ни воды, даже песка. Слезы грустных гигантов дарят соленую воду, как море. Вот почему песок часто встречается как пляж, где есть море.

люди

Люди существуют только во множественном числе. Человек не может быть один. Человек как стадное животное становится «народом». Толпа состоит из людей. Кровь людей - это кровь их клана. У человека, с другой стороны, есть свой кровоток. Со старыми евреями кровь Авраама течет к его покойным внукам. Люди и архаичные народы имеют свою идентичность в группе, а не в себе.

Вавилон

Вавилон не был ребенком: он был слишком большим для самых высоких. В Нью-Йорке также есть небоскребы. Но они должны быть уничтожены террористами, потому что они хотят поцарапать Бога. Вы танцуете вокруг золотого тельца, об экономическом росте и косметическом хирурге. Когда Божий гнев наконец придет и сместит грешных людей в мусорное ведро?

мельчайшие частицы

Фред получил несанкционированный доступ к большому ускорителю частиц недалеко от Женевы ночью и теперь ползет по круглому кольцу: он видит летящие ярко-зеленые частицы.

Фред: Привет частицы, ты тоже можешь говорить?

Зеленая частица: у меня болит голова, и это плохо, потому что я всего лишь голова. С тех пор как физики обнаружили меня, я больше не могу ткать мир. Даже политика выходит из-под контроля.

Красная частица пролетает мимо: она торчит языком, который даже краснее самой частицы.

красная частица: я зажигаю деньги под задницу Обычно деньги это просто информация. Мой огонь дает ценность информации. Пролетает треугольник, у него глаз на лбу.

Треугольник: я самая большая частица. Действительно маленькие частицы существуют только в аду физики. Маленькое не имеет реальности. Чем более всеобъемлющие вещи становятся, тем более реальными они становятся. - Фред просто поражен.

Хаос - это заблуждение, которое творческие инопланетяне используют, чтобы выйти из-под контроля защиты в мир без помех. Хаос красочен. Хаос удаляет мусор прошлого. Хаос танцует и не знает зачем.

запись

В письме язык говорит тихо в звуке, но ярко в сознании. Писатели - скульпторы определенности. Письмо всегда пишется, даже во время письма. Письмо является окончательным и длится дольше, чем хорошее вино. Слово пишет во все времена.

танец

Танцы смелые. Тот, кто танцует, безумен. Танцы также могут быть крутыми, если вы безрассудный человек. Мыслители не должны танцевать. Танец разрушает ее ясность ума. Отчаянно нуждающийся в недостатке любовной пищи, безумие тигра съедает испорченный порок зла: сладкие мези делают фресси-фресси!

Erwin

Капли слез падают с неба. Они собираются на земле, образуя ручей, который впадает в реку. Эрвин садится в каноэ и плетет сквозь слезу. Река течет в гору. Горят огни в честь Вотана на правом берегу реки. На левом берегу - дерево с каменной птицей. Эрвин продолжает кататься в гору на каноэ. Сейчас идет снег. Каноист видит снеговика на берегу между сосновых иголок. Глаза снеговика живы, это глаза мощного плюшевого мишки. Эрвин продолжает грести вверх по реке. Кто-то слева играет на арфе. Бог рядом.

вулкан

Женщина в черном с разноцветными осколками борется с прохладой. Они летят вместе над звездами, под звездами, между звездами. Жизнь Титаника проявляется в его погружении. Бумажная складная лодка случайно плавает в воде, осторожно дрейфует к болотному водному источнику: Пэн! Эш падает сверху. Eyjafjallajökull наконец-то лопнул.

пригодный

Наоборот, подгонка может быть найдена как любовь. В связи с этим Fit дополняет один и другой аналогичным сервисом. Все соединяется в одну структуру. Пиво, сигареты и пепельницы на кухонном столе мистера Алки. Это имеет смысл, это подходит. Кухонный стол мистера Алки - это структура. Хинз и Кунц в большом мировом каталоге вместе в Интернете. Гинз и Кунц связаны только своим существованием. Интернет - это не структура, а глупость.

вещь

Вещь является серой в своем существе; больше ничего Вещи безличны. Безликая мировая машина вещей управляет землей: Интернет вещей. Вещи накапливаются в мире вещи. У сатаны долгое время был мир в когтях. О живых существах не говорят, потому что они сами двигаются. Тем не менее, молодая вещь может двигаться сама. Это вещь.

мера

Мера может быть правильной, с любовью испеченной дружественными богами. Как учитель, больная мера устанавливает пределы для силы ученика. Тогда ученик полон, его жизнь отстает, и промышленность может вырабатывать электричество из плотины.

все

Все это является дополнением многих вещей к пределу беспокойства. Это все целое сейчас? Все это, по крайней мере, круглая вещь. Как и ожидалось, все это должно сиять на краю, но оно остается серым там. Тогда промышленный священник говорит: «Целое больше, чем сумма его частей!» Даже после этого предложения все не сияет, больше не видно. Целое остается голым дополнением всего. В этой книге есть только один.

ничего

Ничто - это мир всех не-вещей. Чашка не стул. Платье не облако. Не говоря уже о собаке: собака просто не кошка, как воробей. Все не-вещи сходятся в мире ничего. Некоторые говорят, что ничего не приходит после смерти. Ты хочешь жить там среди всего небытия? Это будет довольно тесно в шкафу с не-вещами.

удовольствие

Для наслаждения нужно больше, чем нужно. Так что удовольствие связано со счастьем. Но в то время как счастье - это дар жизни, наслаждение является произвольным. Наслаждение длится и остается. Наслаждение жирным. Удовольствие - это жажда, которая переедает. Наслаждение не думает, оно слишком медленное для этого. Когда кишечник переваривает больше, чем нужно, он счастлив. Удовлетворение - это подсластитель, а сахар - это счастье.

german / deutsch

Der Psychosaurus stellt sich vor:

Ich denke dichtend und wurde nicht das Opfer eines Biofanten. Diese außerirdischen Fanten reisen in der Dunkelheit illegal aus dem Weltraum ein und saugen mit ihren langen Rüsseln die Phantasie der Schlafenden aus deren Gehirn. Ich benutze nur widerstrebend Wörter, die andere schon im Mund gehabt haben. Das finde ich unhygienisch. Darum erfinde ich häufig neue Wörter, wodurch sich das Problem ergibt, dass mich keiner mehr versteht. Folglich muss ich wieder gebrauchte Wörter verwenden, die der deutsche Volksmund nur ungenau gebildet hat. Sprache kann sprechen, weil sie die allgemeinen Bilder des Daseins beherbergt. In der Sprache geht es hauptsächlich darum, den Bildern der Welt ein Zuhause zu geben. Tragisch ist es, wenn ein Mensch den Wörtern der Sprache folgt und dies dann für Denken hält. Wirkliches Denken formt aktiv die Sprache. Die Sprache ist das ICH eines Psychosaurus, sie ist sein Zentrum. In der Sprache lebt die Welt als Welt erst richtig auf, denn Sprechen heißt: Die Welt erschaffen. Im Anfang war das Wort!

Angsthase

Ein Angsthase ist auf dem Weg zum Osterhasen. Unterwegs wollte er seinen Onkel besuchen, doch der liegt wieder mal im Pfeffer. Der Angsthase ist kein Frosch, er stellt sich dem Affen, auch wenn der Affe ihn laust. Die Laus läuft dem Floh über die Leber. Der Hase hört diesen Floh husten, der nun mit Kanonen auf Spatzen schießt. Der Angsthase überwindet seinen inneren Schweinehund und macht den Floh daraufhin zur Schnecke. Auf der linken Seite sieht er einen Esel, dem es zu wohl ist. Der Esel geht mitten im Sommer aufs Eis. Das geht auf keine Kuhhaut, und die Hühner lachen über den Esel. Rechter Hand kriegt eine graue Maus die Motten, weil der Elch sie geknutscht hat. Die Mücken in der Luft sind an sich harmlos, wenn sie nicht zu Elefanten werden und sich im Porzellanladen wie solche benehmen. Herr Specht läuft wie ein Hase und führt seinen begossenen Pudel aus, damit dieser nicht in der Pfanne verrückt wird. Herr und Hund haben wohl einen Vogel, aber es kräht kein Hahn nach ihnen, denn dieser ist im Korb mit seinen Hennen. Auf seinem weiteren Weg findet der Angsthase einen Affenzahn, der keiner Fliege mehr etwas zuleide tut. Nun hat der Angsthase es geschafft, er ist beim Osterhasen angekommen.

ein Gespräch

Maulwurf: Sag mal Psychosaurus, worum geht es in diesem Buch eigentlich?

Psychosaurus: In diesem Buch spricht die Sprache selbst. Und da Sprache

über alles redet, so hat dieses Buch jedes Thema.

Ente: Mal eine persönliche Frage: Wo ist der Unterschied zwischen dem

Psychosaurus und dem Carsten?

Psychosaurus: Darüber möchte ich nicht reden,

das Thema belastet mich total.

Ente: Is gebongt, Alter!

Maulwurf: Es handelt sich bei diesem Buch offensichtlich um eine automatische Übersetzung!

Psychosaurus: So ist es. Dadurch steigert sich das Bizarre ins Unermessliche.

Die Sprache sagt mehr als tausend Worte.

Kichermaus: Falls ich dem Carsten mal schreiben will, hat der auch ein

Online oder so?

Psychosaurus: Im Moment hat der die Mail-Adresse

carsten-stemm@web.de und ein eigenes Online hat er auch.

Werwolf: Sunt reprimat de această carte!

Kichermaus: Ich verstehe kein Wort, nicht mal Bahnhof.

Rabe: Man muss nicht alles verstehen. Es reicht manchmal, sich von den Worten durchs Irrationale tragen zu lassen.

Detlef Doppeldoid

Detlef Doppeldoid kann mit beiden Gehirnhälften nicht ordnungsgemäß denken. Detlef denkt schneller als das Licht, was zu Raum-Zeit-Verquellungen seiner Logosphäre führt. Dann vertauscht er rechts mit links, rein mit raus, und brutto mit netto. Er weiß nicht, ob man in ein Zimmer hineingeht oder herausgeht. Es steht schlimm um Detlef Doppeldoid: Neulich hielt er Leute für Menschen. Detlef kann sich auch nicht merken den Unterschied zwischen Albert Einstein und Konrad Adenauer. Detlef fragt sich: Sind "dasselbe" und "das Gleiche" nicht dasselbe? Manchmal macht Herr Doppeldoid auch lagesthenische Rechtschreibfehler. Wenn er völlig verwirrt ist, dann erinnert sich Detlef sogar an die Zukunft.

Detlef sagt:

"Immer wenn ich nicht mehr weiß, wer ich bin, dann schaue ich in meinen Personalausweis: Dort habe ich auch eine eigene Nummer; eine Nummer, ganz für mich alleine, nur für mich. Einmalig und unverwechselbar. Der Staat hat mich lieb. Doch bringt mich das weiter? Wer steckt hinter dem Namen Detlef Doppeldoid? Und was beweist schon so eine kleine Karte aus Plastik? Plastikkarten kann man leicht fälschen. Man kann heute alles fälschen. Sogar eine Identität kann man fälschen. Mir wird ganz blümerant."

Sprechhase

Den Hasen, der sprechen kann, den nennt man den Sprechhasen. Der Sprechhase isst beim Sprechen und spricht beim Knabbern. Wortwurzeln sind ihm nicht unbekannt. Gerade verzehrt er die Liebe. Liebe ist ihm nur ein Wort, mampf, mampf. Liebe kann man essen, ohne zu fressen, das ist Sprechhasenweisheit.

Es gibt Enten!

Der Biologe interessiert sich für die Federn der Enten, der Ontologe interessiert sich für das Sein der Enten. Wer gibt die Enten? Antwort: Das 'Es'. 'Es' und Geben ergeben ergiebig das Sein. Man könnte die Frage auch alternativ wie folgt beantworten: Die Evolution gibt Enten, die Enteneier geben Enten, der Entensex gibt Enten, Gott gibt Enten. Es regnet. Eigentlich müsste man sagen: Die Wolke regnet.

Diesem 'Es' ist nicht mal Gott gewachsen, denn es heißt: Es gibt einen Gott. Das wiederum heißt: Das 'Es' ist größer als Gott. Eine andere Schlussfolgerung wäre: Das 'Es' ist der eigentliche Gott, der Gott erst gibt. Es gibt Enten. Man sagt nicht: Es nimmt Enten. Geben ist seliger als Nehmen. Geben ist wohl auch ontologischer als Nehmen. Das 'Es' ist so unklar, dass man seinen Nebel nicht mehr sehen kann. Das hat zum Ergebnis: Man denkt gar nicht mehr darüber nach, wo die Enten eigentlich herkommen. Das 'Es' ist trügerisch. Es gaukelt uns Wissen vor. Wenn wir nicht mehr wissen, dass die Wolke regnet,

dann regnet 'Es'. Auch die Verneinung gibt das 'Es': "Es gibt keine Elwetritsche!" Wer kann bloß dieses 'Es' sein, das fähig ist, diese Nichtenten zu geben?

Goldmarie und Pechmarie

Es war einmal eine Motivationstrainerin, die hatte zwei Töchter, die beide Marie hießen. Die eine war fleißig, die andere faul. Eines Tages kam die Fleißige an einen Brunnen, auf dem stand:

"Kein Trinkwasser!"

"Das steht da nur aus rechtlichen Gründen", dachte sich die Durstige. Das Mädchen trank von dem Wasser und fiel aus Versehen in den Brunnen hinein, woraufhin sie ihr Bewusstsein verlor. Irgendwann erwachte sie wieder in einer ihr völlig unbekannten Gegend.

Am Fenster eines sanierungsbedürftigen Hauses stand eine alte Frau und schüttelte ihr Kopfkissen aus. Frau Holle, so hieß nämlich die Mieterin, sagte zu dem Mädchen: "Kompetente

Seniorenpflegerinnen wie du sind heute selten, bei mir gibt's viel Arbeit." Und weil die Fleißige so arbeitsgeil war, machte sie der Frau Holle den Haushalt.

Nach einiger Zeit bekam das Mädchen jedoch Heimweh und äußerte das Begehren, nach Hause zurückkehren zu dürfen. Frau Holle gewährte ihr diesen Wunsch. Die Alte führte das Mädchen zu einem Tor, durch das sie gehen sollte. Als die Fleißige durch das Tor schritt, regnete es von oben dioxinverseuchtes Pech auf sie herab, das nicht mehr von ihrer Haut abging. Das Mädchen sagte: "Fucking bullshit! Ich werde mich am Schicksal bitter rächen. Ich studiere Mathematik und promoviere über Paradoxietheorien."

Als die Mutter ihre Tochter so pechverschmiert sah, nannte sie ihr Kind Pechmarie. Aus Gründen des sozialen Ausgleichs schickte die Mutter nun auch ihre faule Tochter zum Brunnen. Der geschah fast dasselbe. Nur kam ihre zweite Tochter statt an Frau Holles Haus zu einem anderen Haus, in dem eine gewisse Frau Hölle wohnte.

Nach zehn Minuten Erwerbstätigkeit ließ die Arbeitsdisziplin des faulen Mädchens erheblich nach. Frau Hölle sagte: "In deinem Alter war ich auch ziemlich faul. Ich habe nicht mal einen Hauptschulabschluss. Wir lassen uns jetzt mit einem Château Mouton-Rothschild 1945 zulaufen, den hat mein Schwiegersohn selber geklaut.

Zum Glück ist der ganz Keller voll davon." Nach einem wochenlangen Saufgelage bekam auch die Faule Heimweh und begehrte, nach Hause gelassen zu werden. Frau Hölle führte sie zu demselben Tor, durch das auch Pechmarie geschritten war. Als das faule Mädchen durch das Tor hindurch ging, regnete es Gold auf sie. Nun war das Mädchen um einiges wertvoller, denn auch das Gold ließ sich nicht entfernen. Zu Hause angekommen wurde sie von der Mutter Goldmarie genannt. Vor lauter Zorn über die Ungerechtigkeit des

Lebens trat die Mutter aus der Kirche aus und ging vor ein weltliches Gericht. Pechmarie wurde später die erste Professorin für Logik mit Dioxinnarben im Gesicht. Ihr Leben war völlig verpfuscht. Goldmarie jedoch lebte glücklich und zufrieden bis an ihr Lebensende. > Happy End

Käse des Schafs

Hirte: Sag mal, was trägst Du denn da für ein Buch unter Deinem Arm?

Wolfgang: Das Buch hat mir einer deiner Schafe zum Geburtstag geschenkt. Sein Titel lautet: Schafskäse selber herstellen!

Hirte: Soll das ein Witz sein?

Wolfgang: Mit Witzen ist nicht zu spaßen. Ich mache nie Witze. Wer Witze macht, ist bloß zu feige, es ernst zu meinen. Nie habe ich einen Scherz gemacht. Und falls doch mal irgendeiner lacht, so haue ich dem Arsch eine auf's Maul.

Ein Schaf: Excuse me if I interfere, but I'm genetically modified, so I can talk. Is there a new tax on sheep cheese soon?

ein anderes Schaf: Auch ich bin ein gentechnisch verbessertes Produkt des Schöpfers, und ich sage euch: Männer sind wie Frauen, nur umgekehrt.

Wolfgang: Ich dachte immer, es wäre anders rum!

Hirte: Von so komplizierten Gesprächen wird mir immer ganz schwindelig ... Ah, schau mal, wer da kommt! Der hinkt ja!

Wolfgang: Dann kann er nur ein Vergleich sein!

Hirte: Wieso denn das?

Wolfgang: Weil man immer sagt: Jeder Vergleich hinkt!

ein geschorenes Schaf: Bedeutung ist immer mehrdeutig. So verspricht sich der Sprecher schnell in seiner Spreche. Das Doppeldeut ist ein Lapsus Freudianikus, die undichte Stelle in der allzu glatten Selbstdarstellung.

Wolfgang: Was ist denn das für ein Schwätzer?

Hirte: Das Schaf hat studiert. Psycholinguistik, oder so.

(Der Hinkende ist nun bei der Gesprächsgruppe angekommen.)

Hinkender: Sie sind hinter mir her. Mein Handel mit geklautem Plutonium aus russischen AKWs ist aufgeflogen!

Hirte: Mach keine Sachen, Otto!

Schaf: Kann man Plutonium fressen?

Hirte: Nicht alle Schafe haben studiert!

alle Schafe gemeinsam: Mähhhh!

Otto: Mir bleibt nur noch ein Ausweg: Selbstmord!

Wolfgang: Ich hätte da einen alternativen Ausweg. Ich kenne einen guten Zauberer beim Zirkus. Er leidet unter einer Allergie, aber fachlich ist er in Ordnung.

Otto: Wer ist dieser Zauberer?

Wolfgang: Er ist all das, für den man ihn hält, denn er hat ganz viele Planeten im siebten Haus, darunter den Pluto.

Otto: Ich glaube nicht an Astrologie!

Wolfgang: Aber die Sterne glauben an Dich!

Otto: Fein, ich will es versuchen, denn ich habe nichts mehr zu verlieren. Ich lasse mich in ein Kaninchen verzaubern und schreibe meinen Namen rückwärts, damit mich niemand erkennt.

Hirte: Tolle Sache! Das ist jetzt echt ein Happy End!

In der Not frisst der Apfel Birnen.

Tötungsdelikt

Affe: Guten Tag, Schrägäugin, du hast schräge Augen.

Schrägäugin: Und du bist ein Affe, du Affe.

Affe: Ich habe hier eine Stange Dynamit.

Wem stecken wir die in den Arsch?

Schrägäugin: Mir natürlich! Bei TNT sag ich nicht nee!

Du genialer Affe, du hast den Nobel-Preis verdient!

(Der Affe schiebt der Schrägäugin das Dynamit in den Arsch und zündet die Lunte an. Nach nervenaufreibenden Sekunden des Wartens gibt es eine heftige Detonation: Staub, Trümmer und Fleischreste bedecken den Ort der Explosion.)

Affe: Geil! Es hat gekracht!

Für uns Tiere gibt es keine Grafen oder Paragrafen.

Jetzt wird erst mal eine Banane gegessen. Haha!

Stahltussi

Einmal war ein kleiner quietschender Wagen, der fährt durch pralle und milde Natur. Das Wägelchen fährt, es wird gezogen von einem Pferd. Ein Gefährt, das heute nicht mehr fährt. Als die Gefährte anfingen, vom Motor gefahren zu werden, da wird Wägelchen zu Stahl, als man Wägelchen noch zog, da blühten Blumen und die Wasser rauschten dazu. Im Mühlrad lebte das Geheimnis des Lebens, hier lief das Rad im Wasser. Das Automobil war die Geburt des Stahlmädchens. Der Himmel streckt sich, der Himmel reckt sich, er ist erregt. Stahltussi ballert mit einer Abwehrkanone in den Himmel. Es ist Weltkrieg, ein sinnloser Versuch des Stahls, wieder zum Pferd zu werden. Stahltussi ist nun selber Pferd, darum trägt sie einen Pferdeschwanz. Pferde sind wirklich elegant, so wie man Eleganz im Zeitalter des Stahls nicht mehr kennt. Kunststoff ist auch Stahl. Alles, was nicht vom Pferd gezogen wird, das ist Stahl. Da kriegt man Ehrfurcht vor einer Schönheit, die nicht Modepuppe ist.

Mehrraum

Ein Mehrraum ist ein Raum, der innen größer ist als außen. Der Mehrschrank zum Beispiel sieht aus wie ein gewöhnlicher Schlafzimmerschrank. Wenn man sich aber notfalls in dem Schrank verstecken muss, so stellt man erstaunt fest: Hier befinden sich ganze Galaxien im Schrank. Und das sind keine Halluzinationen als Folge eines Sauerstoffmangels. Die Welt ist voller Realitätslöcher. Und es werden immer mehr.

Gefahr

Gefahr bedroht einen. Das Unglück hat noch nicht zugeschlagen. Es könnte aber in Zukunft zuschlagen; das ist ein Risiko. Das Leben ist unsicher. Man weiß nicht, ob das Leben im nächsten Augenblick schon kaputt ist. Gefahr steht vor der Tür, Gefahr ist unberechenbar, sie kann zum Alptraum werden. Raubtiere sind gefährlich; Kapitalisten auch. Gefährlich ist es, Stromkabel in einer Wanne voller Wasser zu verlegen. Heiraten ist auch riskant. Eine Lebensversicherung dagegen verspricht Schutz: Wenn man ein Leben verloren hat, so kriegt man ein neues erstattet. Doch Vorsicht vor Versicherungsbetrug: Versicherungen betrügen einen ganz schön!

Denken

Denken wandert im Land der Bedeutung. Die Wege des Denkens laufen in den Wald des Wissens. Durch seine Wanderung wird das Denken schwerer und verschmilzt schließlich mit seinen Gedankenbäumen und seinem Traumschnee.

Olymp

Fred sieht auf dem Olymp einen Gott mit Handy:

Fred: Grüß Gott, Gott!

Seit wann benutzen denn die Götter ein Handy?

Gott: Ja mei, man passt sich halt an. Ich könnte mich auch telepathisch mit meinen Kollegen verständigen, doch wollen wir Götter uns den Menschen begreifbar machen.

Fred: Also, ich begreife es nicht!

Eierköpfe

Hirnwichser sind die Hasen der pneumistischen Agglation. Man nennt sie auch Eierköpfe. Ihre Neurolanten sind nicht sehr geschmeidig, dafür aber sehr lang. Man sollte ihre kahlen Köpfe mit nackten Walnüssen bewerfen, denn diese enthalten viel Hirnschmalz. Neurolanten sind die Stäbchen des Verstandes. Neurolanten können auch die Stämme der Bäume sein, durch die man den Wald vor lauter solchen nicht mehr sieht. Aber eigentlich sind Neurolanten die Stäbchen zum Essen von geistigem Sushi.

Manche Hirnwichser nennt man Philosophen. Die Philosophie denkt ohne seelisches Trinken, sie ist Licht ohne Liebe. In der Wüste der Erkenntnis kann der Denker schlecht scherzen. Kakteen lachen nie. Die Gedanken der Philosophie sind hart wie alter Käse. Philosophen auf dem Weg der Heilung fangen an zu dichten.

Halbgott

Fred: Weißt du was Detlef, ich bin zum Halbgott befördert worden.

Detlef: Echt?

Fred: Is so! Ich kann jetzt auf jede Frage eine Antwort finden, wenn auch nur ungenau, aber ich finde die Antwort heraus.

Detlef: Wer hat dich denn befördert?

Fred: Der große Chef!

Detlef: Aha!

Fred: Ich bin halt nur Halbgott. Unsterblich bin ich noch nicht, aber ich arbeite dran.

Detlef: Mm, tu das.

Fred: Endlich weiß ich zum Beispiel, warum die Banane krumm ist.

Detlef: Ja, warum denn?

Fred: Sie sehnt sich nach Einheit, die Banane will wieder zurück ins Paradies, sie möchte gerne Kreis sein, aber der Sündenfall verbietet ihr das, nur bis zur Krümmung reicht ihre Kraft.

Detlef: Was ein Halbgott alles weiß!

Geist

Der Begriff "Geist" ist ein sehr einsames Wort. Das Wort muss so vieles erklären. Intelligenz hackt Steine; der Geist verbindet. Geist beleuchtet sonnengleich die Teile der Welt und gibt ihnen eine Gestalt. Der Geist ist das Bild für die Dinge. Geist kleidet die kleinsten Teilchen mit Mehr. Der Geist kann denken, Intelligenz kann nur klügeln oder kombinieren.

Ursache und Wirkung

Ein Billardspieler stößt mit seinem Stock gegen eine Kugel, die wiederum eine andere Kugel anstößt. Dieses Denken aus Ursache und Wirkung ist die Urlogik der Wissenschaft. Logik begründet nur, sie erklärt nichts. Der freie Wille des Billardspielers wird in dieser Weltansicht völlig ausgeblendet. Ursachen sind stumpfe Tiere, fast Stiere. Ursachen überzeugen durch Energie, nicht durch Sinn.

Logik

Fred: Ich glaube an die Logik. Der gesamte Kosmos ist logisch aufgebaut. Frauen gehören allerdings nicht zum Kosmos. Durch logisches Denken kommt man an jede Rätselnuss heran. Man muss sich im Denken nur tüchtig anstrengen.

Arnold Heitermann: Logik bringt uns in der Erkenntnis nicht weiter. Ein Beispiel: Es sitzen drei Krähen auf einem Zaun. Da kommt ein Vogelmörder vorbei und erschießt einen der Vögel.

Arnold: Wie viele Vögel sitzen jetzt noch auf dem Zaun?

Fred: Es sitzen noch zwei Krähen auf dem Zaun.

Arnold: Falsch! Es sitzt noch eine Krähe auf dem Zaun!

Fred: Das ist doch völlig unlogisch!

Arnold: Das ist logisch. Der erschossene Vogel fiel tot zu Boden. Die zweite Krähe hat sich durch den lauten Knall erschreckt und ist sofort davon geflogen. Die dritte Krähe bekam durch den Knall eineSchrecklähme und bleibt als einziger Vogel sitzen.

Fred: Dieser Fall kommt mir sehr konstruiert vor, aber logisch ist es.

Arnold: Tja, mit Logik kann man alles und nichts erklären.

Fred: Vor allen Dingen im Nachhinein.

Arnold: Ja, immer hinterher.

Die Wirklichkeit war allerdings vorher da.

Fred: Was wäre, wenn nach dem Schuss plötzlich fünf Krähen auf dem Zaun gesessen hätten?

Arnold: Dann hätten sich ein paar lebensmüde Krähen dazugesetzt, in der Hoffnung, auch erschossen zu werden.

Fred: Echt toll, was alles logisch ist.

Arnold: Man kann sich mit Logik alles erklären, sogar die Unlogik.

Fred: Mensch, Mensch, da muss ich echt mal drüber nachdenken.

Arnold: Aber bitte dabei streng logisch bleiben!

Fred: Äh ... ja ... also ...

Dialog

Sokrates: Was siehst du heute Morgen wieder scheiße aus, Platon!

Platon: Halt's Maul, du Arsch!

Sokrates: Du bist einfach nicht dialogfähig!

Kugel

Eine Kugel ist furchtbar eingeschnürt in sich selbst. Sie hätte das Begehren, gebären zu wollen, wenn sie gezündet würde. Aber niemand zündet sie. Die Kugel bleibt stumpf wie Matsch und kennt sich nicht. Warum rollen Kugeln nur? Sie berollen den Weg, doch ändern sie dabei nicht ihre Form. Letztendlich werden sie von der Bewegung gerollt. Kugel bleibt Kugel. Jetzt fällt's mir wieder ein: Kugeln sind weiblich!

(un) vollkommen

Der Hund an sich ist die Idee eines Hundes. Sieht die Idee eines Hundes nun aus wie ein Dackel, ein Golden Retriever, ein

Schäferhund, oder gar wie ein Pudel? Wie ein Kreis an sich ausschaut, das wissen wir. Es gibt nur einen Kreis, und der ist vollkommen rund. Schon bei Dreiecken wird es schwieriger: Welchen Winkel hat die Idee eines Dreiecks? Der Kreis ist die einzige Idee, die man haargenau zeichnen kann. Den Hund an sich kann man nicht zeichnen, nur einen bestimmten Hund. Der Kreis an sich ist zeichenbar. Sollen wir den Kreis anbeten? Gibt es überhaupt ein „an sich"? Die Dinge zeigen sich doch nur „für mich"? - Das Perfekte in der Realität wäre zu unvollkommen für das Leben. Das Leben braucht eine Ecke im Kreis oder ein Loch im Quadrat. Das Perfekte existiert nur als Idee, denn in der Realität kann das Perfekte nicht bestehen. In der Perfektion des Lebens hat der Kreis Ecken. Eine Kastanie ist eine eckige Kugel. Sie fruchtet in unvollkommener Perfektion als vollkommenes Leben. Trotzdem ist eine Kastanie irgendwie krank. Warum das? Das weiß wohl nur der Igel!

Kreis

Ein Kreis kriegt keine Luft. Nirgendwo hat er ein Loch, durch das er atmen könnte. Der Kreis selber kann als Loch aufgefasst werden. Ist der Kreis das Tor zu einer anderen Welt? Ich kann das nicht nachprüfen, denn der Kreis lässt mich nicht rein. Er ist einfach zu verschlossen. Mit solchen Typen soll man sich nicht abgeben. Der Kreis redet nicht mit mir, er wird immer geheimnisvoll bleiben. Wahrscheinlich hat der Kreis nicht mal was zu verbergen: Er ist naiv, langweilig und leer. - Das Runde ist die Farbe des Kreises. Diese Farbe ist sehr selten und ohne Namen. Am leichtesten lässt sich die Farbe noch mit ''bunt'' benennen. Das Runde kann ohne Kreis und Bogen auf Abenteuer gehen. Ein Abenteuer ist ja das Leben selbst. Heute denkt das Runde etwas Neues. Doch ist das Runde so alt, dass sein Denken des Neuen nie Wahnsinn hervorbringen kann. Spießer treiben sich jedoch nie mit dem Runden herum. Dazu ist es doch zu hupfig. Das Runde wollte zum Kreis werden und hat bei der Agentur für Arbeit um eine Umschulung angefragt. Der Sachbearbeiter war ein Quadrat. Es hat bös geendet.

Der Apfel denkt, und Birne lenkt.

Schlagen ist der Hammer

Schlagen ist das universellste Verb, das es gibt. Schlagen ist echt der Hammer. Schon in der Steinzeit war diese Tätigkeit vollentwickelt. Man kann die Augen aufschlagen, ein Buch gleichermaßen. Im Duden nachschlagen, die Scheibe einschlagen, oder jemanden in die Fresse schlagen. Musiker machen mit dem Schlagzeug Krach. Da trifft einen der Schlag. Der 1.FC Meniskus schlägt die Rosenheimer Plattfüße mit 2:1. Wer schlägt, der gewinnt. Mit Steinen kann man am besten schlagen. Ein vornehmer Stein heißt Hammer. Schlagen an sich ist roh und unbehauen. Ein Schlag ist geistlos und atomar. Schlagen zertrümmert, macht kaputt, Schlagen trennt. Ein Kind des Schlagens heißt Schneiden. Ein übles Kind. Ein anderes Kind des Schlagens heißt Stoßen. Dieses Kind ist sympathischer, denn es hat mehr Sonne im Vorwärts. Schlagen macht eine Faust, dadurch kriegt sein Tun einen Bauch.

Werkschatz

Ein Werkschatz ist die Ablagerung aller endgültigen Erfahrung des Menschen. Es gibt Erfahrung, die hat sich so bestätigt, dass sie sich als Werkschatz verfestigt. Der Werkschatz orientiert wie ein Magnetfeld alle Wesen vom Geistigen her. Der Werkschatz ist das natürliche Wikipedia des Lebens. Leider gibt es auch schwarze Schafe im Schatz des Wissens: Sie heißen Werkschmutz.

Herrschen heißt für König Orthos, die Dinge nach ihrem eigenen Inneren sich ordnen zu lassen. Nicht seinen eigenen Willen überträgt Orthos den Leuten. Der König will die Dinge nicht zwingen, sondern er erforscht ihre Eigenart und lässt sie sich selber ordnen. In Orthos Reich leben Menschen, Ziegen und andere Wesen, alle stehen und gehen an ihrem rechten Platz. Nach seinem Tod wird König Orthos im Wasser seines Lieblingsflusses zerfließen, der sich schließlich ins Meer ergießt. Vom Meer aus wird sein Werkschatz die Menschen weiterhin orientieren.

Hunger und Durst

Hunger will ständig etwas essen. Hunger ist völlig abhängig vom Objekt seiner Begierde. Aber gerade das macht den Hunger so sympathisch. Er steht voll im Leben, manche munkeln sogar, er sei das Leben selbst. Hunger hat auch eine Schwester: Sie heißt "Durst". Die ist aber nur was für ganz durchgeknallte Typen.

Brauchen ist die Abstraktion von Hunger und Durst. Brauchen ist arm dran und hat Not. Brauchen ist sehr weltlich und sieht immer gleich grau aus. Man kann Brauchen bei jeder Temperatur lagern. Brauchen fruchtet niemals, es bleibt immer mager. Wer was braucht, der geht einkaufen.

Wer braucht schon Ballaststoffe? Vor allen Dingen, wenn sie nur noch aus Ballast bestehen. Füllstoffe belasten. Sie füllen die Leere, bleiben aber selber hohl. Die Essenz ist es, die glänzt.

Der Psychosaurus ist völlig am Ende:

Eine Eismacht als Statur hat gehoben ihren Arm. Eine Trehne aus Wasser kullert vom kalten Gesicht herab. Die Augen der Schattenfrau leuchten als zwei Sonnen in der Nacht. Doch nicht lange. Ihre Lichter sind nun erloschen. Die Schattenfrau fliegt als schwarzer Engel in den Himmel. Verwaist ist der Unbekannten Platz. Wo niemals jemand gewesen ist, da steht auch jetzt niemand. Mein Wissen vom Nichtsein steht neben dem leeren Platz. Ich bin warm, doch nur als Hitze, denn einen anderen Körper habe ich nicht. Ein Schrei ohne Zunge geht verzweifelt im leeren Raum umher. Überall ist nur Leere, wo eigentlich etwas sein müsste. Wo nichts ist, kann man auch nichts sehen, gerade wenn man keine Augen hat. Doch sehe ich den Schrecken, und ich weiß nicht warum.

Loch

Ein Loch bezeichnet ein eher rundes Fehlen. Löcher sind leer. Ein Loch ist häufig ein Durchgang, bei dem es rein und raus geht. Manchmal geht der Blick durch das Loch raus, und der Ausblick kommt durch das Loch rein. Löcher haben Hunger, sie möchten gerne gestopft werden. Der Drang allen Seins ist wohl, satt zu werden. Die Realität hat Löcher. Diese sind so durchsichtig, dass niemand sie sehen kann, auch kein Physiker mit seinen tollen Apparaten. Das Fehlen von Kleidung kann man bei nackten Leuten sehen. Das Fehlen in einer Kluft dagegen bleibt hungrig und unsichtbar. Fläche hat die Tendenz zur Leere. Wird diese Leere gefüllt, verschwindet die Fläche schnell, sie macht sich dünne. Der Ästhet verordnet der Fläche Farbe, damit diese mehr Selbstbewusstsein kriegt.

Tier

Das klassische Tier hat vier Beine, es macht „miau", oder es bellt. Der Begriff des Tieres ist ein Setzkastenwort für viele Wesen, die kaum etwas gemeinsam haben. Tiere tragen keine Blätter, und sie können keine Atombomben bauen. Tiere sind zurückgebliebene Menschen. Jedoch: Eines Tages werden auch Tiere den Unvollständigkeitssatz von Gödel verstehen. - Nur wann?

Natur kann roh und unbehauen sein. Es gibt auch die Natur der Träumer: Diese Natur ist das Paradies der Menschen noch vor dem Sündenfall. Die Natur des germanischen Charles Darwin sieht so aus: Ein Kampf des Starken gegen einen noch Stärkeren. Unsere zweite Natur ist die Kultur. Unser drittes Reich heißt Künstlichkeit. Dort mag keiner leben.

Eisblume

Eine fremde Macht aus Schweden ist aus kältestem Eis. Diese Macht geht auf der Erde in Gestalt eines altes Mädchen namens Eisblume. Eine Blume aus Eis, eine wunderschöne Blume. Blumen erinnern an Frühling, weil in dieser Zeit gewöhnlich frische Blumen in junger Wärme blühen. Unsere Eisblume jedoch blüht in der mörderischen Kälte des Winters. Alle anderen Leute, die ebenfalls aus Eis sind, die sind hingerissen von Eisblume. Auch Agnis ist aus Kälte, sie ist aus brennendem Eis. Agnis sieht Eisblume und ist begeistert. Die Frigiden sind immer die heißesten. Herr Sumpfstein ist als Verkäufer von Speiseeis eine Wucht. Seine Eiskugeln verfügen über Sprengstoff, welches dann zündet, wenn er längst über alle Berge ist. Eisblume sieht Herrn Sumpfstein: Sie kriegt einen Schock, die Roulettekugel rollt in ihrem Kopf. Keiner weiß, dass die Kugel im Fach der Siebzehn zum Stillstand kommen wird. Bei Agnis wird es die Drei sein.

Eiskugeln oder Roulettekugeln, Kugeln sind alle gleich. Kugeln sind die Bad Bank des Schicksals. Und in diese Bank brechen wir jetzt ein und befreien den Wahnsinn. Total irre werden alle: Eisblume, Agnis und Herr Sumpfstein in einem Karton zusammen sind. Sie atmen den Wahnsinn ein: Ah, das tut gut. Endlich sind sie frei!

Blut

Blut fließt als dicke und kräftige Wärme im Inneren. Sehr persönlich ist das Menschenblut, solange es noch in seinen Adern kreist. Das Blut kreist, also ist es rund. Blut kraftet in seinem Kreis. Äußeres Blut in der kalten und herzlosen Arztspritze ist schon tot. Wie furchtbar! Nur Reptilien bluten kalt. Es sei denn, die Sonne scheint dem Reptil auf sein grünes Fell. Jeder Vampir weiß: Beim Schein des Mondes ist Blut schwarz. Tagsüber sieht man ja nichts.

Feuer

Feuer tanzt mit heftigen Flammen. Wildes Brennen zertrümmert die Beständigkeit des Brennstoffs. Hitzestacheln piksen in den Raum, Fieberzähne beißen sich selbst. Die Kraft des roten Sturms gibt seiner Umgebung eine Aura von Wärme. Des Feuers Glut erstirbt in Asche. Feuer ist eindrucksvoll, doch leiht es sich seine Substanz vom Brennstoff. Sein Essen ist schneller gegessen als gekocht, sehr viel schneller. Des Feuers Wärme schläft flauschig im Raum der Unvergänglichkeit. Wenn Wärme durchdreht, so wird sie zur Hitze.

allgemein

Das Allgemeine zeigt gerade mal so viel Gesicht wie nötig. Das Besondere zeigt viel klarere Kanten. Das Allgemeine ist überall dasselbe, es drückt sich häufig durch das Gleiche aus. In der Landschaft von Allem ist das Allgemeine an jedem Ort zu finden. Der graue Onkel des Allgemeinen heißt Durchschnitt. Das Allgemeine muss sich auf das Besondere immer neu einstellen, das macht Stress. Das Allgemeine gibt Sicherheit, wenn man im Ungewohnten Urlaub macht.

Stehschatten

Ein Stehschatten muss immer stehen bleiben, obwohl er hingehen kann, wohin er will. Will sich der Stehschatten bewegen, so bewegt sich die Umwelt an seiner statt an ihm vorbei, er selber bleibt stehen. So kann sich der Stehschatten fortbewegen und muss dennoch ewig an derselben Stelle stehen bleiben. Ein Stehschatten hat keine Gesellschaft. Selbstverständlich gibt es noch andere Stehschatten, aber die stehen woanders.

Kurzschluss

Der Weg führt zum Ziel, solange kein Esoteriker auf ihm wandelt. Ein Kurzschluss kürzt den Weg des Lebens ab. Ganz schnell geht er einen Weg, den es nicht gibt. Dadurch fehlt ihm die Erfahrung. Sein Erfolg ist heiß und leer und ohne Fleisch, aber charismatisch wirkt der Kurzschluss. Der kürzeste Weg ist immer ein Kurzschluss, sein Ziel heißt Unsein. Der Kurzschluss handelt ohne Wachstum, er geht ohne Weg. Joachim Ernst Berendt schrieb ein Buch: "Es gibt keinen Weg, nur gehen: SEIN in der Natur". Auf dem Weg zur Vorstellung seines Buches wurde er von einem Auto überfahren.

Gehen

Man kriegt Angst, das Gehen könnte umfallen. Doch das Gehen hat es super raus: Es bleibt ständig im Gleichgewicht. Im Gang bewegt sich das Stehen. Das Liegen jedoch läuft nie.

Himmel

Spitze Berge haben keine Probleme und freuen sich, dass sie so ragen und groß sind. Der Himmel freut sich auch, wenn er von den Bergen Besuch bekommt. Auch der große Himmel braucht Geselligkeit.

Grund

Der Grund ist unten. Er ist Basis, Boden, Sockel und Begründung. Wenn man in den Grund hineinschaut, dann wird er zum Abgrund. Man kann die Schwerkraft dort nicht entdecken. Grund und Abgrund beruhigen die Nerven ungemein. Die beste Tätigkeit für den Menschen ist es, den Dingen auf den Grund zu gehen. Nur Angsthasen machen lieber etwas Nützliches, denn nützlich geht die Welt zugrunde.

Unterwelt

Die Unterwelt liegt unterhalb der Welt. Fast gehört sie nicht mehr zur Welt, man kennt sie nicht, deshalb ist sie einem nicht geheuer. Unter dem Boden liegen die Toten, dort ist auch die Quelle der Fruchtbarkeit. Wie sonst sollten all die Pflanzen wachsen?

Wolke

Die Wolke ist ein Schaf im Himmel. Wolken sind immer traurig. Häufig müssen sie weinen. Sie beschützen aber auch das Vieh vor der aggressiven Sonne. Eine Wolke saugt das Gute und das Böse der Menschen auf. An ihren Formen kann man erkennen, was die Stunde geschlagen hat. Bewegung und Wasser tanzen in der Wolke miteinander.

Schmutz

Schmutz soll man nicht in den Salat reinmachen. Sonst droht Krankheit! Schmutz ist die körperliche Entsprechung zur Sünde. Eine Wunde kann man als Verunreinigung auffassen, denn häufig bildet die Wunde eine eklige Kruste am Rand, die aussieht wie Dreck. Verunreinigung oder Flecke wiederum zeigen Schuld an. Jemand ist befleckt. Wurden wir verletzt, weil wir zu unvollkommen waren? Oder sind wir unvollkommen, weil wir verletzt wurden? Oder sind wir schuldig, weil wir etwas verletzt haben, ein Gesetz oder einen Menschen? Aber wir verletzen doch nicht! Wir sind ja vollkommen und unschuldig! Wer so etwas behauptet, der ist verletzend, somit schuldig.

Sex im Knast

Die Mauern des Gefängnisses formen ein Herz. Seine Außenwände sind von außen schwarz und von innen rot. Der Strafgefangene Rasputin ist nicht mehr der Jüngste, aber auch nicht der Älteste, denn schließlich hat er noch Akne. Auch Germania ist inhaftiert: Rasputin und Germania gehen zusammen ins Bett. Rasputin befürchtet, sich bei Germania mit Syphilis zu infizieren. Germania verlässt Rasputin. Wahrscheinlich muss sie nur kurz Pippi machen, doch weit wird sie nicht kommen, denn wir befinden uns im Gefängnis des Herzens. Ein Gefängnis ist ein Gebäude, dem man nicht entkommen kann. Rasputin stellt sich vor den Spiegel und drückt sich seine Pickel aus. Der Eiter spritzt auf die silberne Unschuld: Voll eklig, ey.

Ratte und Atombombe

Ratten sind Mäuse, die größenwahnsinnig geworden sind. Sie vertragen Radioaktivität am besten von allen Lebewesen. Sicherlich werden sie eines Tages Könige der Erde. Ratten töten sich gegenseitig, sie sind den Menschen sehr ähnlich. Ratte sich, wer kann! Allerdings sind Ratten klüger als Menschen, denn sie lernen sehr schnell, keine giftige Nahrung zu fressen, wenn sie merken, dass ihre Artgenossen daran eingehen. Darum ist Rattengift keine dauerhafte Lösung zur Ausrottung dieser Höllenviecher. Im Mittelalter wurden die Menschen von Ratten gefoltert, heute werden die Ratten in wissenschaftlichen Labors gefoltert. Das ist ein Sieg der Menschheit! Vom Opfer zum Täter! Im indischen Karni-Mata-Tempel werden niedliche Ratten gehegt und gepflegt. Im Abendland jedoch gibt es nur miese Kanalratten. In China gibt es die Ratte sogar als Sternzeichen. Doch der keimfreie Psychosaurus meint: „Wir leben doch nicht mehr im Mittelalter! Fort mit den ekligen Infektionsträgern! Warum tun die Politiker nichts? Die tun nie was!"

Knick

Man kann einen Knick nicht anfassen, weil er so weit weg ist von der Reihe, aus der er tanzt. Wenn das Nichts knickt, dann gibt es Dinge. Eine Linie geht von hier nach da. Sie ist so was von normal, dass man davon depressiv wird. Wissenschaftler und Architekten mögen Linien. Eine Linie frisst kein Leben. Die Linie staut das Leben und gewinnt daraus Energie, um das Zimmer bis auf moderate 20 Grad aufheizen zu können.

Neige

Die Neige ist eine Neigung, die gemäß der Beliebtheit des Geneigten sich neigt, sich zuwendet einem Winkel, der der Neigung des Geneigten entspricht. Eine solche Neige ist nicht beliebig, sondern entspricht der Liebe des Geneigten.

gut

Das Gute ist ein Baum, der das ganze Jahr Früchte trägt. Sein Holz ist aus festem Blut; seine Blätter können lachen. Das Bunte ist gut, das Graue ist böse. Der Teufel frisst das Gute. Das Gute kann aus sich selber bestehen. Das Böse jedoch ist auf die Zerstörung des Guten angewiesen. Daher kann das Böse niemals siegen.

bestehen

Salz besteht aus Natrium und Chlor. Das Stehen steht auf eigenen Füßen, doch Bestehen braucht als Boden eine Substanz. Ein Bestehen braucht Teile aus denen es besteht, von alleine kann es nicht sein. Am gröbsten besteht Bestand. Der Begriff „Bestand" kommt dem der Substanz sehr nahe.

Maus und Fledermaus

Mäuse haben vier Beine und laufen so herum, wie es Gottes Auftrag entspricht. Einige Mäuse jedoch haben ihre Bestimmung missachtet und sind in die Luft gegangen. Den ganzen Tag hängen sie faul rum (mit dem Kopf nach unten) und nachts wird Party gemacht (Blut trinken und so Sachen). Die Maus als Fledermaus ist blind. Das ist die Strafe Gottes für ihre Sünden. Als Notlösung müssen die fliegenden Mäuse nun mit ihren Ohren sehen. Voll krass ist das.

dünn

Dünne Frauen sitzen schnell auf der Anklagebank der Magersucht. Angeklagt von schwabbeligen und fetten Artgenossen. Wenn das Dünne zunehmen will, dann muss es sich „schlank" nennen. Das Dünne hat bisweilen intensivere Wirkung als das Dicke, denn es kann viel Essenz in seinem süßen Bäuchelchen beherbergen. Daher ist das Dünne oft intelligenter als das Dicke. Das gilt nicht für Dünnbrettbohrer, denn diese haben ein dickes Brett vorm Kopf.

Pyrrhussieg

Mein Name ist Schmidt, und ich bin tot. Ich führte ein sündiges Leben. An meinem Arbeitsplatz bei der Firma Satan & Söhne verwandelte sich mein geldgieriger Chef in einen 100-Euro-Schein. Ich witterte meine Chance für ein seliges Leben nach dem Tod: Schnell steckte ich den Geldschein in meine Geldbörse und malte ein Kruzifix auf ihr Außenleder. Mein Chef war gefangen. Nur nach seiner Zusicherung, dass ich nach meinem Tod nicht in die Hölle komme, entferne ich das Kreuz wieder. Kurz darauf rutschte ich vor der AOK unglücklich auf einer Bananenschale aus und fiel mit dem Hinterkopf auf das harte Pflaster. Ich war sofort tot. In die Hölle kam ich wie versprochen zwar nicht, doch in den Himmel wollte man mich auch nicht reinlassen, da ich zwar das Böse besiegt hatte, das Gute aber dennoch nicht getan hatte. Nun irre ich ständig zwischen Himmel und Hölle hin und her und weiß nicht mehr ein noch aus.

Leiden

Fred: Leiden ist total überflüssig. Welcher Idiot hat eigentlich die Welt erschaffen?

Detlef: Leiden schützt vor idiotischen Handlungen. Es verhindert, dass du zu viel Bier trinkst. Das Böse führt zum Guten.

Fred: Geht das nicht auch anders? Irgendwie liebevoller?

Papst: Gott ist unfehlbar (so wie ich), er wird schon wissen, warum er die Welt so erschaffen hat.

Mephisto: Ich bin ein Teil von jener Kraft, die stets das Böse will und stets das Gute schafft.

Bert Hellinger: Auf einer höheren Ebene ist das Böse auch gut.

Fred: Ich lebe auf der Erde; die Erde ist eine niedere Ebene, die höhere Ebene nützt mir nichts. Das alles ist nicht sehr überzeugend.

Detlef: Der Sonnengott hat auch gelitten. Er ist am Kreuz als Mensch gestorben und ist am dritten Tage wieder auferstanden.

Fred: Das ist solidarisch von ihm. Mir geht es schon viel besser.

Allahu Akbar

Gott ist größer als ... Gott ist immer größer, als sich ein Mensch nur vorstellen kann. Ich will sicherheitshalber nix Böses über Gott schreiben, man weiß ja nie. Es sei denn, Gott ist der Teufel. Sind böse Götter eigentlich echte Götter? Oder zehrt ihre Existenz vom Fressen des Guten? Gibt es nur einen Gott, so kann man ihn eigentlich nur Allah nennen. Die zwei neutralen und allumfassenden A-Laute flankieren den unendlichen L-Laut. Wenn es mehrere Götter gibt, dann wird es bunter und liebevoller und auch begreifbarer für den Menschen. Jeder Gott unter anderen Göttern hat seinen eigenen Zuständigkeitsbereich. Allah braucht nicht mehr 99 Namen zu haben, denn es gibt ja 99 Götter. Und der hundertste Gott wird wohl wieder alle Götter vereinigen, so vermutet man. Die fanatische Polarisierung in Gut und Böse löst sich in der Vielheit der Götter auf. Manchmal werden die Götter auch Engel, Erzengel oder höhere Wesenheiten genannt.

Knoblauch

Knoblauch ist abgestandene Frische. Seine Zehen sind gespalten. Eine echte Persönlichkeitsspaltung hat die Wurzel. Nach außen hin jedoch demonstriert die Zwiebel Einheitlichkeit. Knoblauch hilft gegen Vampire und Hexen. Die Knolle stärkt das Blut und macht es so ungenießbar für Schmarotzer, dass sogar den Vampiren der Appetit vergeht. Der schizophrene Lauch tötet auch körperliche Schmarotzer ab, wie etwa Bandwürmer oder Fäulnisbakterien. Knoblauch spaltet die Menschheit wie der Zigarettenrauch. Die einen mögen es: Das sind die guten Menschen. Die Bösen jedoch (z.B. Vampire, Hexen, Nazis, Kinderficker, Kapitalisten und Grünen-Wähler) fühlen sich von seinem Geruch abgestoßen.

Vertrag mit dem Teufel

Man kann schnell zu den Schönen und Reichen gehören, indem man einen kleinen Vertrag im Servicebüro der Firma Satan & Söhne macht: Der Vertragsnehmer (Teufel) erfüllt einem jeden weltlichen Wunsch. Als Gegenleistung vermacht der Vertragsgeber seine nachtodliche Seele den Anatomen der Hölle zu Forschungszwecken. Der Vertrag ist durch einen Tropfen Blut des Vertragsgebers rechtsgültig.

Seuche

Arnold phantasiert eine Seuche, die über die Erde kommt und alle bösen Menschen tötet. Die Guten werden erst gar nicht krank oder überleben den Infekt spielend. Arnold gehört natürlich zu den Guten. Obwohl, wie kann er sich da so sicher sein? Wie wäre es, wenn die Seuche tatsächlich nur die Guten tötet? Das wäre gemein, aber typisch für die Ungerechtigkeit dieser Welt. Arnold kriegt Angst und will sich gegen das Schicksal impfen lassen, obwohl er weiß, dass das gar nicht geht.

schneiden

Das Bewusstsein schneidet das Sein in Dinge. Schneiden ist vornehmer als Stechen, darum trägt eine Stechmücke auch keinen Adelstitel. Kräftige Seelen haben den Schneid zum Mut, Feiglinge haben überhaupt keine Klinge zu Hause. In den Finger sollte man sich nicht schneiden! Darum Leute: Seid bloß vorsichtig! Die Farbe des Schneidens nennt sich Schärfe. Peperoni und Sexbomben können auch manchmal ein bisschen scharf sein.

Arme

Arme strecken sich aus. In den Händen fangen die Arme an zu blühen. Arme verfeinern sich in den Händen, die Hände verstärken sich im Werkzeug. Zweige sind die Arme der Bäume.

Grenze

Eine Grenze trennt das eine vom anderen. Bei der Grenze fängt es an, oder es hört auf. Die Grenze formt ein Gefäß für das Leben. Das Blut braucht Adern, um zu leben. Ein Haus begrenzt das Wohnen durch seine Mauern. Wenn das Wohnen aus seinem Haus auszieht, dann ertrinkt es im Meer der Obdachlosigkeit.

Der Teller hat einen runden Rand. Im Gegensatz zum Rahmen schließt der Rand das Wachsen seines Eigners ab. Ein Rahmen ist Schmuck, er ist ein Zwang zum Beenden des Wucherns.

Mit dem Begriff „Welt" bezeichnet man die Landschaft von Allem. Welt kann verstanden werden als mörderische Größe. Diese Welt hat kein Ende. Des Menschen Blick findet keinen Halt in den unendlichen Straßen. Eine geborgene Welt ist in ihren Rändern geschlossen. Dort umarmt die geborgene Welt die Grenzenlosigkeit mit den Armen der Endlichkeit.

hell und dunkel

Gustav ist auf beiden Hühneraugen blind. Seine Füße können nichts sehen. Das ist gut so, denn wer nichts sieht, der wird auch nicht depressiv. Daher ist Gustav glücklich. Es gibt Leute, die haben ein

Blind Date. Sie sind zu blind für ein Stelldichein. Auch Fledermäuse sehen schwarz, doch hören sie hell. Ist das Licht blind für die Dunkelheit? Sieht die Dunkelheit das Licht?

die Mondin

Der Mond lacht in der Dunkelheit. Er ist voll zu sehen. Als Vollmond ist er männlich. Ansonsten ist sie weiblich. Oder war es umgekehrt? Der Mond huscht ängstlich über den Himmel. Er mag nicht gern gesehen werden; nur Werwölfe, Fledermäuse und Raben dürfen das. Der Mond herrscht heimlich im Reich des Bösen, er ist die Hinterlist mit runden Backen, eine alte Liebe ist er, eine leuchtende Dunkelheit namens Mond. Der Mond leuchtet dann am stärksten, wenn anständige Leute schlafen.

Augenblick

Es gibt nur einen Augenblick, und der ist immer derselbe. Nur der Augenblick ist ein Augenblick. Die Mehrzahl „Augenblicke" macht da keinen Sinn. Also gibt es keine Zeit. Und doch tickt die Uhr. Deshalb sind Uhren Lügner.

Erinnerung

Menschen können sich gar nicht erinnern. Wir sehen die Vergangenheit von unserem heutigen Augenblick aus. Jeden Tag erinnert man sich an eine andere Vergangenheit. Wie es wirklich war, das ist unwiederbringlich verloren.

Urkuh

Im Anfang war die Milch. Das Weltall ist aus Milch entstanden, deshalb spricht man auch von der Milchstraße. Die Milch kam aus dem Euter der Urkuh, der großen MUU.

frisch

Das Frische singt als Leichte in der Feuchtigkeit des Lebens. Frischfleisch ist gesünder als Gammelfleisch. Fruchtsaft frischer als Blut, denn das Tierische vergammelt in seiner Gier.

Schildkröten

Schildkröten sind uralte Embryonen. Sie sind noch aus einer Zeit, als es überhaupt noch keine Zeit gab. Auch ihre Materie ist anders. Sie besteht nicht aus kleinsten Teilchen, sondern milder Brei als Härte läuft in einer Linie von hier nach dort. Echte Erde stirbt nie.

Ruine

Durch die Ruine des zerfallenden Schlosses weht heimlich der Wind. Dunkle Mauern sind leer von Geschehen. Feuerstürme waren gestern, die Narben sind heute. Eine Maus kann schreiben und erzählt dem Papier die Geschichte der toten Ruine. Vögel überfliegen die rote Abendsonne und verschwinden im Nirgendwo.

Ur

Das Ur kommt immer zuerst. Die Ursache, der Ursprung, die Ursuppe, der Uranus, das Urvieh, der Urahn, der Urwald, der Urknall, und natürlich Urkunden und urige Urgroßeltern. Letztere kannten noch nicht den Begriff urgefährlich. Urgefährlich meint in Wien eine Sache, die besonders gefährlich ist.

fake-news

Die Erde ist eine Scheibe! Wenn die Erde eine Kugel wäre, dann würden die Menschen in Neuseeland ja von der Erde herunterfallen. Soll sich die NASA ihre gefälschten Fotos doch in den Arsch stecken. Die haben wohl zu viel Mondluft geschnuppert!

Anfang

Ein Anfang kann plötzlich starten wie beim Sprint oder schleichend auftauchen wie der Nebel im Herbst. Pflanzen keimen aus, und Babys werden keimfrei im Krankenhaus geboren. Ein Anfang setzt ein Ende voraus: Die Geburt eines Babys beendet die Schwangerschaft. Der Anfang kennt sich selber noch nicht: Erst am Ende weiß der Anfang, wer er gewesen ist.

Kinder

Kinder essen Kinderschokolade. Erwachsene essen Erwachsenenschokolade. Beide Produkte schmecken nach Schokolade. Man sieht: Kinder sind nichts besonderes. Sie sind Schokofresser wie du und ich. Kinder müssen auch nicht gegossen werden, obwohl sie in den Kindergarten gehen.

Agaric

A toadstool loves its freedom. It needs rain from above. But the red mushroom refuses to receive God's impulses. The fly agaric would like to keep everything under control. It is even a owner of a whip. Dominance is important to it. Rain falls on the fly agaric. The fungus notices, that there are other things than dominance, but the agaric does not dare to open itself. Then he does it, because he is brave. Fear comes from the top down into the mushroom. He dies. He is now no longer a toadstool, but a little mouse, who wants to live a middle class life in its cave. But this does not work. The mouse studies philosophy and renews the world and becomes famous.

Blitz

Martin Luther und Paulus wurden vom Blitz getroffen. Schnell wie der Blitz wurden sie zu erleuchteten Menschen. Bessert uns ein Blitzschlag? Oder ist der Blitz nur einen Kurzschluss, der Scheinheil hervorbringt? Das müsste man beim nächsten Gewitter mal ausprobieren.

J.F. Kennedy in Bielefeld

Eine angebliche Verschwörungstheorie besagt, dass die Stadt Bielefeld gar nicht existiert. Ab einem gewissen Zeitpunkt war es den Schatten nicht mehr möglich, die Nichtexistenz von Bielefeld zu vertuschen. Darum war ihnen daran gelegen, die Verschwörung als bloße Theorie oder Scherz darzustellen, damit niemand auf die Idee kommt, dass die Fälschung Bielefelds die nackte Wahrheit ist. Doch zum Glück gibt es Bill. Am 24.07.1963 besuchte Bill Clinton den amerikanischen Präsidenten John F. Kennedy im weißen Haus und schüttelte ihm die Hand. Clinton rief aus: "Ich werde Präsident!" Durch diese magische Handlung stahl Clinton dem damaligen Präsidenten Kennedy sein Schicksal und seine Identität. Das Ergebnis: Kennedy musste sterben. Oder vielmehr sein Doppelgänger. Der wirkliche Kennedy wurde tiefgefroren. Als die gefälschte Existenz Bielefelds ans Licht der Öffentlichkeit zu kommen drohte, wurde Kennedy wieder aufgetaut. Nach einer Schönheitsoperation und Intensivtraining in deutscher Sprache ist Kennedy heute unter dem falschen Namen Pit Clausen der Oberbürgermeister der Schattenstadt Bielefeld.

Die Bärte

Sindbart: Ey du, ich kann dich sehen!

Windbart: Wahnsinn! Ich dich auch. Erstaunlich, wenn man bedenkt, dass es uns beide nicht gibt.

Sindbart: Wenn sich zwei Leute treffen, die es gar nicht gibt, so werden sie im Verhältnis zueinander und füreinander real, denn sie begegnen sich beide auf derselben Ebene, nämlich der Ebene der Nichtexistenz.

Windbart: Man trifft selten seinesgleichen. Man wird selten real. Wir sollten die Gelegenheit nutzen und ein ausführliches Gespräch über Täuschung und Wahrheit führen.

Sindbart: Prima, ich bin dabei.

Meer

Meer kann sich Größe erlauben, weil es Geheimnis bewahrt. Das Meer besteht aus den Trehnen der Götter (Tränen enthalten Salz). Das Meer ist Nahrung für die Erde. Der Durst der Wüste jedoch ist längst ausgetrocknet, die Wüste braucht nicht mehr zu leben.

Informationsgesellschaft

Arnold Heitermann sieht kein Fernsehen und liest keine Zeitung. Nur die Überschriften. Für Otto Normal ist wichtig, was aktuell ist, alles andere ist unwichtig. Arnold interessiert sich für die größeren Zusammenhänge, nicht für die Eintagsfliegen. Außerdem weiß man bei einer Information nie, ob sie stimmt. Falls in der Überschrift einmal stehen sollte: "Morgen geht die Welt unter!", so würde Herr Heitermann die Info sicherlich vollständig lesen. So ein Weltuntergang kann einen echt betroffen machen, schon aus persönlichen Gründen.

Wasser

Wasser bewegt sich gerne. Wenn die Natur es zulässt, dann fließt es auch. Wasser ist frisch und singt in sich selber. Licht verglitzert mit den Bewegungen seiner Wellen. Wasser ist überall, wo Leben ist. Wasser ist unstet, solange es noch nicht im Unten ruht. Nässe kleidet das Wasser, des Wassers Nacktheit bleibt unberührbar.

Frösche

Man soll kein Frosch sein, kein Angstfrosch. Wer so nah am Wasser gebaut ist wie der Frosch, der lebt noch im Seelischen. Seele und See sind dasselbe Wasser, das wissen Fisch und Frosch. Im Wasser kann man gar nicht richtig Angst kriegen, nur Trockentiere können das. Fragt den Angsthasen! Nicht den Angstfrosch! Frösche kommen aus der Pubertät nie heraus. Der Frosch ist ein Fisch, der es nicht bis zum Landtier geschafft hat: Ein Versager der Evolution. Nicht mehr Fisch ist er, aber zum Affen hat es auch nicht gereicht. Frösche sind noch grün hinter den Ohren, und nicht nur dort. Häufig kriegen Frösche Pickel, dann aber nennt man sie Kröten.

Wildschweine

Wildschweine springen vom Dach eines Hauses in der nebelheißen Stadt Rom. Die wilden Schweine schlagen unten mit dem Rücken auf dem Straßenpflaster auf. Die Wildsau hat sich nichts gebrochen, locker grunzt sie und lebt weiter. So eine Wildsau ist echt robust. Ihr Blut verwelkt nicht. In kräftigen Schlägen pulsiert zeitlos ihr Feuersaft durch die Rennstrecke ihrer Adern.

Gefühle

Gefühle haben keine Farbe. Sie sind untreue Strolche, ihr einziger Halt ist die Unbeständigkeit. Würdest Du dein Herz an Gefühle vermieten? Gefühle sind geil auf Menge und Masse, sie werden stärker und schwächer, einfallslos kehren sie wieder wie die Pferde auf dem Karussell.

Untergang

Der Welten Breite versinkt in die Tiefe. Alles geht schlafen, und der Mond steht am Himmel. Sein Silberlicht fließt in den Untergang. Eine Hand will den Mond greifen und schafft es auch: Sie hat den Mond zerquetscht. Silberblut, das gleichermaßen schwarz ist, es läuft herab aus einer Kugel, die einmal der Mond war. Die Welt erzittert.

töten

Der Tod verneint das Leben und ermöglicht es gleichermaßen. Von was sollte der Adler leben? Was sollte er hinten ausscheißen? Er kann nur leben, indem er andere Tiere tötet. Wie der Mensch! Veganer sind Gutmenschen. Aber auch sie müssen dem Ruf der Natur folgen. Schließlich sind Pflanzen auch Lebewesen. Veganer haben einen Vitaminmangel. Ihre Unschuld lässt sie fahl im Gesicht werden, sie sind Biovampire. Veganer trinken das Blut der Moral. Das größte Raubtier ist der Mensch.

Der tote Fernsehzuschauer

Der Fernseher läuft, vor ihm sitzt ein Skelett. Seine leeren Schädelknochen kriegen nichts mehr mit vom Programm. Jemand schaltet den Fernseher aus: Der Knochenmann merkt nun, dass ihm etwas fehlt, und er kriegt die Wut. Im Entzug erst merkt der Tod, dass er tot ist.

Sinn des Lebens

Der Sinn des Lebens ist es, den großen Agrarökonomen zu füttern. Das ist jedenfalls die Ansicht von Dr. Lightbrain. Er glaubt folgendes: Aus fernen Himmels sät der große Agrarökonom den Samen unserer Seele in den Boden der Verwirklichung. Durch Lebenserfahrung wächst der Seelenkeim zu einer ertragreichen Seelenähre. Diese Ähre erntet der große Agrarökonom nach unserem Tode ab und verzehrt sie. Dr. Brainlight ist der Zwillingsbruder von Dr. Lightbrain. Jeden Morgen muss Dr. Brainlight nach dem Vollkorn-Müsli kotzen, wenn er an die krude Theorie seines Bruders denkt.

Sonne

Die Sonne ist das Herz der Welt, in ihr ist mehr Raum als im Weltraum. Sie hat einen dicken, leuchtenden Bauch. Die Sonne gebiert die Welt. Die Sonne frisst die Welt. Beides gleichermaßen. Die Sonne ist einfach alles. Sie ist weiß bei alten Leuten, sie ist gelb bei jungen Leuten. Die Sonne hat keine Falten im Gesicht.

Tollwut

Ein Vampir sieht in den Spiegel: Aus dem Silber schaut ein Mann mit schwarzen Haaren und Brille, er hat ein fahles Gesicht. Der Vampir denkt, im Spiegel sieht sie aus wie ein normaler Mensch. Der Untote erkennt sich aber nur im Spiegel, wenn er seine Hände und seinen Körper direkt anschaut, dann sieht er niemanden. Das ist nicht normal, auch nicht für Vampire. Sicherlich hat er die Tollwut.

Pflanzen

Pflanzen sind grüne Tiere, die nicht laufen können. Ihre Blätter sind Steine aus Wasser. Durch das Sonnenlicht werden sie ganz grün. Stein, Wasser und Sonne ergeben auf einmal Leben. Eine Pflanze besteht hauptsächlich aus Wachstum, sie genießt ihr Wachstum. Wachsen kennt keine Gene, es lernt sie jeden Moment kennen. Ein Plan wächst nicht, auch wenn man ihn ausführt. Pflanzen hingegen wachsen planlos mit dem Leben.

knallhart

An der Härte hat sich schon mancher Dickschädel den Kopf gestoßen. Härte bietet Widerstand und Beständigkeit. Ein Skelett ist hart. Gewöhnlich bleibt das Harte hart. Ein Penis ist jedoch nur zeitweise hart. - Warum nur? - Die Kante der Härte steht als imposante Linie im Raum. Kanten sollte man nicht übersehen, man könnte sich den Kopf stoßen an ihnen. Wenn zwei Wände zusammenprallen, dann nennt man den Zusammenstoß eine Kante. Eine Kante ist also das Ergebnis einer Karambolage. Sie ist demnach nichts für zarte Gemüter. Steine sind auch hart. Ein Stein ist ein Ding, er hat kein Gesicht, denn ein Stein sieht aus wie andere Steine auch. In ihrem Dingsein sind sich alle Dinge gleich. Schrank, Tisch oder Zahnbürste, das alles sind nur Dinge. Die Steine, die überall herumliegen, die nennt man Realität. Mit einem Stein kann man anderen Leuten den Schädel einschlagen. In der Steinzeit war das wichtig. Heute können einige Steine schon sprechen, man nennt diese Steine „Handys". Wenn ich es recht bedenke: Es gibt auch schöne Steine, nämlich Edelsteine. Drachen sammeln sie.

sammeln

Das Gesammelte ist dicht, manchmal auch eng. Das Gesammelte gibt Sicherheit als Bestand. Oder es ist eine Last. Das Gesammelte ist schwerer als das Sammeln. Wenn das Sammeln schwerer ist als das Gesammelte, so spricht man von "jagen".

Müll

Das Überflüssige ist im Gewachsenen nicht integriert. Das Überflüssige hat das Flüssige während seines Wucherns nicht kennengelernt. Während das Überfließende reichhaltig sein kann, es spendet mitunter, so ist das Überflüssige nicht nur zu nichts zu gebrauchen, sondern es behindert auch noch die lebende Substanz in ihrem Weitergang. Das Überflüssige ist einfach Müll.

Macke

Hugo hat eine Macke. Seine Macke besteht darin, dass ihn die Macke auf seinem Bildschirm stört. Das macht Hugo wahnsinnig. Jahrzehntelang hatte Hugo eine Macke im Gesicht. Ständig vorm Spiegel stehend schaute er seine Macke an, bis ihm sein Hautarzt den Knubbel weglaserte. Hugo hat eine Macke bei Macken. Aber nur bei einzelnen Macken. Wenn alles eine Macke hat, wie zum Beispiel eine total zerkratzte Fensterscheibe, so stört es Hugo nicht. Hugo hat echt eine Macke.

Spinner

Der leere Gedanke füttert seine welke Schneefrau. Die graue Schneefrau heißt Neurose. Sie ist vollkommen harmlos, sie ist Woody Allen. Über eine Neurose kann man lachen, denn Spinner sind witzige Leut. Aber so harmlos ist der Altschnee in Wirklichkeit nicht. In der Schneefrau fließt kein Blut, sondern der Schnee von gestern langweilt sich in ihr. Der Altschnee geht in Psychotherapie. So eine Therapie ist ebenfalls eine Neurose, sie ist weiß wie neuer Schnee.

Paartherapie

Hund und Katze gehen in Paartherapie. Der Therapeut ist eine Hyäne. Hund und Katze wollen ihre Beziehung retten. Die Therapie scheitert. Warum nur? Woran kann das liegen? Sicherlich am Therapeuten, die haben doch alle selber ein Problem.

Humorverbot

Cheplin geht zum Lachen in den Keller, um seinen Leichen Gesellschaft zu leisten. Viele Leute musste er schon töten, um an Geld zu gelangen. Mit dem Leiden dieser Welt und Frauen ist nicht zu spaßen. Cheplin setzt sich für ein generelles Humorverbot für ganz Deutschland ein, Ausnahmen sind sogenannte Lachzentren, in denen nach Entrichtung einer Humorgebühr lauthals gelacht werden darf.

Lachen

Lachen freut sich mit seinen Lippen. Ernsthaftes Lachen kriegt einen Lachanfall. Humoreskes Lachen kann sich nicht vom Sofa der Bürgerlichkeit erheben. Wirkliches Lachen ist nicht witzig, es freut sich bloß. Nur Zwanghafte reißen Witze vom Baum des Leidens.

total witzig

Isolde: Detlef, bei dir weiß man nie, ob du nur Spaß machst, oder ob du es ernst meinst.

Detlef: Das ist doch ganz einfach: Wenn ich Spaß mache, dann meine ich es ernst, und wenn ich ernst bin, dann ist das nur Spaß.

Isolde: Wie kann ich denn das eine vom anderen unterscheiden?

Detlef: An geraden Tagen ist das Erste der Fall, und an ungeraden Tagen das Letztere. Oder war's andersrum? Ich bin ganz durcheinander.

Isolde: Ich werde wahnsinnig mit dem Typen!

Klimawandel

Otto furzt.

Frau Dr. Kackebart-Struller: Mensch Otto! Weißt du eigentlich, was du der Ozonschicht da antust? Mit jedem gelassenen Furz wird nicht nur dein Arschloch größer, sondern auch das Ozonloch. Mit jedem Furz strömt Methan in die Atmosphäre, was die Erde aufheizt. Furz bloß nicht! Wir müssen unsere Umwelt retten!

Otto Struller: Du hast recht, Mausi, ganz recht. Ich geh jetzt auf den Dachboden, die Tauben füttern.

im wilden Wald

Im wilden Wald verlassen die Wurzeln der Bäume ihr Erdreich und laufen über das Land. Ruhe kehrt nicht ein, sondern sie geht auf Abenteuer. Sie geht über Berge, sie geht in den Tälern. Manchmal springt sie auch.

rollen

Rollen oder Kreisen ist die Bewegung eines Rundlings um seinen Mittelpunkt. Das Rollen des Rads ist gefangen. Das Rollen rollt selber nicht, es bleibt unbeweglich in Bezug auf seinen Mittelpunkt. Würde das Rollen sich vom Kreis zum Quadrat bewegen, so wäre es frei beweglich. Das Rad merkt nur, dass die Landschaft sich an ihm vorbei bewegt, das Rad selber bleibt stehen.

Ruhe und Bewegung

Ruhe genießt ihre Identität. Man kann Ruhe als Abwesenheit von zwanghafter äußerer Bewegung definieren. In der Disco gibt es demnach keine Ruhe. Auf der Autobahn auch nicht. Bewegung aus dem Inneren mit Ruhe ist durchaus möglich. Das Dasein hat Ruhe. Es gibt auch die zwanghafte Ruhe des Zen-Buddhismus. Eine solche Ruhe ist der gepflegte Tod auf Erden, sie beruht auf der Unterdrückung und Abtötung der Zappeligkeit. Echte Ruhe jedoch lebt in Freiheit.

spaulen

Der Kolibri fliegt zu einem lustigen Palast, wo die Leute spinnen. Im Palast wohnen 52 kronenlose Menschen. Keiner und jeder ist König und Narr zur gleichen Zeit. Die Leute im Palast sind alles Zwitter. Sie könnten es mit sich selber treiben, wenn sie dazu Lust hätten. Aber sie haben mehr Lust am Gestalten von Spielwelten: Sie spaulen. Spaulen ist ernstes Spielen. Sie spaulen hier mit Jojos, die Könige. Als Narren haben die Könige ihre Krone im großen Saal unter dem Brunnen abgelegt. Die Kronen dienen den Kolibris als Nest. König Purpur schreibt ernsten Unsinn. Mit so einem Mann kann man nicht reden.

Arbeit

Arbeit schwitzt in ihrem Niemandsland, was anstrengend ist, denn statt einem Rückgrat hat Arbeit eine Brust aus Anerkennung, geschmückt mit Stolz. Ihre Erfüllung findet Arbeit im Herzinfarkt. Wer arbeitet, kann seine Leichen im Keller schnell vergessen. Arbeit hat Sehnsucht nach Erlösung, doch das würde sie nie zugeben. Arbeit ist blind, sie merkt nicht, dass sie arbeitet, sie weiß es nur. Christus als Erlöser ist längst out. Der Mensch erlöst sich durch Arbeit: In der Psychotherapie arbeitet man an sich selbst.

Wahre Bewegung ist innerlich. Ein Pferd bewegt sich selbst, ein Auto jedoch wird von den Pferdestärken seines Motors getrieben. Bewegung hat die Tendenz, sich schlangenförmig zu bewegen, nämlich in Wellen. Gehen, Schwimmen, Fliegen oder Fahren, das alles sind Bewegungen. Heutzutage bewegt man sich hauptsächlich fort. Man könnte sich auch hinbewegen. Doch am Ort hält es keiner mehr aus. Man bleibt vor Ort.

Wind

Der Wind streicht um das Gesicht von Frigg. Die Zeit, sie läuft ab. Das Wasser verschwindet im Loch. Alles läuft, es läuft davon. Der Urin läuft, die Tränen laufen. Niemand ist bei Frigg, nur der Wind. Ihre Füße sind verdeckt durch dicke Schuhe. Wie wäre es, wenn sie nacktfuss ginge? Dann würde sie der Wind empor tragen, und Frigg wäre frei. Ihre schweren Schuhe sind die Last ihrer Vergangenheit. Ein Wind mit Namen Wahuna streicht durch ihr Haar hindurch. Sleipnir, ein Pferd mit acht Beinen gleitet an Frigga vorbei. Frigga ist fasziniert, sie lässt sich auf das Pferd zum Windgott setzen und ganz fest freitragen, barfuß, mit Ohne.

Besser eine Birne in der Hand

als ein Apfelbaum auf dem Dach.

Das reinste Machen macht die Maschine. Eine Maschine empfindet
nichts, daher arbeitet sie vor lauter Verzweiflung. Sie macht all die
Handgriffe, die die stumpfen Arbeiter damals in der Altzeit machten.
Griffe ohne Gefühl und Leben, Mechanik eben, Bewegung ohne Sinn,
nur Zweck. Wie schön ist es doch, wenn eine Maschine uns die
stumpfsinnige Arbeit abnimmt. Doch den Stumpfsinn haben die
Schöpfer der Maschinen einst selbst gepflanzt. Die Maschinen
werden uns mit ihrem Stumpfsinn weiter von außen tyrannisieren.
Künstliche Intelligenz ist zwar differenziert, doch bleibt sie blöde. Wir
selber sind nur noch ein Rädchen der großen Weltmaschine.

Der Eigner nennt seine Hände sein Eigen. Die Atome seiner Hände
gehören dem Eigner nicht. Nur leihweise eignen sich die Atome
seiner Hand für die Gestalt seines Ich. Nach dem Tod des Eigners
eignen sich die ehemalige Atome seiner Hand für eine andere
Erscheinung. Der Eigner fühlt sich zuhause in seiner Hand, er wurzelt
in seiner Hand. Diese Wurzel ist seine Identität. Die Hand selber ist es
nicht.

Der irre Apfel

Im Apfel leben Schale und Fruchtfleisch zusammen. Ob beide wohl
verheiratet sind? Noch viel mehr lebt im Apfel zusammen: Das
Kugelige, das Grüne, das Fruchtige, sein Hängen am Baum. Der Apfel

denkt: "Ich habe zwar Eigenschaften, aber ich bin nicht meine Eigenschaften. Schaue ich mich selber an, so finde ich nur Eigenschaften, aber kein Sein." Der Apfel wird wütend über diese Selbsterkenntnis: "Alles Verarschung! Ich existiere ja gar nicht!" Jede Eigenschaft des Apfels geht nun ihren eigenen Weg. Das Kugelige geht nach Norden, das Grüne nach Süden. Das Fruchtige nach Westen, und das Hängen des Apfels nach Osten. Es ist kein Apfel mehr, es hat ihn nie gegeben. Der Apfel hat sich von seiner vorgetäuschten Identität scheiden lassen. Er war nur zusammengeworfen aus seinem Das-Gehört-Zu-Mir. Wo bleibt die Frische des Apfels? Sie sitzt in der Kneipe und lässt sich zulaufen!

Poesie

Dichtung heißt, die Bedeutung zu verdichten auf ihr Konzentrat. Die Dichtung der Schreiber ist jedoch manchmal so abgedichtet, dass der Leser die Bedeutungsdose nicht mehr aufkriegt. Den Inhalt der Dichtung versteht nur der Autor, während er schreibt. Und selbst dem Autor ist seine Dose am nächsten Morgen zu dicht.

durchsichtig

Das Durchsichtige fliegt im Offensichtlichen frei herum, ohne sich verstecken zu müssen. Durchsichtig sind hauptsächlich Löcher. Obwohl das Durchsichtige durchaus Gewicht haben kann, ist es nicht leicht durchschaubar. Das Durchsichtige wird dann durchschaubar, wenn es plump wird.

fangen

Fangen greift mit Erfolg im Beweglichen nach seiner Beute. In besondere Gefangenschaft geraten deshalb hauptsächlich Fische. Sie sind glitschig und leben im beweglichen Wasser, können aber trotzdem gefangen werden.

Gefängnis

Verbrechen lohnen sich nur dann, wenn man sich nicht erwischen lässt. Ein Affe kommt in den Zoo, auch wenn er nichts verbrochen hat. Ein Zoo ist ein artgerechtes Gefängnis für Tiere. Manche Wildtiere sind im Zirkus inhaftiert. Kinder sitzen im Gefängnis der Pädagogik ihrer Eltern. Ehefrauen sitzen im Gefängnis der finanziellen Abhängigkeit von ihrem Ehemann.

streng geheim

Das Geheime darf das Augenlicht der anderen nicht sehen. Es sitzt alleine (oder mit Verschwörern) in seinem Bunker und tut dort möglicherweise folgendes: Es verwest, es vereitert, es freut sich, es dreht krumme Sachen, es entzündet sich, es entzündet andere, es lacht sich einen ab, es hat Angst, es schützt sich, es verweigert sich, oder es kriegt ein Kind. Das Geheime: Wir wissen nicht, was es tut. Das bleibt geheim.

fliegen

Fliegen gleitet ohne Füße durch das Meer der Weite. Im Fliegen werden Oben und Unten gegeneinander ausgespielt. Ein Vogel hat Macht, ohne die Welt zu vergewaltigen. Das ist genial. Fliegenpilze jedoch können nicht fliegen, ihre Flügel sind verzaubert. Die Flügel der Vögel strecken sich ins Gewagte. Dort sind sie zu Hause. Die Flügel sind die Arme des Fliegens, sie sind aus Kraft. Ein Vogel kann frei fliegen, ohne dass er in der Luft mit einer Katze kollidiert. Ein Arbeitnehmer jedoch kollidiert sehr schnell mit seinem Chef oder mit dem Ernst des Lebens.

leicht

Locker fliegt das Leichte über Rätselnüsse, es geht an schweren Bäuchen einfach vorbei. Das Leichte ist tendenziell im Oben zu finden. Holz schwimmt auf Wasser, weil es leichter ist als Wasser. Der Heißluftballon entschwebt der Erde im blauen Himmel. Das Leichte wird schnell leichtsinnig. So etwas Blödes passiert leicht.

Schneeflöckchen

Eine Schneeflocke fällt vorsichtig. Leise ist sie. Die Flocke kommt aus einer anderen Welt. Sie gibt dieser Welt Struktur, denn sonst würden alle Magnetfelder zusammenbrechen. Beim Nord- und Südpol fällt das Magnetfeld in den Schnee hinein. Von den Erdpolen aus organisiert der Schnee geheime Veränderungen in der Welt. Sein Magnetismus durchdringt die Erdbewohner, und macht sie zu Schwerebürgern.

Schutz

So ein Schutz ist eine feine Sache. Schutz ist die erste Sache, die man braucht: Verfassungsschutz, Saalschutz, Pflanzenschutzmittel, Datenschutz und der Gedankenschutz. Du hattest noch gar keinen Besuch vom Gedankenschutz? Der kommt noch, warte nur ab.

Darm

Verdauen kaut und kaut und kaut. Verdauen kaut immer feiner, bis die Nahrung so fein ist, dass sie ins eigene Fleisch integriert werden kann. Ein bisschen giftig bleibt die Nahrung allerdings immer. Die Erde ist giftig. Sie ist nicht unsere Heimat. Tiere können besser verdauen als Menschen, sie leben näher an der Erde.

Erde

Das, worauf wir stehen, das nennt man Erde. Manchmal nennt man es auch Boden. Stehen und Erde sind fest. Erde kann auch Humus oder Stein meinen. Besonders auffällig ist das Substanzhafte an der Erde, sie ist dicht und schwer. Der Boden ist friedlich, der Boden ist dumm. Die große Urmutter hat kein Gesicht. Hat sie Wärme? Wurzeln greifen in die Erde, sie begreifen die Erde auch. Wurzeln sind eins mit der Ruhe der Erde.

Bienen

Bienen leben im Dicklichen der Materie, innerlichst. Eine Biene geht nach draußen, wo es kalt ist. Sie fällt als Schneeflocke tot zu Boden. Als kalte Flocken haben die Bienen ihre Innerlichkeit entäußert. Solange die Schneeflocke gefroren ist, solange ist es Tannenbaumzeit. Taut die Flocke auf, so ist die Einsamkeit nackt. Im Schlürfen des Nektar verbinden die Bienen alle Teile der Welt und erkraften die Schwere, sie erkauen die Schwerkraft. Der Nektar war ein Buch, das noch nicht gelesen wurde. Nicht einmal von seinem Autor.

Schwere

Schwere ist meist groß in ihrer Menge. Im Blei jedoch ist Schwere klein. Schwere kraftet. Sie übt Wirkung nur aus durch ihre Masse, nicht durch ihre Farbe, denn Schwere ist viel zu dunkel, um bunt zu sein. Nicht begreifen tut die Schwere das Lustige. Nur im Zucker schlafen das Lustige und die Schwere zusammen. Kommt die Schwerkraft von oben oder von unten? Wenn Wärme fester wird, so wird sie zu Schwerkraft. Wie ist es mit dem Stein, den man nicht wälzen kann? Ist er zu schwer oder zu fest? Er ist zu brutal! Schwere ist weicher als das Brutale. Ist das Leichte dann hart? So ist es wohl!

Wind

Wind rennt körperlos über Bäume und Häuser. Des Windes Kraft ist nicht sichtbar, nur seine Auswirkung sieht man. Wind verweht den Bestand. Eine Pusteblume verweht im Wind, die Asche gleichermaßen. Wind ist sehr vergänglich. Doch weht er immer.

Risse im Hirn

Eigenschaft ist einmalig. Sie ist seinem Ding eigen. Menge ist relativ, sie bemisst sich immer aus dem Vergleich. Menge hat keinen Eigner. Isolde hat einen dicken Bauch, doch das Fett gehört ihr nicht. Alles Überflüssige hat Menge. Es ist völlig egal, wie viel Risse das Gehirn von Einstein hatte. Des Gehirns Eigenschaft macht es eigen, nicht die Zahl seiner Risse. Man kann Äpfel und Birnen nicht vergleichen, nur ihr Gewicht.

Sand

Die Splitter der Steine heißen Sand. Sandsplitter sind so klein, dass sie als Gemeinschaft der Isolierten wieder eine Einheit bilden. Der Sand wird dann als Ganzes empfunden. Das Ganze ist zum Heulen, doch der Sand kann nicht weinen, weil er zu trocken ist. Steine haben weder Blut noch Wasser, auch nicht als Sand. Die Tränen trauriger Riesen spenden Salzwasser als Meer. Darum findet sich Sand als Strand oft dort, wo Meer ist.

Leute

Leute gibt's nur im Plural. Ein Leut allein kann nicht sein. Der Mensch als Herdentier wird zu "Leute". Eine Menschenmasse besteht aus Leuten. Das Blut der Leute ist das Blut ihrer Sippe. Ein Mensch hingegen hat einen eigenen Blutkreislauf. Bei den alten Juden läuft das Blut Abrahams hinab bis zu seinen Spätenkeln. Leute und archaische Völker haben ihre Identität in der Gruppe, nicht in sich selbst.

Babylon

Babylon war kein Baby: Es war zu groß für den Größten. Auch in New York gibt es Skyscraper. Diese aber müssen von Terroristen zerstört werden, weil sie Gott kratzen wollen. Man tanzt um das goldene Kalb, um Wirtschaftswachstum und den Schönheitschirurgen. Wann kommt endlich Gottes Zorn und fegt die sündigen Menschen in den Abfalleimer?

kleinste Teilchen

Fred hat sich nachts unberechtigten Zugang zum großen Teilchenbeschleuniger bei Genf verschafft und krabbelt nun in den runden Ring hinein: Er sieht hellgrüne Teilchen an sich vorbeifliegen.

Fred: Hallo Teilchen, kannst du auch sprechen?

Grünes Teilchen: Ich habe Kopfschmerzen, das ist schlimm, weil ich nur aus Kopf bestehe. Seit mich die Physiker entdeckt haben, kann ich nicht mehr richtig Weltweben. Sogar die Politik gerät schon außer Kontrolle.

Ein rotes Teilchen fliegt vorbei: Es streckt dem Fred seine Zunge raus, die noch roter ist als das Teilchen selbst.

rotes Teilchen: Ich mache dem Geld Feuer unterm Arsch. Normalerweise ist Geld nur eine Information. Mein Feuer verleiht der Information Wert. Ein Dreieck fliegt vorbei, es hat ein Auge auf der Stirn.

Dreieck: Ich bin das größte Teilchen, das es gibt. Richtig kleine Teilchen gibt es nur in der Hölle der Physik. Das Kleine hat keine Wirklichkeit. Je umfassender die Dinge werden, desto wirklicher werden sie. - Fred staunt nur.

Chaos ist eine Verwirrung, die kreative Außerweltliche benutzen, um ungestoppt vom Gedankenschutz in die Welt zu gelangen. Chaos ist bunt. Chaos beseitigt den Müll der Vergangenheit. Chaos tanzt und weiß nicht wozu.

schreiben

Im Schreiben spricht die Sprache stumm im Laut, aber hell im Bewusstsein. Schreiber sind die Bildhauer der Gewissheit. Schreiben ist immer Geschriebenes, auch während des Schreibens. Das

Geschriebene ist endgültig und hält sich länger als guter Wein. Das Wort schreibt durch alle Zeiten hindurch.

tanzen

Tanzen ist gewagt. Wer tanzt, der ist wahnsinnig. Tanzen kann aber auch cool sein, wenn man ein leichtsinniger Mensch ist. Denker sollten nicht tanzen. Der Tanz zerrüttet ihre Geistesklarheit. Verzweifelt aus Mangel an Liebesnahrung frisst der Wahnsinn als Tiger die verdorbene Ordnung des Bösen: Süße Miezi machen Fressi-Fressi!

Erwin

Tropfen aus Tränen fallen vom Himmel. Sie sammeln sich auf der Erde zu einem Bach, der zu einem Fluss anschwillt. Erwin sitzt in einem Kanu und paddelt durch den Tränenfluss. Der Fluss fließt bergauf. Am rechten Ufer des Flusses brennen Feuer zu Ehren Wotans. Am linken Ufer steht ein Baum, auf dem ein Vogel aus Stein sitzt. Erwin fließt paddelnd weiter mit dem Kanu bergauf. Nun schneit es. Der Kanufahrer sieht am Ufer zwischen den Tannennadeln einen Schneemann. Die Augen des Schneemanns sind lebendig, es sind die Augen eines potenten Teddybärs. Erwin paddelt weiter den Fluss bergauf. Auf der linken Seite spielt jemand Harfe. Gott ist nahe.

Vulkan

Eine Frau in Schwarz mit bunten Splittern zecht mit dem Coolen. Sie fliegen zusammen über Sterne, unter Sternen, zwischen Sternen. Das Leben der Titanic taucht in ihrem Sinken auf. Ein Papierfaltboot schwimmt lässig im Wasser, es treibt vorsichtig auf eine Sumpfwasserfeder zu: Peng! Asche fällt von oben. Der Eyjafjallajökull ist endgültig geplatzt.

passen

Passen findet sich selber in seinem Gegenteil als Liebe. Als Verwandtes ergänzt Passen das Eine und und das Andere durch ähnliches Dienen. In einem Gefüge passt alles zusammen. Bier, Zigaretten und Aschenbecher befinden sich bei Herrn Alki auf dem Küchentisch. Das macht Sinn, das passt. Der Küchentisch von Herrn Alki ist ein Gefüge. Im Internet befinden sich Hinz und Kunz im großen Weltkatalog beieinander. Hinz und Kunz sind nur verbunden durch ihr bloßes Existieren. Das Internet ist kein Gefüge, sondern Unfug.

Ding

Ein Ding ist grau in seinem Sein; es ist, mehr nicht. Dinge sind unpersönlich. Die gesichtslose Weltmaschine der Dinge beherrscht die Erde: Das Internet der Dinge. Dinge türmen sich zum Weltending. Der Satan hat die Welt längst in seinen Krallen. Bei Lebewesen spricht man nicht von Dingen, weil diese sich selber bewegen. Ein junges Ding jedoch kann sich selber bewegen. Das is'n Ding.

Maß

Ein Maß kann das rechte sein, liebevoll gebacken von befreundeten Göttern. Ein krankes Maß setzt als Herr Lehrer dem Schüler Grenzen aus Macht vor die Nase. Für den Schüler ist das Maß dann voll, sein

Leben staut sich, und die Industrie kann aus dem Stauwerk Strom gewinnen.

alles

Das Alles ist eine Addition von Vielem bis zur Grenze der Restlosigkeit. Ist das Alles nun schon das Ganze? Das Ganze ist zumindest eine runde Sache. Das Ganze sollte erwartungsgemäß an seinem Rand glänzen, doch bleibt es dort grau. Da spricht der Industriepriester: "Das Ganze ist mehr als die Summe seiner Teile!" Auch nach diesem Satz glänzt das Alles nicht, ein Mehr lässt sich nicht blicken. Das Ganze bleibt die nackte Addition von Allem. Ein Mehr gibt es nur noch in diesem Buch.

Nichts

Das Nichts ist die Welt aller Nichtdinge. Eine Tasse ist ein Nichtstuhl. Ein Kleid ist eine Nichtwolke. Ganz zu Schweigen vom Hund: Ein Hund ist doch auch nur eine Nichtkatze wie der Spatz auch. Alle Nichtdinge finden in der Welt des Nichts zusammen. Manche sagen, nach dem Sterben kommt nichts. Möchtest Du dort unter all den Nichtdingen leben? Da wird es ganz schön eng werden in der Abstellkammer der Nichtdinge.

Genuss

Genuss braucht mehr als das Notwendige. Somit ist Genuss mit dem Glück verwandt. Während aber das Glück ein Geschenk des Lebens ist, so genießt Genuss ganz willkürlich. Genuss verweilt und bleibt. Fettig genießt der Genuss sein Genießen. Genuss ist Lust, die sich überfressen hat. Genuss denkt nicht, dazu ist der Genuss zu träge. Wenn der Darm mehr verdaut als er braucht, dann ist er glücklich. Zufriedenheit ist Süßstoff, aber Zucker ist Glück.